NOR

—AND THE—

CENTAURS

A Tale of Woe

RON BACA

PAGE PUBLISHING, INC.
Conneaut Lake, PA

First originally published by Page Publishing 2021

ISBN 978-1-6624-3143-2 (pbk)
ISBN 978-1-6624-3563-8 (hc)
ISBN 978-1-6624-3144-9 (digital)

Printed in the United States of America

For my brothers Mitchell, Bill, and Bryan. You live on in my memories, always on my mind, and forever in my heart.

CONTENTS

CHAPTER 1

A FORTUITOUS MEETING

I AM YNEW, daughter of the Seventh Tier of the Morning Star of Nezer or, as I call him, Father; to others, he is called Grumpa. I shall tell you a story of a king and his people who dwell in the deep of the northern forestlands. A life unlike any other, this king shall endure and more.

One day in a time long past, a Greek traveler came upon these people for the first time. The Greek became mesmerized as his eyes beheld a gaze of these magnificent-looking giant warriors and their tiny beautiful women; it left him in awe. He felt the need to meet these people and learn more about them, no matter the consequences or the cost. He was said to have witnessed these warriors run with and catch wild horses with their bare hands. Their strength was like that of ten men, and they were as tall as the horses they captured. Hence, he named these people the Centaurs. He insisted and believed them to be favored and touched by the gods. He was said to have compared the women's beauty to that of a Greek goddess he called Aphrodite. She was to the Greeks, the most beautiful of all women and goddesses. The Centaur women were of a smaller and more curvaceous stature than that of their men. Most were thin with tiny waist, larger than average breast, legs that ran forever, behinds that were shaped like the hearts that they could melt. They all possessed beautiful long hair that surpassed their amazing derrieres and beautiful faces that would make even the most beautiful goddesses envious.

The men were all very tall and broad with muscles that would rival that of Adonis and they were warriors with skills that could challenge even that of Achilles. They were all war-hardened veterans, with the scars to prove it. Their weapons were much larger in size than he had ever laid his eyes upon. Their weapons were magnificent pieces of art as were their shields; they were made of a metal stronger than bronze with an inner layer of dense wood covered with hardened leather and straps with a handle to hold them securely.

When this Greek man and his companions made first contact with these Centaurs; he made an offering of gold, fine linens, and exotic foods. He had the offerings placed at the center of the main road leading to the Centaurs' village. He and his companions then placed themselves a short distance behind these offerings and knelt down in a sign of respect and to display their nonaggressive intent. No sooner had they knelt, they were surrounded by these large mighty warriors carrying large swords adorned in furs, cloth, metal armor plates, and chains. A young man of large stature and extremely muscular, carrying a large sword wrapped in a mixture of furs, cloths, and metals, approached the Greek and his companions. The young man pierced the ground with his sword directly in front of the Greek, which prompted the Greek to look up to this young man.

The Greek smiled and said, "Nice sword."

The young warrior smiled down at the Greek and simultaneously reached his left hand out to aid the Greek up. The Greek did not hesitate in this generous gesture. The Greek stood up and greeted the young warrior in his native tongue. The young warrior nods at the Greek and begins (to the Greeks' amazement) to speak in a Greek tongue back to the Greek.

"I am William. I am king of this village. We have been watching you and your friends for some time now. What brings you to our village?"

The Greek, still in awe responds, "We are traders and travelers from the land called Greece."

William responds, "I know this, but why our village?"

The Greek, in a nervous tone states, "We seek to trade our goods and get to know the customs of your people."

William smiles and replies, "Trade and our customs?"

The Greek, in haste responds, "Yes, we have some goods that may interest you, and perhaps we could exchange some knowledge of both our people's customs?"

William retorts, "You could be spies for our enemies or the information we give you may be used as a weakness against us. What say you?"

The now very nervous Greek hesitates. "We intend you no harm. We are not spies or have ill intentions for that matter."

William laughs as he looks around at his men. William motions to his men to gather the goods left on the road. William then motions to all to follow him as he heads back in the direction of the village. They all proceed to the center of the village where there are several large tables that are surrounded by chairs and stools, which are surrounded by the people of the village. The village was made of stone homes with wooden and straw roofs. The homes were laid out in a circular fashion with stables on the outer perimeter of the homes. Out front of each of the homes are lines hung with woven goods, jugs, and furs.

The warriors led by William and the Greek along with his companions, reach the center of the village then gather near the tables. William sits down and is joined by a voluptuous dark-haired beauty that appears to have affection for William as he to her. William looks around then jesters to all to sit. All do as William has indicated them to do, except for a few of his warriors who take a defensive stance surrounding the backs of the Greek and his companions. The Greek and his companions appear somewhat uneasy as they look up and around at the intimidating presence of the warriors that surround them.

The Greek looks to William and states, "We are no threat to you or your people!"

William replies with a cocky smile as he caresses the beauty seated next to him and with a chuckle, "My warriors are simply protecting you and yours from our beautiful women. Their beauty is only surpassed by their fighting skills and their passion! So I warn you and yours, tread lightly and gaze upon them with caution!"

The dark-haired beauty seated next to William gives him a stern gaze with a slight nudge of her elbow. William looks to her with a cocky yet concerned gaze.

The beauty seated next to William, still with a scowl upon her face, turns to look at the Greek then states, with a pleasant smile and a confident manner, "I am Einirt, queen of this village and wife to this big brute. Please excuse my husband and his motley crew. They simply wish to impress upon you their manly exposition."

The Greek, with a look of surprise, replies, "Your Highness, you speak my language as well?"

Einirt smiles, then chuckles, "Well yes, we speak many languages, don't you?"

The Greek responds in amazement, "Yes, but I just..." He pauses.

Einirt intercedes, "You did not expect us barbarians to speak many tongues?"

The Greek, with a smile, replies, "No, that is not what I meant to imply nor did I mean it as an insult. I was just surprised to hear my own language spoken back to me by someone as beautiful as you."

William laughs as he looks to the Greek. "That was a wise reply!"

Einirt gazes at William, then lays her head upon his massive chest as she places her hand in his and then places his arm between her impressive bountiful breasts.

Einirt then turns to the Greek as she speaks out, "Yes, it was."

The Greek and his companions look on with astonishment as the king and queen demonstrate a passionate affection for each other.

The Greek questions the two, "So what are your people called, or what do you call yourselves?"

Einirt responds, "We are simply called the people of the forestland."

The Greek, with a serious look on his face, questions, "That is what you call yourselves?"

William replies, "Yes, we take care of the forestland and the forestland takes care of us, so we find the name suiting, do you not?"

Cautious and with hesitation, the Greek responds, "I would call you Centaurs for not only are you and your men the size of horses, you also all demonstrate the strength and speed of that of a horse."

William cuts in, "What the hell is a Centaur?"

The Greek, with a concerned look replies, "A Centaur is a magnificent being. They are half man and half horse. A gift from the gods to mankind and they are mighty warriors and their females are a sight for the gods as well."

William grins, then speaks, "I like this name, Centaurs. It sounds fierce, yet it has a beauty about it." William looks down to his beautiful queen, then asks, "Well my queen, what have you to say about this name?"

Einirt answers as she turns with a seductive gaze to William, "I like it." Einirt then looks to the Greek and speaks in a soft yet firm tone, "How does one spell this word, *Centaurs*?"

The Greek, in a calm voice, spells the name out to Einirt, "C-e-n-t-a-u-r-s."

Einirt spells it back to the Greek, "C-e-n-t-a-u-r-s."

The Greek, with a cautious view upon his face, looks to William and notices the expression on William's face. William then lowers his eyebrows, as if to warn the Greek.

The Greek nods as he smiles then replies, "Yes."

Einirt then replies, "Yes."

William looks to the Greek with a slight grin, then lets out a laugh as he announces, "We are now called Centaurs! That is what our queen has decided, so it shall be done and now this is law!"

William stands up then announces, "Everyone, drink!"

William is joined by all in a drink or, in the case of the Centaur men, a chug. The women, on the other hand, sip their drink in a delicate and feminine manner. William motions to the Greek to join him.

William says, "Come."

The Centaur warriors place their hands on the Greek's companions to restrain them from joining William and the Greek. With the look upon the Greek and his companions, it is evident they have demonstrated fear of the Centaurs.

William says, "Worry not my Greek friend. We shall speak in private, yes?"

The Greek nods as if to agree. William places his arm on the shoulders of the Greek. They then proceed to walk away from the group.

In the distance, hiding in the forest near the Centaur village, a shadowy figure appears and hides behind a large tree, as if spying on the Centaurs and their guests. Suddenly, the shadowy image darts from the cover of the tree and into the open area where he is ran down by two very large Centaur warriors. The figure is lying on the ground with one of the Centaurs holding him down with one very large foot on his back and a sword to his neck. William and the Greek proceed toward the area where the two Centaurs have the figure captive. William and the Greek reach the three where William motions to his warriors to raise their prisoner up to his feet. The warrior, with his foot on their new prisoner, takes a step back and grabs the man by the back of his neck, then raises him to his feet. The prisoner is much shorter than the two warriors and nowhere near their massive size.

In a subtle and nonchalant manner, William states, "Speak or die."

The prisoner looks up to William with a disrespectful glare, and before he can say a word, the warrior, who is standing near William, stabs the prisoner in the chest, then spits on him as he remarks, "This is what happens when your kind disrespect our king!"

The Greek looks on in amazement, then asks, "Why did you kill him before he could speak?"

The warrior grins, then explains, "Did you not see the look he gave our king?"

The Greek responds, "Yes, but why did you kill him? For his angry glare?"

In a casual manner, the warrior states, "Yes!"

The Greek looks to William. William shrugs his shoulders, then nods in approval to his warriors as he motions for the Greek to join him as he turns and walks away.

The Greek appears bewildered and somewhat disturbed as he then asks William, "Did you not wish to question him first?"

William shrugs his shoulders, then in a baffled manner he asks, "Why?"

The Greek says, "He may have had some information you could have found useful."

William replies, "No, he didn't."

The Greek says, "But how can you be certain of this?"

In a nonchalant manner, William replies, "He would have not spoken."

The Greek comments, "But how can you be sure?"

William answers, "He was a Tartan."

The Greek, with a confused look on his brow, questions William, "What is a Tartan?"

William chuckles as he answers, "Our enemies."

The Greek in amazement asks, "Your enemies? You have enemies?"

William states with a chuckle, "Yes, don't the Greeks have enemies?"

The Greek replies, "Yes, we do, but who in the gods' name would want your people as enemies?"

William looks to the Greek with a baffled brow, then responds, "The Tartars for one!"

Surprised, the Greek responds, "You have more than one enemy?"

William laughs as he states, "Yes!"

The Greek shakes his head in disbelief, then replies, "They are of little wit and lacking in wisdom to wish your people as enemies!"

William grins as he responds, "I agree, but they attack in strong numbers and many more than we can place on the field of battle, but we always prevail."

The Greek looks to William in amazement as he shakes his head in disbelief. The Greek asks, "What kind of numbers are you outnumbered by?"

Calmly and with a smile, William responds, "Usually ten times or more of our force."

The Greek looks to William with an expression of awe, then states, "You must employ some great strategies and your men are great warriors for sure then!"

William smirks, "Of course."

The two continue to talk and walk.

CHAPTER 2

AN ENEMY FROM WITHIN

LATER THAT EVENING, William is lying in bed with his beloved Einirt sitting by his side at the edge of the bed. The two appear to be having a pleasant conversation and being affectionate with each other.

Einirt gazes upon her man and whispers to William in a sultry voice, "Guess what?"

William grins and glares as he places his right hand upon Einirt's thigh as he proceeds to slide her dress up. Einirt gently slaps, then caresses and stops William's hand.

Einirt looks to William as she shakes her head ever so slightly from left to right, signaling no with a happy smile, then says, "No my love, not that."

William appears displeased, then bewildered.

Einirt, in a soft voice, states, "I am with child!"

William sits up abruptly with a smile on his face, then wraps his massive arms around Einirt. The two embrace in a loving manner, and they kiss. William holds Einirt's face with his hands in a caressing and tender manner. William, in a soft voice, says, "Thank you, my love."

Einirt smiles as the two touch foreheads in an affectionate manner. Suddenly, there is a knock on the door.

A voice from outside the door is heard. "My king!"

William gets to his feet and places his fur robe about his shoulders, then ties the fur robe together at the waist. William then walks over to the door as Einirt, still dressed in her gown, turns and faces the doorway with a concerned look.

William opens the door and is greeted by his general, Cantor. Cantor is unattractive and scarred-faced man; he is tall but slender compared to William. Cantor is dressed in his cloths, furs, and metal plating with his sword at his side.

William questions his general, "What news have you brought me?"

Cantor responds, "Our scouts have spotted a Tartan army approaching our northeastern territory."

William asks, "How many men?"

Cantor responds, "Our scouts report infantry of three hundred men and one hundred cavalry."

William orders Cantor, "Prepare the guard to secure the village, then gather our cavalry to the east road and send Moats with his infantry to the north bridge. I shall join you shortly."

Cantor questions his king, "My king, should we not join our forces to fight as one?"

William, in an assertive and displeased manner responds, "Do as I instruct you and never question my orders again."

Cantor bows and states in an apologetic yet cocky manner, "My apologies, my king. I'm just trying to learn from your wisdom!"

Cantor then turns and walks away toward the center of the village. William turns back into his home, closing the door behind him.

Einirt, with a stern look, comments, "I do not care for that man. He gives me an ill feeling every time he looks at me."

William replies, "He is a good warrior and a good horseman."

Einirt smirks as she states, "Perhaps, but not very bright and I do not trust him. Besides, he is a pig with our women and they all loathe him."

William is changing into his battle gear as he responds to his wife, "I need his sword, not his wits or his manners my love."

Einirt helps William with his sword, then caresses his face with her two hands as she speaks, "Come back to me and your child, my love!"

William replies, "Yes my Queen, as soon as I am able, my love."

William kisses Einirt passionately and wraps her in a loving embrace as he affectionately gazes into her in the eyes. "I love you, my queen."

Einirt gives William a frown, then blows him a kiss as he exists the doorway. Escorted by some of his men, William proceeds down the road to the center of the village to meet up with his men.

Moments later, there is a knock on the back door. Einirt turns, then proceeds to the back door. Einirt then opens the door, and to her shock and amazement, standing there beaten, bloodied, and breathing heavily, Einirt can see that it is her friend Holga. A woman of Einirt's height, size, shape, stunning hazel green eyed beauty, with long beautiful deep red hair, Holga appears to have been beaten badly and bleeding profusely from her mouth. Holga's eyes are swollen and her face is covered in blood. As she opens her mouth to speak, Einirt can see that Holga's tongue has been cut out. Holga stands weeping with her hands, arms, face, and clothes covered in blood and soiled with leaves and twigs tangled in her hair, as well as her clothes. Einirt takes her into her arms and holds her as the two weep a pitiful and sorrowful mourn.

Einirt asks, "Who did this?"

Holga is unable but tries to speak as only unintelligible sounds come from her mouth. With her right arm, Einirt supports Holga from her left side as the two proceed to walk out the front door of Einirt's home.

Einirt speaks in a determined but shaken manner, "I'm taking you to the healer!"

The two proceed out the front door and out to the open area in front of Einirt's home.

Einirt shouts out for help, "Help us!"

An older man dressed in a dark cloak and a young man dressed in a night robe rush over to help. The two look upon Holga with surprise and shock.

Einirt instructs the two, "Young man, rush over to the healer and fetch him! Here, hold her from the other side, for she has lost much blood and is very weak!"

The older man moves over to aid Holga from the right side, and together he and Einirt walk Holga to meet the healer. Suddenly, an old man dressed in a dark cloak approaches in haste with the young man at his side.

The young man shouts, "There they are!"

Einirt looks to Holga. "There's the healer, Holga!"

The healer takes a quick look at Holga, then motions for them to follow him. They reach an older structure made of stone and wood with a wooden and a straw roof. Strange items such as animal skulls, feathers, jars, bones, and small sacks hang from the edge of the poles that overlap the walls from the roof. They all enter the structure, then lay Holga down on the cot in the center of the room. The healer motions for the older man and young man to depart the room, and they leave the structure as indicated by the healer.

Now alone with the healer, Einirt asks her friend Holga, "Who did this?"

Holga tries to speak, but no words can be formed. The healer gives Holga a drink of powders he has mixed with some water. Holga tries her best to drink it, but some spills from her mouth as she coughs some of the mix out. The healer motions for her to drink more, so she does her best to finish the concoction as the look upon her face demonstrates the lack of fondness for the concoction she is drinking.

The healer asks Holga, "Did a man take you and cut out your tongue so you would not talk of his horrible deed?"

With a sorrowful expression covering her beautiful face, Holga looks to the healer with a nod to indicate yes.

The healer then asks, "Do you know who it was?"

Holga nods as if to indicate yes; she recognized her attacker.

The healer then asks Holga, "Were you two alone?"

Holga shakes her head to indicate no, that they were not alone.

The healer asks, "Was there more than one man?"

Holga shakes her head to indicate no.

The healer, surprised by this, then asks with a curious expression on his brow, "Was there another woman there?"

Holga again nods her head up and down to indicate yes.

The healer questions, "Was this woman also taken against her will?"

Holga nods again to indicate yes.

The healer asks, "Where is this other woman now? Do you know?"

Holga shakes her head to indicate no.

The healer questions, "Did you know this other woman?"

Holga nods her head to indicate yes.

The healer asks, "Can you show us where she lives? Is her home nearby?"

Holga nods her head to indicate yes.

Einirt asks the healer, "She is very weak still. Do you think it wise to have her walk there?"

The healer takes out a rolled-up leather map and unrolls it on the ground next to the bed where Holga is lying, then hands Holga a long stick. Holga takes the stick and points to a home near the healer's compound.

Einirt shouts, "That's Angelina's home!"

Holga nods her head to indicate yes, then she points the stick to a home near the center of the compound and looks to Einirt with a scowl.

Einirt speaks in an angry voice, "Cantor!"

With an angry scowl, Holga nods her head to indicate yes.

Einirt says, "I should have guessed!"

Holga nods as huge alligator-sized tears flow from her beautiful sad eyes.

Einirt, in a sorrowful manner, tells Holga, "I'm so sorry, my friend. I will have William punish him accordingly!"

Holga nods, then rests her head upon Einirt's chest. Einirt takes Holga's head and lays her back on the bed. The healer takes a piece of cloth and dips it into a bowl of water, then begins to clean up Holga.

Einirt looks to the healer. "Please take care of her. I shall gather some of the others and search for Angelina and, sir, speak of this to no one!"

The healer responds, "As you wish, my queen. Please take heed, for the warriors are a fair distance from our village by now."

Einirt replies confidently, "My husband left his guard here. I shall seek their aid."

Einirt bends down and kisses Holga on the forehead, then turns in haste and departs the healer's home. Einirt locates two of William's guards as she walks down the center of the village's main road.

Einirt says to the guards in a firm tone, "Go to the healer and guard his door. Allow no one in or out but him and me. I mean no one!"

The guards nod and proceed to the healer's quarters. Einirt spots several of the women near the center of the village.

Einirt speaks to the women in a firm and concerned voice, "Ladies! Gather around! Have any of you seen Angelina?"

The women look to one another, shaking their heads then to Einirt and indicate that they have not seen Angelina.

Einirt asks the women, "Are your children safe and secure?"

The women nod to indicate yes.

Einirt commands in a soft yet firm tone, "Arm yourselves with your daggers."

The women all reach for their hidden daggers and appear all are properly armed.

Einirt orders the women, "You four search to the north, you four search to the west, you four search the south, and the rest of you come with me and we shall search the east. She may be harmed and unable to respond, so look cautiously and carefully!"

The women nod in agreement.

Einirt directs, "We shall all meet back here when the moon is high. If anyone should spot her, bring her to the healer immediately!"

One of the women questions their queen, "My queen, what has happened?"

Einirt responds in a firm voice, "We do not know. We must find her and no one is to question her until I have spoken to her myself. Understood?"

The women all nod in agreement. All depart in the four directions as instructed by Einirt. Einirt leads her group into the forest as they search the bushes and pathways for Angelina.

Now deep in the forest, the women, led by Einirt, search for their missing friend when one of the women nearest Einirt whispers but does not motion to her, "My queen, someone is watching us to the east behind the trees."

Einirt responds in a whisper, "They are two Tartan scouts. Tell the others, but do not alert them that we see them."

The woman nods and then begins to whisper to the other women, alerting them as instructed. The women continue as if they do not notice the Tartans. Suddenly, the two Tartans, in a cocky and confident manner, dart out with their swords drawn in front of the women's path. Without hesitation or fear, every woman throws her dagger into the Tartans' bodies, catching them off guard and before they could raise their shields. The Tartans both drop to their knees, pulling at the many daggers now stuck in their chests, necks, and stomachs. Einirt calmly and stoically approaches the two Tartans, then takes her dagger from the neck of one of the Tartans, then slashes his neck as she then turns without expression to the other and does the same to him. The other women approach and remove their daggers from the dead Tartans' bodies, then wipe them clean on the two dead bodies lying in front of them.

In a calm voice, Einirt orders, "Let us continue to look for our friend and be alert."

Einirt continues to lead the women in the continued search for their beloved friend.

As they walk farther down the path and into the bushes, one of the women speaks out, "Here!"

Then she motions for all to join her. Einirt is the first to join her. Einirt can see that it is Angelina, a tiny figure of a woman with long black beautiful hair that reaches her feet, very plush thick red lips, light olive skin color; she has been beaten badly and is unconscious. Angelina's clothes are ripped, soiled, and covered in blood, as well as leaves and twigs. Her face has small cuts, it's swollen, and bloody mess. The women, including Einirt, appear visibly shaken and sorrowful as several begin to cry.

A teary-eyed and visibly upset Einirt orders the women, "Pick her up, but be gentle with her!"

The women lift Angelina in a very cautious manner, then proceed to turn back to the village, carrying Angelina ever so cautiously. As Einirt leads her group closer to the village, the healer's quarters comes into sight with the two guards standing by the door as ordered. They can't help but notice the women carrying an injured woman. The two guards react with an angry but concerned state.

One of the guards calls out to Einirt, "My queen, may we assist?"

Einirt responds, "Yes, come and take her into the healer's quarters!" The guards throw down their spears and place their shields onto their backs as they rush over to help the women with Angelina. The guards take command of Angelina and rush her into the healer's quarters in a cautious manner.

Einirt says to the women, "You shall speak of this not, not to anyone. No one must know what we have learned here! Is this understood?"

All the women nod and respond in unison, "Yes, my queen!"

Einirt, in an angry tone, says, "Whoever is responsible for this horrible act must not know we have found her, yes?"

All the women nod in an angry but agreeable manner.

Einirt orders the women, "Go and gather the rest of our women and tell them we have found her, but by order of the queen, no one is to talk of this!"

The women nod in agreement.

Einirt then instructs them, "When you have located all our women, proceed to the safe house and I shall meet you there as soon as I am able."

The women again nod, then turn and depart. Einirt enters the healer's quarters where she can see the two guards have laid Angelina upon the bed in the center of the room and Holga is lying on a bed against the wall and appears to be sleeping. The two guards appear very shaken and angry.

Einirt instructs the two, "You are not to say anything to anyone about this!"

The two guards appear baffled and confused.

Einirt addresses the two once again, "No one is to know what we have discovered here. We don't want the guilty one or ones to flee their punishment, and our king will punish them. I swear on my husband's name!"

The two guards nod in agreement as the shorter guard responds angrily, "Our king shall dispense justice and kill whoever did this!"

Einirt orders the two, "Guard the door and allow none to enter."

The two guards nod, then exit the room.

The healer, in a somber manner, approaches Einirt, then speaks in a sorrowful voice to his queen, "My lady, Angelina is badly injured!"

With her eyes full of tears and in a pitiful tone, Einirt responds, "Can you help her?"

The healer looks at Einirt with a doubtful expression. "I can only keep her alive for a while. The damage is more severe than my skills can provide. I fear we will lose her if I don't ask for aid!"

In a surprised manner, Einirt questions, "Aid from whom?"

In a humble manner, the healer responds, "I have an old friend whose wife is a more powerful healer than I, my queen."

Einirt questions him again, "Who is this friend you speak of?"

The healer retorts, "He lives in a very hard-to-find village past the Tree of Sorrow and is very secretive of its location. In fact, he will find you and bring you to his village. I can never find it on my own."

Einirt responds, "Do we have a choice?"

The healer answers, "No. No my Queen, we do not!"

Einirt, with a stern glare, looks the healer in the eyes. "You will need to make preparations and will you require an escort?"

The healer replies, "No guard will be permitted and will not be necessary, my queen. As I said before, he is very secretive."

Einirt nods, then questions the healer once again, "What of Holga? Will she not require your services?"

The healer smiles a brief smile, then responds, "She has you, my queen, to look after her."

Einirt grins and responds, "Yes she does, ole wise one."

The healer hands Einirt a pouch, then informs her, "Give her a small spoonful of this and mix it with water in the morn, noon, and at night. She should be better but will not be able to speak properly, if ever again."

Einirt shakes her head with a mournful expression. Einirt then approaches Angelina lying on the bed. Einirt, in an affectionate, caring, and gentle manner, brushes Angelina's hair as Einirt begins to weep ever so softly as tears run down her beautiful face.

"Look what he did to my beautiful Angelina. She was the most beautiful of us all and the best of us. Her eyes, they are so swollen I cannot even see those beautiful sapphire blue eyes of hers!"

Einirt wipes the tears from her checks as more just fill the void she has created. Einirt continues to weep ever so softly, then whispers, "My beautiful, sweet, little Angelina. I fear I will never see your beautiful face and smile ever again. Please, little one, come back to us. Please!"

Einirt takes Angelina's hand into hers and kisses it gently, rubs Angelina's hand across her face, then kisses it one more time as she then places Angelina's hand back on the bed next to her body. Just as she begins to release Angelina's hand, to Einirt's amazement and shock, Angelina's hand tightens around Einirt's hand.

Einirt bends down over Angelina and speaks in a soft, pitiful, and mournful tone, "I am here, my little one. I am here!"

Angelina, unable to open her eyes, begins to speaks in a weak and frail voice, "I'm sorry my Queen! I did not mean to be so much trouble!"

Tears now start to pour in droves down Einirt's face as she attempts to speak; the words Einirt tries to speak won't come out. Then after a clearing her throat, Einirt speaks softly and her words are tattered. "No, my little one. You have never been trouble, and you will never be. You are much too sweet to ever be trouble!"

Angelina attempts to smile but is unable to; just as soon as she awoke, she passes back out.

Einirt shouts to the healer in a startled manner, "Quick! Is she okay?"

The healer places one hand on Angelina's chest and the other touching Angelina's neck.

The healer responds, "Yes, she is just sleeping."

Einirt questions the healer, "When will you depart with her?"

The healer answers, "In just a bit. I need to gather some food for the journey and place her in my cart."

Einirt calls the guards to assist. The two guards enter the room.

Einirt instructs the two, "Place Angelina upon that flat board, then take and place her on the healer's cart. Just make sure she's comfortable!"

The two guards nod in agreement, then do as their queen has instructed them to.

With his bags full, the healer approaches Einirt. "My queen, I shall do my very best for her, and I shall return once I know she is going to be better." He nods to his queen.

With tears in her eyes and a pitiful gaze, Einirt grasps his cloak and addresses him one last time before he departs, "Remember, speak of who done this to no one, and please bring her back to us once she is herself. I beg you, please do not allow her to pass into the next world. Please!"

The healer responds, "I shall do my very best, my queen, but she is in bad shape. The sooner I leave, the better chance she has!"

Einirt nods, then responds, "Make haste, and I shall wish you a successful and safe journey!"

The healer turns and exits the room. Einirt joins her friend Holga. Sitting next to Holga now, with a sorrowful frown and tears running down her beautiful face, Einirt begins to stroke her friend's hair and whispers a soft tune into Holga's ear, which only Holga can hear. Holga begins to awaken as she turns to Einirt.

Einirt looks down to Holga with a strained smile and asks, "Are you feeling any better?"

Holga nods to indicate yes.

Einirt takes her hands and places them upon Holga's face and speaks to her in a soft tone, "I will always be here for you."

Holga smiles a gentle smile as she places her hands upon Einirt's and nods in agreement.

Einirt speaks in an eloquent manner, "We will get him and punish him properly for what he has done, but until then, we must not speak of this to no one, yes?"

Holga nods in agreement. Suddenly, there is a knock on the door.

Einirt responds, "Yes, who is it?"

One of the guards responds, "It is I my queen, one of your guards. I am Hogar."

Einirt speaks, "You may enter."

The guard enters the room and bows, then looks to Holga with a look of tenderness and concern. The guard speaks, "My queen, how is Holga? Is she feeling better?"

Einirt responds in a questioning manner, "Yes, she is a bit better."

Holga attempts a smile as she gazes at the guard.

The guard says, "I am Hogar, son of Lux."

In a confident manner, Einirt responds, "I know who you are and who your father is, Hogar. My husband selected you for his guard because of your loyalty and your battle skills and because of who your father is."

Hogar nods his head, then replies, "With all due respect my Queen, you must be very tired. It has been a trying night for you."

Einirt tilts her head then replies in a questioning manner "Yes, it has, but what purpose brings you into this room?"

Hogar, in a nervous fashion, states "My lady, I know Holga. She and I have been friends for some time now, so I have come to ask if I may look after, protect, and care for Holga so you may get some rest."

Einirt looks to Holga with a grin. Holga smiles, then nods to Einirt to imply she would be satisfied with Hogar attending to her. Einirt comments as she pretends to yawn, covering her mouth, "It has been a long and stressful night. Perhaps I could use a bit of a rest. Perhaps I could just use the bed here and take a brief nap."

Holga nudges Einirt with her elbow and gives Einirt a slight scowl.

Einirt looks to Holga and announces, "Well, if Holga approves of you taking care of her, I'm sure she'll give me a nod of approval."

Einirt looks to Holga as Holga is nodding in approval very eagerly as she appears smitten by Hogar.

Einirt says to Hogar, "Remember, no one is to know of what happened to her, yes?"

Hogar nods his head and announces, "No one, yes my queen."

Einirt stands up and stretches as if she is tired and sleepy. Einirt looks to Holga and asks, "You will be fine in his hands?"

Holga grins and nods to confirm yes.

Einirt states, "I shall leave you two alone then, and I will return in the morn to give you your medicine."

Holga and Hogar cannot seem to take their eyes off each other, so Einirt grins and departs the room, leaving Holga and Hogar to themselves.

Einirt tells the guard outside the door, "Come with me."

The guard joins her as they make their way down the main road to the main compound.

As Einirt and the guard approach the main compound, the Greek and his companions meet the two.

The Greek asks, "My lady, is there anything you would like me and my men to do?"

Einirt responds, "You may join us in the main hall, which is where we gather when our men go off to battle."

The Greek seems embarrassed. "I had wished William would have asked us to join him and his warriors. We have been in battles before."

Einirt chuckles, then announces to the Greek, "The Tartans are not your enemies. They are ours."

The Greek responds, "Yes, but we would like to become your friends and allies, so we would gladly help if we were invited."

Einirt responds, "Well, you are both. Perhaps my husband did not wish you harm and put an end to our new found friendship and risk the future of you becoming our allies, yes?"

The Greek nods his head as he realizes he cannot persuade Einirt to allow him and his men to arm themselves or join William and his army in battle.

Disappointed, the Greek replies, "What wisdom you have displayed here, my lady."

Einirt grins and with her hand, motions for the Greek and his men to follow her as she then leads them to the main hall. They reach the hall with the double doors open and then enter. There are several well-armed guards surrounding the main hall. More guards are on top of the main hall with bows and arrows barely visible as they are protected by the ramparts surrounding the top of the main hall. The rest of the village appears abandoned as the night has silenced the darkened village. The doors to the main hall are closed, and the four guards posted at the doorway make themselves invisible as they place themselves behind the stone walls to the front of the main hall.

* * *

We now find William on top of his large steed, and he is amalgamated by his fearsome and intimidating cavalry as they have gathered at the end of the northeastern area of the forest. William's cavalry is well armed with their shields at their sides, swords sheathed, spears at hand, and sitting tall in their saddles dressed in their furs, clothes, and metal plates covering their massive chests. William appears to be giving orders to his men as he sits upon his beautiful black and proud steed, ready and heavily armed.

William orders his men, "Hold your positions men!"

Cantor is mounted on his brown horse next to William to his right. Cantor looks to see if he can spot the enemy as he stands up in his saddle.

William speaks to Cantor, "Anything?"

Cantor shakes his head to indicate no.

William asks Cantor, "Any word from Moats?"

Cantor replies, "No sir."

Now on the north end of the Centaur territory, General Moats, an older and seasoned warrior, stands ready with his infantry, blocking the bridge to the Centaur village. Moats is dressed in his battle gear which is like the rest of his men. They are covered in cloth, furs, and metal plates covering their huge chests, with their swords in their sheathes, shields barred covering the front of their large bodies, spears at their sides, and archers with their bows loaded but in a rested position at bay, standing behind the shielded men. They are all standing tall and proud as they await the oncoming battle.

Moats addresses his men in a confident manner, "Patience my boys. They will be here soon enough." Moats lets out a cocky laugh, then announces, "No quarter is to be given! I want them all dead!"

His men look to one another and smile as they nod in agreement.

Meanwhile, at the edge of the northeastern forest, William appears to notice a movement in the distance between the hills that leads to the path of the Centaur village. William and his cavalry maintain their position in a calm and confident manner. Moments later, the Tartan army has exposed themselves as they march and ride through the hills and onto the path leading to the Centaur village. The Tartans are a larger army outfitted in cloth attire, most are suited with bronze chest plates, all wearing bronze helmets, dawning capes of green cloth, some carrying axes, some with swords, many with spears, and archers carrying bows and arrows strapped to their backs. The Tartans appear to be of average human size compared to that of the massive-sized Centaurs. The Tartan cavalry appears to ride in the middle of the formation as they make their way southwest down the path. The Tartans appear unaware of the Centaurs' position in the forest ahead of them. The Tartans continue to approach nearer and maintain their formations in doing so. The Centaurs continue to maintain their positions, and in a very calm manner, they continue to watch the Tartans pass in formation.

Back at the northern gate leading to the Centaur village, the Centaur infantry remains steadfast in their position. They all have a look of confidence and pride as they remain loose and apparently joking, as well as actually laughing, with one another. Suddenly and at full speed, two riders appear from within the valley as they make their way from the opposite side of the northern bridge.

Moats shouts out to his men, "It is but our scouts!"

The riders cross the stone bridge and make their way over to Moats's position and stop directly in front of General Moats. The two scouts nod in respect to General Moats, then one of the scouts begins to speak.

Scout 1 says, "The Tartans have made themselves visible and are crossing near King William's position. They should be here within the hour, sir!"

Moats responds to the scout, "Very good, just as William had predicted. Now take your places with the archers."

The two scouts ride near the archers' position, dismount then tie their horses up to a tree, then join the archers.

Meanwhile, Moats instructs his men, "Boys, the enemy draws near. Prepare for their destruction!"

The men nod and grin in an eager fashion. Moats, with a red rag in his hand, waves it in the air which prompts a flagman in the front of his infantry formation to raise, then wave his long red banner in the air back and forth some three times. This action has prompted a pair of horsemen to take off from the rear of their position and ride off with haste. Moats grins and nods confidently.

Back at William's position, the Centaur cavalry continues to watch as the Tartan army marches unaware of the Centaur position.

General Cantor asks William, "Shall I give the word to attack?"

William looks in puzzled manner to Cantor. "No, I've given no such order. Now be patient. We have yet to hear from General Moats."

Cantor seems anxious and behaves oddly.

William asks, "Are you ill?"

Cantor responds, "No, just eager to go to battle!"

William shakes his head in disbelief and with a sarcastic grin. The Tartan army finally appears to pass as the last of the Tartans' archers pass the Centaurs' position. Just then, the two riders from General Moats appear and make their way to King William's position.

The first rider, now in front of William, bows his head; he then proceeds to address his king, "Sir, General Moats is ready at the bridge, and he sends word that the plug is in and ready for you to break the jar."

William smiles, then motions for the riders to head to the back of their position. William looks to his men on his right, then motions with his right hand for those men to advance forward. The entire right side of William's cavalry makes their way out of the forest and onto the path behind the Tartans. William then motions with his left hand, and as he looks to his left, his cavalry to his left make their way out of the forest and join the rest of William's cavalry on the path behind the Tartans. William, now joined by General Cantor, proceeds to make their way to the front of the cavalry as they form in a four-line wide formation. William raises his left arm, bearing his impressive and large shield with his bow in the same hand; he then lowers his arm. Immediately after William's arm is lowered, the Centaur cavalry, in unison, all reach for their bows with their left hand; even though their large shields are in their left hand, they then place an arrow with their right hand into their bowstrings as they continue to ride their large, shiny, impressive, and beautiful stallions toward the Tartans' position.

Now at the northern bridge, the Tartans gather in a wide formation with some fifty men wide and the rest piling up behind them, and they begin to rush the bridge. The width of the bridge will only allow the Tartans to send a six-man line to engage the well-armed Centaurs. The Tartans rush the bridge anyway, and as their six-man wide wave collides with the Centaurs' spears and shields, the first wave of Tartans are brutally slain. As hundreds more Tartans engage the well-positioned Centaurs, the Tartans continue to get crushed and annihilated in the same manner. It is a bloodbath of Tartans. As more and more Tartans try to break the Centaur line, they too are decimated and fall like waves crashing on a rocky shore, but it is not water falling; it is the Tartans' blood-covered bodies. In a distance, safe from the ensuing battle, the Tartan king appears mounted on his horse and appears to be giving orders to his men.

Suddenly and without warning to the rear of the Tartans' position, the Centaurs appear with King William and General Cantor leading the way. The Centaurs form a wide line of mounted archers, and following William's lead, they draw their arrows back, then release them into the air as the arrows cascade down upon the Tartans;

the Tartans fall like rain to the ground. The Tartans appear unaware of what is happening behind them; as they look back, they realize that they are now trapped between the bridge and Centaur mighty mounted cavalry they now face. The Tartans, now in disarray, charge mindlessly toward the bridge and the Centaur cavalry. The Tartan king appears in vain to take control of his men. It is useless as the Tartan soldiers have lost the ability to hear their king's orders. The Centaur cavalry now began to ride in waves into the mindless unorganized Tartans. With their spears and swords drawn, the Centaurs began to devastate in mass the foot soldiers and charging mounted riders of the Tartans.

As the battle continues, the battlefield begins to widen and spread deeper behind the Tartans' original position. Most of the men have dismounted on both sides and are engaged in a gruesome and brutal battle. Arms are being hacked off, as are legs and hands. Headless bodies roam and lay at the feet of the men still fighting. It is a gruesome and bloody display of warfare.

As the bridge is covered in dead bodies, the Centaur infantry is taking them and tossing them aside and over the bridge walls. General Moats is shown ordering his men to remove the dead so that his infantry may go to the aide of his king. The bodies are numerous and laden with blood, which makes them very slippery and difficult to move. The Centaur infantry labor to clear the bridge of the dead and eventually make a path so that some of General Moats's men can join in to aide their brave king on the other side. The two sides are engaged in a blood-thirsty battle, and it appears that the Centaurs are beginning to take the Tartans to task. So much more of the ground is littered with the weapons, body parts, and bodies of the Tartans. Very few of what lies on the ground are that of the Centaurs.

As the battle continues, William and Cantor appear to be farther away than most in battling the Tartans. William cuts down two more Tartans with Cantor engaging with two others. Three more Tartans surround William, but to their dismay, William slices through the shield of a Tartan, cutting the Tartan deeply down the chest, then another is beheaded by William; the third charges William, but William simply slices the Tartan at the knees, leaving

31

him legless. Suddenly, four more Tartans led by their General Erick, a younger man who is brandishing a highly decorated shield, wearing gold-laden armor, directs his men to attack William. William sees the threat and reacts with urgent vigor. William slays the first Tartan nearest him with a swing of his mighty sword and then with one swift and powerful blow; he crushes the Tartan that chose to hurdle himself at William. William turns and can see that Cantor is still battling the two Tartans he has been fighting for some time now.

William is then challenged by two more Tartans, one to his left and another to his right. William makes a move to his right, slaying the Tartan soldier with ease, but then from behind, William feels a pain in his back. William peers down to see a sword has pierced his chest from behind. William drops to his knees as blood rains down his chest, stomach, and armor. William turns only to see that the man who stabbed him from behind is his General Cantor. William appears heartbroken as he shakes his head in disbelief and lets out a woeful last word, "Why?" Cantor appears pleased with himself as he draws back his sword out of William. Cantor then turns rapidly, and with his long and bloodied sword, he beheads William. William's head falls from his body, then rolls to the ground as his now bloody and limp body flops down to join his decapitated head. Cantor, now with a grin on his ugly mug and a gleam in his eyes, looks to the Tartan general, Eric, and nods.

Eric nods back then lets out a holler, "Retreat!"

Eric and the Tartans begin a full retreat led by their king. What Cantor does not realize is that up on the hill stands a very somber Moats who has witnessed what has happened to his king. Moats falls to his knees and appears to weep in a pitiful and sorrowful manner for the loss of his friend and king. Moats places his head into his hands as he continues to weep. Moats's men soon join him on top the hill and see what has happened to their beloved king. The Centaurs, who have seen their fallen king, now join Moats in the mourning of their now-late beloved and respected leader. Cantor looks to see if anyone else has seen their king fall, then realizes that there are men on top the hill mourning their king's death. Cantor then reaches for William's sword, and as he lifts William's sword, he appears to grin, then looks to the men up on the hill. Cantor hollers to the men up on the hill, "Our king has been slain by the Tartans!"

Cantor then, in an arrogant manner, raises what was once William's sword into the air and shouts, "By our laws and by William's wishes, I, Cantor, do hereby proclaim myself king of our people and all the lands we possess!"

Cantor looks around and can see that the Centaur men are not very pleased with this move by Cantor. The Centaurs look to Cantor with a glare in their eyes, and almost in unison, they tilt their heads as if to indicate they disagree and question Cantor's actions.

Cantor then announces in a condemning tone, "Those who question my right as king should stand in front of me and speak his last words!"

Cantor peers around as if he expected a challenge, but none has been made, so he then boldly announces, "All that was once William's is now mine, which was William's wish. And who am I to disobey our former king's last wishes? For he had no hire and has bestowed this burden upon me!"

Cantor continues to look around for someone to second his action. Still, no one speaks as Cantor continues to seek approval.

Just then, a Centaur warrior steps up next to Cantor and proclaims, "Hail King Cantor," then raises his sword and looks to his comrades in arms to affirm his action.

Some Centaurs speak but not in a loud voice, "Hail King Cantor."

With a look of disgust and a shake of his head, Cantor sheaths his new sword, then motions for his men to follow.

* * *

Back at the Centaur village in the main hall, the villagers seem eager to the news of the battle.

The Greek approaches Einirt, then asks, "Your Majesty?"

Einirt smiles as she looks to the Greek. "You may call me Einirt. I never cared for the title. I just married the man I loved and he became king and I became his queen."

The Greek, with a stunned look on his face, asks, "So how did your people come to learn all these trades, skills, and languages?"

Einirt responds with a pleasant tone, "We send out our women to scout our neighbors both near and far. They then learn of these things, and then they teach us these skills and tactics once they have gathered what they need to know."

The Greek, with a surprised but approving look, questions, "But they learn of war tactics, fighting skills, weapons, and strategies?"

Einirt chuckles. "Yes, our women are not just beautiful and intelligent. They are great warriors too!"

The Greek responds in an embarrassed fashion, "I meant no disrespect, my Queen."

Einirt smiles. "None taken. You just learned a lesson which will make you all the wiser!"

The Greek nods in agreement, then asks, "So if I may ask, why don't the men do this quest for knowledge?"

Einirt smiles, then laughs. "Have you not seen the size of our men?"

Einirt shakes her head, then replies, "No my friend, our men would stand out like a lion amongst sheep!"

The Greek nods in agreement, then lets out a chuckle. "Yes, they would not go unnoticed or without troubles!"

Einirt nods in agreement. "This is true and why we do not send them. We have learned from the past not to do this." Einirt then chuckles.

Suddenly, two guards open the main doors and one announces, "Our men are returning!"

Einirt rises to her feet and leads the people of the village out the doors to meet their men. The villagers appear concerned yet excited and in good spirits as they prepare to welcome their men.

CHAPTER 3

A SHATTERED QUEEN

Now IN A distance down the main road, the Centaur army appears but led by Cantor. Einirt, with a surprised and concerned expression on her beautiful face, rushes over to meet the army. Cantor speeds up his horse to meet Einirt, then upon reaching Einirt, he dismounts his horse. Cantor places his hands on Einirt's arms when he informs Einirt of the battle and its outcome.

Cantor, with a stern yet arrogant tone, announces, "We have chased off the Tartans, my queen, but we have lost William!"

Einirt, in shock and mortified, attempts to step back, but Cantor will not release her.

Einirt appears weak and somewhat faint as she lets out a scream, "No! No! Not my William! Not my love!"

Einirt weeps uncontrollably and is inconsolable. Cantor tries to hold her, but she pushes away and forces him to release his grip on her. It is apparent by the shocked expression on her tear-covered beautiful face that Einirt can see now the cart that carries William's body. Einirt suddenly bursts out in a loud, piercing, mournful, and painful scream. Einirt's screams and weeping are so perturbing and heart-wrenching that even the hardest of war veterans cannot help but shed tears and weep for their queen's loss; it appears that all have witnessed this earth-shattering scream and display that, almost in unison, everyone bows their heads and attempts to cover up their own weeping eyes and quivering lips. Einirt is so horrified she turns blindly and then begins to rush over to the cart which contains her fallen beloved William's body.

General Moats suddenly appears from within the army's ranks as he then rushes over to stop and aid Einirt. Einirt is so mortified she can only take a couple of steps before she begins to collapse when Moats, in the nick of time, grabs her and holds her from falling to the ground. Cantor looks to the two with an angry glare. Moats looks down at his queen and can see she is weak and in no condition to see her fallen beloved, and he does not want her to see the condition of what remains of William. So in a loving manner, Moats bends down and holds her as she continues to weep, then faints and collapses from shock and heartbreak into Moats's arms. Moats lifts her up with his huge arms, then proceeds to carry her away in the direction of her home. Moats and Einirt are followed by several warriors and women. As they reach her front door, Moats kicks the door open and enters with Einirt in his arms.

Back in the center of the village, the rest of the army make their way to their loved ones. All are in poor spirits; some weep as others appear simply subdued from grief and pain at the loss of their beloved king—all but Cantor, who appears cheerful and eager to take rule of the Centaurs.

Cantor announces to all that will listen, "I, Cantor, have taken up William's sword, and as William wished, I have claimed the crown and title of king of our people!"

Most of the villagers and warriors glared at Cantor and shake their heads in disbelief and disgust. It is obvious that they do not care for Cantor, especially his actions. Cantor and a few of his followers make their way to the doors of the main hall, then stop and turn to face the villagers.

Cantor announces, "We shall feast and drink to our fallen and honor them as we will our former king. Then we shall proceed in honoring our new king, King Cantor!"

The villagers just look to Cantor in disbelief, then some walk off in disgust, some just stand there in amazement, and others walk toward the main hall doors to join Cantor and his followers. Cantor enters the main hall, then proceeds to the king's throne where he sits and makes himself comfortable. His followers form two lines in support, one line on his left, which is on the other side of the queen's throne, and another to his right closer to him. The villagers who have entered the main hall look at Cantor's actions with a puzzled and bewildered look.

Cantor realizes he is not a favorite of the people and whispers to his follower to his right, "If any speak poorly of me, kill them immediately!"

The follower nods in agreement, then appears to whisper to the other followers next to him. Cantor motions to the follower to his left, the follower makes his way over to Cantor, and Cantor whispers the same instructions to him as well. The follower makes his way back to the line left of Cantor's position and begins whispering to the followers with him on the left line.

Cantor shouts, "Bring us some drink, and be quick about it! We are thirsty and wish to celebrate our new king—me!"

The young women who are acting as servers bring drinking mugs, jugs of ale, and containers of wine to Cantor and his followers. Cantor and his followers begin to drink and celebrate their new king.

Cantor hollers, "Bring us some food! We are hungry from battle!"

The young women now appear nervous and bewildered at Cantor's behavior and tone, but they bring Cantor and his followers the food he has demanded. Shamelessly, Cantor and his followers begin to grope and harass the young women. Some of Cantor's followers follow Cantor's lead and pull some of the young women to them as they grab their breasts and behinds. Cantor and his men laugh, joke, and belittle the young women as they molest them. One of the young women slaps one of Cantor's followers; the follower slaps the young women and knocks her to the ground. A guard who is standing at the door rushes over to aid the young woman.

The guard helps the young woman up, then turns and he punches Cantor's follower in the jaw as he reprimands the follower.

The guard commands, "We are Centaur. We don't treat our women in such a manner. Now apologize to her!"

The follower looks to Cantor, and Cantor responds on the follower's behalf, "He was just having fun, as was I. You will apologize for striking him. Do you understand?"

The guard rears back in shock and disgust. The guard replies, "Me, apologize to that piece of shit? No, I think not!"

Cantor rises to his feet with rage in his stance and tone. "I am your king, and you will do as I order. Do you understand?"

The guard shakes his head in disagreement.

Cantor shouts, "You disobey your king's order!"

The guard gives Cantor a look of dismay, then steps back. The guard, in a confident but angry tone, announces, "William may be gone, but his wife is still our queen and you have not been properly crowned, old friend!"

Cantor is outraged and incensed with anger as he has been disrespected by his old friend and lower-ranking guard.

Cantor shouts, "When I am properly crowned, you will pay for your disobedience, you hear me!"

The guard now holds the injured young woman and leads her out of the main hall. As the two depart, they are joined by several other guards and villagers who appear disgusted by the events that just took place.

Now in the home of Einirt, Einirt is lying on her bed, sobbing in a pitiful and distraught manner. Holga rushes into the home of her queen, then bends down to hold and console her friend and queen. Moats, Holga, and several other men and women attempt to console Einirt but to no avail. Einirt is simply inconsolable and just continues to weep in a pitiful, grief-stricken, and excruciating manner. Einirt's pain can be felt by all, and her cry is contagious as the others are unable to prevent themselves from sharing her sorrow and her tears. Holga, sitting next to Einirt, holds her, then places Einirt's head on her lap and proceeds to pat her head and stroke Einirt's hair as she attempts to console the inconsolable. Einirt just keeps crying a heartbreaking weep as tears continue to pour down her face. Even Moats, an old battle-hardened warrior general, cannot control the tears flowing down his face as he watches his queen and sister weep for her lost love.

Moats wipes away his tears, then kneels down next to Einirt and places his battle-hardened face and his scarred forehead gently on Einirt's head and whispers to her in a soft, compassionate tone, "We all miss William, but we need your strength, my Queen. My little one, please take the time you need to mourn your husband. He was a great man, a great king, and my good friend."

Moats's eyes fill with tears and his lips begin to quiver as he rises to his feet. He again wipes the tears from his eyes. Moats looks to Holga and speaks in a soft voice, "Take care of her. I will need to speak privately with her before she speaks to Cantor."

Holga nods in agreement, then shakes her head in displeasure of the mention of Cantor's name. Holga looks away, then spits on the floor as she attempts to speak Cantor's name, and it is garbled because of her missing tongue. "Can Hor!"

Holga then looks back at Moats and nods. Moats gives her a serious and obliging look as he nods. Moats then turns and walks out of the home, closing the door behind him.

Moats spots several loyal guards, then calls to them, "Guards!"

Four very large guards walk over to meet Moats.

Moats addresses them, "You four are all good men and were loyal to William, yes?"

The four guards nod emphatically in agreement.

Moats then orders, "Guard the queen. Allow no one in without Holga's approval. She's in there with our queen, so knock lightly and ask her for permission before anyone enters. Understand? No one!"

The guards nod and give Moats a salute by thumping their right fist to their heart. Moats walks off with his head down in a grieving and somber manner. Two of the guards stand watch at the front door as the other two make their way to the back door.

Back at the hall, Cantor and his followers appear to be somewhat intoxicated and in good spirits. The Greek approaches Cantor in a respectful yet suspicious manner.

The Greek addresses Cantor, "General Cantor, may I?"

In a disrespectful and angry manner, Cantor interrupts the Greek, "General! No! I am not general. I am King Cantor!"

The Greek is shaken by Cantor's tone and action, so he bows in respect and fear, then apologizes, "Forgive me my King, I spoke poorly as I am not aware of all your people's traditions. I am terribly sorry, Your Majesty!"

Cantor now grins as he appears smitten and pleased with the word choice the Greek has utilized in his apology to Cantor. Cantor addresses the Greek, "Your Majesty? I like it. From now on, that is what I will be called, Your Majesty Cantor." Cantor laughs as he looks to his followers, as if he is seeking approval, then announces, "Better than king, yes?"

His followers grin as they nod in approval. Cantor then slaps the Greek on the shoulder and lets out a hardy laugh.

The Greek is unsure of what he should do now, so he smiles, then compliments Cantor, "A fitting title for a man of your stature."

An uneducated, unintelligent, and paranoid Cantor appears angry at the Greek's compliment.

Cantor grabs the Greek by the shoulder and demands, "What the hell is that supposed to mean?"

The Greek, now in clear visible fear, responds, "It was a compliment, Your Majesty! I meant you no dishonor or disrespect!"

Cantor appears embarrassed, then gets angry. "I know what it means!"

Cantor then pushes the Greek back, then releases him as he looks to his followers, then laughs. "Look how afraid he was of me! I will truly be a great and fearsome Your Majesty!"

Everyone in earshot looks puzzled and somewhat embarrassed by their new king's actions and choices of words. Cantor seems oblivious of his surrounding and people's feelings toward him. Cantor and his followers continue to drink and make fools of themselves as the villagers can't help but notice their behavior.

Meanwhile, near the stables stands Moats with several very large, rugged, and heavily armed Centaurs.

Moats is in a somber yet angry mood as he speaks to his brave warriors, "I saw him strike our king, our friend, and from behind as William was lying waste to many Tartans. Then as William fell to his knees, I saw the Tartan General Eric, nodding to Cantor. Then that coward Cantor, took William's head from his body with a swing of his sword!"

The Centaurs warriors, all demonstrate their anger and their discontent as they shake their heads in disgust, with an angry scowl on their faces upon hearing what their new king has done to their beloved and brave former king and friend.

Moats tells the men, "Do not speak of this to anyone, not even your women, understood?"

The men all nod to agree with Moats's order and its meaning.

Moats continues, "When the time is right and our beautiful brave queen and I have spoken, I shall give you her order on how to proceed, yes?"

The men again agree with a nod of their heads and salute to their respected old general by pounding their hearts with their right fists.

Back at Einirt's home, sitting on the bed in a somber mood are Einirt and Holga. Still weeping but in a less dramatic manner, Einirt and Holga are sitting next to each other with their foreheads touching ever so gently.

Einirt tells Holga, "I miss him so much!"

Holga holds Einirt's hands in hers as she rears back slowly, then she looks into Einirt's eyes and tries to speak in a sincere but muddled manner, "I know my dear. William was the best man I ever knew, even better than his father."

Einirt nods in agreement, then speaks in heartbroken fashion, "Yes, he was the best thing that ever happened to me. He made me so happy. I could never stay mad at him, and he knew it!"

As tears pour down Einirt's face, she lets out a gentle smile, then speaks to Holga, "Sometimes he'd make me so mad I wanted to hit him, but it would do no good. He would just laugh anyway. I couldn't hurt him even if I wanted to. That big ox!"

The two teary eyed beauties chuckle.

Einirt says, "By the gods, I loved that man so much it hurt! I told him that once, and he just smiled and asked, where does it hurt? He then placed his hand on my breast and asked, here? He then he grinned and chuckled. I gave him a very angry look, then he stares into my eyes with his handsome looks and those piercing eyes, then he said, 'You're so beautiful when you are angry!' So I got even angrier, and yet I was strangely seduced. What was I to do? I was so angry all I could think of was to keep him from talking, so I just grabbed his face and kissed him like I never kissed him before!"

Holga grins, then asks in her mumbled voice, "Did it work?"

Einirt chuckles. "No, he just lifted my gown, then made love to me, and I forgot why I was mad at him. He always had his way of making me happy no matter how mad I got at him and then I would forget why I was mad at him!"

The two ladies giggle, then begin to weep in a tearful moaning embrace.

Einirt is weeping softly. "I miss my William, my love!"

Suddenly, there is a knock on the front door. Holga gets up and motions to Einirt that she has this handled; she then makes her way to the door and answers the knock by opening the door. Standing in front of the door is one of the guards with a follower of Cantor's next to him.

The guard asks, "Holga, Cantor wishes the queen to meet him at the main hall when she has finished weeping for her William."

The follower intrudes, "You mean King Cantor!"

The guard gives Cantor's follower a glare, then turns and grins to Holga. "Like I said, Cantor wishes to see our queen when she is ready!"

Holga nods, then speaks in her mumbled voice, "Not now. She's not ready."

The guard turns to Cantors follower, then states, "When our queen is ready. Got that? Not till then!"

Cantor's follower, now clearly frustrated, turns, then kicks the ground and storms off in a bustle. The guard grins, then chuckles as he looks, then nods to Holga. Holga smiles, then closes the door and locks it from within.

Holga walks over to the bed and sits next to Einirt, then Holga, with a combative look, says, "Can Hor can eat shit and die. He does not deserve your company!"

Einirt looks to Holga with a smug look as she nods in agreement.

Meanwhile, in Moats's home, Moats is seated at the dinner table with his dark-haired, young, massive, bearded, and handsome son, Brock. Brock is clearly a giant of a man with the bulk to match

Brock asks his father, "Would you like me to send Alecia over to comfort and care for our queen, as well as help Holga?"

Moats smiles, then nods as he grunts, "Uh-huh."

Brock turns and looks to an open door that clearly leads to another room and calls out, "Alecia, come to me woman!"

Suddenly, from out of the room walks a tiny, stunningly beautiful, young woman with very long beautiful shiny black hair that reaches her tiny feet. She is wearing a tight form-fitting white dress that also reaches her petite feet.

She glares at Brock with her mesmerizing sky blue eyes and hands on hips. "What did you say?"

Brock grins as he leans back and, in a cautious tone, says, "I was calling my beautiful lady to join me!"

Alecia storms over to Brock, and with her right hand, she slaps Brock from behind the head as she speaks out loudly, "I heard you, *woman*!"

Brock's head doesn't move a bit from the strike, yet he apologizes with a pout as he gawks at his Alecia. "My lady, I needed you, my love!"

Alecia leans in as she places her arms upon her massive husband's shoulders; she announces with a sexy smile and in a sultry voice, "Yes, my lover!"

Brock smiles as he lays his huge head upon Alecia's thin arm, then asks, "My lady, would you be so kind as to go over to our queen's home and tend to her needs and give Holga a rest?"

Moats, with a look of disbelief, shakes his head, then announces, "You two are going to make me toss my dinner up. Enough of that!"

Brock tilts his head, shrugs his shoulders with a smug look, and smiles as he speaks, "Father, we cannot help it!"

Alecia smiles at Moats as she makes her way over to Moats, who appears somewhat bewildered by her approach. Alecia then places her tiny and gentle hands upon her father-in-law, then speaks in a soft voice, "Father, your son takes after his fearless and handsome father."

Moats melts in her hands, then blushes as he responds in an embarrassed yet confident manner, "Yes, yes, he does." Moats chuckles, then looks at Alecia as he asks in a curious but affectionate manner, "How do you have this effect on me, little one?"

Alecia simply smiles at Moats, then kisses him on his forehead and gently places her forehead upon his as she responds in her sweet and loving voice, "It is because you love me and I keep your son in line."

Brock looks on as he nods his head in agreement, then announces in humble and agreeing manner, "True."

Moats nods his head as he peers into his beautiful daughter's eyes, and in a complimentary and loving manner, he speaks, "It is your voice and your eyes. They remind me of Brock's mother."

Alecia kisses Moats once again on his forehead, then looks to her husband and asks, "Would you like me to go to our queen now, my husband?"

Brock smiles at his wife, then lifts his arms and with his hands, motions for her to join him. Alecia walks in a very sultry manner over to her husband, which forces Brock to gaze upon her with awe, his mouth open as his jaw drops to the floor. Alecia places her tiny hands on her husband's face, then kisses him a very romantic way.

This causes Moats to react. "Enough!"

Alecia turns her head as she gazes over at her father-in-law and lets out a chuckle as she speaks, "Yes, Father."

Alecia steps back, then turns and proceeds in a very sultry manner to the doorway. Brock is sitting, staring at his wife with his mouth open in a kissing expression as his father is shaking his head in disbelief. A grinning Moats then looks to Brock and comments, "Son, your mouth!"

Brock finally closes his mouth as his wife exits the home, closing the door behind her.

A bewildered and love-stricken Brock looks to his father and proclaims, "That beautiful woman has some kind of magical power over me!"

Moats, drinking his ale, abruptly lets out a snort as ale shoots out his nose while he coughs the rest in his mouth out in a spay toward Brock. Brock, now covered in ale, looks at his father in disbelief and shock.

Brock questions his father, "Why did you do that?"

Moats responds, "Fool, it is no magic. It is her beauty and her heart that owns you!"

Brock nods in agreement, then proclaims, "By the gods, I love that woman!"

Moats shrugs, then replies in a grumpy manner, "That's obvious! I need to speak to our queen soon."

Brock nods in agreement, then asks, "Father, would you like me to eliminate Cantor?"

Moats answers, "No, it cannot be you. You have much to lose if all goes poorly!"

Brock, somewhat bewildered, questions, "But it will not go poorly. I can kill Cantor."

Moats, with a glare in eyes, addresses his son, "What of Alecia? Should someone seek revenge for Cantor, Alecia would be in danger, yes?"

Brock, in agreement, nods with a look of humility and concern upon his brow, then states, "Yes, Father, you are correct as usual!"

Now with a concerned gaze and in a loving fashion, Moats appeals as he looks to his son, "I wish no harm to come of that beautiful lady of yours or you, understand?"

Brock, in an appreciating manner, nods in agreement, then states, "Your wisdom is always appreciated, Father."

Moats looks to his son in a confident manner as he announces, "I have a plan, but we must first have our queen's approval."

Both Moats and Brock lean in to whisper and discuss the plan to deal with Cantor.

Back at Einirt's home, Einirt is handing Holga a cup of her medicine the healer has provided for Holga. Holga gives Einirt a frown of disappointment and shakes her head in disapproval of the cup Einirt is handing her.

Einirt says in a soft tone, "You must drink this. It is for your own good!"

Holga takes the cup, then looks to Einirt with pouting lips, then states in her muttered voice, "It tastes horrible!"

Einirt gives Holga a firm glare, then speaks in a reassuring but firm tone, "But it will help you to heal, so as your queen, I must insist you drink all of it now!"

Holga lifts the cup to her mouth as she then proceeds to consume all the contents from the cup. Holga then places the empty cup upon the table; she then appears to struggle to hold the concoction down. Suddenly, she covers her mouth with both hands, then begins gagging and convulsing as she attempts to retain the mixture within her mouth. Some of the concoction makes its way through her fingers, but Holga manages to retain most of it in her mouth, then swallows what remains of the mix that still resides in her mouth. Holga gives Einirt a sorrowful frown as she attempts to keep the substance within her. Einirt attempts to keep from displaying her emotions of laughter as she covers her mouth with her right hand. Holga can see that Einirt is attempting to refrain from laughing and glares at Einirt as Holga fights to keep the mix down. Einirt can no longer hold in her laughter; she then let's out a hardy laugh. Einirt holds her stomach as her laughter is from deep within and is apparently so contagious that even Holga begins to chuckle. The two are now laughing uncontrollably as it is apparently hysterical to both women.

The two are caught off guard as there is a knock on the door; it is one of the guards and he asks, "My Queen, are you okay?"

Einirt and Holga are laughing so hard neither is able to respond to the guard's question. The guard knocks harder then attempts to open the door but is unable due to the lock that secures the door. Finally, Einirt makes her way to the door, then proceeds to unlock the door. Einirt opens the door as the guards appear ready to battle. Einirt motions with her hand that all is well.

The guard asks, "My Queen, may I ask what has happened in there? We thought we heard choking and laughter."

Einirt points to a red-faced and giggling Holga. Holga responds with a wave of her hand to dismiss the guards at the door. The guards begin to chuckle, then nod in approval and understanding. Just then, in her body-hugging white dress, Alecia appears with an unsure smile on her face as she can see what is happening with Einirt and the guards.

Alecia reaches the door and asks, "My Queen, are you laughing?"

Einirt nods to indicate yes.

Alecia places her arms around Einirt and smiles as she comments, "I am so pleased to see you in such good spirits, my Queen."

Einirt retorts with a hug and then kisses Alecia on the cheek. Einirt nods and waves to the guards; she then pulls Alecia into her home and closes the door behind them. Now inside, the three ladies begin to hug one another in an affectionate manner as they are all very close friends. Einirt and Holga appear to treat Alecia as a younger sister in a close family.

Alecia asks, "What happened in here that brought my Queen to laughter?"

Holga, with a smiling glare upon her still-beautiful brow, looks and points to Einirt, then nods as if to say, tell her why. Einirt continues to struggle to talk but manages to point at the cup on the table that once held the concoction that Holga drank. Alecia steps up to the table and lifts up the cup, then sniffs the cup. Alecia makes a sour face, then turns to Einirt, then to Holga with a scowled gaze upon her beautiful face.

Alecia, now looking at Holga, asks in an astonished tone, "You drank what was in here?"

Holga nods, then points to Einirt with angry glare. In all her futile efforts to conceal her laughter and grinning face, Einirt bursts out laughing once again in an uncontrollable manner. And again, her laughter is contagious that both Holga and Alecia let out a hardy laugh as well. All three beautiful ladies continue their laughter for minutes on end.

Finally, after several minutes of laughing, Alecia, with a serious look, asks Einirt in a soft and pleasing manner, "My Queen, would you like me to bring you some food or drink?"

Holga looks to Einirt with a bitter glare, which prompts Einirt to begin laughing once again, and again, Einirt's laughter is contagious and loud. The three lovely ladies can't seem to stop themselves from the laughter they are sharing. It is very obvious that they may continue this behavior all night long as the apparent image of Holga's reaction to the concoction she drank will not go away so easily.

Back at the main hall, Cantor and his followers have drunk themselves into a very inebriated state. Some of Cantor's followers have passed out on the floor, some on the tables, and others on the chairs to which they are seated. Cantor is beyond drunk and can't seem to rise from the throne he is seated in. He obviously is attempting to rise but is unable as he is unstable. Some of the villagers that remained in the main hall appear to be laughing at Cantor and whisper among themselves about his appearance and behavior.

Cantor notices the villagers' reactions, then attempts to addresses them, "What the hell are you looking at? What?"

The villagers smile at Cantor, then turn and continue whispering among themselves. Cantor is now visibly upset as he attempts to rise from his sitting position. Cantor, after several more attempts, finally makes it to his feet, then without warning, he falls face-first onto the table directly in front of him. Cantor has bloodied his nose and lips from the fall and is clearly unconscious from the liquor or the fall. The villagers all let out a loud and continuous laugh as they point and mock Cantor.

Meanwhile, the Greek and his party stand in a corner of the main hall and appear to be discussing the events that have taken place earlier and just now. As they continue their discussion, in walks Moats with a few of his men.

Moats and his men make their way over to the Greek's position. Moats asks, "So, Greek, what do you think of Cantor?"

The Greek, unsure of how he should respond, answers in a hesitant and unsure manner, "His Majesty appears to be a tough and ambitious king."

Moats grins, then let's out a chuckle, "Really?"

The Greek, not sure of how to respond, asks Moats cautiously, "What do you think of him?"

Moats grins, then responds, "He is a fool and will not make for a good king as he is not a good man, is he?"

The Greek looks unsure but gives Moats a shrug of his shoulders and tilt of the head, then lifts his hands as he turns them over as if to say I don't know.

Moats chuckles. "You are among friends here. Speak your mind or depart with haste from whence you came!"

The Greek, taken by surprise, responds with haste to Moats's demand, "Yes, we feel that William was a great king and Cantor will not be!"

Moats smiles, then ask, "Now that wasn't so hard to say, was it?"

The Greek and his men smile in relief.

The Greek, now feeling more assured, speaks more plainly to Moats, "Cantor says he will marry Queen Einirt, and she will have no choice in the matter. Is this true?"

Moats retorts with a frown and in disgust. "It is our tradition that our king, if not married, may wed any single women of his choice so long as she is of no kin to him, for breeding purposes!"

The Greek appears taken back by Moats's words.

The Greek questions Moats again, "So he can marry Queen Einirt at any time he chooses then?"

Moats's response is deliberate and rapid. "No! Cantor must give Einirt seven nights to grieve for William before he can take her as his wife and queen!"

The Greek nods as if to demonstrate his understanding of the situation, then states, "Queen Einirt is a good queen and a good woman. She deserves better than Cantor, yes?"

Moats smiles at the Greek, then responds, "William said you were a smart and wise man. He was right as usual."

The Greek grins, then nods to Moats as he thanks him for the comments. "I thank you, General. William said the same of you."

Moats laughs, then speaks, "He was a good friend before he became king, then he became a great friend and an even better king. He was my best friend, my brother, and my sister's husband!"

The Greek, with a shocked look, then asks, "Einirt is your sister?"

Moats gives the Greek a proud smile, then asks, "Do you not see the resemblance?"

The Greek, now with a baffled look upon his brow and unsure of how to respond, mutters in a soft tone, "Yes."

Moats laughs, then states, "She is my beautiful sister, and no, she looks nothing like me!" Moats laughs. "Thank the gods!"

The Greek, now relieved, appears to relax once again and laughs with Moats as well as all those in earshot of Moats's comments.

Moats leans and whispers to the Greek, "That is why I cannot be king. My sister is queen."

The Greek nods as if to demonstrate he understands.

Moats smiles at the Greek and announces, "You know, I raised her after our father and mother died. She had only seen one winter. She was very young."

The Greek nods, then speaks, "You did well. She is a fine lady and a great queen!"

Moats nods with a look of pride upon his rugged mug, then states, "Yes, yes I did!"

The Greek grins and nods in agreement with Moats. All within the hall seem to be in better spirits after Moats has arrived and brought a sense of stability and honor back to the people of the village. Moats then turns and glares over at an unconscious Cantor. Just then, two of Cantor's followers aid him back to his feet and place him back on his stolen throne, where he remains passed out. The two followers of Cantor look around in a suspicious manner as the try to present their new king as a respectable leader.

* * *

Now at a dark stone-built, gloomy, moss-laden walled fortress up in a wooded covered mountainside sits the fortress of Grimmcock. Inside a stone-walled room, standing in front of what appears to be a stone-built circled water well stands the old warlock, Grimmcock. He is a very aged, wrinkled, white-bearded, white-mustached, thin, grayish-skinned, evil-looking man with two different colored eyes and dressed in his purple-and-gold embroidered cloak. Grimmcock appears bent over as he stands staring into the well. He appears stoic and without expression as he glares into his well with an evil stare. In the water appears a vision, which brings a half-sinister grin to Grimmcock's mug.

Suddenly, the door to his chamber opens and in walks two of his disciples; the first to enter of the disciples is a large man, adorned in bronze-colored armor trimmed in black unpolished metal, a scar-riddled pale-faced strange-looking bald man with bizarre-colored eyes who is named Brummel. Brummel is the apprentice warlock and second to Grimmcock. The other disciple enters with an awkward walk, a gangly yet a muscular-built man adorned in a ribbed armor which is red color and laden in silver chain mail. He has long red hair with bright red mustache and beard; his eyes are as black as his heart, and he is a terrifying presence of man who answers to the name Cetan. He is Grimmcock's grand warrior general and beast master. The two make their way next to Grimmcock, Brummel to the right and Cetan to Grimmcock's left.

Brummel asks, "My lord, your plan appears to be working as you imagined."

Cetan, with an evil grin, nods in agreement.

Grimmcock grins as he turns to Brummel, then responds, "Yes, my child. Yes, indeed."

Cetan speaks out in a creepy tone, "Cantor and the Tartan king both get what they wanted, and now we get what we want!"

Grimmcock smiles, then announces, "Cantor is such a fool. He betrays all just to have William's woman and his throne!"

Brummel speaks, "Yes, my lord. He should have asked for more. What a fool!"

Grimmcock nods as he smiles, then makes his way over to the large wooden table sitting in the middle of the room, which is covered with scrolls, books, small pouches, small glass bottles, small pots, large and small bowls. Brummel turns, then walks up to the table and joins Grimmcock. Grimmcock appears to be mixing some powders he has poured from some of the pouches into a bowl. Brummel appears to reach his hand out over the table to grasp a large dark-colored book with some strange insignias on the cover.

Grimmcock slaps Brummel's hand, then gives Brummel a very angry scowl as he addresses him harshly, "Don't ever touch that book or for that matter, anything else on this table!"

Brummel retracts his hand with a look of fear upon his face.

Brummel then bows to Grimmcock as he takes several steps backward; he humbly apologizes to his master, "I apologize, my lord. Please forgive me, Master!"

Grimmcock glares at Brummel, then announces, "Let that not happen again. In time, I shall share with you what you need to know, but not now. Understand!"

Brummel nods in agreement. Cetan stands by and watches on as a slight grin forms on his strange-looking mug.

* * *

Back at the main hall in the Centaur village, Moats and the Greek are engaged in a deep conversation.

Moats looks to the Greek with a serious expression on his face. "Perhaps in tomorrow's morn would be a good time for you and your people to depart this village and get as much safe distance as possible between yourselves and this village."

The Greek, with a puzzled look, asks, "Are we in danger from Cantor?"

With a slight grin, Moats replies, "It is possible. However, I say this because you may not want to be around when we send out our young men on their journey to become men."

The Greek curiously questions Moat, "What happens on this journey, if I may ask?"

Moats explains in a very serious tone, "Several of our young men are selected to go on a long and dangerous journey to a place we do not speak of often. They must enter a dark forest where evil lurks, and then they must reach the Tree of Sorrow where their hearts are tested as is their duty and loyalty."

The Greek appears suspicious, then asks, "What happens at this tree?"

Moats reluctantly answers, but in a whisper, as he leans down and tells the Greek, "The young men must take the sick, deformed, and deathly ill children to this tree and bind them for Grimmcock to take."

The Greek, not as surprised as expected, reacts, "Oh, I see, much like the Spartans discard their undesired or weak children."

Moats gives the Greek a glare, then, in a resolute voice, proclaims, "Discarded! No! We sacrifice them to that evil piece of shit of a warlock so we won't have to battle his creatures or his army of cannibals!"

The Greek, now with a traumatized looked on his face, questions, "Creatures and cannibals!"

Moats says, "Yes!"

The Greek asks, "Sacrifices to Grimmcock, how long has this been going on?"

Moats responds in disgust, "Since before I was born!"

The Greek asks, "Why didn't anyone try to put a stop to this ritual long ago?"

Moats shrugs his massive shoulders, then answers, "I'm not the king and no king to my knowledge has ever desired war with both Grimmcock and the Tartans. One mighty foe is enough for even us to deal with."

The Greek nods and comments, "The Tartans are a large army, but they don't seem to pose any peril to your army of mighty warriors as demonstrated in this last battle!"

Moats chuckles, then responds, "They are led by a fool of a king, but that fool's time will end, then General Eric will take over, and he is no fool, so we must always choose the wise and less harmful path for our people!"

The Greek nods in agreement, then announces to Moats, "I am grateful for your advice, your wisdom, your kindness, your friendship, your honor, your guidance, and your strength, General Moats."

Moats laughs, then slaps the Greek on the back and responds, "William and Einirt both liked you and so do I, Greek. It was my pleasure. Perhaps one day you can help my nephew with the same."

The Greek smiles, then appears somewhat bewildered as he asks, "What is your nephew's name?"

Moats shrugs his shoulders once more, then responds, "I do not know. He has not been born yet! When he is, he will be Einirt's son and our future king."

The Greek, with a puzzled gaze, looks up to Moats, then asks, "Is Einirt with child?"

Moats, with a determined look, replies, "One day she will have a son and he will be a great king!" Moats nods in a very positive manner, then begins to smile. "The best king our people will ever know!"

The Greek smiles, then nods in agreement.

Back over in the queen's home, the three ladies sit and talk as they have in the past many times before, but this time there is a suspicious and secretive manner about them.

Einirt, in a soft voice, "Things will be different under Cantor's rule."

Holga, with a look of despair and in a worried manner, asks with her muttered voice, "But why is he allowed to be king? Did William tell you Cantor was to take his place if he should fall?"

With a depressed look on her face, Einirt responds, "Cantor is the top-ranking warrior and general, so the crown falls to him. It is our way as William and I have no heir to bestow William's crown upon."

Holga asks in a dejected manner and in her muttered voice, "What of your brother? He is of higher rank and a better warrior than Cantor."

Einirt responds sadly to her friend, "Yes, this is true, but he cannot. He is brother to our current queen and he cannot challenge Cantor because of this, because of me!"

Holga bows her head, then places her hands over her face in a dejected and disenchanted manner.

Einirt places her hand on her friend's back, then announces in a determined and firm tone, "You have my word. Cantor will never harm you again!"

Alecia asks, "There is talk that Cantor will take you as his bride. What you will do, my Queen?"

Einirt turns as she looks to her niece, then responds in a deliberate manner and tone, "I shall marry the bastard and retain my position so that I may protect our people, especially those that I love!"

Alecia grins, then inquires, "How will you punish him for what he has done to our friends?"

Einirt grins, then places her hand under Holga's chin, raising it just to make eye contact with her friend, then responds very deliberately, "I shall have a conversation with our healer when he returns. Then I shall inquire as to certain remedies he can grace his queen with to aid in my protection and my designs to grace our new king with!"

The three smile a mischievous smile, then give one another a nod of agreement. Suddenly, there is a knock on the door. Alecia rises up, then unlocks and opens the door.

Alecia turns and announces, "It is your brother and my husband, my Queen."

Einirt motions with her hand to have the two enter. Moats and Brock enter the dwelling where Alecia immediately embraces her loving husband, Brock. Moats feels ashamed and is apprehensive as he approaches his queen, for he knows what he is about to tell his little sister will pierce her heart and cause her only more agony and sorrow.

Moats also fears Einirt may not forgive him, yet he steps up and with a slight bow, asks in a respectful manner, "How is our Queen?"

Einirt shakes her head with grin and a glare in her eyes, then replies in a determined manner, "I was your sister before I was your queen, and you should address me as such, my brother."

Moats nods, then, in a sarcastic tone, responds, "Yes my Queen, as you wish."

Einirt grins as she makes her way to her big brother, then gives him a loving embrace, "You see, this is where I get my stubbornness from!"

Einirt then gives Moats a kiss on the cheek. In a somber but confident manner, Einirt tells Moats, "I am doing my best, my brother. It is all I can do."

Moats looks down into the eyes of his beautiful but saddened sister, then in a soft tone, he states, "It is urgent that I speak to you in confidence and in secret."

Einirt releases her hold on Moats, then steps back in a serious fashion. Einirt asks, "What is it about my brother?"

Moats looks around, then states in a whisper, "Perhaps we should speak alone."

With a stern gaze and concerned but confident tone, Einirt responds, "My brother, we are all family here. You may speak of what you wish in confidence among them as well."

Holga speaks up as she makes her way to her feet, then proclaims in her muttered voice, "I am tired, my Queen. May I have your pardon to go to my home and get some sleep?"

Einirt nods her head, then calls to the guards, "Guards!"

The door opens, then the senior guards asks, "Yes, my Queen?"

Einirt orders the guard, "Please take another guard with you and escort Holga to her home and see that no harm comes to her."

The guard nods, then escorts Holga out of the home, closing the door behind them. Brock, still standing near the door, locks the door with one arm and caresses Alecia with his other arm. Moats then motions for his queen to sit in a chair at the table that lies in front of them. Moats sits directly across from his queen as he places his coupled hands on the table. Einirt gently but firmly caresses her hand over his, then looks him in the eyes with a concerned look on her beautiful yet intrigued face.

In a very serious manner, Einirt asks her brother, "Tell me my brother, what is that ways so heavy on your mind?"

Moats looks Einirt directly in the eyes with a heavy and stern frown. "I wish to tell you what I saw on the battlefield, but I find it difficult to say, especially at this time!"

A now determined yet reluctant Einirt asks as she clears her throat, then peers into her brother's sad eyes and pleads in a soft voice, "Please tell me. As your sister, I beg you, and as your queen, I demand you tell me!"

With a tear in his eye and a look of despair upon his rugged, bearded face, he begins to speak in a soft voice, "William and the cavalry attacked the Tartans from the rear as he had planned. While we were battling our way over the bridge, it took us time as it was covered with hundreds of Tartans dead. When we finally made our way through and battled to the top of the hill, I could see William was engaged with three Tartans and Cantor was engaged with one. William slew two of the Tartans. As I was making my way down the hill, I saw Cantor slay William from behind. He drove his sword through William's back, then took our king's head. Cantor then looked to the Tartan general, Eric. They nodded at each other, and then Eric withdrew his army. Cantor then took William's sword and proclaimed our king dead and that he was, by the wish of William, to take the throne. All I could do was fall to my knees and mourn our king, my brother, and my best friend!"

All this time, Einirt simply sits there and listens with a stoic gaze as tears flow down her beautiful face. Einirt begins to open her mouth to speak; the tears continued to flow down her beautiful face and now down her plush rosy red lips and into her mouth. She swallows the tears as she attempts to speak once again. Alecia is weeping uncontrollably with her beautiful face now buried in her husband's chest. With his Alecia in his embrace, Brock looks on as his lower lip begins to quiver; he is unable to hold off any longer. His eyes fill with tears.

Moats shakes his head with tears flowing down his rough and hardened face, then in a sad and apologetic voice, he says, "I am sorry my little one. I could not get there in time to save him!"

Einirt squeezes her brother's hands as she looks to him in a consoling manner. With tears flowing and mouth quivering, she speaks in a soft and choked-up voice, "No, my brother, you need not apologize! I know how much you loved my William as much as he loved you!"

Moats looks to Einirt in such a pitiful manner it causes Einirt to rise up, then hug her brother from across the table as the old rugged and battle-hardened general lets out a loud cry, "I am sorry my little one. I am so sorry!"

Einirt grasps her brother's face in her hands as tears continue to run down both their faces. She then addresses him in a reassuring yet sorrowful manner, "We need to be strong my brother. That is what you taught me and what William would expect!"

Moats nods in agreement, then announces in a still mournful but clearing voice, "Yes my lady!"

Einirt releases her brother's face, then sits back in a stoic manner as tears continue to run down her somber and beautiful face. Einirt announces in a clearer but still somber manner, "We must all be strong and take heed of our emotions and thoughts! We must also make preparations for all that may come our way!"

Moats nods as he clears his throat. "Yes, my lady."

Einirt looks to her family as she attempts to smile; as the tears continue to run down her face, she announces with an attempted grin and in her soft but stern voice, "William lives on!"

Moats sits back in surprise and is speechless with both eyes and mouth wide-open.

Brock looks to his aunt with a sorrowful frown and with a disparaging stare as he states, "Auntie, I saw King William lying there!"

Einirt announces in a heartfelt and soft tone, "He left me with child!"

Now they all look to Einirt in a mix of amazement, confusion, and glee. Einirt strains to smile but only manages a glimpse of one. All appear excited and happy for the news they have just received.

Moats, without hesitation, asks, "That is great news! Do you think it is a son?"

Einirt, in a gleeful manner, responds, "Yes!"

Alecia speaks out in glee, "So you have an heir to your throne!"

Einirt looks to all with a serious but distraught gaze. "Not if Cantor finds out!"

Moats speaks up in a protective and forceful manner, "I have a plan to deal with that piece of shit. You will have no need to fear Cantor!"

Einirt raises her hand to calm her brother down, then announces in a stern yet loving tone, "No, my brother. You will do no harm to Cantor, and neither shall you Brock!"

Brock looks to his aunt in a disgruntled and confused manner, then speaks, "But, Auntie, we must do something to protect you!"

Einirt gives Brock a look of wrath and utter resolve, then speaks to all in a determined manner, "Neither of you will act against Cantor as I will not allow any harm to come to you or my unborn son! Is that understood?"

All nod in agreement; they then bow to their queen.

Moats looks to his little sister, and in a somber tone, he speaks, "I would do nothing to place your son in harm's way, my little one, but we will protect you both with our lives! This I swear!"

Moats and Brock both nod, then place their fists to their chest, covering their hearts, and state in unison in a firm and proud manner, "That we swear, my queen!"

Einirt announces in a confident and firm tone, "I shall deal with Cantor in my own way, in my own time, and he will never have an heir to our throne. This I swear to you all!"

Moats speaks up confidently, "Is there anything you wish us to do?"

Einirt replies with a cocky guise and yet in sweet tone, "Yes, there is, my brother. Come all of you and sit. This is what I wish you to do for your sister, your aunt, and your queen."

With a nod and a serious gaze, they all sit at the table, then lean in closer to hear Einirt's plan.

Now with a tilt of her beautiful face, Alecia, in an understanding manner, asks, "That is why you said you will marry Cantor, to make him believe he is father of your and William's son, yes?"

Einirt grins as she nods, then replies, "Yes, my wise little niece."

Moats chuckles, then proclaims, "You are wise beyond your years and have learned much, my little one." Moats nods in approval of his little sister.

Einirt places her hand over her brother's hand with a smile on her face as she announces in a content and complimentary manner, "I have you and William to thank for that, my brother."

Brock smiles, then comments proudly, "You are a great queen, my aunt, and a wise lady to learn from." Brock then looks to his beloved and smiles.

Alecia makes eye contact with her rugged and handsome-faced husband; she then turns to look at Einirt as she speaks in a calming voice, "Yes my Queen, this is true. I will be honored to learn from you."

Einirt smiles at her beautiful and elegant niece, then nods as she gracefully speaks, "You would have made a wise and beautiful queen, my precious, wise, and trusted Alecia!"

Alecia smiles back at Einirt with a slight blush on her cheeks.

Einirt, in a determined and confident manner, addresses her family, "We must maintain our positions and await the return of the healer. He is vital to our success and the justice we seek."

All nod in agreement with a bit a snarl upon their faces.

As he looks to his sister in an understanding and agreeable manner, Moats speak up, "We must act as if we do not know of what Cantor has done, yes?"

Einirt nods in agreement, then says in approving tone, "Yes, my brother. Cantor must never know what we have learned and only those whom we trust shall. That is the way I wish it to remain."

Again all nod in agreement.

Brock, in somewhat of a puzzled manner, asks, "Auntie, what does the healer have to do with your plans?"

With a glare of discontent and disbelief, Alecia looks to her husband, then gives him an elbow to his massive rib cage, then says in a lecturing tone, "The healer has potions and spells he can prepare for our queen to give to Cantor to make him ill or worse!"

Brock sits on the bench, still with a confused look on his face, then realizes what his beautiful wife has said. Brock appears to understand when his expression turns from bewilderment to a grin, which then turns into a smile as he nods; it is clear that understanding has overtaken him. He nods in a more pleasureful manner as his beautiful wife's words have finally set into his slow but well-meaning mind.

The rest look to Brock as Moats shakes his head in disbelief, then rolls his eyes when, suddenly, Brock speaks out excitedly, "I get it, I get it!"

The ladies let out a smile and sweet chuckle as Moats gives his son a contemptuous glare.

Moats then speaks, "Yes, you understand now?"

Brock nods to indicate yes he does.

Einirt, with a pleasant smile upon her beautiful face, speaks in her soft voice, "Then it is understood. We must not act until I speak with the healer, yes?"

The rest of the family look to Einirt, then with a nod and a smile, they all place their hands upon Einirt's folded hands in the center of the wooden table.

The next morning, we find many of the villagers have gathered near the main hall in the center of the Centaur village where they appear somewhat unpleased with the event that is soon to take place. Cantor and his followers make their way from the main hall as they clearly appear the worse for wear. Cantor is staggering to keep his balance with his bloodshot eyes and nearly closed from the morning sun as he attempts to gather his composure as he spurts out words that cannot be understood. Cantor's followers look no better as they attempt to listen to his mumblings. Cantor stops near a bucket which appears to hold some type of liquid, then he pours the liquid contents over his head. What appears to be water pours down his long snarled, dirty hair and scarred, unappealing face, which appears to awaken him. Cantor appears to gather his senses as he then looks to his men as he stands upon a pile of horse feces.

Unaware of his predicament, Cantor addresses his followers in a gruff and unclear voice, "Cooome with meee and shhaa maaan queen and get sheee baaack Eeeinirt."

A follower of Cantor's looks to him with a baffled look on his face, then asks, "What?"

Cantor appears angered by the question, then attempts to respond in a more clear and precise voice, "I said, get Queen Einirt and tell her I demand her presence here!"

The follower nods; he turns, then begins to make his way from Cantor in the direction of Einirt's home.

Meanwhile, in the front of Einirt's home stands a surprisingly happy-spirited and smiling Einirt. Einirt is standing with her arms crossed behind her back and is clearly a true vision of beauty in her long, white, somewhat sheer dress gown and her barely visible white leather elegant braided sandals. Truly a vision of natural beauty with her long black hair flowing down her shoulders covering her bountiful breasts, smiling with her plush ruby red natural lips and deep blue sultry eyes that could freeze even a god in his tracks. She appears to be having a pleasant conversation with the Greek and his people. And standing alongside her in a pleasant and cheerful manner are Moats in his usual battle attire, Alecia in a form-fitting white gown with her smiling beautiful face, which is flanked on both sides by her gorgeous long, flowing locks, Brock in his characteristic daily battle gear, and a beautiful yet surprisingly smiling Holga, draped in a yellow-laced deep cleavage-baring waist-wrapped elegant, flowing gown with her long beautiful hanging mane wrapped in braids just tickling her tiny waist.

The Greek speaks in a grateful manner, "Again, I am very grateful for all you and your people have taught us, my Queen."

Einirt smiles, and in a proud yet soft tone, she replies, "My friend, it was our pleasure, and we thank you for what you have brought and taught our people."

The Greek humble replies, "This was an experience I will never forget, and you, my queen, are, without a doubt, the kindest, wisest, and most beautiful queen these old eyes have ever laid eyes upon, and I thank you for that."

As a slight blush arises to her cheeks, Einirt smiles, then in an honored manner, she nods to the Greek and speaks in a humbled tone, "I thank you for your kind words, my friend!"

Moats interjects in a firm yet friendly manner, "Perhaps it is time our friends depart for their home, my queen."

Einirt reaches for the Greek's hands with hers; the Greek simply complies with his hands stretched out and upended as he humbly nods his head down in respect and admiration of his newfound friend and queen.

Einirt, in a soft and almost emotional voice, says, "You and your people are welcome in our village anytime, just as William so desired and as long as I am queen."

The Greek looks up to Einirt, then realizes her eyes are beginning to swell up with tears, so without notice or fear, the Greek takes Einirt into his arms, placing his hands around her tiny waist and back, then gives her a loving hug. Shocked by this action, Moats, Brock, and several guards react as they almost rush to the Greek as the women gasp at the action, but they all suddenly realize that Einirt has placed her arms around the Greek's shoulders and neck in a very reciprocating manner.

Tears began to flow from Einirt's beautiful blue and now-saddened eyes as she struggles to speak; she then finally pries the words from her beautiful succulent lips, "Thank you. He thought very highly of you!"

The Greek, with his eyes full of tears, manages to speak in a choppy voice, "I thought he was a great man, not just a great king, and I, too, shall miss him, but it saddens my heart to see you be so strong knowing what you have lost. If you ever need me and my people, please send word and we shall be here. Anytime, my lady."

The Greek then gives Einirt a peck on the cheek. Einirt places her hands on his cheeks as she gazes into his eyes with her tear-filled beautiful eyes, then kisses him on the forehead.

Einirt tells the Greek in a very sincere way, "Thank you and your presence shall be missed. Perhaps one day we will meet again in a less mournful time." Einirt then pulls the Greek's face in closer to hers, then whispers in very soft tone, "Perhaps one day you will meet my son, but this must never be spoken of until his birth!"

The Greek, with a surprised look on his face, pulls back as Einirt, with a grin, releases his face from her hands.

As a smile begins to form on the Greek's aged mug as he then begins to slightly nod his head repeatedly, then happily states, "Yes, my lady, perhaps then and only then."

Einirt lets out her subtle and elegant smile with a slight tilt of her head; she nods to indicate her satisfaction with the Greek's response though the pain is prevalent as tears run down her beautiful face. She still manages her composure and queenly stature. The Greek and his people begin to bow continuously as they step back to their small caravan of goods and horses.

The Greek and his people now begin to depart as the Greek looks to Einirt, and in a very respectful manner, he bows down from his horse, then states, "My lady, until we meet again. May the gods protect you and bless you!"

He nods as he tilts his head ever so slightly as he smiles, then slowly turns his head and waves goodbye with his right hand as he and his party depart then make their way down the path exiting the Centaur village.

Moats steps up to his little sister and asks in a concerned yet calming manner, "Are you all right, my little one?"

Einirt smiles with a sincere gaze at her brother as she wipes the tears from her beautiful face and tear-filled eyes; she then replies in an assuring yet reluctant voice, "Yes, yes, I am fine."

Moats steps up and places his huge left arm over his little sister's shoulders as he smiles down at her as he confirms, "Shall we go and do this shameful duty forced upon us? Then while we are at it, take Cantor's mind for a dark and mysterious journey!"

Einirt looks up to her big brother with a cagey grin upon her beautiful brow as she grasps his scarred, massive, and manly hand with her elegant and feminine hand; she then leads her family and friends down the path in the direction leading to the main hall.

Suddenly, Cantor's follower reaches the royal party, then stops in front of his queen and nods in respect to Einirt; he asks in a respectful manner, "My Queen, Cantor requests your presence at the main hall."

Einirt responds in a positive and kindly manner, "Please tell Cantor I shall be there shortly."

The follower nods, then turns and dashes away from the party. Einirt continues to lead her family and friends in the direction of the main hall area. The party soon reaches the front of the main hall area where all that see Einirt bow their heads in respect to their beloved queen and friend. Cantor is standing with his followers and can't help but notice Einirt in her form-fitting, elegant, somewhat sheer gown, with her long black flowing hair, beautiful face, and sultry yet commanding walk. Cantor is mesmerized by Einirt's beauty and elegance as he cannot help but stare and drool at the vision of beauty which has been presented to his nondeserving malevolent eyes. Einirt makes eye contact with a stunned and speechless Cantor; she simply smiles, and with a slight tilt and nod of her head, she turns to speak to her subjects that have come to speak to her. Cantor's followers gawk at the presence of their breathtakingly beautiful and stunning queen.

Cantor notices his men, then reacts in an angry tone, "Do not gaze upon our queen in such a way. She is to be my bride soon. Show respect!"

His followers look down to the ground in accordance to Cantor's orders, but unlike his followers, Cantor continues to gaze upon Einirt's beauty. Einirt is made well aware as to Cantor's behavior by several of the ladies whom she is speaking with. Several of the ladies let out a giggle as they smile and grin as they admire their beautiful queen. In her elegant and skillful manner, Einirt begins to sway side to side as she strokes her long beautiful hair, then gives a quick and sultry gaze in Cantor's direction, then turns as if to act shyly away and back to her friends and subjects. Einirt continues her discussion as she grins at her fellow ladies and friends; she then glances to her massive older brother with a gentle nod. She turns back to continue her conversation with her friends and subjects. Moats, on cue, steps up to his little sister's position, then stands to her right side, as if to protect her, as does his giant of a son, Brock, who takes position to Einirt's left as the guards who escorted them stand nearby in formation and attention. Shortly after, Cantor appears to have summoned the courage to approach his queen.

Cantor, flanked by some of his followers, now stands near his queen as he clears his throat; he asks nervously, "How is our Queen today?"

Einirt, in a subtle manner turns and in her elegant way, peers over to Cantor, then smiles as she speaks in her soft sultry voice, "I am better than yesterday, thank you."

Einirt now turns back in a coy fashion and continues to converse with the ladies whom she was speaking with previously. Cantor appears smitten and, in a somewhat baffled manner, attempts to get Einirt's attention by clearing his throat once again. Einirt pays him no mind.

Cantor then, in a hesitant manner, asks, "So, my Queen, would you be so kind as to accompany me into the main hall?"

Einirt looks to Cantor in a subtle and demure manner, then responds in a soft and sultry tone, "But of course, since you asked in such a pleasant manner."

Cantor is visibly smitten by Einirt, and no matter how hard he tries, he cannot succeed in hiding his feelings for her. In a delighted manner, Cantor steps up to Einirt both nervously and clumsily. Cantor raises his right arm so as Einirt may hold his long but average-sized arm. Einirt grins as she looks to Cantor with a confident look about her; she gently places her hand upon Cantor's arm, then nods to indicate she is ready. Cantor then awkwardly attempts to lead his queen in the direction of the main hall so that they may proceed in the commencement of this important day.

Einirt stops in her tracks, which causes Cantor to also stop; she looks down, then addresses Cantor in a whisper as she attempts not to cause too much embarrassment for Cantor, "You have horse waste on your feet!"

Cantor, clearly embarrassed and red-faced, responds in a low voice to his queen, "I apologize, my lady. I must have just stepped in it!"

Einirt smiles as she looks up to Cantor, and in an understanding and reassuring manner, she quietly speaks, "I am sure it will all come off before we enter the hall."

She nods with a smile, then continues her sultry and confident walk as Cantor continues to escort his queen proudly. The two lead the procession into the main hall. As the others begin to fill the large room, it is clear that not all are pleased with what is about to take place. Some of the women inside the hall are weeping as the men standing next to them; it is apparent that they are none too pleased either. Cantor escorts Einirt to the thrones, which rest against the eastern wall near the center of the large room and resting upon a stage some three steps high. Cantor holds his arm out so as to aid Einirt to step up to the throne where she sits, then to everyone's amazement, she waves her right arm over the throne, which resides next to her to indicate to Cantor to sit next to her. Cantor, with a duplicitous grin, takes the throne next to Einirt.

Einirt then stands and proclaims in a confident yet compassionate manner and tone, "As your queen, I do hereby proclaim the day of sorrow and rebirth to begin."

Einirt regains her seat as Cantor, who appears visibly shaken and unnerved, looks to Einirt, and in an unsure manner, he questions his queen, "I thought the king was to begin the day?"

Einirt, in a confident yet calm manner, retorts "Yes, but you are not yet king."

She then smiles and tilts her head ever so gracefully, then turns to look at her subjects. Cantor is left flabbergasted and visibly confused. Near the side of the stage area sit three young children. One of the children, a young boy no more than three years old and is dressed in a simple white robe, appears to be riddled with excessive skin tags, a larger-than-average forehead and his face appears slightly deformed. Next to the young boy sits a young girl, perhaps two years of age, with little, if any, hair on her head; she also appears somewhat disfigured with one eye black in color and the other blue. She is also adorned in a simple white robe. The last child is also draped in a simple white robe and is a young girl not more than one year of age and appears blind as both eyes are covered with a bluish, blackish film. Standing behind these three young children are eight teenage boys, large for their ages but still no younger than twelve years of age but no older than fourteen based on their appearance. They are all darned in similar clothing, all wearing pants, shirts, small fur cloaks, and fur-covered leather strapped boots. The teenage boys do not appear pleased that they are bound for the duty they are about to endure. Several of the teenage boys and ill-fated children's parents appear saddened as they have gathered near the group.

Einirt glances over to Cantor and asks, "Will you be so kind as to address the parents of these ill-fated children and the boys who must take this sad journey?"

Cantor bravely and eagerly nods to his queen in agreement; he then stands up with a gleam in his eyes and announces to the group of parents in a harsh uncompassionate fashion, "We all know what must be done here, so let us move on!"

Einirt looks up to Cantor in a surprised manner, then gives Cantor a slight nudge with her elbow. Cantor looks down at his still-seated queen and can see by her facial expression that she is somewhat perturbed at his uncompassionate display.

Cantor immediately attempts to defuse the situation he has created with his failed and heartless speech; a now-embarrassed Cantor turns to his queen. "Perhaps it would be best to hear from our Queen in this matter."

Einirt composes herself as she smiles, then rises to her feet whereby she announces in a compassionate tone and manner, "My friends, this is truly a trying time for us all, and for some of us, a mortifying one, I can assure you!"

Einirt, in a compassionate fashion and a somber gaze, first looks to the children, then to the teenagers and finally to the parents who are weeping and saddened by the events taking place. With a graceful yet saddened expression, Einirt then looks around to all her subjects and friends.

Einirt then announces in a very compassionate tone, "We all have these families to thank, and we need to show our condolences as well as our strength and appreciation for what they have yet to endure. We must be there for them as you have all been there for me in my time of mourning!"

All the Centaur people nod in agreement as they all look to one another for compassion and strength.

Cantor speaks out from his seated position, "Yes, we must all show strength."

Cantor smiles as if he was proud of himself as well as the words he has chosen to speak. All look to Cantor in dismay and disappointment as some even shake their heads in disbelief.

This prompts Einirt to react in her elegant and queenly manner. Einirt smiles subtly, then looks to all the parents who are involved in the day's matters and announces in confidence, "I would like to personally thank each and every one of you for the sacrifice you are making today for your people. It is no easy thing to do, but it serves us all in the days to come, and may the gods be gracious for those who shall return to us. May they return us men!"

Einirt bows to the parents, then takes her seat as she appears to wipe a tear from her eyes. The people begin to nod and discuss the matter at hand.

Cantor, unsure what to say, stands, then proclaims, "We should all be as strong as our queen and do what is necessary for our people to prosper and live well!"

It appears that the Centaur people do not pay much attention to Cantor as they continue to discuss the matter at hand. Cantor appears pleased with his short speech and begins to look around for praise but does not receive any as the people appear to converse among themselves and pay no heed to Cantor.

Einirt looks to Cantor with a pleasant smile, then asks, "Do you wish to lead the procession out the door and prepare the cart?"

Cantor nods eagerly, then arises to his feet once again and proclaims, "Let us make our way to the sacrificial cart and begin the ritual."

Cantor steps down the stage and proceeds to the main doorway, followed by his loyal followers. Cantor turns, and to his dismay, he notices no one is following him. Cantor looks over to Einirt in a disbelieving and baffled gaze. Einirt retorts with a look of disappointment as she shakes her head in disapproval of his rushing off. Cantor, realizing he did not behave correctly and forgot his place, suddenly rushes over to Einirt, followed by his loyal followers. Cantor steps up to the stage and places his arm out for Einirt to grasp. Einirt smiles down at Cantor, then stands up as she takes Cantor's arm and makes her way elegantly down the stairs, and in her sultry walk, she makes her way to the doorway, followed by her family, friends, and personal guard. The villagers follow them from the rear of the procession, the parents with their teenage sons, and, lastly, the parents carrying the young children who are to be sent away. Now all have gathered around a small horseless cart and standing nearest to the cart are Einirt, Cantor, Moats, Brock, and the royal guard of Einirt.

The parents of the teens say their goodbyes to their sons, the mothers with tears in their eyes and the fathers raising their hands to their chests and giving a simple nod to their sons. The parents of the ill-fated children place their children onto the cart with heavy hearts, and the pain is plain for all to see as the mothers weep and moan, and the fathers look down as if ashamed and sad at the same time. The parents of the ill-fated children now bend down and kiss their children for the last time; they are then escorted away by the guards appointed to this harsh and woeful task.

Now with the children's parents out of sight, the order is given by a sorrowful but determined Einirt, "May you have a safe and prosperous journey. Always remember, you are our future, and we will need you all to return to us a men. The guards shall escort you to the edge of the village, and there you will began you journey to manhood. This may be the hardest thing you shall do, but you must for the good of our people. Now with the God's blessings and protection, be on your way and return to us as men."

Escorted by several guards, the teens grab the cart handles and proceed to pull the cart away to begin their journey down the path leading out of the Centaur village. A mournful Einirt turns, then proceeds to walk away with tears in her eyes, then is joined on walk by her family, friends, and royal guard. Unsure what to do, Cantor stands confused, watching Einirt as she walks farther from his position.

Cantor finally speaks out in an unsure tone, "My Queen, I had expected to discuss a matter with you."

Moats turns, then addresses Cantor in a firm yet polite manner, "Our queen is still in mourning. She will send for you when she is ready to discuss matters of our people, not until then."

Moats turns and continues to escort his beautiful little sister. Cantor appears displeased with this response, but he is unable to challenge their traditions for losing the people at this time would be an unwise and nonreversible mistake.

One of Cantor's followers leans in and speaks to Cantor in an advisory tone, "Our queen has six more days to mourn and then you may demand her presence!"

Cantor nods in agreement as he stands with an angry scowl upon his brow. Cantor in a low voice says, "Yes, and we shall bury her king on tomorrow's morn."

The next morning, we find a richly decorated long box lying on the back of a cart; it is apparent that the box is a coffin and the box apparently contains the former King William's body. Standing to attention in rows besides the cart with their right fists to their chest, covering their hearts, are a well-dressed royal guards, adorned in gold-colored armor and donning their gold-dressed helmets, each and every one of them unable to restrain their tears from running down their rugged, battle-hardened faces as they try ever so hard to maintain their composure. To make it even harder on the loyal royal guards, now arrives their beloved and heartbroken queen; she is being escorted by her loyal and loving family.

With Moats to her right, dressed in his best gold battle armor, he is clearly moved by the situation at hand and is trying to resist the tears forming in his bloodshot saddened eyes. To Einirt's left is her giant nephew Brock; he is adorned in his gold shining armor as well, and he is not doing as well as his father to hold back the tears. They simply continue flow down his bearded and hardened, rugged mug. With her arms wrapped around his massive left arm walks his beautiful and dainty wife, Alecia. Alecia is dressed in a lovely black gown that hugs her magnificent sculpted body like a well-fitting glove. Her long beautiful hair hangs low and is free-flowing as gusts of wind move her hair ever so lightly; she is visibly distraught and unable to withhold her emotions and flowing tears as she struggles to keep up with her giant husband's stride. Finally, we have Einirt shrouded in a long sheer black veil covering her mournful beautiful face.

As usual, Einirt is stunning in a long black dress adorned with beautiful and elegant lacework that appears as if the dress was painted on her. Her long beautiful flowing hair is blended in with the color of the veil covering her upper body and face. It is very apparent to all that Einirt is very grief-stricken as she continues to weep profusely in a pitiful and heart-wrenching fashion. It is apparent that if her brother and nephew were not holding her up, she would collapse from her very visibly unstable state and degree of her mourning. Their queen's presence has a domino effect on all who are present, and the tears, like rain in storm, just steadily increase and pour down in droves. Cantor is present with his followers who are all dressed in their best gold-and-silver armor; they are all standing in the distance, appearing not to want to be a distraction from the proceedings at hand, yet none seems to mourn at this woeful event.

Now standing in front of the casket cart, Einirt and her family bow to their beloved and fallen king; they then turn and begin to walk slowly down a well-beaten roadway as they are followed by the royal guard pulling the casket cart. As the procession passes the people of the village, they gather in lines behind the royal guards and walk slowly as they grieve in their own manner for their deceased beloved king. The procession reaches the graveyard which is lined with many well-cared-for graves; the procession stops, and the royal guard pull the casket cart in front of their beloved and respected queen. Still flanked by her loved ones, a still-weeping and grief-stricken Einirt nods from within her black sheer veil to her royal guards, who are teary-eyed with quivering lips, yet they still manage to turn to the casket resting in the cart, then begin to remove the casket from the cart. The royal guards, in unison, look down to their fallen king's casket, then nod in respect.

The royal guards then take the casket to a deep hole that lies near the cart, where they stand holding the casket. They then lay the casket upon several ropes, which lay on the ground beneath them. The royal guards then step away and grasp the ropes on each end very tightly as they pull all at once to lift the casket of their former king, then they walk closer to the hole where they slowly release the ropes, setting their former beloved king to lie in his final resting place. The past events and ceremony have clearly taken their toll on Einirt, and she simply faints as her big brother Moats lifts her with his huge arms, then carries her away where they are followed by his giant of a son, a petite daughter-in-law, and six of their loyal royal guards. All are still weeping as they make their way down the well-traveled road from which they came. The rest of the villagers remain with the still-large presence of Einirt's royal guards as they cover their fallen and former king's casket with the earth from which we all once came from. It is a very somber and mournful time.

CHAPTER 4

A PLAN TO SAVE THE FUTURE KING

THE FOLLOWING MORNING, we find Cantor flanked by several of his followers walking down a well-traveled path, and in the clearing ahead, they can see several women dressed in dirty pants and blouses with their hair tied up in buns or braided bundles atop their heads. As Cantor and his followers move ever closer to the women, it is clear that the women are practicing their battle skills and exercising. Cantor also notices that there are several royal guards standing, watching over the practice session. Cantor can now see that one of the women is Einirt; he is somewhat aghast as Einirt appears utterly engaged in a battle with another Centaur woman. Both women appear to possess a wooden carved practice knife and are attempting to get the better of each other.

Cantor approaches the two women engaged in combat, then shouts out, "My lady, what are you doing?"

Einirt pays Cantor no mind as she continues the battle with the other woman. Einirt suddenly grabs, then flips the other woman on to the ground, then presses the wooden knife to the woman's throat, then asks, "Do you submit?"

The woman looks up to Einirt and, with a smile, proclaims, "Yes, I concede, my Queen."

Einirt smiles down at woman, then in a respectful and good sportsmanlike act, Einirt offers the woman her left hand then helps the woman to her feet. The two nod in a show of respect for each other, then they hug. Einirt and the woman step back from each other, then bow and walk away.

A scuffed-up and tarnished Einirt walks up to Cantor, then asks in a curious tone, "So, General, what brings you to our practice field?"

In an arrogant manner and tone, Cantor looks to his queen, then asks in a surprised voice, "Why are you participating in these sessions?"

With a sarcastic gaze and a cocky tone, Einirt responds, "This is a requirement for all our women. You know that!"

Cantor grimaces, then replies in a disapproving tone, "You are our Queen and should not partake in this unladylike session. This will come to an abrupt end when we are married and I am king!"

Einirt steps back with her hands on her hips and with an angry scowl on her beautiful but soiled face; she then proceeds to dress down Cantor in a verbal assault and in a very angry tone, "You will not tell me what I can and cannot do, not now and not even if we get married! Understand?"

Einirt then looks angrily at Cantor; it is clearly visible to all who have witnessed the event that Cantor is a bit embarrassed and shaken by Einirt's verbal aggression toward him.

Cantor suddenly steps back, then bows as he begins to apologize to his queen in a shaking voice, "My apologies, my lady. I did not mean you any disrespect. I was just concerned for your well-being and did not wish your beautiful face or body to be harmed in any manner from this brutal routine, that is all."

Einirt, with a firm gaze, responds to Cantor in a more friendly tone but with the same determination, "I choose to partake in this and many other activities. As a Centaur woman, I decide when to cease them, not you! Yes!"

Cantor nods to his queen, then grins in a tentative manner as he steps back. Cantor, in a more humble fashion, asks, "I wanted to ask you if we could meet and discuss the future of our situation as well as the people's business as soon as you are ready, my queen."

Einirt grins, then replies in a much softer tone, "Perhaps tomorrow morn in the main hall, if that is acceptable, General?"

Cantor smiles, then in a more confident display, he responds in a pleasant voice, "That would be more than acceptable, my Queen."

Einirt smiles, then, in very sultry manner, places her hand on Cantor's chest, then gently and slowly, she glides her hand down to his belt and grasps his belt as she speaks in a low and soft voice, "Until then, General!"

Cantor and his followers are stunned and aroused by Einirt's display, and it is plain to see that Cantor is smitten by this turn of events and Einirt's mannerism. Einirt then turns and walks in a sultry manner away from Cantor and his followers, leaving them in awe as they stand with their mouths dropped wide-open. Einirt is well aware of how she left the befuddled general and his followers as she smiles a grand smile and attempts to keep from laughing as she then makes eye contact with her female friends, and they all let out a cute chuckle. Einirt glances over to her royal guard, and they smile, appreciating the show and gesture their beautiful queen has exhibited. The guards just grin and smile as they shake their heads in jest. Einirt gives the guards a smile and a wink and then covers her mouth, as if to guard her silent laughter. In the meantime, Cantor and his followers are walking away and are unaware of what is happening behind them.

One of the guards steps up to his queen, then asks, "My lady, perhaps it is time we adjourn so you may prepare for your meeting with your brother as you had planned."

Einirt places her right hand on the very large shoulder of her very large guard, then smiles and proclaims in her soft agreeable voice, "Yes, yes, of course. You are most attentive to my needs and my agenda, are you not?"

The guard, with a slightly embarrassed smile, nods, then states, "Yes, my lady, it is what you and—"

The guard's face draws a blank as he realizes he was ordered to take care of his queen by personal order of his former King William, but he is afraid to say William's name to Einirt.

Alerted by her guard's predicament, Einirt smiles at the guard, then in a compassionate manner, she speaks softly, "It's okay. William will always be in my heart and my thoughts. You are a good man, and William could not have chosen a better man to look after me, and yes, you may speak his name in my presence."

The large guard smiles down at his queen, and with a nod, he then addresses his queen with a tear in his eye and with respect, "It is what you and King William asked of me, and I am honored. Therefore, I demand no less of myself!"

Einirt smiles, then nods as she removes her hand from his huge shoulder. Einirt turns, then walks away from the practice area as she is escorted by her huge royal guards.

The next morning, we find Cantor sitting in the king's throne, eagerly and nervously awaiting the arrival of their beautiful and elegant queen. In the hall, sitting at the large rectangular table in front of Cantor and his followers are twelve much-older men and women all draped in long white cloaks. There appears to be an equal number of elders in the hall, of which there are six older gray-bearded men and six older women.

Cantor looks to the elders in disgust, then addresses his follower next to him in a low voice, "Elders? We don't need them, and I don't trust them anyway."

The follower leans down and whispers to a nervous and fidgety Cantor in a low tone, "It is our laws, and they are a powerful ally and could be very useful when the time comes."

Cantor's followers attempt to ease his stress and very apparent displeasure as they motion with their hands to be patient and to calm down.

Cantor looks around, then gives his followers a look of disdain as he asks one of his followers in a very unhappy tone, "Go to the door and check to see if she is even on her way!"

His follower rushes over to the doorway, looks outside, then suddenly turns to Cantor and announces in an excited manner, "She is coming, she coming!"

The follower rushes over to Cantor and takes his place alongside the rest of Cantor's men up close to the wall next to the thrones. Cantor and his followers attempt to regain their composure as they fix themselves in preparation for their queen's arrival. Soon enough, Einirt's entourage enter the doorway to the main hall, led by the giant of a man Brock and his beautiful, tiny, and elegant wife, Alecia, who is dressed to kill in a body-hugging royal blue gown with her beautiful shiny black hair flowing over one shoulder. Following the couple are several of Einirt's royal guards, which take their places to the sides of the doorway.

Next to enter the hall is Queen Einirt, escorted by her massively large devoted and proud brother Moats, who is blocking Cantor's view of Einirt, then Moats steps aside and reveals the beautiful queen in all her elegance and beauty. Einirt is a vision of pure unadulterated beauty as she is adorned in a body-hugging, cleavage-baring, thigh-high slit, sheer white, and toe-revealing gown. Her beautiful black shiny locks are free-flowing as the wind plays with the strands of hair, moving and swaying with her sultry and sexy walk. Her eyes are highlighted with a complementary bluish color, and her plush rose-red lips are enhanced with some form of accentuating lip color cover which make them stand out and shine like a bright star in the dark of night. Einirt, in her sultry and teasing way, gazes with a sexy smile over to Cantor, and she can see that he is in awe of her appearance, so she turns back to her entourage in a meek yet sultry fashion.

Cantor is visibly mesmerized as he sits glaring at Einirt with drool dripping from his lips; he is paralyzed and is unresponsive to this followers' gestures and whispers. Einirt's people whisper to her as she begins to chuckle in her cute and sexy mannerism, knowing what it will do to Cantor. As anticipated, Einirt was right. Cantor's mouth drops wide-open, and he is unresponsive to his surroundings.

Einirt giggles as Alecia smiles at her queen, then leans in and whispers, "You were right. It's working just as you planned!"

Einirt grins and slowly nods in agreement. Moats grins and nods with his giant of a son. Now enter the rest of the royal guards; the last two guards close the doors behind them, then stand, blocking the exit.

The two guards nod to Moats; this prompts Moats to nod back as he then turns to his little sister and whispers, "Are you ready, my Queen?"

Einirt nods and smiles at her very large brother, then on cue, Moats raises his left arm into the air where Einirt places her right arm and hand on his. Moats then leads his queen to the steps and walks her up to her throne where she is now seated next to a speechless and dumbfounded Cantor.

Einirt appears to gather herself, then looks to a gawking Cantor with a pleasant smile, then asks in her softest of voice, "What would you like to address first, my general and future king?"

Cantor is taken aback by her appearance, tone, and blunt question, so he not only hesitates to respond, he also appears rather discombobulated and confused.

As she gazes at Cantor, Einirt smiles a very friendly smile, then with her right hand, she gently places it upon Cantor's left hand, then asks in a very sultry and sweet way, "Cat got your tongue?"

This action by Einirt has an earth-shattering effect on Cantor as he blushes and attempts to speak, but no words come from his mouth.

Einirt lets out a slight chuckle, then with her right hand, she pats Cantors left hand and states in her most seductive manner and softest voice, "Perhaps I will initiate the conversation and agenda!"

All Cantor can do is nod his head in agreement as drool begins to drip from his jaw-dropped mouth. Einirt smiles at Cantor, then she turns to address the parties in front of them.

Einirt, in a more serious tone and mannerism, states, "First order of business we must address in this day's matter is that of replacing our former and beloved king. As your queen, I do hereby make a motion to officially make General Cantor our new king as per his standing and our laws. This is the way of our people. It is our tradition and our law. No one person may have rule over our people, and every queen must have a king and every king a must have a queen to share rule of our people equally. That is our law."

Einirt then looks to Cantor with a more serious gaze, then turns back to address her subjects as she goes on to announce in just as serious tone and manner, "Cantor, by law, when he is officially made king of our people, shall have his choice of any unwed woman from our village to share the throne with him, equally and for life."

Einirt again looks to Cantor with a serious stare, then turns back to her subjects to announce in a firm tone, "Once we have made General Cantor our king and upon his wedding day, I will no longer be queen. This, of course, is our way unless he chooses me as his queen, and should I accept is another question. This is our law!"

Einirt looks to Cantor with a manufactured smile, then asks, "Is there anything else you would like to add, General?"

Cantor seems out of place and appears indecisive as he looks at Einirt in confused manner, then attempts to respond in a mix of shambled words, "I think, well, we covered most of what I had hoped for, but…ah…ah…ah…What day will my coronation be, and when will we wed?"

Einirt gives Cantor a disparaging glare, then responds in a harsh manner, "Well, as king you will have to be more decisive and confident. As to marrying you, well, let us just say that you have not asked me and have not asked me in an appropriate manner, General!"

Cantor rears back flabbergasted, then in a more confident manner, he retorts, "Well, you have not made yourself available for me to ask for your hand in an appropriate manner, my Queen!"

Einirt bows her head, then turns to Cantor and gives him a more gracious gaze as she allows a smile to grace her beautiful face. She responds in a more softer and graceful manner, "Yes, General, I have not made myself available to you because of the death of my beloved husband and king of our people. For that, I am very sorry!"

Cantor smiles and nods as if Einirt was apologizing to him for the inconvenience she has caused him.

Cantor turns to Einirt with a proud smile and a more confident tone. "I understand, my Queen. You are forgiven."

All who hear this, including his followers, are taken aback and, in unison, comment, "What?"

They all then give Cantor a look of disbelief as his follower nearest to his right bends down and whispers to Cantor, "Our queen was not seeking your approval or acceptance. She was explaining that she was mourning her late husband's death."

With an embarrassed expression clearly covering his face, Cantor attempts to explain himself to Einirt, "Yes, I understand, and it was rude of me to think otherwise, my Queen. Please accept my most humble apology, and if you would be so kind as to give me a time when we can speak in private, I would be honored!"

Einirt gives Cantor a gentle smile, then asks in her typical soft and sensual way, "A private moment! For what, may I ask?"

Cantor, in a somewhat baffled manner, asks, "So I may ask for your hand?"

Einirt grins, then retorts in her sultry fashion, "My hand? You wish me to wed you and remain queen?"

Cantor, with a smile, responds, "Yes, yes, I would like that very much!"

Einirt, in a very elegant and confident fashion, peers at Cantor, then demands in a commanding yet sultry manner, "If you wish to wed me, get on one knee and ask me in an appropriate manner!"

Cantor immediately reacts to his queen's requested demand and rises from his throne, steps down the stair, and kneels in front of Einirt, taking her left hand into both his hands, and asks in a very begging tone, "My Queen please honor me in becoming my wife and my queen."

Everyone in the hall appear shocked, some in disbelief and yet others with disappointment.

It appears that all but Einirt react in a surprised manner. Einirt simply responds in a coy manner and tone, "We will have to establish rules, make agreements, and have an understanding witnessed by our high council first, yes?"

Cantor, on his knee, gazes up at Einirt with a confused look, then replies, "Is all that necessary?"

Einirt smiles, then leans down and gazes into Cantor's eyes as she speaks in a very sultry voice, "Yes, yes, it is, should you wish my hand in marriage. Remember something, I am no common woman. I am a queen and have been for some time."

Cantor bows his head, then looks up at Einirt with a smile and, in an excited voice, asks, "So does that mean yes, you'll marry me?"

Einirt chuckles, then looks to Cantor with a half grin, then replies softly, "Perhaps after we come to an arrangement, but only then."

Cantor appears very pleased, and as he rises to his feet, he looks to Einirt, then announces, "Let us begin the negotiations then!"

Einirt shakes her head in disbelief, and with a smile, she addresses the elders sitting at the large table in front of her in a commanding voice, "Are the elders ready to hear and write down the terms of Cantor's proposal of marriage to Einirt, Queen of the Centaurs?"

The twelve elders nod in agreement as one elder man and one elder woman each pull out a blank scroll with a feather and jar containing some kind of ink. The two elders appear ready to write down the terms and agreement and make a nodding motion to confirm they are prepared and ready.

Einirt begins to make her position and conditions known in no uncertain terms as she addresses the council and Cantor in a firm and confident manner, "Should I accept Cantor's proposal? Let it be understood by our laws and traditions that we, as king and queen, will have equal say in the ruling of our people. Our marriage is until death. I, as queen, shall have the right of naming the firstborn child we may have. Should I ever be with child, the child's life will not be at risk to please either of our desires and I must remain untouched so as not to harm our unborn child. No punishment or death shall come to any Centaur without both the king and queen's approval and a witnessed signed agreement. In the event of a disagreement in any manner, the final decision will be made by the Council of Elders as per our laws. No wars may be engaged or raids be made without both the king and queen's approval. All common laws and traditions shall remain in effect for the duration of the king's and or queen's rule."

Cantor looks puzzled as he is not familiar with all the laws and does not like what Einirt has proclaimed and asked for, so he speaks out in a disagreeable manner and tone, "I do not care for some of those conditions, and I am not aware of all the laws you speak of. I am a warrior and a soldier general, not a law keeper!"

Everyone looks to Cantor with smug grins or disdain.

Einirt smiles, then, in her sultry voice, reassures Cantor, "Worry not, for I do know all the laws and traditions, and as a good queen should, I will advise my future husband and king of all matters that concern him. All that has been discussed here is within that realm of trust, honor, and our customs."

Cantor looks to Einirt with an untrusting guise but says nothing to his queen, for it may shame him and he is aware of this.

Einirt smiles, then asks in a calming tone as she tilts her head ever so slightly, "Is there anything or any question I or the elders can help you understand, or perhaps all is understood and we are agreed?"

Cantor nods, then looks to his followers for approval; they all nod as if to indicate they are pleased and agree to what they have heard. Cantor then looks to Einirt and nods again as he states, "We are agreed. When is my coronation, and when will our wedding be?"

Einirt smiles, then with a confirming tone, she announces, "Cantor shall be crowned king on tomorrow's sundown. Our wedding shall take place on the sunset of the day after he is crowned. Is that satisfactory, General Cantor?"

Cantor smiles and nods in agreement, then in an excited voice, he responds, "Yes, hell yes!"

Cantor then lays his hand out to shake Einirt's hand, but she does not retort.

Einirt instead looks to Cantor with an angry glare, then questions him, "Is that how you seal a proposal with your future wife and queen?"

Einirt steps up to Cantor and wraps her arms around his neck, so Cantor, in awe, simply wraps his arms around Einirt's tiny waist, then no sooner than they embrace Einirt pulls back and announces in an embarrassed, sexy, and cute manner, "We must save this behavior for our wedding night, silly!"

Cantor blushes and grins. Einirt gives him a simple but sultry glare, then tells him in a sexy sweet voice, "Off with you now, and we must not see each other until your coronation and then not until our wedding day!"

Cantor nods as he walks away, walking backward, gazing at Einirt, for he cannot take his eyes off his beautiful future bride. It is obviously apparent that Cantor is excited as he makes his way out of the main hall, followed by his loyal followers. The guards open the door so Cantor and his followers may exit, and after they depart the hall, the guards immediately close and secure the large doors.

Einirt makes her way to the table and addresses the council in a very gracious and elegant manner, "I wish to thank each and every one of you for your time, your trust, and your honor."

Einirt curtsies and bows her head in the most respectful, elegant and feminine manner. It is breathtaking to the elder men and greatly appreciated by the women elders as they nod in approval to her actions, presentation, and choice of words.

Einirt then asks the elders, "I do fear that many times your judgment and decisions will be needed in the future as our soon-to-be king may be found to be hardheaded and without good judgment. So it is with heavy heart that I implore you now. Be prepared for his appeals, and please be as wise with him as we all know you have the wisdom to be and soon the power to guide him away from the dangers he may bestow upon our people."

Einirt looks to all the elders, and in a graceful style, she speaks, "I thank you now and when I am unable to."

All look a bit perplexed by her comment but say nothing. Einirt now looks to her family and nods, then turns and walks toward the door, followed by her loving and supportive family. The royal guards open the doors and follow behind their beloved and respected queen outside, then up the path leading to Einirt's home.

We join Cantor and his followers sitting on benches surrounding tables outside the rear of the main hall; he is in a very pleasant way, and it is very apparent to all. They are all drinking ale and wine, and the effects of the drink are very apparent as they all appear quite intoxicated now.

A very inebriated Cantor shouts in an excited manner, "Tomorrow I shall be king and ruler of our people!"

All shout, "Yes, hail King Cantor!"

They all slam their drinks together in cheering their future king and friend.

Cantor hollers in a drunken fashion, "I shall change many of our traditions so that the loyal followers of Cantor may have more pleasures and rewards!"

The followers shout and raise their cups to their future king in a glorious manner.

Now at Einirt's home, Einirt is sitting at her table with her beloved family and friends. Einirt has changed her attire to a more comfortable white short tied-at-the-waist wrap dress with a cleavage-baring neckline and is barefoot. Moats is in his usual attire of military garb, as is his giant of a son Brock. Alecia is also dressed in a similar dress as Einirt's but red in color and is wearing black knee-high strap sandals. Holga is seated near her queen and is dressed in a simple yellow everyday gown and is also barefoot, and flanking her is Hogar. Hogar is also dressed in his usual guard's uniform.

Einirt has the group's attention as she addresses them, "Yes, I agree we have the support of the elders and most of the people, so Cantor will have to be cautious in his actions should he wish to be held in their favor, and more importantly, he must maintain an appropriate behavior from the start."

Moats grins, then speaks out, "Imagine if he does not. Perhaps we could help him with that!"

Moats makes a mischievous facial expression, then lets out a chuckle, which makes the rest of the group laugh out loud as this is very unlike Moats, who is usually serious and resigned.

Einirt laughs so hard she is unable to speak but manages to gather herself, then looks at her much older brother and asks with a huge smile, "When did you ever make faces like that? You have never made a funny face in your life."

Moats smiles, then proclaims with a serious but sarcastic grin, "Did you not tell me it is never too late to start?"

Everyone laughs. Moats grins, then winks as he takes a drink from his large mug which he has been drinking from. All are in good spirits.

Einirt, with a pleasant smile, then grabs Holga's hand and gives her a sincere gaze, then asks, "My dearest friend, I would appreciate it if you would join me and Alecia in the wedding party and stand with me as my witness and bridesmaid."

Holga looks to Einirt with a smile and nods in agreement, then responds in her muddled voice, "Yes, I would be honored, but I'll not give Cantor a pleasant smile when we are up there."

Einirt gives Holga a gleaming smile, then, in a serious manner and tone, leans in closer to Holga and states with sincerity, "My Holga, you must not act as if you remember anything of that horrible night or our plan will be at risk. I promise you, I shall get you the justice you so deserve, but you must give me the time I need to succeed please. Can you restrain your justified hatred for just a little longer?"

Einirt, with a compassionate gaze, then peers into Holga's beautiful green eyes as she gently presses her forehead to Holga's.

Holga, in a soft tone, mumbles out, "Yes, for you, my friend, my Queen, my lady, I shall do as you ask."

A single tear rolls from Holga's right eye, but she bravely gives her queen a compassionate smile, and then with a gentle caress of her hands, she squeezes Einirt's hand.

Einirt smiles at her friend as she pulls back; she then announces, "We shall all look amazingly beautiful, and we will make Cantor's ugly mouth water with envy!"

They all smile and chuckle as they nod in agreement.

The next morning, we find a gleaming and very happy Cantor in his home, pacing back and forth as he appears to be speaking to himself, practicing his acceptance speech for his upcoming coronation. He is wearing nothing but his underwear, which is a simple wrap cloth, as he appears to gloat over his speech. Cantor stoops down as if he is practicing to be crowned as he begins grinning; he then takes a seat which, in this case, is the bench in front of his dining table. There is a knock at the door. Cantor stands up, then walks over to the doorway, opening the door wide-open to see that it is one of his followers. Cantor motions to the follower to enter.

The follower enters the home. Cantor closes the door, then addresses his follower in pleased tone, "How are the preparations for my coronation coming along?"

The follower nods, then responds, "As you have requested, sir."

Cantor nods happily, then states, "All is going as planned, just as I imagined it would."

The follower replies, "Yes, yes, it is."

Cantor asks in an unsure manner, "Are all the villagers excited about the upcoming event?"

The follower hesitantly and nervously then responds, "As is could be expected, sir."

Cantor is overcome with a disturbed and apprehensive mannerism as he then asks, "What does that mean? Are they not excited as they should be?"

To his dismay, the follower replies sadly, "No, not all of them. Some still miss William. Others we will have to win over, and some just don't think you are ready to be king, but they won't come out and say the words!'"

Cantor becomes angry, then, with a glare and a very angry tone, demands, "Get the names of those who feel that I am not prepared to be their king and we'll deal with them at a later time!"

The follower nods, then replies, "Yes, sir, it will be done. Is that all for now, sir?"

Cantor glares at the follower and, in a softer tone, commands, "Yes, for now."

The follower bows, then turns and exits the home, closing the door behind him. Cantor stands in a still position, staring at the wall, in deep thought, pondering the upcoming day's events.

CHAPTER 5

THE GIFTED ONES

MEANWHILE, LATER THAT day, on the path leading to the northeastern woods en route to the land of the Chin, in a clearing off the ridden path sits the Centaur's healer. He is seated on top the cart bench which is being led by his trusty steed. The healer appears to be resting as is his steed. Lying in the back of the cart is a sleeping Angelina wrapped in a blanket with her head propped up on a pillow. Suddenly, from out of the woods appears a dark-cloaked image which simply stands still in a nonthreatening manner with the image's head hanging down and holding a twisted cane in the right hand. The healer does not notice the image, but his trusted steed appears to notice the image and is somewhat startled in its reaction. The steed takes a step back as it turns to look at the image when the healer pulls the reins to control his horse, then he turns to see what the horse is looking at.

The healer, with a surprised look, is overcome by glee as he rapidly dismounts his seat; he then jumps to the ground and rushes over to the image and, in a very pleasant fashion and tone, greets the image, "My friend! How the hell are you?"

The image, with its left hand, pulls the hood of the cloak back to reveal an old wrinkled-face, long white-haired, white bearded-faced man with a pleasant smile.

The old man, in a very happy and welcoming tone, speaks, "I am well, my friend."

The two hug each other in a warm-hearted embrace; they then let out a happy laugh as the two look into each other's old and worn but gleeful faces.

The respectful healer says, "My friend, it is good to see you. You are like the sun shining on a cloudy cold winter's day."

The old man grins, then tilts his head as he speaks with a short chuckle. "You are here for my aid, are you not? And who is the lady you bring me?"

The healer acts somewhat surprised, but then in respect, he nods and bows his head as he replies humbly, "Yes. I have a very big favor to ask, and the beautiful lady is called Angelina. I need you to heal her."

The old man walks to the back of the cart where he is joined by the healer. The old man stands still for a moment as he takes in the scene, then with his left hand, he grasps Angelina's ankle in a gentle manner.

The old man bows his head momentarily, then turns and looks to the healer with a serious glare in his eyes, then speaks in vexed tone, "This lady is injured badly and is pregnant!"

The healer, with a shocked look, responds in the same manner, "Pregnant! I did not see this!"

The old man then turns back to Angelina, then places his staff into his left hand and leans over to Angelina, and with his eyes closed, he reaches his right hand out and places it upon her hip as he mutters several words that the healer cannot hear, then the old man removes his hand and steps back.

The old man appears to gather himself, then turns back to the healer and announces in a calm manner, "We need to get her to my village as soon as possible."

The old man, in a nonchalant manner, then turns and begins walking down an unclear path that, as he proceeds toward the vegetation blocking the path, it all magically seems to move from his path as he draws nearer to it. The healer, with a surprised look, rushes suddenly, then jumps onto the cart's seat and pulls the reins to make his horse follow the old man down this mysterious path. Now as the healer follows his old friend down the strange path, he notices that the vegetation behind him closes ranks as if it had never moved before. The healer turns back to see his old friend has entered a small village which is similar to that of the Centaur village in its construction of homes, pathways, stables, circular configuration of its design, and even the attire of its people. The healer's old friend stops in front of one of the homes there and is greeted by an older lady who was standing near the doorway; she then approaches the old man, then gives the old man a welcoming familiar hug and kiss. The old man reciprocates the affection. The old man leans in and appears to whisper something to the old lady, and the old lady, with a surprised look, glances to the healer, then rushes over to the healer's position.

The old lady looks up to the healer and curiously asks, "Are you just going to sit there, or are you going to help me with the girl?"

The old lady then motions with her hands in a questioning manner, so the healer, now somewhat embarrassed, jumps from the cart and gives the old lady a warm hug and asks, "How have you been, my lady?"

The old lady chuckles and then nonchalantly pulls and then leads the healer with her toward the rear of the cart. The two stop behind the cart, then affectionately and gently, the old lady places both of her hands onto Angelina's ankles, then in a surprised fashion, the old lady begins to tremble; she then starts shaking in a very traumatic fashion. The healer is surprised by this reaction but has failed to notice that his old friend has joined them and is standing to the healer's right curiously but stoically. The healer begins to reach for the old lady's hands as if to pull her back from the situation but is stopped by the old man's staff which has blocked him from reaching the old lady.

The old man, in a calm voice, says, "She is fine, my friend. Leave her be."

The healer steps back as he looks to his old friend with an amazed gawk.

The old friend simply smiles, then states, "She is very good at this, but she has gotten a little slower in her old age!"

The old man then lets out a slight chuckle. Without looking or missing a beat, the old lady releases her left hand from Angelina's ankle, and then in a continuous motion, she slaps the old man's head, then replaces her hand back onto Angelina's ankle and acts as if nothing has happened.

The old man acts as if he was stuck with harsh force as he comments, "Old woman, you're being violent and rude in front of our guests!"

The old lady just ignores the comments and continues to hold Angelina, then begins to mutter very softly as she continues hold on to Angelina.

Suddenly, she releases Angelina as she steps back, then looks to the two and she speaks bluntly, "Well, what are you two are waiting for? Take her into the house and lay her onto the bed!"

The two men step up and carry Angelina to the home nearest them as indicated by the old lady. The old lady follows the men carrying the motionless Angelina.

Now inside the home and lying on the bed is a statuesque and still-sleeping Angelina. From out a side room enters a lovely young beautiful girl dressed in a long white gown. It is clear the young girl has been blessed with long flowing auburn reddish hair that reaches her tiny feet, the most hauntingly devastatingly beautiful green eyes, and perfect light olive skin. The young girl sees Angelina lying on the bed, so she rushes over to Angelina, then in a compassionate manner, the girl places her tiny hands upon Angelina's forehead and stomach as she then begins to slowly raise her head, finally looking up to the celling. She begins to speak in a very soft and strange language.

The healer is taken aback by this and asks his old friend in amazement, "Who is this girl?"

The old man smiles, then proudly yet nonchalantly replies, "She is my daughter."

The healer, now even more surprised, asks in a dumbfounded manner, "I did not know a wizard could conceive children!"

The old man shrugs and then responds with a cocky smile, "Neither did I!"

The healer asks in a tentative manner, "May I ask who her mother is?"

The old man gives the healer a stern gaze, then responds in an apparent agitated manner, "Why, Nana, of course! Who else would have me?"

He then laughs as he places his right hand upon the healer's shoulder. The healer is unsure of how to respond, so he just smiles in an uneasy fashion and nods.

The old man looks to his friend, then proclaims, "It could have been anyone of the beautiful women I have enchanted but—"

He is unable to finish his statement due to the smack he has just received on the back of his head from a passing and nonchalant Nana.

As she passes the two, Nana glimpses over to the two old men, then announces in a calm and soft tone, "As if any of them wanted your old bones, ha!"

The old man, in an insulted manner, speaks out, "Hey, old woman, you are tarnishing my reputation with the ladies and my friend's opinion of me!"

Nana giggles, then looks back at her old man and proclaims, "What reputation?"

She then lets out a quiet chuckle, as does the healer.

The old man, now with a insulted look, glances over to his friend, then the old man joins in on the chuckle and states, "Oh yes, I don't have one, not anymore!"

They all let out a laugh.

The young girl now removes her hands from Angelina, then places them on her hips as she looks to the three elderly people and proclaims, "Seriously, Father!"

The elders all give the young girl a smile.

The old man addresses his daughter, "Can you mend her, my child?"

The girl smiles, and softly but confidently, she declares, "Yes, Father, I have healed her insides and have stopped the bleeding. However, I am unable to give back her sight, but her daughter is healthy and will be born on time."

The healer appears amazed at the young girl, then asks pleasantly, "I am the healer of the Centaur or, as we were once called, the people of the forest. What, may I ask, are you called, little one?"

The young girl smiles; she then curtsies and bows her beautiful head and looks up, and in a confident and proud manner, she speaks, "I am Ynew, sir. It is a pleasure to meet you."

The healer appears impressed by the girl, then nods and states in a very complimentary fashion, "The pleasure is all mine. May I say that you are as beautiful as you are talented? You clearly take after your beautiful and gifted mother!"

They all smile and nod, but then the old man gets offended and states in a jealous manner, "Hey, she did get some of my good qualities, too, you know!"

Nana speaks up in a smugly, "Oh really? What exactly did my little beauty get from you?" Nana now gazes at her old man with looks that could kill.

The old man simply smiles smugly, then proclaims, "She has my perfectly shaped ears, so there!"

The old man gazes at Nana with smug look, then turns to his friend and nods with a cocky grin and announces, "Yes, it is obvious my little Ynew has some of my natural charms and, perhaps, even some of my gifts. She is just too young now to know which ones!"

Nana shrugs, then leans down to tend to Angelina.

The healer asks Ynew in a concerned manner, "So Angelina will never regain her sight?"

Ynew shakes her head, and in a soft and sad tone, she answers, "I am sorry, but her eyes were so badly damaged I could not reverse the damage. I am truly sorry. She is a very beautiful lady. The man that did this, is he dead yet?"

All turn in shock to Ynew's question.

The old man looks to the healer, and the healer responds in a shameful fashion, "No. He is not. He is to become king!"

Ynew looks to the healer with an angry glare and responds with an even angrier tone, "What! Are you serious! Your people reward a man like that with a crown? What kind of people are you?"

The healer looks down in shame.

Ynew's father cannot help but notice his friend's shame, then responds to his daughter in an instructional manner and tone, "My daughter, there is more to this situation than either of us must know. I have known these people for more than two hundred winters, and they are good people. They must have a very good reason for this, yes?"

The old man now looks and waits for a response from his friend.

The healer looks to his old friend, then the healer begins to explain, "On my journey here, I was informed that our king was killed, and I know by our own queen's voice that he had left our queen with child. If this man finds out she is with child, he will kill them both. He is in line next for the crown, and our queen must wed him to save our former king's unborn child. This is not an easy time for us, but we must do whatever is deemed necessary to save our queen and our future king. William's blood will prevail, and his son will make a great king for our people. I have seen this in a vision."

They all nod as if to approve of the healer's words and vision.

Ynew curiously asks, "Is your queen a good woman?"

The healer responds proudly and defensively, "Queen Einirt is possibly the greatest queen our people have ever had, little one!"

Ynew replies, "Then she is worthy of saving, as is her son then, yes?"

The healer responds positively, "Yes, they are both worth saving at any cost! Einirt's and William's son must be saved no matter the costs!"

The old man speaks up in agreement but strangely adds, "Yes, my daughter, we must see that their son is not only born but also takes the throne, for he shall be a great king and ally to us!"

Ynew gives her father a curious look, and in return, he smiles.

The healer asks in a curiously, "You are very wise beyond you years. If I may ask, how old are you, Ynew?"

Ynew smiles, then replies, "I have seen nineteen winters, and you, sir?"

The healer shockingly replies, "What?"

Ynew and her parents simply smile, then Nana whispers to the healer in a soft and assuring voice, "Yes, Ynew stopped aging as humans do when she saw ten winters, and now she ages one winter for every thirty. So our little Ynew has seen a hundred winters since we were blessed with her birth. She did come as a surprise to us as you know! Wizards are not supposed to be capable of having children of their own!"

The old man pumps his chest out, then cockily announces, "Yes, I am more than just a great wizard as you can plainly see!"

The old man proudly points to his beautiful mesmerizing daughter with a very proud gaze.

Nana chuckles, then she pops her man in the stomach with the back of her hand and proclaims, "My husband is too boastful for his own good. Grumpa, stop behaving in such an embarrassing manner! You should know better, old man!"

The healer asks, "What are we to do with Angelina? Should she return, Cantor will kill her. I promised my queen I would not allow Angelina to die, and returning her to our village would surely be the end of her and her child!"

Grumpa speaks confidently, "When Angelina has healed from all her wounds and has given birth to her daughter, I shall take them both to a safe place that no one will find them or bring them harm. This I swear to you, my friend."

The healer nods in agreement, then asks, "Where will you send them?"

Grumpa rears back and shakes his head, then replies, "This you must not know. Only I will know, for the less you know, the less this Cantor can draw from you, yes?"

The healer nods in agreement, then replies, "Yes, yes, you are a wise man, my friend."

Grumpa asks, "Come, let us feed you, for I am sure that belly is in need of some nourishment and some good drink, yes?"

The healer nods with a smile. The two men exit the home, closing the door behind them. Ynew and Nana are tending to Angelina's needs and have acquired a new dress for her to wear as well.

Ynew asks, "Mother, what do you know of this son that King William and Queen Einirt have created?"

Nana, in a nonchalant manner and tone, responds, "Not much, my daughter, as your father has not discussed that with me."

Ynew acts suspiciously, then states, "Then I will have to ask him then."

Nana replies, "Yes, you should."

Ynew responds rapidly, "I shall."

Nana smiles at Ynew, then nods in agreement.

Outside, the two elderly men are sitting at a table, eating meat from some kind of large bird, eating vegetables, and drinking some concoction Grumpa has brewed up.

Grumpa asks, "So, my old friend, what do you think of my firewater? Good, yes?"

The healer finishes the drink in his mouth and then gives Grumpa a look that can only reflect how strong the drink is. The healer responds after burping, "This is very good, but it burns going down!"

Grumpa smiles, then takes a large drink from his cup; he swallows the drink now in his mouth, then he responds, "Yes, I use it to keep the torches burning at night also."

The healer, with a surprised look on his face, asks, "What?"

Grumpa retorts, "I also use it to keep the torches burning at night. Good stuff, yes?"

The healer smiles as he rears back in his seat, then responds with a laugh and states, "You crazy old bastard. You could have told me that before I drank it, but it is good and has a warming effect too!"

The two men laugh as they consume even more of the firewater Grumpa has produced.

Back at the Centaur village, the villagers are preparing for the coronation of Cantor. Outside the main hall, the villagers are setting up several long tables with benches and chairs surrounding them. Several types of food are being placed on the tables as many different types of meats are being slowly cooked on several different spits. The women are placing and tying flower decorations on the tables and chairs as the men stand around, talking and drinking.

Inside the main hall, villagers appear to be doing the same—decorating, talking, and drinking. Standing near the two thrones are several of Cantor's followers; they appear to be talking within their small group as some appear to be gawking at the women and girls who are doing the decorating.

Now inside Einirt's home, a stunningly beautiful Einirt is brushing her long beautiful black hair as she stands dressed in a form-fitting white long high-slit gown, with a neckline baring her very bountiful cleavage and a beautiful dainty gold necklace to cap off her captivating vision. Her eyelids bare a hint of blue-colored powder, and her lips are painted an even rosier red than usual. Sitting on the table she is standing next to is a beautiful, dainty, gold jewel-encrusted, twisting, and braided crown. Einirt looks up to what appears to be a shiny silver platter hanging on the wall, which acts like a mirror. Einirt appears to be gazing at her reflection in somewhat of a daze as she stops brushing her hair, as if frozen in time, and she appears to be in deep thought as a saddened look develops on her beautiful face.

Meanwhile, in Moats's home, sitting at a table are Moats and his giant of a son, Brock. They are dressed in their usual attire and drinking from their mugs they hold in their hands. A noise is heard from one of the adjoining rooms when, suddenly, walks out a stunningly beautiful Alecia. Alecia is dressed in a long body-hugging, cleavage-baring light blue and delicately laced gown. Her long shiny hair is hanging off her left shoulder in a long single braid. Her lips are painted a deep shiny red, and her eyes, as usual, are in no need of compliment; they are mesmerizing and naturally beautiful. Brock gazes at his stunningly breathtaking tiny wife with awe and a grin that would rival the crescent moon. Alecia notices out of the corner of her eye her gawking massive husband.

Alecia says with a surprised look, "What? What is it?"

Brock just smiles, then states, "Just admiring my beautiful wife!"

Alecia smiles, then approaches her adoring husband and kisses him on his cheek as she then proclaims, "You're so sweet. That is why I love you so, my handsome and kind husband!"

Moats grunts, then speaks out, "Enough of that. We need to make our way over to Einirt's home soon. Are you finished dressing, my daughter?"

Alecia gazes over to her rugged-looking father in-law, then with a pleasant grin, she replies, "Yes, Father, I am ready."

The two huge men stand up, then proceed to make their way behind a tiny and stunningly beautiful Alecia as she leads the two out the door.

At this time in Cantor's home, we find a well-groomed and nicely dressed Cantor. He is wearing his best off-white fabric pants, shirt, golden-colored armor breastplate, golden greaves, and gold-laced jewel rings.

Cantor appears anxious as he stands in place, talking to himself, "Be confident, be proud, be commanding in your acceptance."

Suddenly, there is a knock at the door. Cantor turns, then responds, "Enter."

The door opens, and standing in the doorway is one of his loyal followers. "Sir, the hall is prepared, and the people are gathering."

The follower bows, then asks, "May I be excused, sir?"

Cantor replies in a confident and cocky manner, "Yes, but come for me when it is time for me to make my entrance!"

The follower bows and nods, then turns and exits the home, closing the door behind him.

Now back at Einirt's home, gathered and standing around the table are Einirt with her loyal and loving family.

Einirt asks, "Well, are we ready?"

They all smile and nod to signify that they are, indeed, ready for the upcoming event.

* * *

At the same time, back at Grumpa's village, in front of Grumpa's home, sitting on his cart is a very hungover healer. Standing near the cart are Grumpa, and he is flanked by his wife, Nana, and daughter, Ynew.

Grumpa asks, "Would you like some more firewater for your journey, my friend?"

A bloodshot-eyed healer slowly turns to Grumpa and responds, "That would be great!"

A smiling Grumpa hands the healer a jug of his firewater; as the healer reaches out and grabs the jug, Grumpa announces, "This is a fresh brew and much more potent than what we drank last night!"

The healer retorts in a sluggish tone, "Oh, great."

Grumpa laughs as he looks over to Nana and Ynew, then suggests, "Perhaps it is time to say farewell to our friend."

Nana addresses the healer, "Have a safe and fast journey, and worry not, for we will take good care of Angelina."

Ynew adds, "Yes, Angelina is in very good hands. Have a safe journey."

The healer nods, then speaks in a rough manner, "I thank you all for all you have done."

Grumpa reaches into his pocket, then hands a pouch to the healer. "I almost forgot. Give this to Queen Einirt. Tell her to give him small daily doses at first, then at the end of the first week all the rest."

Grumpa winks with a smile as the healer gives him a curious look as he takes the pouch from Grumpa's hand.

Grumpa then adds, "You must make haste to aid Queen Einirt. Go through the path I have opened for you, and once you have reached the end, you will be at the Centaur village. Hurry, my friend. Make haste!"

Nana and Ynew give a smug smile to the healer as he commands his horse to depart by whipping the horse's reins; the healer departs through the dense forest trail as instructed by Grumpa.

CHAPTER 6

THE CORONATION OF CANTOR

Now BACK AT the Centaur main hall, it is a lively scene full of villagers talking, laughing, and drinking as all appear to be having a good time. From the open doors of the hall, one can see the villagers are moving into two lines, creating a pathway. Suddenly, it is clear why the villagers formed the two lines. Einirt, wearing her dazzling yet delicate and elegant crown, escorted by her family and a procession of her royal guards are making their way toward the main hall. The villagers all bow in respect to their beloved and beautiful queen. Einirt, in her standard elegant style and typical sultry walk, acknowledges all with a smile as she nods to her subjects. The villagers all appear very pleased to see their queen in such good spirits and elegant form as they reciprocate the smile and nod to their respected queen in approval and with admiration.

Einirt, with Moats to her right side, makes her way into the main hall where she greets and is greeted in the same fashion by all the villagers inside. Einirt finally makes her way to throne area and is escorted up the short stairs by Moats where she takes her seat in her throne. Moats makes his way next to Einirt's right side where he stands sword sheaved at his side, with his massive arms crossed, and a serious gaze upon his rugged mug. Both Brock and Alecia stand next to their father with Alecia to Brock's right, holding his huge right arm. Einirt sits in her throne in her usual ladylike manner, and with her customary commanding presence, she smiles and nods to her adoring subjects. Einirt's attention is now drawn to the front-row table where the twelve elders are seated all dressed in their usual white cloaks; they all nod and smile in unison with respect and admiration to their queen. There is a commotion at the front main entrance of the hall which draws the attention of all inside as they all turn to see what is happening.

One of the two guards stationed at the doorway announces the arrival of General Cantor; the guard slams a gong hanging on the wall next to him, then announces, "Attention, attention! Our future king has arrived!"

Cantor enters the hall with his loyal followers trailing behind him in two separate rows. Cantor stops once he has entered the main hall, as does his small procession of followers.

Queen Einirt stands, then turns to recognize General Cantor. Einirt, with a slight smile, looks to Cantor, then announces in a commanding tone, "Everyone, it is time to begin the coronation of our new king."

Everyone stands to their feet and form a pathway for Cantor to walk.

Queen Einirt then announces, "Please, my fellow citizens, let us welcome General Cantor to join your queen to the throne stage."

All nod in the direction of Cantor. Cantor then proceeds to make his way to the front step of the throne stage, then stops and bows to his queen.

Queen Einirt looks down to Cantor, then states, "As we have done in the past and shall continue our tradition of crowning a new king, I ask who here shall stand to confirm General Cantor's right to be proclaimed king of our people?"

To everyone's surprise, Moats speaks up in a very affirmative manner, "I, Moats, senior heir of the second family to the throne, do hereby proclaim General Cantor, heir of the third family, to be in compliance and of proper rank to hold the position as our new king!

Anyone who does not recognize my position and standing in this matter, come forth and be recognized!"

Moats looks around to see if anyone challenges his conformation; no one comes forth or makes any comment. In apparent shock, Cantor looks up to Moats with a look of amazement on his face when, suddenly, Queen Einirt peers down and gives Cantor a look of displeasure, along with a slight tilt of her disapproving head. Cantor immediately bows to his queen, then remains still and silent.

Queen Einirt begins to address her people, "Since no one is in disagreement with General Moats and since we have no apparent challengers to General Cantor's claim, then as it is in our tradition and our custom, we shall precede in the coronation of General Cantor without interruption."

Moats turns to Brock, who has in possession the king's crown. Moats then takes the crown handed by Brock and, in return, turns to Queen Einirt and bows to his queen and hands the crown with both of his large hands to his queen.

Einirt takes possession of the king's crown, then turns to General Cantor. Holding the crown over his head, she begins to speak in a very serious and commanding voice, "I, Einirt, queen of the people of the forest and who proudly call themselves the Centaurs, do hereby proclaim the passing of the king's crown to be made this day. Now may each and every elder of the twelfth council please render your decision of this proclamation and allow General Cantor to accept your wisdom and give homage to honor your decision."

All twelve nod their heads in unison, then, one by one, place their hands out in front of them, palms up.

Queen Einirt then announces to Cantor, "General Cantor, you may now accept and give homage to our elders for their acceptance of your claim and conformation thereof."

General Cantor rises to his feet, then turns to the twelve elders; he then bows his head into their open hands as he makes his way down to each and every one of them.

Now that he has paid homage to all twelve of the elders, he walks up to the throne stage in front of Queen Einirt, then bows his head. Einirt then proclaims, "I, Einirt, proud queen of our people, do hereby proclaim and crown Cantor, heir of the third family, our new king, and may he rule our kingdom and our people as our great, wise, and beloved king before him."

Einirt then places the king's crown upon Cantor's head. Einirt then bows to Cantor as she reaches out her right hand to authorize Cantor to take her hand and rise to his new throne. Cantor takes Einirt's hand, then makes his way up the steps and sits in his new ill-gotten throne with an arrogant and cocky grin. Cantor looks around to see that not all are in harmony with his joy. To his displeasure, Cantor begins to display a bit of a scowl, then not realizing he has acted inappropriately by not allowing Queen Einirt to be seated first, he immediately jumps to his feet, then looks over to his queen and motions with his hand for her to take her seat. In her unique style and with her typical class, Einirt nods to Cantor, then gracefully takes her seat in her throne. Cantor then takes his seat with a look of embarrassment, which then turns to glee. Einirt simply smiles at her new king, then turns to her massive brother, Moats. Moats looks down to his queen, then places his left hand upon Einirt's shoulder; she compassionately places her right hand upon his left hand and smiles as she nods contently.

Now appearing jealous, Cantor turns to Einirt and asks, "We wed tomorrow, yes?"

Queen Einirt smiles as she glances over to King Cantor, then gives him a confident nod and states in a calm voice, "Yes, tomorrow."

The people continue to celebrate as they eat, drink, talk, and converse with one another.

Suddenly and unexpectedly, Einirt stands up, then addresses the new king, "I congratulate you King Cantor. Now if you'll excuse me, we have a long day ahead of us tomorrow."

Einirt begins to take a step down the stairs when, suddenly, King Cantor grabs Einirt's left wrist and stops her from going any farther.

With a smile on his face, Cantor questions his queen, "Why not stay a bit longer and celebrate with your new king and future husband?"

Seeing this and reacting without any hesitation, Moats, Brock, and every royal guard proceed to draw their swords in anger.

Einirt immediately motions with her right hand for all to stop; she then turns to Cantor with a pleasant smile and states, "My lord, please let us not resort to physical restraint or unwise behavior. I am a queen, and I expect to be treated as such, yes?"

Cantor appears more embarrassed than angered as he releases Einirt's wrist. All but Cantor's followers react in a very negative manner to the behavior they have just witnessed.

Einirt looks around to take in the reaction of her people, then in her classic style, she addresses her people, "My friends, please continue your celebration, for tomorrow we shall have another reason to feast and celebrate. I must retire for now, and I shall look ever so forward to having your friendly faces appear here again tomorrow. With that said, I wish you all a good night."

Einirt then proceeds down the throne stairs accompanied by her loved ones and all her royal guards as they make their way to the large front doors.

Cantor stands up and shouts to the royal guards, "Royal guards, you shall stay and guard your king now!"

Einirt stops as does all who are accompanying her. Einirt turns, and in a calm and commanding tone, she addresses Cantor, "My King, the royal guards are my royal guards and only answer to me as this is what your friend, our former king, and my now-deceased husband gifted me before he passed, and I am sure you would not wish that to be undone, would you now?"

Cantor, now again visibly embarrassed, responds in a shaken manner, "No, no, I would not. Your King wishes you a pleasant night. Now be on your way."

A very embarrassed and angered Cantor turns and drinks from his cup as Einirt and her entourage turn with smiles and exit the main hall.

CHAPTER 7

THE WEDDING

THE NEXT DAY, we find the women and girls of the village redecorating the main hall, both inside and out, with new flowers and wraps of white lace and linen. Many of the men appear to be somewhat the worse for wear as the previous night's drink has yet to leave their systems as they tend to the meats they have cooking on the spits.

Back at Einirt's home, we find her royal guards standing outside her home in their best-dressed gold-colored armor and draped in their blue capes in an imposing stance; they are a very impressive sight. Several of the young children approach then stand away from the guards with their little fists clinched to their chests. The guards look to one another, then in unison, the guards raise their right fists to their hearts as they let out small grin to the little ones. The little ones are flattered by this kind gesture, then smile at the guards and rush off in glee as they chuckle.

Meanwhile, inside Einirt's home, we find a stunningly beautiful Holga draped in a bright green, cleavage-baring, high-slit, almost-sheer gown. Her beautiful red hair is hung over her right shoulder freely. With her rose-red lips shining and complementing her hazel green eyes, Holga is a true vision of utter beauty. Holga is talking to a stunning vision that is Alecia. Alecia is adorned in a chiffon-colored, body-hugging, one-sided high-slit gown, and it has a very low cut V-neck. Alecia's long black hair hangs behind her and touches the delicate tan sandals she is wearing. Her lips painted a bright ruby red, and a hint of blue powder over eyelids enhances her mesmerizing sky blue eyes. Standing like proud peacocks are Brock and Hogar as they can't take their eyes off their stunningly beautiful ladies. Both Brock and Hogar are dressed as Moats is—in their best gold-colored armor and white fabric linen clothing underneath their shiny armor and rich blue capes. The five are standing around, talking and laughing as the men sip from their cups of brew.

Alecia calls out to Einirt, "My queen, do you require some aid?"

From the room which Alecia is directing her conversation toward comes a soft response from Einirt, "No, my dear, I am almost done, but thank you."

Alecia looks up to her giant of a proud husband and states, "She does not need much to look beautiful as she is the most natural beauty I have ever laid eyes upon!"

All nod in agreement.

Brock speaks out as if insulated, "My aunt is beautiful no doubt, but so is my natural ravishingly beautiful wife!"

Brock then lifts Alecia by her tiny waist up to his level where he kisses her on the lips as Alecia reciprocates in a very passionate manner; she then gazes into her giant husband's eyes.

Alecia requests, "Put me down, my love. You will wrinkle my dress."

Brock complies with her request and places Alecia down in a very slow and gentle fashion, then kisses her on her forehead.

Moats just grunts, then comments, "Really, just can't keep your hands off her, can you?"

Brock smiles at his father, then states very proudly, "No!"

This brings a chuckle for a response from Hogar as Holga gives him a back hand to the gut. Hogar just smiles adoringly at Holga, and she gives Hogar a very sexy grin in response to his flattering behavior. The two seem very content and very much in love with each other as noticed by the other three as they just smile and nod in acceptance of the relationship.

From the other room, Einirt announces her entrance, "Okay, I am as ready as I will ever be, I guess."

Einirt enters the room where her party is awaiting her entrance; they all look to the doorway which Einirt enters from, and she is breathtakingly stunning in her toe-touching long, white-laced, almost transparently thin, body-hugging, and V-neck gown. Her hair is free-flowing and grazing the back of her ankles as she approaches her loved ones from the other room. Her eyelids are touched with a bluish powder and her lips painted a glossy ruby red. All look to their beautiful queen and nod in approval to her appearance.

Moats compliments his little sister, "My sister, you are as beautiful as you have ever been and that dog-faced pig does not deserve you!"

All nod in agreement as they agree with Moats's words.

Einirt, in a subtle tone, says, "I must do as I must regardless of how I feel about my future pig of a husband. I wish the healer would return soon. Any word about him yet?"

With depressed looks, they all shake their heads to indicate no.

Alecia speaks up, "Let us hope he returns soon!"

They all nod emphatically with hopeful grins.

Brock announces in a depressed tone, "It is almost time, Auntie."

Once again, they all nod in agreement and in a not-so-happy manner.

Einirt announces, "Well, let us get this over with. You all know what to do. Please remember, we do this for my son and my William!"

They all gather around Einirt and give a group hug.

Now in the main hall stand King Cantor flanked by his loyal followers. Cantor is wearing his best gold-colored armor, his cleanest white linen clothes, and his blue robe as are his followers. Cantor wears his crown on top his head and is careful not to allow it to fall, so he moves very slowly and rigidly; it is very obvious to all that the crown does not suit him very well.

Now outside, making their way to the main hall are Einirt and her large entourage. Einirt, as usual, is being escorted by her massive brother Moats to her right and they are flanked by her royal guards. Behind the queen walk Brock with his stunning wife, Alecia, followed by Holga and a very proud Hogar, who are flanked by Einirt's royal guards, and they are followed by the balance of the royal guard. The entourage makes their way down to the main hall where they are honored by the queen's loyal and loving subjects. The subjects greet their beautiful queen with smiles as they bow and nod in approval of their beloved queen. Finally, the entourage make their way to the large doors of the main hall where the royal guards lead the way by creating a path to the throne stage where very pleased King Cantor is seated, awaiting his future queen bride. Einirt makes her way escorted by Moats to the throne stage and stand just before the steps. Cantor rises from his throne, then steps down to meet and greet his future bride. Now standing besides Einirt, Cantor takes her left hand into his right hand, then both turn to face the tables where the twelve elders are seated as do the rest of the wedding party turn to face the elders.

Moats then speaks up, "To begin this ceremony, I would call upon the twelve elders to give their approval of this union. The elders shall now nod and bow if they approve of this union. Those that do not approve shall turn away from the two as required by our tradition. Should more turn than bow, the union shall not take place. This is our law and shall be binding now and forever."

The first of the elders nods and bows as do the all the rest of the elders. Moats then steps in front of the king and queen, then takes their joined hands into his. Moats then places a rope made of hair around the two hands of Einirt and Cantor.

Moats then wraps the two hands together, then announces as he glares into Cantor's eyes and in a very serious tone, "As the eldest member of our queen's family, I do hereby proclaim Cantor King of the Centaurs and Einirt Queen of the Centaurs to officially be wed and shall rule as equals, live as equals, and be equals with those they rule. Now let it be said, let it law, and let be written!"

Moats stands back and to the side of his sister.

Cantor and Einirt now turn and step up to their thrones. Einirt takes her seat in her throne with a stoic gaze upon her face as Cantor announces, "Eat, drink, and celebrate the marriage of your king and queen!"

Cantor then takes his seat in his throne with a large grin upon his brow and asks Einirt, "Are you happy to be married again, my beautiful queen?"

Einirt looks to Cantor with a pleasant smile, then replies, "I am pleased."

Cantor shouts out, "Our queen is very excited to be married to me, King Cantor! Drink to our happiness and to our many children that we shall bear!"

The villagers shout and cheer; Einirt turns her head and looks to her loyal family and friends with a look of discontent and disgust.

Cantor looks over to Einirt and notices Holga standing next to Einirt's family, then he asks in a strange fashion, "What is wrong with Holga? She seems to be acting rather suspicious and strange."

Einirt gives Cantor a glare, then replies cynically, "She was injured by a stranger sometime back."

Cantor in a suspicious manner asks, "Was she damaged and penetrated by this attacker?"

Einirt responds in a very deliberate and nonchalant voice, "He removed her tongue and beat her. If he penetrated her, he must have been very small, for she said she could not feel him down there."

Cantor appears embarrassed and acts suspicious, but to her credit, Einirt changes the subject so as not to alarm Cantor to the truth that she knows what he has done and that will not be forgotten.

Einirt states, "I did not compliment you on your attire. It is nice."

Cantor projects an image of confidence now and smiles, but being the fool that he is, he asks, "Where is Angelina? I have not seen her. Is she not coming to our wedding?"

Einirt turns her head to gather herself, then faces Cantor with a calm gaze, then speaks, "Angelina is gone. We have asked the healer to seek aid in finding her, but he has not returned as of yet. We fear she was captured by the Tartans but are not certain and have not received a ransom notice, so we wait. That is all we can do for now."

Cantor nods as if he understands, then comments, "If there is anything I can do, let me know."

Cantor turns his head and takes a drink from his cup. Einirt turns and looks to Moats with a half grin and nods as if to indicate all is going as planned. Moats nods with a grin, then drinks from his mug.

All of a sudden, Cantor grabs his new wife's hand, then leans over to her and asks, "Are you ready for our wedding night to begin?"

Einirt smiles at her new husband and chuckles, then replies, "Patience. We must not be rude with our subjects, for we are not a normal couple. We are king and queen. We must first tend to our people. They have all come to honor us, my king."

Cantor nods, as if he understands; he then speaks out, "Yes. Then we can fulfill our obligations to each other afterward, yes?"

Einirt gives Cantor a slight smile, then responds, "Yes, of course."

Einirt smiles, then asks Cantor, "Will my new husband fetch me some wine?"

Cantor smiles and nods, then stands up; he proceeds down the steps to the table in front of them. He grabs a cup and a wine jug. He proceeds to fill the cup with wine, then realizes they have servants for this, so he turns and makes his way back up to his throne and hands Einirt the wine cup. Cantor then takes in his seat in his throne next to his queen.

Cantor looks over to his queen and remarks, "Foolish me. We have servants that can get you wine!"

Einirt smiles pleasantly, then retorts, "Yes, but as tradition has it, my king, the first drink of wine a wife has is served by her new husband, yes?"

A humiliated and red-faced Cantor nods, then states, "Yes, my queen wife, how could I forget?"

Einirt smiles at Cantor, then takes a sip of her wine from the cup. Cantor unexpectedly rises to his feet, then announces to all, "Everyone! Everyone! Let us all raise our cups to our new king and our beautiful queen."

All those that were seated now rise and lift their cups as they face their new king and queen. Einirt then rises to her feet and raises her cup as she faces Cantor. Cantor, in a classless move, raises his cup, then begins to chug his wine from his cup, not realizing Einirt is facing him with her cup raised. Einirt simply smiles at Cantor as all around continue to hold their cups, awaiting their queen's action. Cantor finishes the drink, then realizes that no one has joined him in his toast. Cantor then looks to his queen, and it is plain to see he realizes that he did not toast his queen as tradition has long set for a newlywed couple. Cantor drops his head in shame. Einirt, in her typical, classic style, places her hand under Cantor's chin, lifting it slowly and directing his face to view her smiling, charming, and beautiful face.

Einirt stylishly toasts, "To our new king and my new husband, please join me in drink to honor him."

Everyone smiles, then proceed to drink from their containers. Cantor simply stands there, glaring at his queen in what appears to be a very unhappy manner. Now in a very modest and humble manner, Einirt smiles, then nods to her new husband. All Cantor can do is smile and nod back to his queen. Cantor then reaches out his empty cup for a servant passing by to fill his cup; the servant complies and fills his cup. Cantor then peers over to his queen, then nods and raises his cup to her. Einirt mimics his actions as they both then sip from their cups. After the drink is completed, the two simply smile at each other, then look back at their subjects to view the reactions and happenings. Moats leans in to get his queen's attention; he has noticed that the healer has returned and entered the main hall without anyone else noticing.

Moats whispers to his queen, "My lady, the healer has returned and is surely awaiting your presence."

Einirt nods, then turns to Cantor and requests, "My husband, will you thank our guest for their presence and happy tidings while I excuse myself for a moment?"

Cantor nods in agreement as Einirt rises, then steps down, flanked by her family; they make their way to the position of the healer. Cantor rises, then proceeds to comply with his queen's request.

Cantor announces, "My Queen and I would like to thank all our subjects for this very pleasant celebration and for your attendance."

All the people raise their cups, mugs, and containers in joining Cantor in a drink. As this takes place, Einirt has now reached to position of the healer.

The healer addresses his queen with a bow, then speaks, "My Queen."

Einirt nods, then asks, "How was your journey? And how is my Angelina?"

The healer leans in and whispers in his queen's ear, "My journey was successful. However, I had to leave Angelina with my friend and his family. Angelina is going to live but has lost her sight, and we were unable to restore it. I am sorry, my queen!"

Einirt lowers her head and attempts to refrain from demonstrating any unfavorable reaction; she takes several moments, then leans in to whisper to the healer's ear, "She will not be able to return, will she?"

The healer dejectedly replies, "No, my Queen, she will not." The healer lowers his head in disappointment and shame.

Einirt gently places her hand on the healer's shoulder, then whispers, "You did well, my friend, and I am sure you did the best you could as usual, and that has always been up to our high standards. I am so very grateful!"

The healer raises his head and leans closer to his queen then whispers softly, "Angelina and her daughter will live. They will be protected and will be looked after. I do apologize, my queen, for I did not return her to you as I had promised."

Einirt rears back in amazement; she then leans in to speak into the healer's ear in a surprised yet soft voice, "My little Angelina is with child?"

The healer replies quietly, "Yes, my Queen."

The healer then hands Einirt a small pouch in a very sly manner. Einirt takes the pouch and places it in her dress, just fitting it into her impressive cleavage.

Einirt asks, "What are your instructions?"

The healer responds, "Pour a little into his drink every day, then the rest on the seventh day, and it shall have the effect you wished, and it shall be permanent!"

Einirt smiles, then nods and gratefully says, "Thank you, my friend!"

The healer responds in a sorrowful tone, "I only wish I could have done more, my Queen."

Einirt whispers back, "One day I would like you to take me to see my little Angelina, if you can arrange this."

The healer retorts softly, "I will ask my friend if this is possible."

Einirt replies softly in a begging manner, "Please tell him I beg of him to permit me to do so. Please!"

The healer whispers, "I'll ask, my Queen."

Just then, Cantor approaches the group and asks, "So where have you been, healer?"

The healer replies respectfully, "I was away gathering some roots, mushrooms, and other ingredients for my tonics and cures, my king."

The healer bows in respect, then comments, "If I may have your pardon, my King and Queen I am tired from the journey and would like to get some rest."

Einirt immediately grants the healer permission to leave. "Yes, of course, my friend. Thank you for appearance."

Cantor appears a bit aggravated by this but says nothing for fear of being embarrassed by his queen. The healer nods, then bows as he turns and exits the main hall. The group acts as if nothing significant has happened. Cantor is none the wiser and continues in his immature and clumsy ways. As the evening wears, both Einirt and Cantor are seated in their thrones. Einirt appears tired and Cantor is visibly drunk. Einirt covers her mouth as she yawns while Cantor continues to drink. Cantor notices his queen is tired, so he asks in a drunken state, "Is my queen ready for bed?"

Einirt simply smiles, and then in her classy fashion, she replies, "Yes, my king, I am tired and very sleepy."

Cantor smiles and appears somewhat feisty as he asks, "Are you ready to make your new husband a son?"

Einirt smiles, then leans in and whispers, "I shall pardon myself and await your arrival in my home. I mean, in our home, yes?"

A very intoxicated Cantor smiles at this queen, then has the servant walking by fill his cup once again.

Cantor says, "Yes, I shall be there shortly after I finish this last cup."

Einirt simply nods, then smiles. All of Einirt's friends and guards that heard Cantor's words now nod and smile at Einirt suspiciously.

Einirt says in a gentle soft tone, "Take your time, my king. No need to rush."

A very obviously drunken Cantor smiles at his queen; he then nods as he raises his cup to drink some more wine. Einirt makes her way down the steps where she is followed by Alecia, Holga, some friends, and all the royal guards out of the main hall. At this time, Moats refills Cantor's cup as Brock appears to make a toast, prompting Cantor to drink. These toasts are now shared between Moats and Brock as they continue to refill Cantor's cup over and over again.

Later that evening, lying in her bed, Einirt hears her drunken new husband at the door, talking to someone. Cantor opens the door and stumbles into the home with drink in hand. Cantor attempts to speak to his new wife but is unable to speak in an understandable voice. Einirt sits up, then rises up out of bed. She is naked and her beautiful body is revealed, but no one is there to appreciate her natural stunning beauty. Einirt then places a white sheet around her and makes her way into the room where she finds a very drunk Cantor. Cantor is leaning over the table and clearly unable to do much, much less consummate the marriage. Einirt chuckles, then makes her way to the door where she opens the door and addresses her guards.

A very happy and smiling Einirt says, "Will you two come and aid our sleepy king into bed?"

Einirt lets out a cute and short chuckle as the two smiling guards accommodate their queen's wish. The two guards enter the home, then take Cantor by his arms and lead him into the bedroom where they lay him on the bed in front of them. Einirt has followed them in and instructs the two guards to aid her.

One of the guards comments, "Your plan worked, my lady."

Einirt smiles. "Yes, our new king does love his drink. If not for all of you and the wine, of course, I would not have such a pleasant wedding night. I am very grateful to you all."

The guards nod with a smile.

The guard says, "He does not deserve you, and we will always be loyal to you, my queen."

Einirt smiles, then places her hands on both guards' chests, and to their amazement, Einirt gives each guard a kiss on the cheek, which causes both to blush and smile. Einirt says, "William would be so very proud and grateful for how you care for your queen. I thank you for that."

The two guards proudly smile and nod.

A very elated Einirt laughingly and candidly asks, "Now if you would you be so kind as to help me undress our king please?"

The two guards, at first, appear shocked at their queen's request but then laugh and nod. The two laugh as they proceed to undress their now passed-out and unconscious king. Cantor is now undressed and only wearing his underwear as the two guards step back with a mischievous glare. Einirt laughs as she then thanks the two loyal guards and hands them each a gold coin. The two guards seem apprehensive to take the gift.

Einirt, in a very pleased tone, speaks, "Here, take it. You both earned it." Einirt chuckles. "Thank you so very much. Remember, you are not to speak of this to anyone. William would be proud of you both and thank you for your loyalty."

Both guards take the coins, then turn and exit the home, closing the door behind them. Einirt then pours a cup of wine and adds a bit of what the healer gave her earlier. She sits on the bed next to Cantor, then raises his head, placing the cup to his lips, then speaks to her drunken new husband in a soft yet commanding voice, "Cantor, open your mouth and drink this."

Amazingly, Cantor opens his mouth, then consumes the drink in its entirety. Einirt releases his head as it falls back upon the bed. Einirt then places the cup on a stand next to her. Cantor begins to snore and smiles simultaneously as Einirt proceeds to remove his underwear. A buck naked Cantor now lies in Einirt's bed in an open-legged fashion. Einirt grins and lets out a cute chuckle as she lies in bed next to Cantor, covering herself.

As the next morning arises, we find Einirt in her bedroom overlooking Cantor. She stands dressed in her casual white gown, holding what appears to be a platter of meats, fruits, and vegetables.

Einirt announces, "Cantor, Cantor! Wake up, my husband. Eat this and you will feel much better."

Cantor, with his bloodshot eyes, sits up as he went to sleep buck naked. Einirt hands Cantor the platter of food, then turns around and reaches over to pour a cup of wine as she adds the daily mixture the healer has given her. Einirt turns, then hands Cantor the cup of wine in a very sultry manner, "Here, my husband, something to wash that down and mend your headache I am sure you have."

Cantor mumbles something as he reaches for and takes the cup from Einirt. Cantor then chugs the drink down, emptying the cup. Cantor, with cup in hand, reaches out for Einirt to give him more wine. Einirt pours more into the cup, then places the container back on the stand.

Einirt speaks questioningly, "So, my husband, I must go see the healer. I fear I may be getting ill. My stomach feels rather strange, and I feel warm."

Cantor looks at his new wife with a suspicious grin. Cantor says in a cocky manner, "It was probably from too much of my manhood inside you last night, ha ha ha."

Cantor appears very proud of himself as he attempts to display that he is manly by pushing out his chest and giving Einirt a cocky snarl. Einirt smiles as she attempts to cover her embarrassed reaction with a chuckle beneath her covered mouth. Einirt begins the facade of convincing Cantor that he was an amazing lover last night though she knows better.

Einirt embarrassingly says, "Oh yes, my husband, you were quite the lover last night, and you just kept going and going. I am so sore still."

Cantor arrogantly boasts, "Yes, I was amazing, was I not?"

Einirt responds, "Yes, you were, and now I must go see the healer. Thank you, my husband!"

Cantor commands, "Yes, go see the healer and have him give you something to make you able to hold up to all my manhood. We cannot have you getting sore and tired all the time!"

Einirt, with a smile and a soft sultry tone, says, "As you wish, my king. I shall return shortly."

Einirt walks out of the home, leaving Cantor on the bed eating and drinking.

Einirt walks up to the healer's home and enters. The healer is sitting on a bench near his large table. The healer greets his queen, "Enter, my queen."

Einirt responds, "Thank you, my friend."

The healer requests, "Please have a seat and tell me of your success."

Einirt happily says, "Well, I gave him the first dose last night and the second this morning. He was so drunk last night he thinks we made love all night. He is sitting in bed now, trying to eat and drink his headache away."

The two let out a laugh.

The healer asks, "Perhaps he was so good he left you with child and has made you tender in the midsection as well as in your female parts. Therefore, you will not be able to accommodate his needs until after the birth of his son?"

Einirt smiles and, in her classic soft voice, responds, "Thank you, my friend. Perhaps I shall go and tell our king he has accomplished his duty and in such great fashion!"

The two let out a great laugh. Einirt rises to her feet, as does the healer. Einirt leans in and gives the healer a grand hug. The healer, in amazement, simply hugs his queen back in somewhat of a hesitant manner. Einirt releases her hug and steps back as she announces her intentions in an excited tone, "I shall go now and inform our king of his grand accomplishment! Once again, thank you, my friend!"

The healer, in a humble and honored manner, says, "The pleasure is all mine, and it shall always be, my lady!" The healer nods, then bows as Einirt turns and makes her way out of the healer's home, closing the door behind her.

Moments later, we find Cantor still sitting naked, eating and drinking on the bed. Suddenly, the door bursts open, and Einirt rushes in with an excited look upon her beautiful glowing face. She is excited, then confronts Cantor on the bed in an excited voice, "You did it! I am with child! It is a boy!"

Cantor rises to his feet with excitement, knocking the tray of food on the floor in excitement. Cantor excitedly says, "I got you pregnant! Yes! I am a great man indeed!"

Einirt smiles, then chuckles, "Yes, Cantor, you are that!"

Cantor arrogantly remarks, "You see, all I needed was one night and you are with my child and a son at that!"

Einirt responds, "Yes! The first time and now we must both suffer for the next several full moons!"

Cantor's face drops. Cantor asks, "What do you mean, suffer for the next several full moons?"

Einirt rubs her belly, then tilts her head as she gazes at Cantor. Einirt, in a concerned manner, replies, "The baby's health concerns, of course. You know we cannot partake in pleasures of the flesh until the baby is born, and I am done breastfeeding, silly."

With a depressed and shocked look upon his brow, Cantor drops both the chicken leg he was eating as well as the cup of wine he was holding. A saddened Cantor now stands buck naked with a look of total despair as a tear slowly runs down his hardened and ugly face, as Einirt stands smiling rubbing her belly with glee.

CHAPTER 8

THE FUTURE HAS ARRIVED

SEVERAL MONTHS LATER, we find a very pregnant Einirt standing at the doorway of the healer, and she appears to be in pain. Einirt is flanked by two of her very nervous large bodyguards. The guards appear somewhat frantic in their attempts to get their queen into the healer's home. Suddenly, the door of the healer's home opens, and standing in the doorway is a calm and gleeful healer.

The healer calmly says, "My lady, it appears your son wishes to enter this world."

Einirt gives the healer a look that would frighten even the fiercest of beasts and the bravest of man. The two guards appear even more shaken as they attempt to aid their queen into the home. Einirt gives the two guards a glare that would give the devil himself chills. Einirt then pulls her arms out of the grasp of the two guards, which they immediately comply with her assertion and will.

A very angry Einirt says, "I can do this by myself!"

The two guards take a step back and bow to their very pregnant and angry queen. The healer, on the other hand, reaches out his hand for his queen to hold but is rejected by the very pregnant, very irritable, and yet a beautiful queen. Einirt appears to be fighting off the pain but is not her usual sweet self.

Einirt speaks angrily, "I said I can do this by myself, dimwit!"

The healer steps back cautiously, then motions for his queen to enter the dwelling. Einirt is in severe pain and is extremely harsh with those all around her, especially the men, as she makes her way to the doorway. Suddenly, both Alecia and an also very pregnant Holga appear from behind Einirt.

Alecia calls out, "My lady, we are here to help!"

At this time, the two women have reached Einirt and are allowed by Einirt to aid her into the healer's home and then on to the bed that was made ready for her expected arrival.

Einirt attempts to make herself comfortable on the bed but is unsuccessful and is clearly very irritable as she addresses the men at the doorway, looking in on their queen with extreme concern. Einirt screams, "Get out! And close that fucking door!"

Everyone reacts in a shocked manner as they have never heard their elegant queen speak in such manner. The two ladies let out a slight chuckle, immediately covering their mouths, but the men simply back up and nod as they close the door behind them. Now outside, the two somewhat frightened and shaken guards see Moats approaching. Both guards put their hands out as to indicate General Moats to stop. Moats notice the look on their faces, then begins to chuckle a bit.

Moats asks, "Did my tiny little sister frighten her two elite and very fierce guards?"

The two guards look at each other and then they look at Moats as they nod simultaneously to indicate yes. Moats laughs and questions the two, "What has my little sister done to make her fierce elite guards react in such a fashion?"

One of the guards speaks out, "Our queen screamed at us to get out and close the fucking door! She was very unhappy—very!"

Both guards nod furiously as Moats lets out a chuckle.

Moats, in a more calming tone, says, "Don't take it personal, my friends. Our queen is about to give birth to our future king and is a bit out of herself. I am sure she will make it right with you once she has delivered our new king."

Moats pats both guards on the shoulder, then gives them both a smile.

Moats commands, "Allow no one else to enter here by order of the queen, yes?"

Both guards nod in agreement. Moats makes his way into the healer's home and closes the door behind him. The healer acknowledges Moats with an approving and welcoming nod. Moats makes his way closer to his little sister, then stands next to her right side near Einirt's shoulder. Einirt is lying with her head on a pillow and her legs open and up in the air as her very large brother attempts not to look at the area in question. Einirt realizes her brother is now standing next to her and is, at first, unpleasant to him.

Einirt screams, "What the hell are you doing in here! Can't you see I am giving birth and I am in great pain!"

Moats calmly gives his sister a pleasant smile, then places his massive hand upon Einirt's sweaty forehead as he speaks to her, "I remember when you were about to pass through Mother. She was not very pleasant to be near either, but we loved and cared for her enough to tolerate her rage and sharp tongue as I will yours, my little one!"

Einirt first gives Moats an evil glare, then all of a sudden, at the drop of a hat and in a more pleasant state of mind and with a softer voice, Einirt asks, "Did Mother take long to deliver me?"

In a compassionate and calm voice, Moats speaks, "Yes, you gave her quite the time, and like you, Mother was brave and strong as she finally gave you to us. When you were finally born, it truly was the best day of our lives, and Mother was never so proud as she was when she gazed upon her little Einirt's beauty."

Einirt gives a tearful smile to her massive brother. Einirt reaches out her right hand for her brother to hold. Moats places his tiny sister's hand in between his massive paws with a compassionate embrace and comforting smile. Both Alecia and a very pregnant Holga look on very pleased at the calming effect Moats has had on their friend and queen. The healer gives a slight smile and a nod of approval as they are all pleased with Moats's choice of words and calming effect. Einirt, now with both hands, grabs her brother's hands and squeezes as she lets out a piercing scream and then a moan as she appears to be having a severe contraction. Einirt's squeeze must be intense as her brother displays a touch of discomfort in his face from the strength Einirt has displayed. Being the great man and brother he is, Moats gives his little sister the approval to squeeze and give him the pain she has.

In a show of compassion and strength, Moats speaks, "Squeeze as hard as you can, my little one. Show me the strength my nephew and future king shall possess. Give me the pain you contend with."

With the prevalent pain in her beautiful face and as tears flow from her mesmerizing and stunningly beautiful eyes, Einirt attempts to smile at her doting brother. Alecia has now made her way to Einirt's left shoulder area and is attempting to comfort her queen with a compassionate smile. Einirt notices her beautiful niece now standing next to her and, for some reason, lashes out at her in an unprovoked display.

An irritated Einirt scolds, "What the fuck are you doing? Are you trying to scare my child from me!"

Alecia jumps back with a look of fear and shock upon her beautiful face. Holga, also with a shocked and fearful gaze, steps back as she covers her mouth. The healer gives Einirt a compassionate glance as he appears to be preparing a concoction for her. Moats gives a slight but quick grin but clears this look from his rugged handsome face before his little sister can see it. Now Moats, in an effort to calm the situation, speaks up, "Come now, my little one. Alecia was only trying to add comfort to your situation. Please allow her to aid in your comfort."

Einirt turns to look upon her brother, then responds in a unexpected manner, "The bitch snuck up on me and startled me!"

A very emotional Alecia, now with tears in her eyes, in a soft and unsure manner, Alecia speaks, "I'm not a bitch."

Einirt turns and notices the effect her words have had on her loving beautiful niece, and a look of compassion overtakes Einirt. An apologetic Einirt says, "I am so sorry, my Alecia! I meant you no ill manner. I am not myself and I am truly sorry!"

Alecia smiles with the tears in her eyes and nods to her aunt. Alecia softly responds, "Thank you, Auntie. I understand."

It is apparent by Einirt's facial and body expression that she is having another severe contraction, and it is demonstrated in her tone as in her words.

Einirt screams at Alecia, "Now stop acting like a fucking baby and quit crying!"

Alecia's jaw drops to the floor as she steps back with a look of shock and anguish. Holga, in the same manner as Alecia, begins to shed a tear and covers her mouth, as if not to speak in fear of Einirt's wrath. Moats looks to his daughter-in-law with a brief head shake and a wink of the eye in an effort to aid in her understanding of the moment. The healer places his mixing stick on the table, then approaches Einirt as he stretches out his hand with the concoction in it to Einirt.

The healer, in a commanding and confident tone, says, "Here, my queen, this will help with the pain and your mood swings."

Einirt gives the healer a very angry glare as she reaches out to grab the cup.

Now in a sweet voice Einirt speaks, "What mood swings?"

All but the healer give Einirt a shocked big-eyed look as they are amazed at her new swing in tone and attitude. Einirt takes the concoction and drinks it all, then gives the empty cup back to the healer. Einirt replaces her hands onto her big brother's, and Moats compassionately caresses his little sister's hands once again. The healer places the empty cup upon the table, then makes his way down to Einirt's feet.

The healer asks, "My queen, I must now lift your garment to view the status of your condition. Do I have your permission?"

Einirt gives the healer a strange look, then responds in a more pleasant tone, "Of course! It is you after all that shall be delivering my son."

The healer lifts Einirt's dress and proceeds to examine her nether region. The healer lifts his head with a bit of a surprised look, then announces, slightly excited, "My queen, your son is about to arrive, so if you would be so kind as to pull both your legs back as far as you can, it will make the delivery much easier."

Einirt prepares herself and braces for the next contraction.

Alecia again attempts to aid her queen and steps up to comfort her. Alecia, in a sweet, concerned voice, says, "Auntie, if you wish, I would like to offer my hand for you to hold."

Moats reacts immediately to Alecia's request as he looks at his daughter-in-law, shaking his head in somewhat a dramatic fashion, then speaks up abruptly, "Your auntie is very strong and has quite the grip, my daughter!"

Alecia notices the look on her father in-law's face, an indication that he does not recommend her holding Einirt's hand. Einirt attempts to take her left hand from Moats's grasp, but Moats will not release her hand. Einirt gives her big brother a gaze of disapproval.

Moats speaks up, "My sister, I should be the one who holds and comforts you as a good brother should, yes?"

Einirt gives Moats a compassionate look and smiles as she replies in a soft and appreciative manner, "Well, of course, that is so sweet of you, my brother."

All of a sudden, Einirt's face changes from a pleasant gaze to a frown of extreme displeasure as she lets out a loud and sharp scream. At this time, Einirt is squeezing Moats's hand so hard he actually makes a face with the discomfort and pain plainly visible for all to see. Alecia gives Moats a look of concern and, at the same time, relief as she can see the pain she avoided due to Moats volunteering to absorb and endure the pain she foolishly almost encountered. At this time, Holga is standing next to the healer with several sections of cloth in her hands. The healer again looks down at Einirt's nether regions. The healer looks up and announces the situation is about to get more intense, "My queen, I will need you to push when the next contraction begins and every time thereafter, yes?"

Einirt dramatically replies, "Yes!"

Just then, Einirt begins to have another contraction, and this one is very hard for her as she proceeds to push as indicated by the healer. Einirt squeezes her brother's hand very hard as she lets out the loudest scream of the night. Moats's face indicates the pain and power his sister is displaying with the grimace upon his mug.

Einirt screams, "By the gods, take him out!"

The healer speaks up calmly, "Once more, my lady, once more."

Einirt screams out, "It hurts so bad! Please take him out!"

All but the healer show their emotions in the saddened faces they are all wearing now.

The healer proclaims, "Once more, my lady, just once more."

Einirt's face is now showing that the pain is building and the next contraction is on its way. Moats can see that his little sister is in severe pain and speaks to her in a calm but commanding manner, "My little one, just once more for William. You can do it, my lady, for William!"

The next contraction now hits Einirt, and she pushes as she stares into her brother's commanding and reassuring eyes. The healer appears to be doing his job as he is bent over between Einirt's legs.

Einirt shouts in a composed but painful manner, "Is he here?"

The healer stands up with Einirt's son in his hands and a very happy look on his face. The healer speaks, "Yes, he is. Here is your son, my lady!"

Einirt smiles and then reaches out for her son. In a very concerned manner, Einirt asks the healer, "Why is my son not crying? Should he not be crying?"

The healer calmly states, "Not this one. He just looked up at me and smiled. Do you believe that? He just smiled at me and grunted."

Einirt takes her son into her arms and kisses him on the forehead, then proclaims his name in a proud and commanding tone, "You, my son, are named Nor."

All smile and nod in approval, and they are pleased to see that their queen is doing well and has delivered a healthy, happy, and strong baby boy.

Moats comments proudly, "Congratulations my little one. William would be so very proud!"

Alecia speaks happily, "Congratulations Auntie! He is a very handsome little man!"

Holga attempts her best voice, but it's still slightly muttered, "I am very happy for you, my lady. He is very handsome!"

The healer comments proudly, "You did well, my queen. He will be a great king and a better man, just like his father."

Einirt smiles as a tear runs down her beautiful and proud face. In a proud and soft voice, Einirt states, "Thank you all. I am so sorry for what I said and my actions, especially to you, my little Alecia. Will you forgive me?"

Alecia, without hesitation, speaks up proudly and in a comforting and humble voice, "Of course, my queen, my Auntie, my friend, but you have nothing to apologize for."

Just then, there is a commotion outside the door. Men are heard arguing. Einirt looks to Moats, who immediately turns and addresses the situation. Moats opens the door to find Cantor attempting to overpower the guards, who will not give way. Moats then commands in a pleasant tone, "It's okay. Our queen has given us a heir to the throne. A strong and healthy boy and our queen has given permission for Cantor to see his son."

Cantor pushes his way past the guards as Moats gives way for Cantor to pass. Cantor enters the room where he finds his queen and her son. Cantor is pleased to see his newly born son as he makes his way to stand next to his queen.

Now several months later, we find Holga in the healer's home, lying on the bed, ready to give birth. Holga is flanked by Einirt and Alecia as they attempt to comfort her.

At the same time, we find at Grumpa's village and in Grumpa's home, lying on a bed, ready to give birth is Angelina. A beautiful and tiny Angelina is lying in the bed with her legs up in the air and is in obvious pain as she breathes and pants heavily. Standing next to her is a stunningly beautiful Ynew, who attempts to comfort Angelina as she holds her hand as Nana is bent over between Angelina's legs, giving directions.

In a calm voice, Nana instructs, "Now push, little one. She is almost out. I need you to push once again, little one. Now push hard."

Suddenly Nana pulls out Angelina's tiny and beautiful little infant girl. Nana wipes the infant clean as she then hands the infant to a relieved and joyous Angelina.

Nana, in a very pleased voice, says, "What a beautiful little angel. She is beautiful just like her mother. You did well, my little one!"

Angelina smiles as she proudly holds her new daughter, then she responds to Nana's comments in a pleased way, "That is what I shall name her, Angel. She is my sweet little Angel. Thank you, Nana."

Ynew steps back and gives Nana a strange and curious look. Then almost as if Nana read Ynew's mind, Nana gives Ynew a shake of her head to indicate no. Ynew gives her mother a bit of a beguiled glare as she shrugs her shoulders in dismay.

Nana announces to Ynew, "Come, my daughter, let us gather some more fresh water and give Angelina a chance to bond with her daughter alone for a short time."

Ynew comments, "We'll be right back, Angelina. You did great, and she is so beautiful."

Nana leads Ynew out of the residence and closes the door behind them. Ynew immediately encroaches upon her mother and whispers into Nana's ear in a very concerned voice, "Mother, why did you not tell her?"

Nana, in a calm and soothing tone, says, "Now is not the time, my daughter. Angelina has enough to deal with at the present time, and we do not wish to lay a dark shadow upon her bright sunny day now, do we?"

Ynew nods her head in agreement and displays her understanding of the situation with a simple smile.

Ynew responds in a calmer voice, "Yes, Mother, you are correct. When will you tell her?"

Nana, in a stoic manner, replies, "I won't. You will in seven days hence."

Now, with a shocked look on her young beautiful face, Ynew asks, "Why me, and why in seven days?"

Nana answers calmly, "The experience will serve you well in the future, and you will need the practice. Besides, Angelina deserves time to enjoy her child before we tell her that her little Angel was born blind."

Ynew, with wide-open eyes, asks her mother to explain, "Yes, I agree. Wait, practice for what, Mother?"

Nana nonchalantly replies, "You'll see my child, you'll see."

Back at the healer's quarters, Holga is ready to deliver her son. The healer is bent over between Holga's open legs as she pants and moans in pain.

The healer instructs, "Push as hard as you can this time."

Holga lets out a painful scream as she attempts to push as the healer has instructed her to.

Holga screams in pain, "Take him out! Take him out now! Please!"

The healer now steps back with Holga's son in his hands, then proceeds to wipe the infant clean. The healer then hands the infant to a now very relieved Holga. Holga takes her infant son into her arms and gives the child a loving caress and kiss. Then in a pleased and satisfying voice, she speaks, "I shall name you Doom, for that is what you shall bring your father's future. You are my avenger and my life from this day forward."

All nod in agreement and with satisfaction to Holga's words.

CHAPTER 9

A KING IN THE MAKING

SOME EIGHT YEARS later, down in the middle of the Centaur village, we find several young boys circling one of their own. The boys in this little gathering are all dressed in similar fashion. All the boys are wearing similar cloth pants, cloth wrap shirts, fur boots, and all have long hair. Though the boys appear to be the same size and have the look of teenagers, they are only eight to ten years of age and yet are all very rugged-looking boys. Standing in the center of the circle is a rugged-featured, stout, husky, and angry-looking boy. The boys circling him appear to be chastising the boy in the center. Two of the boys are much larger than the rest, and they are the two that appear to be the most indignant toward the boy in the center.

The larger of the two taller boys, Ox, shouts, "Hit him, Musse, and make him cry!"

Musse shouts, "He probably would cry like he talks. We won't understand him!"

Ox hollers, "Doom, say something smart!"

Doom, the boy in the center of the circle, just glares at Ox and doesn't say a word.

Musse, in a cocky voice, says, "Doom, can you say your mom's name? It's Holga. Say H-O-L-G-A! Ha ha ha ha ha! Can't say Holga, can you, dummy?"

Just then, another boy rushes in to the thick of things. This is a good-looking and well-built boy who is dressed as like that of the other boys, and he appears very angry. The good-looking boy steps up to the boy called Musse, then, from out of nowhere, punches Musse in the jaw, knocking Musse to the ground. Ox rushes in and is flipped over on to the ground, hitting his back, whereby knocking the air out of him by the handsome boy.

In a shocked and slurred voice, Musse shouts, "That hurt! Why did you punch me, Nor?"

Nor, in an angry and commanding tone, replies, "I told you guys to leave Doom alone!"

Ox, attempting to get his breath, sits up and remarks, "We were just playing with him!"

Nor says, "Well, I was just playing with you and Musse. How does it feel?"

Musse and Ox are sitting on their rumps with very disenchanted faces and demonstrate their frustrations in their body language. Nor then steps up to Doom and escorts him away from the group.

Now several days later, Nor finds Musse holding Doom from behind as Ox is punching on his friend Doom. Nor rushes in, throwing Ox onto the ground, then punches Musse in the face, forcing Musse to release Doom. Musse hollers at Nor in a loud voice, "That's it, Nor! Me and you right now!"

Nor turns and gives Musse a mischievous grin as he confidently states, "Let's do it Musse, me and you right now!"

Musse rises to his feet, then raises his fists as he steps up to Nor. Nor, with his fists clenched and hands to his side, simply nods to acknowledge Musse's action. Musse throws a punch that misses Nor by a good distance.

Musse speaks, "Ready? Because the next one shall hit you in that pretty face of yours and mess it up."

Nor laughs, then speaks, "Ha ha ha ha! Right. Do it! You have the first move. You better make it count, crybaby!"

Musse charges in with a punch. Nor ducks the punch, then returns it, but Nor's punch hits Musse in the gut. The gut punch causes Musse to curl up, then fall to the ground in severe pain as Musse grasps for air. Suddenly, Ox charges Nor from behind. Nor apparently hears the noise that Ox makes as he charges in at Nor. Nor simply bends over, causing a very large charging Ox to flip over Nor's back, and Ox flies over, flipping with his massive feet in the air as he lands very hard onto the ground. Ox is in visible pain as he is attempting to get air into his lungs once again, which he lost due to the impact of the landing he made on his back. Both Nor and Doom let out a smile as they nod in satisfaction to each other.

Now confidently Nor asks, "Are we done here?"

Both Ox and Musse nod in agreement as they continue to attempt to secure the air their lungs lack. With a gaze of satisfaction upon their brows, both Nor and Doom turn and walk away with very large grins on their faces.

Sometime later that day, in an isolated area near the stables, we find Ox holding Nor from behind while an angry Musse is punching Nor in the stomach and face. Out of nowhere, Doom appears and is visibly incensed with what he has gazed upon. Doom rushes over to the group and tackles Musse to the ground; he then sits upon Musse's chest and begins to batter Musse's face, blackening his eyes, breaking his nose, cutting his lips, and then Doom rises to his feet and turns to face Ox. Ox releases Nor with a look of fear and amazement. With a bloodied and bruised face, Nor falls to the ground, then attempts to gather himself. Doom rushes toward Ox, then leaps into the air, kicking Ox in the face, whereby dropping Ox on this back and knocking him out. Doom then bends down and helps his friend Nor to his feet. The two walk off with Doom aiding Nor as they make their way away from the two lying on the ground.

Nor, aided by his friend Doom, make their way to Nor's home. They open the door and make their way inside where they are greeted by an older but still shapely and beautiful Queen Einirt. Einirt is donning a form-fitting white gown with high slits on the side and her long beautiful hair is braided and hanging free behind her. Einirt looks to the two with a bit of a glare as she tilts her head ever so slightly and questions the two. A curious Einirt asks, "Have you two been fighting again?"

Nor looks into his mother's eyes and responds with a nod of acknowledgment as does Doom. Einirt shakes her head ever so slightly, then speaks, "Come, let's wash you two up. Are you injured or just hurt?"

Nor smiles at his mother, then shakes his head as he responds calmly, "Neither, Mother, just a bit dirty from the fight."

Einirt asks, "Did you win?"

Nor replies with a grin, "No, but Doom did."

Einirt appears a bit confused as she asks suspiciously, "What? Doom, did you fight back this time?"

Doom nods to indicate yes as a slight grin begins to form on his rugged face. Both Nor and Einirt smile as they nod in satisfaction of Doom's response.

Einirt states, "Your mother will be so proud of you! You finally fought back against those troublemakers."

In a somewhat muttered voice, Doom responds, "Yes. Musse and Ox jumped on Nor, and I stopped them. Nor is my friend, my only friend, so I beat them as they needed."

Einirt, with a surprised glare which turns into a happy smile, pats Doom on the shoulder, then thanks him. In a grateful tone, Einirt speaks, "Thank you Doom. You did a good thing and helped your friend as you should always do. Nor and I are very grateful for what you have done."

Doom smiles, then blushes a bit as he is clearly smitten with his queen's radiant beauty. Nor just smiles and pats his friend on the back. Behaving as if it a regular occurrence, Einirt takes a rag, then dips it in water as she then begins to wipe the blood and grime from Nor's face. Einirt smiles, then looks to and addresses Doom in a soft tone, "Perhaps you should go home and tell Holga what you have done today. I am sure she will be very proud of you, Doom. I truly am."

Doom smiles, nods, and then makes his way out of his friend's home. Einirt continues to clean up her son. Nor grasps his mother's hand and stops her from cleaning his face and then asks her a question in a sincere voice, "Mother, why does Father drink so much wine at the hall all the time?"

Einirt, with smile, responds, "My son, our king has many burdens upon him, and that is how he chooses to deal with them."

Nor curiously asks, "So our king is very troubled and drinks wine to avoid the issues he should be dealing with then, yes?"

Einirt smiles and kind of chuckles as she responds, "You, are wise beyond your years, my son. Just be cautious how and who you trust with your words."

Nor cautiously asks, "I don't feel that Father is a good king, and he does not show me much attention as he once did."

With a tilt of her head and a concerned gaze, Einirt responds, "Why do you think this is so?"

With a serious gaze and tone, Nor speaks, "Father always gives me a sour look and does not respond to my questions. He always says to ask your mother. And as king, he passes his responsibilities to you and Uncle Moats, then continues to drink more wine. Why is that?"

Einirt responds, "Perhaps he wants you to learn on your own. As king, he may choose to seek the wisdom of those he holds high in esteem, and perhaps he feels we may make a better judgment and decision."

Nor nods, then asks, "When I become king, I would like to make my own decisions and ask those wiser than me for advice, then I would make a decision of my own. Is that not what a king should do, Mother?"

With a grin and a slight chuckle, Einirt proudly responds, "You, my son, will make for a great king and an even better man. Just remember, be cautious to whom you give your trust."

Now with a proud smile, Nor nods in agreement, as does his doting mother as she gazes proudly at her son.

CHAPTER 10

A JOURNEY AWAITS

IT IS NOW some five years later and we find Nor leading eleven of his young male companions walking down a road. They appear to be escorting three small children and one infant lying in a small cart, which is being pulled by one of the young men. All the young men are blessed with a long thick hair and are very large in stature; some even appear the size of full-grown men as well as some with hints of facial hair. All the young men are donned with fur boots, cloth pants, fur capes, cloth shirts, and large knives stashed in their leather belts.

The small children appear ill, sickly, and some even deformed. The children are wrapped in blankets as they sit up while some lay quietly in the cart with their dejected stares. Just then, a rugged, handsome, tall, strongly built, well-groomed, blue-eyed, long dark brown-haired apparent leader Nor raises his right hand to indicate for the party to stop.

In a commanding voice, Nor speaks out, "Let us stop for a while and hold up here and get some rest. Musse, gather some firewood, and Magnus, hunt something fresh for us to eat. This old bread tastes like Olff's mother's cooking."

All laugh as they nod in agreement. Musse, a very tall, lean-built, broad-shouldered, rugged, slightly bearded, blue-eyed, long white-haired, and always-grinning young man, begins gathering wood for the fire. Magnus, a tall, well-built, green-eyed, good-looking, and long blond-haired young man, draws his bow and arrow to hunt as instructed by Nor. A tall, thin, light brown haired, not so handsome, and blue-eyed Olff shakes his head as he chuckles, then begins to nod in agreement.

With a chuckle, Olff speaks out, "This is true. My mother is not a very good cook."

Again, the young men all let out a laugh as they prepare to make camp. Just then, Grimm, a tall, brown-eyed, brown-haired, handsome, well-built young man, asks his friend and leader, "Nor, so how far do you think we are from this evil forest we seek?"

With a smile and a wink, Nor replies, "I would say about thirty more days and nights of travel. If we are lucky, we may find some horses."

Just then, Lugg, another tall, broad-shouldered, handsome, rugged, blue-eyed, black-haired, and lean young man, speaks out, "I would eat them! My gut is like an empty wine jar in need of filling."

All laugh as they continue to prepare to make camp.

* * *

Meanwhile, back at the Centaur village, in the king and queen's bedchambers, we find a frustrated Cantor lying in bed, flanked by an apparently disgusted Einirt and a seemingly unhappy young lady; all three are lying in bed covered with blankets. The young lady is a beauty as well with long black flowing hair, an hourglass-shaped body, blue eyes, perfectly tanned skin, beautiful face, succulent red lips, perfect average-sized breasts, and tiny in size.

In a frustrated voice, Cantor commands, "Get me some more wine!"

The young lady begins to rise but is commanded by Einirt in a strong voice, "Stay! I shall get our king his wine."

Einirt rises from the bed naked as a jaybird; the naked beauty then grabs a blanket from the bed, which she wraps around herself, then proceeds to get the wine Cantor has demanded. As Einirt pours the wine, a sinister smile begins to form on her beautiful face. Einirt immediately composes herself, then turns to her husband lying frustrated in the bed with an angry scowl upon his ugly brow. Einirt then addresses Cantor in a solemn yet considerate voice, "Perhaps it is I. I no longer please you, my husband."

Cantor responds angrily, "I do not know! Ever since our wedding night, we have not mated! That damn healer can't seem to find out what is causing this problem! He is worthless!"

Einirt calmly replies, "Husband, perhaps it is the wine. Too much cannot be good for you, my King."

Cantor, in a frustrated and angry voice, says, "No! It is not the wine! I do not understand why I haven't been able to please my wife since we made our son, Nor!"

Einirt, with a smile and in a soft voice, responds, "Yes, he was quite the gift, and like his father, he shall be a good king. So at least we have that, yes?"

Still angry and frustrated, Cantor pushes the young lady from the bed. The young lady falls off the bed naked and embarrassed; as she stands up, she gathers her dress to cover herself.

Cantor shouts angrily, "That does me no good now, does it? And this little bitch can't do the job either! I am forever cursed!"

Einirt approaches the scared and shattered young beauty. Einirt places her hand upon the still-naked and scared young lady, then commands her in a southing and calming voice, "Get dressed, my dear. You have performed admirably and honorably as your king has demanded. I thank you for your aid and loyalty."

The young lady slips on her dress, then looks to Einirt for further instruction as she can see Cantor drink from his cup of wine. Einirt also slips on her gown as she appears to put an end to the strange situation Cantor has arranged. Einirt motions to the young lady for her to join Einirt. The young lady complies as she joins Einirt.

Einirt, in a comforting voice, says, "I shall walk Nikka to her home to see she makes it safely."

Cantor frowns, then nods in agreement at the two, then simply grunts to his queen's statement as he looks away and proceeds to drink his wine. The two ladies make their way out of the bedroom, then out of the home. Once outside, the two are flanked by Einirt's royal guards, who stand guard at the door. The two huge guards smile at the two ladies and simply nod in acknowledgment.

In her usual sweet voice, Einirt says, "Join us, my friends, and walk with us to Nikka's home."

The guards nod and follow as commanded. Now with a concerned expression on her lovely face, Nikka looks to her queen. In a humble and meek voice, Nikka asks, "Did I do all as you asked, my Queen?"

Einirt smiles, then responds happily, "Yes, my dear. You did great! I am very sorry that I had to ask you to do this unpleasant deed, but you are the only woman that our king has shown any interest in since his problem has occurred."

Nikka responds in a positive manner, "You were right, my queen. He did not penetrate me as you had promised. I thank you for that."

With a stern look and in a grateful manner, Einirt stops the group, then turns to face Nikka. In a very humble tone, Einirt addresses Nikka, "No, my dear! I thank you for doing what you did with no hesitation and no concern for yourself! You have done something that I never thought I would ask anyone to ever do."

Nikka smiles, then nods to her queen as she addresses her proudly, "I did what was expected of my Queen, to help you in your time of need. I know you would have never done this with King William, and I would give my life to protect you, my lady! I am just pleased that I was able to help you prove Cantor is underserving of you, my lady. You are what all us women aspire to be, and your sacrifices are unparalleled! So I would happily do this a thousand more times if needed. For what that man has put you through, you are our rock!"

Tears begin to form in Einirt's beautiful eyes as she reaches out and hugs Nikka. Nikka reciprocates the affection with glee. The two massive guards nod in agreement and smile.

Now back at the young Centaur's camp, we find the young men sitting around the fire, roasting what appears to be a deer. The young men appear to be talking and laughing as they pass the time. The young children and infant lay some distance away from the group as they watch without intervention or disruption. Abruptly, Nor stands and grabs some meat and places it into a bowl he has in his hand. Nor then walks up to the group of young children with a look of compassion and concern; he hands them the bowl of meat. The children all reach for and take some meat, and as they begin to consume the meat, Nor bends down to the infant, then picks the infant up and takes the infant with him and rejoins the group of young men. Nor then feeds the infant some of the milk from one of the pouches he has brought with them. All the young men look up to Nor and nod in agreement with his actions.

In a commanding tone, Nor speaks up, "Let us finish this meal and get some sleep as we have long road ahead of us."

In a concerned voice, Magnus speaks up, "Should we wake up to those black clouds? We may want to take to higher ground. It is said that the rain waters run deep in this valley."

All look up into the air and begin to nod in agreement. Nor continues feeding the infant, then glances over to the young children with a concerned gaze upon his handsome young brow.

In a confident tone, Nor addresses the group, "That is a good idea. We will start up the hillside in the morn, but for now, we must get some sleep. Children, come and join us near the fire. It may get cold tonight."

The children stand, then join the young men. The young men have lain blankets down to sleep on, and in a selfless act, each of the young men motions for the children to lie down on their blanket. The children comply and lie down on the blankets as they grab and pull the covering blankets over them.

Many days later, the twelve young men and the children they are escorting reach an area that is encumbered with darkness and is barren of any living vegetation. In the distance, they can see a large dead tree with many dead branches reaching out and it is an evil-looking tree. As the group gets closer and closer to the tree, they can see chains and ropes hanging and nailed to the malevolent-looking tree. It is truly a tree of sorrow tidings and evil in its presentation.

The group stops short of the tree and gaze upon its dark and bewildering presence.

Grimm says, "This is an evil place."

In a determined voice, Nor commands, "I agree! Grimm! Moordock! Bind the boys to that evil tree! We shall take the baby and the little girl to the Chin road. The boys are too week and ill; they will not make it any farther."

The young men comply with Nor's command and begin to move the children. One of the young men speaks out; he is a tall, strongly built, brown-eyed, black-haired, good-looking young man. A concerned Krom says, "This is not wise, Nor! If your father finds out, he will not be pleased with us! That pig would cut out our tongues and feed them to the dogs!"

Nor turns to his friend in a nonchalant manner, then responds confidently, "Then we shall never speak of this and he will never know! Will he?"

Suspicious, Musse asks, "Why does your father treat you so poorly, Nor?"

A cocky Nor replies, "Because he has the face of a dog and I don't! I wish he would die for how he treats my mother!"

Suddenly, a shaved-headed, tall, stocky-built, blue-eyed, rugged-faced and stoic Doom speaks out in a cold, serious voice, "Would you like me to kill him?"

Calmly and coolly, Nor looks to his friend with a smile. A confident Nor replies, "I would not have you dishonor yourself! Besides, his time will come! Now let us gather our things for the road to Chin, for it is a long way from here."

Now a concerned and curious handsome, tall, broad-shouldered, brown-eyed, brown-haired and rugged Moordock speaks up, "This is a good thing we do! Perhaps we should hide in the forest and see who comes for the other children."

Nor, in a confident manner, nods, then responds, "I agree! Let us take to the trees and wait for this evil warlock! Then we can kill him and put an end to this evil tradition of sacrifice!"

A concerned Musse asks, "What would we do with the two sickly children? They will not make the trip to the Chin road."

Nor responds in a confiding manner, "We shall do what we can for them. The healer gave me some sleeping medicine just in case they were to have terrible pains."

Musse asks, "Terrible pains, like permanent sleep?"

Nor looks at Musse with a stoic gaze, then gives Musse a slight nod to indicate yes. Musse's eyes open wide as he becomes shockingly aware of what Nor has to give the children in order to give them a peaceful end.

Hours later, we find the young men hiding in the forest behind bushes and trees, a sound distance away from the Tree of Sorrow. Unable to get closer due to the lack of foliage, the young men do as they must to gain an edge on what is to come. Suddenly, from seemingly out of nowhere, a man donning a dark head-covering cloak and carrying a wooden staff with some kind of crystal on its top end makes himself visible to all as he approaches the children bound to the evil-looking tree. The figure bends down and picks up one of the children, then gently places his free hand on to the head of the other child.

The child that is sitting on the ground before the cloaked figure looks up in a peaceful gaze and speaks to the cloaked figure in a peaceful and grateful tone, "Thank you."

The little boy then smiles at the cloaked figure, then closes his eyes and appears to die in a tranquil and calm manner as his little body bends over, then slumps to the ground motionless. Now from out of the vegetation, the twelve young men dash out and surround the cloaked figure. The figure then reacts by placing the boy he is holding on to the ground calmly. The figure then grasps his stylistic staff with both hands in preparation to defend himself. Nor, in a bold manner and without fear, approaches the figure head-on. The figure stands with his head down, then unexpectedly, as Nor nears closer, the figure rises his head to acknowledge Nor's presence. Then suddenly, to Nor's surprise, the figure kneels down to one knee, then rises in a very respectful manner.

Before the figure could speak, an angry Nor asks the old man, "So you are called Grimmcock?"

In a calm voice, the figure responds, "No, Nor, I am not Grimmcock."

An angry Nor shouts, "You lie! You evil coward! I shall have your head!"

The figure simply smiles, then replies calmly, "No, I shall now teach you and your friends a lesson in respect and manners!"

The figure then takes up a defensive posture as he continues to smile as if he will enjoy the upcoming confrontation. The young men laugh as they begin to close rank on the figure. Ox, the largest of the group, charges in at the figure. Nor appears a bit baffled by the reaction of the old figure they face and attempts to stop Ox's charge.

In a commanding voice, Nor shouts, "Ox! Stop!"

It is too late as Ox's momentum carries him within range of the old figure's staff and bashes Ox upon his massive head, then the staff strikes Ox's legs, lifting him off the ground and on to his backside. Now the rest of the young men attempt to defeat the old figure but are taken down and comically defeated in a very quick, decisive, and humiliating manner by the old figure. All twelve are now lying on the ground, beaten and battered, with their pride more damaged than their persons, but they seem determined to take the old figure down. Several of the young men attempt to rise to their feet when the old figure questions them in a laughing manner, "Well, have you had enough?"

The young men all appear winded as they demonstrate their fatigue in their slow body motions, along with the aches and pains they have recently sustained in the short battle they have just had.

In a concerned voice, the old figure comments, "I do not wish to harm you any further! Your fight is not with me but with Grimmcock. I am not your enemy. I am known to many as the Seventh Tier of the Rising Star of Nezer, but my friends call me Grumpa. I am a great and powerful wizard. I am no warlock! I am honored to meet you Nor, future king of the Centaurs. You may call me Grumpa, Nor."

With a raised eyebrow, Nor appears somewhat perplexed by Grumpa's words and, most of all, Grumpa's calm demeanor. Nor then rises to his feet and begins to question Grumpa.

Curiously, Nor asks, "How do you come to know my name, and how do you come to know where we leave the children?"

Grumpa smiles as he then pulls back his hood to reveal his old, worn, and long-bearded face. He places his staff in his left hand, then offers his right hand to Nor. With a slight smirk on his face, Nor shakes Grumpa's hand.

In a calm tone, Grumpa replies, "Patience, my young king. In time, you will have the answers you seek, but for now, let us seek shelter and tend to these unfortunate little ones at my village. I shall then enlighten you Nor of all that you seek and need to know. Yes?"

Nor simply smiles and nods in agreement as he and his friends gather themselves and prepare to make for Grumpa's village.

Several minutes later, the group, led by Grumpa, finally arrive at a small but well-kept village. As the group enters the perimeter of the village, they pass by a lodge where they see a seated and very beautiful young lady sewing a garment. She is a vision of perfection with her long flowing auburn hair, devastatingly seductive emerald green eyes, light-colored olive pale skin, well-endowed tiny figure, and covered in a body-hugging white gown. All the young men pass as she looks up with a subtle smile; the young men appear in awe as their jaws drop wide-open while their eyes gaze upon the mesmer-izing young beauty. Now Grumpa and Nor pass in front the young beauty, and unable to resist the charm and beauty of the young lady, Nor is obviously smitten by her and apparently she by him. They young beauty rises to her feet as she stares with a sultry smile at Nor. The young beauty questions Grumpa as she continues to stare at Nor though she is speaking to her father.

In a soft and sultry tone, Ynew speaks, "Welcome home, Father. How was your journey?"

Grumpa glances at Nor, then back at Ynew. Grumpa can't help but smile as he realizes the strong attraction his beautiful daughter has for the young Nor and vice versa. Grumpa responds to his lovely young daughter in a pleasant tone, "As you can see, my journey was rewarded with riches and some surprises."

Ynew, still in a trance, is staring at Nor and Nor doing the same with Ynew. Ynew replies in a soft, sultry tone to her father as she continues to stare in a mesmerizing trance at Nor, "That's nice, Father."

Grumpa chuckles, then begins to get sarcastic with his comments to see if Ynew is even listening to him. "Yes, it was nice. We captured some demons and Grimmcock. We then cooked Grimmcock on a spit and ate him."

Ynew smiles as she gazes into Nor's eyes, as if in an hypnotic trance, then she replies to her father in an unfazed manner and tone, "That's so nice."

Grumpa shakes his head in disbelief, then lets out a chuckle. Grumpa continues his walk as he picks up the pace to join the group. Still with no reaction to this, Nor and Ynew continue to gaze into each other's eyes without so much as a whisper between the two. Nor suddenly makes the first move as he slowly and cautiously reaches out his right hand, placing his fingers underneath Ynew's lovely chin; he then leans in and kisses the young beauty on her lips, and she happily reciprocates the kiss. Ynew, seemingly in a trance, then reaches out both her lovely hands and places them on Nor's face as they continue the passionate kiss. Nor's hands then caresses the tiny waist of Ynew's, then pulls the young beauty even closer to him as their kiss becomes even more passionate. Suddenly, from out of nowhere, a whisk broom end strikes Nor from behind. With his hands still on Ynew's tiny waist, Nor turns to see what struck him. Nor looks back then down to see a little old lady with a broom in her hands as she strikes Nor again. Now Ynew leans over to see what is going on. Ynew then realizes that Nana has arrived and has struck Nor with a broom.

Angrily, Nana speaks, "That is my daughter you are kissing, young man! Release her now!"

Ynew steps to Nor's side, then begins to explain to her mother.

In a surprised tone, Ynew addresses her mother, "Mother! Please stop! It was just a friendly kiss!"

Nana, with an angry scowl upon her old withered face, gives Ynew the evil eye, then looks up to Nor with an even angrier glare. Nana scolds the two, "Your father has not kissed me in such a manner in over one hundred years! So don't tell me it was just a friendly kiss!"

Both Nor and Ynew appear a bit embarrassed by the situation as Nor woefully attempts to make the matter less tense as he begins his to apologize to Nana. For the first time in his life, Nor is at a loss for the wisdom and words he seeks to soothe the matter with Nana.

Uncertain and with a slight stutter, Nor speaks to Nana, "Nana is it? Please forgive me, I, ah, I could not help myself. It is all my fault. I, I initiated the kiss and pulled your beautiful daughter toward me as I kissed her. I, ah, I, ah, meant her no foul malice, and I have the best of intentions for your daughter, my lady!"

Nana continues to give Nor the evil eye as Ynew suddenly steps in front of Nor and confronts her mother in a defensive yet apologetic voice, "Mother, it was just a kiss. I wanted to kiss him, and I have never felt this way about a young man before. Please do not harm him. He is very special to me!"

Nana places her broom down next to the table._Then with a smile on her face and in a joyful and playful manner, Nana addresses Nor, "So you wish to be with my daughter, Nor? Do you love her now? Did you ask her father's permission if you could kiss his only daughter? Well, did you?"

Nor, in a shock, reacts as a blubbering idiot would as he has trouble finding his tongue and the words to answer Nana's questions. Ynew looks to Nana and Nor in a bewildered manner and is unsure of what is about to happen. In a somewhat panicked and unconfident manner, Nor attempts to respond to Nana's questions, "I, ah, I, ah, yes, I wish to be with your daughter. I do. I think I do. I have never been in love before, so yes, I think so. No, I did not, not yet. I will go ask him now if that is satisfactory with you, my lady."

Ynew looks on with an uncomfortable and unpleasant gaze, then within seconds, a very pleasant smile begins to grow on her beautiful face as she can hear Nor speak to Nana, "I think I am in love with your daughter!"

Nana begins to chuckle as she points the way to Grumpa, then motions to Nor to go and ask Grumpa for permission to see his beautiful daughter. Nor looks in the direction to which Nana is pointing and can see that all his friends are sitting at a table, eating and drinking with Grumpa and a few other people. Nor, in a more buoyant manner, looks to Nana, then smiles with a confident gaze at Ynew. Ynew looks up at Nor, then in a sign of unity, she places her arm around his, then they proceed toward Grumpa with a giggling Nana following near behind. The three reach Grumpa's position where they stop, and Nor notices he is being watched by all his friends with suspicious looks on their brows; they then all began to smile at their leader with a very beautiful Ynew at his side.

Confidently, Nor speaks up, "Grumpa, may I ask you a very serious question?"

Grumpa finishes the drink he holds in his hand, then places the now-empty cup onto the table as he turns to respond to Nor with a calm and controlled voice.

Grumpa addresses the couple in a calm and certain voice, "Yes. The answer you seek from me, Nor, is yes. Yes, you may have a permanent relationship with my daughter. Is there anything else you wish to take from me?"

Nor steps back in shock with his now-priceless expression upon his brow as he suddenly begins to smile and nod in agreement. Nor, in a very pleased manner, looks to a very happy Ynew, then back to Grumpa.

In a very satisfactory manner, Nor addresses Grumpa, "No. No, sir. Ynew is all I want. However, I do wish to thank you for such a magnificent and beautiful surprise. Ynew is the most amazing and beautiful woman my eyes have ever beheld."

Nor can't seem to take his bewildered eyes off his beautiful Ynew and she as he. Ynew simply gazes at her Nor with love and passion in her eyes. Grumpa just lets out a laugh as he places his arm around Nana, who has joined Grumpa at his side. Nana leans down and whispers to Grumpa, "He is all that you said he would be."

Grumpa smiles and nods in agreement. Nor's friends look on and smile in agreement as they can see that Ynew and Nor are hopelessly in love and make the finest of couples. Grumpa abruptly stands up, then turns to the doting young couple, with Nana at his side, and begins to speak to Nor in a commanding voice, "My daughter, I shall need to speak to Nor for a moment."

With a somewhat concerned look, Ynew nods in agreement. Nor turns to Grumpa, then the two walk off to talk in private. Nor is seen nodding in agreement to whatever Grumpa is telling him. Meanwhile, the group of Nor's Centaurs continue to eat and drink as their friend walks off with Grumpa.

Later that day, we find a love-stricken Nor and Ynew standing face-to-face with a mesmerized gaze upon their young faces. They appear to be standing in front of what appears to be a cave opening. In a very sultry manner, Ynew takes Nor's hand, then the two proceed to walk hand in hand into the cave entrance, then they disappear into the darkness of the cave.

The next morning, we find the Centaur young men making preparations to depart for home. Grumpa, dressed in his usual cloak, appears with his doting daughter, Ynew, at his side. Ynew is stunningly breathtaking as she is wearing a body-hugging white gown that only enhances her tiny waist and bountiful bosom with her long beautiful free-flowing hair behind her; she is quite the vision. Grumpa looks to Nor and asks in a serious manner.

Grumpa asks, "Nor! I hope you have gained the knowledge you have sought."

In response to Grumpa, Nor nods as he looks to Grumpa in a content manner, then gazes over to view the vision of beauty at Grumpa's side. Nor sees Ynew is staring at him as he then fixates his eyes upon his angelic, statuesque, beautiful Ynew. Nor then walks over to Ynew where he places his hands around her tiny waist, then proceeds to lift Ynew into the air just high enough to gaze into her beautiful smiling face and piercing emerald eyes.

In a very romantic tone, Nor addresses his Ynew, "I shall return as soon as I am able, my love."

Nor leans in and kisses Ynew as she wraps her arms around his large neck and shoulders. The two embrace in a very passionate kiss and caress. All look on with grins and nod in approval of the couple. Grumpa claps his hands, then speaks out, interrupting the two, "That is quite enough, you two."

Nor and Ynew finish their kiss and give each other one last hug. Nor then places the beauty back onto the ground as he gazes into her mesmerizing, sparkling emerald eyes as Ynew gazes back at her newfound love. Nor gives Ynew a kiss on the forehead, then turns to his friends and gives his commands.

Nor issues commands in a confident tone, "Let us begin our journey back home, my friends! For the sooner we get there, the sooner I can return to my Ynew!"

Grumpa speaks up in a cautious and friendly tone, "I wish you and your companions a rapid and pleasant journey. We will eagerly await your return to our humble village, especially my daughter!"

Ynew nods in agreement with a glowing gaze upon her beautiful face.

Nor nods, then responds to Grumpa excitedly, "We thank you and do look forward to returning, especially me!"

Grumpa speaks out in a cautious tone, "Oh, by the way, look to the north, for your enemies not only await you at home!"

Nor nods to indicate he understands while his friends give a look of bewilderment to one another. The group begins to walk off as Nor turns to see his beloved one last time. Ynew waves to Nor as he walks away.

Ynew shouts, "Bye, my love! Be safe and return to me soon!"

Nor nods, then blows Ynew a kiss. Ynew stands waving as tears began to form in her beautiful emerald eyes. Nana approaches the young beauty and places her arm around Ynew's tiny waist as Nana attempts to comfort her daughter in a calm voice, "He shall return to you my dear, he must, for he now has more responsibilities!"

Ynew smiles, then gives Nana a questioning gaze. Grumpa just looks at his daughter with a suspicious smile as he nods in agreement.

Several days have now passed as we find the group of young Centaurs passing through the eastern hills. The twelve seem to be in good spirits as they continue their journey.

Inquisitively, Moordock asks, "So, Nor, are you going to tell us what Grumpa had to say to you, or do we have to torture you to find out?"

Nor begins to chuckle as he turns to Moordock in response, "Be patient, my friend. You will all know in time. I must speak to my mother first and see if what Grumpa tells me is true."

Just then Nor notices some movement on top the hillside. There, Nor can see and points out that there are some thirty-six armed Tartans on horseback and are preparing to charge.

Excited, Nor shouts, "To arms! The Tartans are upon us!"

The young Centaurs draw their daggers from their belts and make ready for battle.

Now Nor confidently orders, "The cart! Grumpa gifted us some swords! Get them and prepare for some fun, boys!"

The young Centaurs rush to the cart, then draw the swords hidden from underneath the blanket in the cart. The young men then stand in a line with the swords and daggers at the ready. The Tartans begin to draw nearer and nearer as the young Centaurs display an amazing display of courage and calm. The Tartans charge in, but to their dismay, the young Centaurs all leap into the air, swinging their swords and beheading the first wave of Tartans. The Tartans then attempt to encircle the young Centaurs, but as the Tartan horses move into place, the horses are slapped on their rear ends by the young Centaurs' swords, and then the horses begin to rise up and throw the mounted Tartans from their saddles. As the Tartans, in a panic, fall from their horses, the young Centaurs lay waste to their much-more experienced and better-armed enemies. Now the odds are even as the twelve remaining Tartans attempt in vain to dispatch the young Centaurs, but to no avail. The Tartans are surprisingly stuck down with ease by the young Centaurs.

Now as sudden as they rushed in at the young Centaurs, the Tartans now depart with only three of their warriors remaining. The Tartans rush off in awe and fear as they continually look back at the young victorious Centaurs. The remaining Tartans make their way over the hillside and disappear from sight. Back at the bloody field of battle, the young Centaurs are gathering the horses, weapons, and whatever riches they can locate. The weapons and riches are placed into the cart and the young Centaurs tie a horse up to pull the cart. Now all are mounted on horseback and appear in even better spirits.

Ox shouts out in glee, "Finally! We have horses to save my sore feet from wear and pain!"

With a chuckle, Musse cockily states, "Now that poor horse will break trying to carry your fat ass!"

Ox, in an offended and wounded tone, responds, "My ass is not fat."

All the young Centaurs let out a hysterical laugh as they continue their journey in a very pleased manner—all but Ox who is still sulking from the fat-ass comment.

Now many days later, the young Centaurs are seen entering the Centaur village. Many of the villagers gather around and look on in amazement at the sight of the young Centaurs' favorable condition and bountiful treasures they have acquired. The young men make their way to the front of the main hall where they dismount their horses, then begin to display their bountiful treasures to the villagers. The young men are shown speaking and laughing with the villagers when Cantor and a few of his followers arrive. Cantor, dressed in his usual attire, appears to be angered by the return of Nor and his fellow young friends. In a huff, Cantor makes his way closer to Nor and his friends.

Cantor asks in an angry yet disappointed manner, "So the sheep have returned with stolen horses and false tales of battle! Do you really expect me to believe you won these treasures in a battle with grown men?"

Cantor and his followers let out a laugh as the other villagers look on in amazement and disbelief of their king. The young Centaurs look to Cantor with a sour stare of disbelief and disappointment as they motion with their hands to indicate they are disgusted with the comments their king has made. Confidently, Nor steps up to Cantor, then replies calmly, "I am sorry to have disappointed you, my king."

Cantor, now even more angered, in a cocky tone, asks, "Did you even make the journey to the Tree of Sorrow? Or did you and your sheep lack the courage to complete the journey?"

Again, confidently, Nor replies, "Yes. We delivered the children as you instructed us to the Tree of Sorrow, and I shall show you what we saw on that wicked and evil tree."

Nor takes his dagger out, then bends down where he begins to draw on the ground the symbol he saw on the Tree of Sorrow. Nor draws exactly the same symbol the young men saw on the tree. Nor stands up and looks Cantor in the eye. Cantor appears upset as he scowls at the drawing and the young man.

Cantor responds sarcastically, "So who told you what the symbol looked like?" Cantor laughs. "I don't believe you had the courage to finish the job, boy!"

In a subtle move, Nor takes out a piece of chain which he took from the Tree of Sorrow and hands it to Cantor. Cantor examines the chain, then glares at Nor.

Nor confidently says, "Does this answer your question and prove we are being truthful, my king?"

Cantor becomes even more enraged and incensed at Nor's gesture. Cantor throws the chain to the ground, and unable to control himself, he then shouts at Nor, "How dare you speak to me in that tone, boy! I am your father and your king! You will show me respect, boy!

Cantor now realizes all the villagers are looking at him with a look of disdain. Cantor attempts to regain his composure and tugs at his clothing, as if to make himself more presentable after the embarrassing display he has demonstrated.

Now in a more controlled tone, Cantor addresses the group, "So you and your friends are now men. I congratulate you. However, I shall meet with the elders to determine your punishment for speaking the lies you have spoken here. I shall dispense with your punishment in the morn. Now leave my sight! You all disgust me!"

The twelve young men turn and make gestures to demonstrate their frustration and disbelief as they walk away. Some mutter under their breath as they depart.

Cantor speaks up again, "Twelve boys defeating thirty-six Tartan warriors! Yes, and I can fly like a bird!" Cantor laughs. "Ha ha ha ha, me fly like a bird!"

Immediately, Nor turns to his young friends in disbelief and with a concerned gaze. In a seriously concerned manner, Nor speaks, "We never told him it was thirty-six Tartan warriors, did we?"

The young men all shake their head to indicate that none had spoken those words to Cantor. Nor then gives his friends a suspicious gaze and begins to nod with an angry scowl upon his brow. The young men continue walking away from the main hall area.

CHAPTER 11

AN UNFORTUNATE TIME

LATER THAT EVENING, we find Nor sitting at a table with his beautiful mother, Einirt, who is dressed in a lovely form-fitting white gown. They appear to be eating their dinner when Nor raises his head, then questions his mother seriously, "Mother, we need to speak about my father. My real father, King William!"

Caught off guard and in shock, Einirt drops her spoon into her bowl of stew as she peers at her son with a look of astonishment clearly visible on her beautiful face.

Einirt, in a frightened and surprised voice, asks, "How? Who told you this?"

Suddenly, tears begin to form in Einirt's beautiful sapphire eyes as her lower lip uncontrollably begins to quiver. A single tear runs down her lovely cheek as she gives Nor a fragile look. To his surprise, Nor is quite taken by this as he has never seen his brave, confident, beautiful, and wise mother in such a fragile and vulnerable state before. Having never seen his mother shed a tear before, Nor appears uncertain how to react to this. Though he is in need of answers, Nor reaches out to his mother, taking her hands into his as he looks deep into her eyes; he attempts to comfort her but still has questions he would like her to answer. A now-weeping Einirt nods in agreement as she peers into her handsome son's eyes.

Nor then answers his mother's question confidently, "I met an old man who said he knew my father. The old man's name was Grumpa. He is a powerful and wise wizard. He also told me that Cantor killed my father during a battle with the Tartans. Cantor did this to become king and take you as his bride! Is this true, Mother?"

A still-weeping Einirt looks into her son's eyes as she caresses his hands tighter, softly weeping as she responds, "My son! You must understand! I had to marry Cantor to make him believe you were his son, or he would have killed you! I loved your father more than life itself and I would have taken my own life if not for being pregnant with William's child, with you! Did this Grumpa also tell you that Cantor was once married before and killed his wife, then sacrificed his only child to Grimmcock?"

Nor, surprised, responds, "No. Grumpa did not speak of that. He did tell me that all your royal guards were poisoned and that Uncle Moats was ambushed, not killed in battle as Cantor said he was. So I am worried about your safety, Mother! There is no telling what Cantor may do with you now, without Uncle Moats or your royal guards here to protect you!"

Now in a more concerned and sure manner, Einirt speaks, "Now do you see what kind of man Cantor truly is now? You must never tell anyone who your real father is, or Cantor will surely kill the both of us! Do you understand? In these past few years, I do believe that Cantor has grown suspicious that you are not his son. You do resemble William. You have his good looks, intelligence, wisdom, courage, and love from those around you as he did. I too fear Cantor's wrath, but my options are limited now, my son!"

Abruptly, the two hear a sound from the back of the home. Nor jumps to his feet, then rushes over to the back window to investigate the noise; he bursts open the window cover and looks around. In the distance, Nor can see an image running, then disappear behind one of the homes. Nor turns, then acting with urgency and in a commanding style, Nor takes control of the situation.

Confidently, Nor speaks out, "Mother! You must leave now! Never return to this place! Here, these are the directions to get to Grumpa's village. Leave now! Please hurry!"

Einirt takes the leather-drawn map from Nor, then she begins to gather some things to take with her.

Concerned, Einirt asks, "Will you come with me?"

Calmly, Nor responds, "No, I cannot. I must stay and buy you some time."

In an unsure voice, Einirt asks, "What will you do, my son?"

Nor gives his beautiful mother a confident smile, then responds, "Worry not, Mother. I will be fine. I am my mother and father's son. Besides, you will finally get to meet Ynew. I am going to make her, my queen, and she will need your guidance and wisdom. So you must hurry and get to Grumpa's as soon as possible."

Einirt goes from state of fear to a state of elation in a split second. The two join in a loving embrace.

A confident Einirt says, "Why do I have this feeling that you will be just fine?"

Einirt gazes into her son's eyes, then gently brushes her fingers through the front of Nor's hair and gives him a gentle smile. Einirt suddenly turns, then runs out as fast as her beautiful legs can carry her.

The next morning, we find all the villagers gathered near the main hall. Cantor and his followers appear as they make their way through the crowd, then enter the main hall. Now inside the hall, Cantor walks up the steps and takes his place in his throne. He is unusually confident in his mannerism. Now the twelve young Centaurs enter the main hall, then make their way to the steps of the stage where Cantor is seated. Cantor's followers make their way behind the twelve young men.

Cockily, Cantor makes his command, "Bind their hands behind their backs and noose their necks!"

Cantor's followers take the ropes they possess, then proceed to bind the twelve young men. The young men simply stand bravely and accept their punishment. Nor looks around, then suddenly, his facial expression begins to speak volumes. Nor notices that the elders are not seated where there supposed to be seated in the main hall. The other young Centaurs notice Nor's reaction then they all give Nor a questioning head gesture.

In a concerned, low-toned voice, Nor speaks, "The elders are not here!"

The other eleven now appear somewhat shaken by this news. Cantor notices the reaction of the twelve, so he begins to smile an evil smile.

In a sinister tone, Cantor addresses the twelve, "So you say that you completed your mission to the Tree of Sorrow, did you? Well, I have proof that says otherwise, not to mention you fools violated the peace treaty I established with the Tartans. You boys killed and robbed one of their horse traders. As if that wasn't bad enough, you disobey my commands! That is a death sentence. But today, I feel merciful. So fortunately for you boys, I will simply banish you. Now on your knees, little girls! I have a pleasant surprise for you, especially you, Nor!"

Cantor looks to his left where a large curtain has been hung from the ceiling. Immediately, everyone turns to see what it is that Cantor is waiting for. Suddenly, the curtain is drawn back and the worst of all possible situations is revealed. Standing with his bodyguards at his side is the evil Warlock Grimmcock. Grimmcock is dressed in his usual attire, as are his evil minions Cetan and Brummel. Brummel is holding a rope which appears to be attached to a weeping and a hooded woman.

In a very commanding voice, Cantor addresses the Centaur people, "For disobeying their king and breaking the agreement with our dear friend and ally Grimmcock, we shall impose the banishment of these twelve disobedient little lambs for the next twelve winters."

Cantor pauses to see the reaction from everyone. The villagers all let out a gasp and with their facial expression, display their displeasure as well as their surprise at Cantor's punishment for the twelve young men. Standing behind but near Cantor, Grimmcock and his cohorts simply smile as Cantor has announced the banishment for the young men. The twelve young men look to one another without expression but simply nod.

Smugly, Cantor continues, "Now should anyone of you decide to disobey me and return sooner than commanded or refuse to stay in the designated place you are banished to, well, then your families shall pay the price of death!"

Just then, a very cocky Cantor turns to Grimmcock and nods. Grimmcock removes the hood from the woman he has bound, and to everyone's astonishment, the woman is a beaten and battered Einirt. Einirt's mouth is gagged, preventing her from speaking out. A very angry and horrified Nor attempts to rise to his feet but is kept down by the very large guard standing behind him.

In a very inconsolable and livid manner, Nor shouts, "Cantor! Make no mistake! Upon my return, I shall have my vengeance! On that day, our people will truly know what you did to King William to steal his crown and his bride!"

An embarrassed yet enraged Cantor shouts, "What! You know nothing, boy! You should not tempt me, boy, for a very long journey awaits you and your death may come to you earlier than you know! However, should you have the misfortune of returning, you will suffer along with your whore of mother!"

The Centaur villagers appear shocked and somewhat angered by the actions and words of their king. Appearing overconfident, Cantor spitefully begins to disperse the punishment areas to which each of the twelve shall be banished to.

In a very evil tone, Cantor commands, "You, Moordock, shall go to Rome. Doom, you shall go to the Badlands. Dread, you shall go to Germania. Ivan, you will go to Persia. Musse, you shall go to the frozen Northlands. Krom, you will go to Carthage. Magnus, you shall go to Espania. Olff, you shall go to Gaul. Grimm, you shall go to Egypt. Lugg, to Mongolia. Ox, you shall go to Chin, and you, Nor, shall go to Sparta. Now should any of you decide to leave sooner than you should, just know this: your loved ones shall die because of your actions. Should you not return here in the twelve years, then your loved ones shall die because of your failure to return. I'm sure you all understand. You will all be unbound once you are a safe distance from our village and do not attempt to return or the deaths of your loved ones is on you.

As each is given their destination for banishment, the Centaur villagers sigh and gasp. Einirt drops to her knees and weeps uncontrollably as she gazes at her brave and handsome son. Grimmcock and his crew laugh as the twelve receive their banishment orders.

In a commanding and angry tone, Cantor orders, "Take them away and keep them bound until they are a good distance from here."

The twelve are led away by their assigned guards. On the way out, Nor turns and addresses his friends. Now Nor speaks but two words, "Bear cave."

The bound young men seem to turn one by one and repeat the words Nor has spoken as they nod in agreement back at Nor. The young men are separated then are led away by two guards, each except for Nor. Nor was taken away by four guards.

Several days later, out on a deserted road, Nor is unbound by his guards. One of the guards grabs Nor in a violent manner, then smiles at Nor as the guard slips a dagger into Nor's shirt and violently throws Nor to the ground. Nor gives the guard a slight nod, then changes his expression to a look of rage as he then shouts at the guards.

An angry Nor shouts, "Tell Cantor, should my mother see any harm done to her, it will take two winters for him to die from the pain I shall inflict upon him!"

Nor stands up and dusts himself off as the guards turn and ride away. Nor turns, then begins walking toward the city he sees in the distance.

Around this same time, we find a very large Musse near an icy riverbed; he appears to be watching a fish. Suddenly, Musse lurches in and grabs the fish; however, the fish is more slippery than he anticipated, and it slips into the air, away from Musse's grasp, causing the very large Musse to fall into the icy waters of the river.

We now find Nor nearing the valley of the southern mountains of the Greek city states and his destination of Sparta. Suddenly, from behind a turn in the road, Nor sees two riders approaching very fast toward his direction. As the two riders near closer to Nor, they draw their swords and appear to have bad intentions for Nor. To the riders' surprise, Nor does not flee; instead, he rushes toward the riders this appears to confuse the two. Nor leaps into the air and hurtles into one of the riders, dismounting the rider and knocking the rider onto a stone, which knocks out the rider. The other rider turns and rushes back to battle Nor, but Nor grabs a rock and hurtles it into the rider's chest, causing the rider to lose his grasp on his sword. The now-injured rider rides away in agony. Nor grabs the sword from the ground, then walks up to a still-knocked-out rider; he then leans down and slaps the unconscious man in the face, whereby waking the man.

A confident yet slightly cocky Nor asks, "Who sent you to kill me?"

The man shakes his head to indicate he will not answer.

With a simple smile and a calm voice, Nor comments, "Have it your way."

Nor then thrusts the sword into the man's heart, killing him rather quickly. Nor bends down and grabs the other sword lying in the ground, then captures the loose horse. Nor mounts the horse, then rides off down the trail leading to his destination.

Now at Grumpa's village, screams are heard coming from his residence. Inside the home and lying on a bed is a very pregnant Ynew. Standing between her long beautiful legs is Nana; Nana is the acting doctor, delivering her own grandchildren with a very prom-inent beaming smile upon her face. Suddenly, from the doorway, Grumpa makes his presence known as he inquires as to the situation at hand.

In a surprisingly excited tone, Grumpa asks, "Well, what news?"

In a very angry voice, Ynew shouts, "Get out! Get out!"

Grumpa's excitement turns immediately to sadness as he exits the room immediately and closes the door behind him. Nana gives Ynew a stern look with a slight tilt of her head to scold her daughter.

In a stern voice, Nana speaks to Ynew, "That was not nice, my daughter, and you know better."

Overwhelmed with pain, Ynew speaks, "I know, Mother! This hurts! I don't want any man in here! Now hurry and get these chil-dren out of me before I die from the pain, Mother!"

Nana gives Ynew a questioning glare, then smugly states, "You're the one that didn't want my mixture to ease your pain."

Ynew gives her mother the most evil of looks with her eyes, then announces in a painful and very harsh voice, "Just deliver my children. Enough with the talking, Mother!"

Nana nods, then gives a slight smile to her daughter. Nana then bends back over as she lifts the sheet covering Ynew's lower body. Nana's face appears to change to an excited expression, then excitedly announces, "Here comes the first one my daughter. Now push!"

With a loud scream, Ynew pushes to extricate the first child. Now with a gleeful smile and the first baby in her hands, an excited Nana announces with pride the first child's arrival. Nana then hands the infant to a nursemaid who is there to assist in the births of Ynew's children.

Ynew asks in a fragile tone, "Is it a boy?"

Nana calmly replies, "No daughter, she is a beautiful and healthy girl."

Nana then leans back in to deliver the next child. Sooner than expected, the second baby makes her arrival known with a loud scream as a very proud Nana takes the infant and places her into the hands of the other nursemaid who takes and wraps the infant in a small blanket as they did with the first child.

In an inquisitive yet demanding tone, Ynew asks, "Is this one a boy?"

Again, Nana replies calmly, "No my daughter, she is also a beautiful and healthy girl."

Ynew appears irritated and somewhat angry by the news. Then seconds later, Ynew lets out a scream, and soon after, the third child is born. Nana takes the infant and wraps her in a blanket, and as she turns to Ynew, Ynew asks again in a sad yet inquisitive tone, "Is this one a boy?"

Nana smiles down at her daughter, then replies in her usual calm voice, "No my daughter, she is a beautiful and healthy girl, just like the other two. The gods have blessed you with three beautiful healthy daughters, and they all look just like their mother."

Ynew smiles, then the smile turns into a frown as she realizes she has not given her love the son and heir she had hoped for. In a

NOR AND THE CENTAURS

saddened voice, Ynew speaks up, "I was hoping to give my love a son."

Nana lets out a chuckle, then speaks, "You will next time, my daughter. Now we shall enjoy these three little ones until he and Nor arrive. Yes?"

Ynew smiles, then nods in agreement.

In a cute manner, Nana leans in and asks, "I think it would be nice if you asked your father to come and see his granddaughters, yes?"

Ynew smiles and nods in agreement. Shouting in a sweet tone, Ynew calls out, "Father! Come and welcome your grandchildren into this world. They would like to meet you!"

Suddenly, the door bursts open and Grumpa comes rushing in with a gleeful bounce in his step and grin from ear to ear as he makes his way to see and welcome his grandchildren, then steps up to speak to his daughter. In a concerned manner, Grumpa asks, "How are you, my daughter?"

With a smile and in a sweet tone, Ynew responds, "I am fine Father. What do you think of your granddaughters?"

With a beaming glare and as proud as a peacock, Grumpa announces, "I think they are beautiful just like their mother. You did very well, very well indeed, my daughter. I am so very proud of you. Nor will be so very proud of you and of his daughters!"

Grumpa compassionately brushes Ynew's hair, then gives her a concerning yet inquisitive gaze and asks, "So what are their names?"

Ynew responds without hesitation, "Their father will have to name them when he returns. It is their way. Besides, I would not deprive him of this honor."

Grumpa nods in agreement, then gives his doting daughter a smile.

In a commanding fashion, Nana takes over the room and announces to all, "Ynew will need to rest now, so let us take care of these little angels and give their mother some time to rest. I shall return in a bit, my daughter."

Grumpa gives Nana a sour face, then in a very immature manner, he sticks his tongue out at her. Ynew sees this and lets out a little chuckle; Nana gives him a very mean look, then rushes him out the room.

Now as Nor is passing through a shadowed valley, he can see four horsemen approaching him. He stops his horse, then turns it sideways as to indicate to the riders he wishes them to stop. The riders suddenly began to charge toward Nor with their swords drawn; with a slight grin, Nor tilts his head, then turns his horse and charges toward the riders with both swords now in his hands. Two of the riders take the lead to charge and engage Nor. In a magnificent display of horsemanship and swordsmanship, Nor charges in between the two riders, beheading one and slicing off the other's sword arm. The other two riders not far behind engage Nor with their swords. Nor slices through one of the riders' legs and guts the other. The rider with the leg injury falls to the ground in pain as the rider with the amputated arm rides away as the other two lie dead on the ground. With a slight grin on his young and handsome face, Nor dismounts his horse, then approaches the fallen rider.

A cocky and confident Nor asks, "So are you going to tell me who sent you to kill me?"

The rider, in obvious pain, responds, "I don't know his name. He just paid us in gold, so we agreed!"

Suspiciously, Nor asks, "What did he look like?"

The rider responds, "He was a very large man. He had a full beard and…and…he appeared to be an older man with a very large sword that had a strange symbol on the hilt. It looked like a dead evil-looking old tree."

With a smile, Nor responds, "I know who sent you."

The rider pleads, "Please don't kill me! I have seven children and I have answered your questions. Have mercy please!"

Nor lets out a chuckle, "Seven children, huh?"

The rider gives a pathetic smile and nods vigorously. Nor just smiles as he shakes his head in disbelief.

A compassionate Nor says, "You better tie that leg off or you will bleed to death and your five children will be without a father." Nor then throws the rider a binding to tie off his leg.

The rider nods in agreement, then speaks, "Thank you. Yes, all five will all be very grateful for your compassion and mercy, sir."

Nor laughs sarcastically. "I thought you said you had seven children."

The rider looks up to Nor with an uncertain and slight smile. "Yes, I meant seven."

Nor just laughs as he shakes his head in disbelief, then asks, "So is this the road to Sparta?"

With a frightened look, the rider responds, "Yes, but you don't want to go there, young man. It is a harsh place for strangers, and they do not fear death!"

With his standard grin and cocky tone, Nor replies, "Well, good luck with those seven children and tend to that leg so they may see their father once again. Farewell."

Nor mounts his horse, then with a smile, he nods to the rider and rides off down the path to Sparta.

Many years later, we find Ivan, now a grown man of some twenty years or so of age. He is walking in the desert with sun-burned face and appears tired and dehydrated.

Around this same time, we look in on Musse who is also a fully grown and a heavily white-bearded man. Musse is cutting up a dead seal; as he looks up to his displeasure, he sees a very large polar bear. The polar bear charges in at Musse, who stands up angrily, then takes his knife and charges the polar bear. Musse, who stands over seven feet tall, stabs the polar bear in the throat and is thrown to the frozen snow-covered ground. With the now-dead polar bear on top of him and bleeding all over him, he lets out several grunts as he makes his way out from under the now dead polar bear. He stands up and begins cleaning off his blade when he notices three baby polar bears standing at a distance, watching him. Musse shakes his head in disgust. He then addresses the three cubs disgustedly, "She gave me no choice! I would have shared the meat!"

Musse shakes his head in disgust, then kneels back down as he continues cutting up the dead seal as the three cubs continue to look on. Slowly but surely, the three cubs approach Musse's position; as he glances toward the three, he grunts, then tosses each cub a piece of the dead seal. The cubs, at first, are unsure, then eventually begin to devour the meat Musse has so selflessly provided them.

Meanwhile, in the desolate Dark Lands a determined and angry young Doom makes his way down a narrow dark pathway.

At the same time, in the barren plains of the steps in Mongolia, we find a grown Lugg walking in chains as he is being led by mounted Mongolian riders.

Meantime, in Egypt, near the Nile River, we find a grown-up Grimm swimming naked in the river; several women and girls look on and appear to be giggling as the gawking crowd stare at Grimm, who does not appear at all bothered by this, for Grimm has no shame what's so ever.

In a small village in Northern Italy, we find a grown Moordock sitting at an outside table surrounded by villagers. Moordock appears to be in good spirits as he continues drinking wine and eating lamb with some other men.

In southern France, near a rocky stream, here we find a grown, bearded Olff attempting to cross the stream. Being ever so cautious, he slips into the stream as he makes his way to his feet; he is now covered in mud and pond scum. Olff is not very pleased with the current events as he stands and attempts to clean the mud off and makes an effort to exit the stream; he slips once again and falls into the muddy stream. This time, Olff just sits in the stream covered in mud and pond scum.

At this time, in cave in the country Cartage to find a very grown and heavily bearded Krom. Krom cautiously enters the cave he finds near a hillside, but unbeknownst to him, it is occupied by a very large male lion. The large lion demonstrates to Krom that the cave is his, but the lion does not realize that Krom has no intention of leaving the cave at this time. The two engage in a fierce battle, but Krom ends up wearing the massive lion for warmth and protection.

Meantime, in Sparta, we see a king of Sparta walking with a now fully grown Nor. Nor is a very impressive sight to see, especially decked out in his oversized-to-fit Spartan armor. To the Spartans, Nor possesses a size to which only the gods could have gifted him. Nor is treated like that of royalty as he has fought in many a battle to aid the Spartans in victory after victory. A very rugged and handsome Nor has been granted many beautiful and willing Spartan women to make his own and to hopefully spread his seed as his hosts have so noticeably desired, and being the generous and selfless man that he is, Nor obligates himself as desired by his hosts.

Several years later, back in the frozen northlands, we enter an ice-covered cave up on a mountainside where we find a fur-covered Musse lying on the ground and flanking him are three very large grown polar bears sleeping and snoring as if not a bother in world.

Meanwhile, in Rome on top a fortress wall, we see a very large and rugged-looking Moordock standing guard with several other Roman soldiers dressed in their Pretorian guard purple capes and golden armor.

To the east, in camp somewhere in Persia, we can see a very large man sitting among other fancy-dressed Persian soldiers around a campfire, it is obvious to all that Ivan is not your average Persian soldier.

In the west, near the great Atlantic Ocean, in a fighting pit somewhere in Espania, we find a bloodied but laughing and very massive Magnus. Magnus is adorned in gladiatorial armor and armed with a small shield and gladius for a weapon. Magnus appears to have eliminated two gladiators already and yet faces two more well-armed gladiators who appear very hesitant to engage the very large and fear-less warrior. An eager Magnus advances on the two now-frightened warriors and dispenses with them with two impressive swings of his sword.

Just south of Espania, we find Krom sound asleep and snoring in a cave; however, the very massive Krom is not alone in the cave. Sitting with a glare and appearing very uncomfortable is a very large female tiger with three cubs. One of the cubs is sleeping next to his mother; a second is sound asleep on top of the very large massive chest of Krom while the third is chewing on Krom's very large boot.

In the cold forest of Germania, we find a huge figure draped in a dark cloak carrying wood, following a tiny old lady who appears to be speaking to the figure behind her. Dread glances up from his hooded cloak to give the old lady a grin and a short chuckle as he nods in agreement.

Meantime, near the Chin road, a massive figure of a giant man Ox is eating and drinking with a large family around a table, and they all appear in very good spirits.

Now back in the dark lands at what appears to be a blacksmith's residence and shop, we find a massively impressive-looking bald-headed Doom standing outside the door of the shop. The door opens and out rushes a young boy of maybe four years of age; he is followed by a younger boy of maybe two or three year of age. The boys are followed by a very beautiful young woman who appears to be their mother, and she appears to be blind. She is a vision of beauty with long beautiful black hair and a body that any goddess would desire. She is tiny in mass and well-endowed as she is dawned in a form-fitting gown that only enhances her tiny figure. Doom lifts the two boys and hugs them with his massive arms, then steps up and leans down and kisses the blind beauty as if it were a familiar action. The beauty wraps her thin feminine arms around the massive Doom's neck as they both smile in a very content manner.

CHAPTER 12

A Sorrowful Departure

IN A VERY dark and gloomy room in the fortress of Grimmcock, we find a very stoic and sinister-looking Grimmcock gazing into his viewing well. Through the open door enter both Cetan and Brummel; they join their evil leader at his viewing well. Grimmcock steps back, then address his cohorts in a concerned manner, "We must make preparation. The son of William is going to return to seek his vengeance on all who have betrayed him and his family."

Back in a Mongolian village, we find the Khan speaking to the exceptionally large Lugg. The Khan then hands Lugg a magnificent bow with a full quiver of arrows, then gives Lugg a short bow. Lugg reciprocates the bow, then turns and mounts his horse; he looks back at a certain woman and gives her a smile and a nod, then rides off down the trail.

Back in Sparta, in the king's hall we find our hero, Nor. Dressed in his Spartan armor and crimson cape, Nor is surrounded by several scantily dressed beautiful young weeping women as he faces the king. The king motions for the young beauties to depart, then he steps up to Nor and gives Nor an uncharacteristic embrace.

The Spartan king, in a saddened tone, says, "As you can see, you will be missed my son. Now take these gifts and may the gods smile upon you and may you achieve victory with your vengeance. Remember, my son, should you ever need your Spartan family to come to your aid, we shall fly there upon the wings of Hermes to be at your side."

Just then, the king motions for a servant to step forward with a large cape-wrapped gift for Nor; the servant hands the gift to Nor. Nor nods and smiles at the king. Nor then turns and departs the chambers as the young beauties continue to weep in the most pitiful of manners. Now outside, Nor straps the gift he received from the Spartan king on a pack horse, then mounts another impressive steed and rides off.

We now join Musse as he makes his way down from the frozen northlands. Musse is covered in a very thick white polar bear fur as he is accompanied by three very large polar bears. As Musse makes his way south, he trips and falls into the snow, but something has caught his attention; he moves some of the snow to discover a long-handled, very well-crafted halberd. Musse stands up as he lifts the very large and impressive halberd; he then examines the blade which he realizes is very sharp and without any rust or marks. Musse smiles and then proudly displays his newly discovered treasure to his polar bears; however, the bears don't appear interested.

Back in Chin, we find a giant of a man who is Ox; he is preparing his horse to depart as his adopted Chinese family has gathered around him to bid him farewell. The old man hands Ox a silk-wrapped bundle and nods to Ox. Ox places the bundle upon his horse, then ties it off. Ox mounts his horse, then nods to his adopted family and then rides away.

In the dark lands at the Alchemist blacksmith's shop and residence, standing in front of the stable is a strange-looking old man with different-colored eyes and a scarred-up, rugged old face. The old man appears to be preparing a horse that is well armored in a dark metal cloak and spikes on the front of the metal face guard the horse is wearing. From out the front door of the residence appears a very large bald and white-bearded Doom donned in a magnificent and wicked-looking set of armor. Doom is followed by his two sons and a very pregnant tiny beauty. The boys are standing with a very saddened gaze upon their quivering faces with tears forming in their eyes as they attempt to put on a brave face for their father. Unlike their beautiful mother, who is openly weeping, she grabs and hugs her man in the most heartbreaking manner; she is relentless in her embrace and refuses to relinquish the hold she has on Doom. Even the hardened and rugged Doom is brought to shed a tear; though small, it is a tear nevertheless. Doom leans down and kisses his beloved on the top of her petite head, then looks to her father the Alchemist, who responds by taking hold of his tiny and beautiful daughter, causing her to relinquish her hold on Doom.

In a forceful tone, the Alchemist asks, "When will you return?"

In a saddened voice, the massive and intimidating Doom replies, "Look for my return upon the next winter's fall. I shall arrive before the new moon sets." Doom then looks to his tiny black-haired beauty and tells her, "I love you, my angel! Thank you, Alchemist!" Doom then looks down to his eldest son and in a manly tone, he commands, "Little Doom! You take good care of your mother and your little brother. Little Nor, you listen to your mother and big brother, you best not get into any trouble while I am gone."

With tears flowing down from the oldest son's big blue eyes and his saddened little face, the young boy nods in agreement as little Nor, with his usual mischievous grin, nods and smiles. Doom then gives the boys a nod and a wink, then without hesitation, Doom takes his beloved's beautiful dainty face into his two giant hands and caresses his beautiful Angel's face and kisses her in the most romantic of ways, then turns to mount his magnificent and wicked-looking steed. Doom nods to the Alchemist, then proceeds to ride down the trail that lay ahead of him.

In an Egyptian palace, we catch up with a fully grown and ruggedly handsome Grimm who is surrounded by several beautiful scantily dressed ladies who are all fitted in short, revealing, and somewhat transparent white wraparound dresses; they all appear saddened by the imminent departure of the man they adore and love. Standing directly in front of Grimm is a well-dressed and jewel-laden prince, who seemingly is very fond of Grimm.

In a grateful manner, Grimm speaks up, "I thank you and your father for all you have generously given to this unworthy soul!" Grimm then nods in a very humble manner.

The prince steps up, then places his hands on the shoulders of the very large Grimm and the two touch foreheads together, then in a sad manner, the prince turns and walks away. Grimm then turns to exit the palace with his hoard of lovely ladies at his side, but all the ladies remain inside the palace as Grimm exits the large fancy-decorated doors.

We then head to Germania to find a sad Dread standing over a grave with a very stoic gaze upon his rugged and scarred brow. Behind the massive Dread stands an old man holding an apparent giant weapon wrapped in a blanket while holding the reins of the giant Clydesdale horse of Dreads. Dread turns to the old man where the old man hands Dread the massive weapon and the reins to his horse. Dread nods to the old man, then mounts his giant Clydesdale horse. The old man simply smiles at Dread, Dread nods with a slight grin, then turns his giant steed and rides off.

On the outskirts of Persia, we find Ivan dressed in Persian battle attire and on horseback where he is flanked by several Persian soldiers on horseback as well. The group stops where the apparent leader of the Persian troops shakes the hand of the very large Ivan. Ivan nods to the Persian leader, then rides off alone into the desert.

Back in Gaul we find Olff. Olff appears to be attempting to mount his horse, but once he is on the horse, he falls off the other side. Olff is obviously very inebriated as he makes his way back to his feet; he is laughing as are his apparent friends that have come to bid him farewell. Olff makes his way back to the other side of his horse where he is aided by his friends on to his mount. Olff adjusts his fur robe he is wearing, then with a drunken grin, he smiles and waves goodbye to his friends, but his horse does not move, so a friend smacks the rear end of the horse, prompting the horse to proceed forward and eventually walks away from the group.

On the outskirts of Espania, we can see a lone horseman riding on a well-traveled trail. The rider is decked out in a magnificent set of gladiatorial armor; upon closer examination, we can see that the rider is Magnus. Magnus appears to be in deep thought as he makes his way up the trail.

CHAPTER 13

A Long-Awaited Reunion

Several winters have now passed. Now the twelve now-grown men have departed their once places of banishment. As the twelve had agreed many years ago to meet the bear cave, we see this cave come into view as we find a very large and well-dressed Moordock on top a large white horse riding then stopping near the cave entrance. Moordock dressed in his Roman Pretorian guard armor and draped in a purple cape; he dismounts his horse, then ties it to a nearby tree where he then enters the cave.

Several days have now passed, and many more of the twelve have arrived while several are still making their way to the cave. In the distance, a large man dressed in gold-colored armor, draped in a crimson red cape, riding a large beautiful black horse, followed by heavily loaded pack horse, approaches on the trail leading to the cave. Standing at the entrance of the cave is a very large and tall white-bearded man draped in a giant white fur coat. The giant of a man stands with a cocky grin on his thickly bearded face as he stares at the figure approaching. The man draped in the red crimson nears the cave entrance, and it is apparent that it is Nor. The large man dressed in the white fur begins to smile, then he lets out a laugh. As he lets out a laugh Musse asks in a loud voice, "Nor? Is that you?"

Just then, the three giant white polar bears exit the cave in a somewhat anxious state. Nor notices the three magnificent and imposing bears, so he draws his impressive and large Spartan sword as his startled horse raises up, nearly knocking Nor off. Suddenly, Musse raises his hands into the air, then addresses both Nor and his three bears excitedly, "Stop! They are my friends! They will not harm you!" Musse then looks down to his bears and disciplines them.

Angrily, Musse shouts, "Stop! Get your asses back here now!" The three bears do as Musse instructs them, as all three of them sit next to the massive Musse.

In a surprised voice, Nor shouts, "What the hell!" Nor then sheathes his impressive sword as he gives Musse a stern gaze. In an inquisitive and suspicious tone, "Is that you, Musse?"

In a laughing manner and with his prototypical smile, Musse replies, "Yes, it is, Musse the Mighty!" Laughing, he announces, "These are my friends and pets!" Musse shrugs his shoulders, then continues as he points to each bear. "This one is called Claw, this one is called Bear, and that one with the bad attitude is called Teeth." Musse then proceeds toward his long-lost friend.

Nor dismounts his horse, then ties it next to several other horses. Nor turns, then is greeted with a huge bear hug that lifts him off the ground by an exuberant Musse. Musse finally places his beloved friend back onto the ground, then places his giant paws on Nor's shoulders and gives Nor a happy smile. Nor reciprocates by placing his large hands on Musse's massive shoulders, then greets him with a smile and a slight chuckle.

A pleased Nor greets his massive friend, "It does my heart good to see your ugly face once again, my large friend! My, have you grown and even uglier!"

Musse looks at Nor with a sour face and a squint of the eye, then lets out a laugh. A very pleased Musse announces, "How has my friend fared after all these winters?"

A serious Nor replies, "I have fared well, my friend. I have learned much from my new friends, the Spartans. Musse, they are the mightiest and bravest warriors I have ever seen!"

With a grin on his mug and sarcastic tone, Musse responds, "That is good for us, for we will need as much help as we can get when we meet up with that ass of a father of yours! So tell me, my friend, in all these winters and on your journey, did you find a woman as fair as Ynew?"

With a cocky smile, Nor replies in a braggadocios manner, "My Ynew's beauty is unmatched! However, the Spartan women are very beautiful and many requested that I teach them the Centaur way, so how could I refuse their desire and needs as I was just a lonely man among strangers and very friendly female hosts? One should not be rude, yes!"

Musse grins, then they both let out a loud laugh. While the two men laugh, they are joined by a very happy Moordock. Moordock and Nor embrace in a very harmonious fashion as they are both overcome with huge smiles. They then release the embrace and give each other the once-over gaze.

In a delighted manner, Moordock comments, "Well, I see you have returned to us with a manly face! It is so good to see you, my friend!"

With a huge grin and a very happy tone, Nor responds, "You are a sight for sore eyes, my friend, and that uniform is quite impressive!"

Moordock smiles, then turns ever so slowly for Nor to examine him. Nor nods in approval, then shoves Moordock, causing Moordock to almost fall. With a smile, Moordock turns to look at Nor, then the two let out a laugh.

Later that evening, from out of the shadows exiting the Centaur forest appear two large mounted figures. The two figures make their way closer and closer to the bear cave. The two figures become more visible as they near closer to the cave; one is Dread, draped in his long dark cloak riding his massive Clydesdale horse and the other is Magnus. Proudly, Magnus is donning his shiny gladiatorial battle armor to impress his fellow friends. As Dread and Magnus draw ever nearer to the cave, they are joined by two more riders from out of the forest. The other riders are none other than Olff, dressed in his black fur-like cloak and the ruggedly handsome Grimm decked out in his fancy Egyptian battle armored uniform.

Suddenly, from out of the other side of the forest emerge three other riders; the riders are the giant Ox dressed in his Chinese battle armor; Krom, to his left, decked out in his mix of animal furs and donning an impressive massive lion's head, complete with a giant mane for a helmet, and following Krom are two very large tigers; to Ox's right is a very fancy dressed Ivan, decked out in his Persian battle attire. Together all the riders converge on the cave in an awesome-looking sight, and once near the entrance, they dismount and tie off their horses, then begin to hug and shake hands as they reunite, but all are cautious of Krom's tigers as they glare and snarl as Krom is hugged by his fellow Centaurs.

Nor, Musse, and Moordock all exit the cave to welcome the new arrivals, then proceed to hug and shake hands as they welcome one another and share a few words as well as laughs. Now from out cave exit Musse's polar bears. Krom's tigers spot the three bears, then begin to snarl and roar, as if to warn the polar bears to stay their distance but to no avail as the bears simply ignore the tigers' warnings and advance in a slow and determined pace. Ivan notices the bears and nudges Ox.

In a loud and startled voice, Ox shouts, "What the hell are those!"

That is when all the Centaurs turn to see that the bears are advancing in a very determined manner. Musse becomes disturbed, then steps in front of the bears where he scolds them; all but Teeth stop and that enrages Musse, so he punches the massive bear in the face, knocking the massive bear to the ground.

In a very angry and aggressive manner, Musse scolds the bear, "There! You dumbass! See what happens when you don't listen to Musse the Mighty!"

The three bears now all sit at attention to Musse's commands. Krom's tigers see this and sit back in a somewhat of a surprised manner. Krom looks to his tigers, then addresses them sternly, "See what happens when you disobey? You get knocked out!"

All the other Centaurs look on in amazement, all but Musse, who gives the tigers a smirk and a shake of his head, as if to display his disapproval of the tigers, then gives Krom the same smirk and headshake, then proclaims his thoughts, "What the hell, Krom? You have two pussycats? What good are pussycats for in a battle? Oh, I see. They are here for your own evening pleasure?" Musse lets out a sarcastic laugh.

Angrily, Krom speaks out loudly, "My pussycats will tear your big ugly ass apart!"

Laughing, Musse grabs Krom from under Krom's armpits, then lifts him into the air as if he were a small child. Musse then states with a smirk, "I was only messing with you, my friend. No need to beat my ass or stick those giant pussycats on me!"

All the Centaurs let out a loud laugh and pat one another on the backs as Musse places Krom back on to his feet.

In a very pleased fashion and tone, Nor displays his pleasure of having his friends together, "It is a good day, a very good day to see so many of my old friends together once again, though it does appear that we are two men short. Has there been any word of Doom or Lugg?"

They all look to one another with a disconcerted gaze upon their brows and shake their heads to indicate no.

In a cocky and undaunted tone, Magnus attempts to defuse the rising stress, "Nah! They're probably just dragging their asses as usual."

Then in the same manner, Ivan states, "Yeah, those two were always the last to arrive and will be late as usual."

Suddenly, from atop the cave entrance, Lugg appears, dressed in what looks to be an outfit made of rat fur stitched together with his bow in hand, loaded with an arrow aimed down at the group.

The group all hear a shout from on top the cave entrance, then all look up in unison.

Shouting, Lugg makes his presence known to all, "Who is late! If I were your enemy, you would all be dead!" Lugg begins to laugh but is interrupted by Nor.

With a grin and a slight chuckle, Nor critiques Lugg, "No! I don't think so! Look behind you!"

Lugg turns to see a massive bald-headed Doom with his arms folded and a stoic look upon his rugged and scarred face. Doom is quite the vision decked out in a very unique and malevolent-looking black armor with chain mail hanging from his waist, covering his tender loins and rear end. Attached to Dooms chain mail is a full-face-cover helmet with white horns attached to the black helmet and has a very intimidating look to it. Malevolent is an understatement for the appearance and manner in which a bald-headed white-bearded Doom appears to look. Doom looks as if hell has sent him to kill an army single-handedly; the Angel of Death would fear the sight of such a warrior. In a friendly manner, Nor motions to the two to come join the rest of them.

Nor shouts at the two, "Come on down you two! Join us!"

Doom and Lugg make their way down and have now joined the rest of the young men in front of the bear cave where the group has a campfire going with what appears to be a deer roasting on the spit. The first person Doom greets is Nor; everyone can see that they still have that very special bond as the two smile at each other, then almost crush each other as they lock in a very heartfelt embrace. Lugg shakes hands and hugs all the other Centaurs.

In a choked-up voice, Nor asks, "How has my friend fared in the dark lands?"

In a similar shaky voice, Doom replies, "I have done well, my friend. I have a beautiful woman and two sons. The oldest is named after me, the other is named after you, and like you, he is smart, unpredictable, and full of piss and vinegar! I see that Sparta has agreed, my brother!"

With his prototypical smile, Nor responds, "Yes, my friend, Sparta was very good to me, and I have learned much to aid us in our quest!"

Nor then accepts the hug from his friend and fellow warrior Lugg. Suddenly, out of nowhere Ox punches Musse, who falls back on to the ground. Musse wipes his lips, then holds his jaw as he looks up to the giant Ox, then with a cocky smile and attitude, Musse responds but first addresses his bears which did not appreciate Ox's action. All three bears rise to their feet, then begin to advance toward Ox but Musse intervenes.

In a sarcastic tone, Musse addresses his very large friends, "Bear! Claw! Teeth! Sit and stay!" The bears all comply with Musse's command. Musse then focuses his attention back to Ox. "I see you still punch like a woman!"

All laugh as they see Musse's reaction.

With a grin and a chuckle, Ox replies, "You still fall like a little girl!"

Shaking his head with a grin, Magnus comments, "Here they go again!"

Musse makes it to his feet, then addresses his massive friend as he points to Ox's face with a concerned expression.

In a concerned tone, Musses asks, "What is that on your face, my friend?"

Ox touches his face in a somewhat bewildered manner. Now in a very vulnerable state, Ox asks, "What? What is on my face?"

Just then, Musse lets go with a punch to Ox's face, causing the giant of a man to fall to the ground. Ox looks up, holding the side of his face where Musse has struck him, then with a slight grin on his face, Ox makes it to his feet.

With a cocky grin and in a brash tone, Musse responds, "The bump I just placed under your eye!" Musse rears back, then lets out a loud laugh.

With this, the other Centaurs laugh and shake their heads in remembrance of the past. Just then, Ox and Musse engage in a battle of giants, exchanging punches, then Musse tackles Ox where the two begin to roll around on the ground. A disgusted Doom looks to Nor, then asks in a bland voice, "Do you wish me to put a stop to this?"

With a shake of his head and in a nonchalant voice, Nor responds, "No, my friend. Let them go for now. They have many winters to make up for."

As Musse and Ox continue their fight, the three polar bears look on in a bewildered state as they appear perplexed and restless. Meanwhile, the other Centaurs are sitting around the campfire, eating meat from the spit and drinking what appears to be wine from flasks they have brought with them.

In a heavy and tired voice, Musse asks, "Have you had enough?"

In just as heavy and tired voice, Ox replies, "Have you?"

In a cocky and resolute tone and a smile on his rugged face, Musse responds, "Never!"

Ox and Musse continue their battle as the others simply ignore the scuffle and continue their discussions. Seemingly hours later, both Ox and Musse are still going at it.

In an inquisitive tone, Nor asks Moordock, "So tell me, Moordock, what did you learn in Rome?"

With a smile and a chuckle, Moordock boastfully replies, "The men wear blankets like gowns and skirts when they go into battle, but make no mistake. They can fight and are very good at it. The women, oh, the women! The women are beautiful and very lustful. Well, when it came to me anyway!"

They all let out a laugh as they continue to eat and drink.

Calmly, Nor nods in agreement, then responds, "Yes, it is the same way in Sparta and Athens!"

Surprised by this Moordock, asks, "You spent time in both Sparta and Athens?"

Smiling confidently, Nor replies, "Yes. Yes, I did!"

Anxiously and inquisitively, Moordock asks, "Are the stories true? Are the women of Sparta and Athens as beautiful as the stories say? Are the Spartan warriors as mighty as gods when they fight?"

With his standard grin and in his usual confident manner, Nor responds, "Yes, the stories are all very true. The women are as beautiful as the goddesses they worship. Oh, their beauty is breathtaking and mesmerizing. The women of Sparta are not only beautiful, but like our women, they can also fight and are very outspoken." All laugh as Nor continues speaking, "The men of Sparta are like that of god warriors. They do not fear death and fight like nothing I have seen before. They call their battle wall a phalanx. It is a wall of impenetrable shields and long spears. It is a sight! In fact, I was told a story of three hundred Spartans who bravely fought against hundreds of thousands of Persian warriors under King Xerxes of Persia. It was impressive and quite the story. It took place in Greece in a place called Thermopylae, and the battle lasted three days until the Spartans were finally outflanked and attacked from behind!"

All the Centaurs look on in amazement and awe of Nor's story as his friends seem can't get enough. The Centaur warriors, in astonishment, are all leaning forward, nearing closer to hear even better. No one seems to take notice of the continuing scuffle between Ox and Musse other than one of the polar bears. While Bear and Claw have fallen asleep, Teeth looks on in a suspicious manner as he swivels his head from the scuffle to the Centaurs, then back again.

Excitedly, Grimm speaks out, "What courage! What glory! These Spartans are truly the greatest warriors of all time, yes?"

Nodding his head in agreement and in an enthusiastic tone, Moordock speaks up, "I agree, very impressive, very impressive indeed!" Now in a disgusted manner, Moordock glances over to Ox and Musse, then asks, "Are you two finished yet?"

In a commanding voice, Nor speaks up, "You should know better, my friend! Neither will cease, and as usual, we shall have to separate them as we did when they were much younger."

Now in a comic tone, Dread announces, "Yes, and much smaller!"

Nor looks over to the two and states, "Yes, much smaller! Musse! Ox! Perhaps you should come and join us in this delicious meal while you two still have teeth the chew with."

Now exhausted and both on their knees, whaling at each other still, Musse speaks to Ox in an exhausted voice, "So ugly one, do you yield?"

A tired and beaten Ox replies as he too, is out of breath, "To you! Never!" then throws another punch at Musse as the two continue their battle.

Now apparently disgusted and exhausted from his two friends going at it for as long as they have, Nor stands up then commands his Centaurs. In his usual commanding manner, Nor orders his fellow Centaurs to aid in his stopping the fight, "Dread, you and Grimm grab the Ox. Doom and I shall grab Musse. Come on."

The four approach Musse and Ox where they separate the two giants.

Sarcastically, Grimm announces, "Damn, Ox! You are as heavy as your mother!"

Now being carried by Grimm and Dread, Ox looks to Grimm with an angry but bewildered glare.

Angrily, Ox shouts, "My mother! You dog! I shall pound you when my arms are able!"

Nonchalantly, Grimm smiles as he looks at Ox, then calmly announces, "No, my friend, you will not."

Calmly, Grimm starts shaking his head in disagreement.

Ox gives Grimm a bewildered glare, then asks in a puzzled voice, "I won't?"

In a composed manner, Grimm smiles, then responds in a calm voice, "No. Your mother is heavy."

A smile forms on Ox's face as he then nods his head in agreement and calmly retorts, "Oh yeah, she is heavy." Ox then makes a face of agreement as he shrugs his shoulders.

Now all the Centaurs have gathered around the campfire as night has taken the place of the day.

Inquisitively, Olff asks, "Tell me, Grimm, what are those structures that everyone speaks of there in Egypt, those triangle things?"

With a confident smile and similar attitude, Grimm responds, "They are called pyramids. They are truly magnificent structures and are the size of mountains. The ancients made them from very heavy and hard stones. Quite a magnificent sight."

With a few bruises and cuts, Musse speaks out happily, "That large? Wow, what a magnificent sight they must truly be. They are large and impressive, like Ox and me then, yes?"

All get a chuckle out of Musse's comments.

In a braggadocios manner, Grimm adds, "Oh yes, they are very impressive but not as impressive as their women. The women there are some of the most beautiful women I have ever seen, and most do not cover their breasts, and when the sun shines at a certain angle, you can see right through their dresses. They, of course, loved it when I approached them and even more when I would bed them. Many beauties have I bedded, many!"

All the men laugh and drink to their friends' success or suggested success. Nor now looks to Lugg and asks of his experience, "So tell me, Lugg, what are the people of the steps like? Do they really call themselves Mongolians?"

Nodding as he looks to Nor and in a confident manner, Lugg responds, "Yes, that is what they call themselves. They are very strong, shrewd, and great warriors. Probably the best horsemen I have ever seen or heard of, and they can shoot a bow from under the neck of their horse and hit any target they so desire. They train their children from a very young age to do this and it has suited them well."

Shaking his head in disbelief, Musse can't help himself but to insult Lugg, "No! That is impossible! It cannot be done! Bullshit! Bullshit, I say!"

Lugg stands up in a rage, then returns the aggression, "You oversized white-haired son of hog! I will show you!"

Lugg storms over to his horse, then hops up on to it as he draws an arrow with his bow, then rides off some distance and returns charging toward the other Centaurs. As Musse watches, he continues eating a deer leg as Lugg launches three arrows into the deer leg from which Musse is eating from, but without getting startled or missing a beat. Musse simply continues eating as he examines the arrows that are now resting in his meal. Ignoring the three arrows, Musse simply smiles, then looks to Lugg as Lugg has halted his horse and stares at Musse, as if to anticipate a shocked response.

Musse smiles, then stoically comments, "Impressive! Not bad for a man dressed in rat fur!" Then Musse continues to eat his meal, ignoring Lugg.

All were impressed by Lugg's archery and riding skills but can't help laughing at Musse's response. Lugg rapidly dismounts his steed, then ties it up; he then marches over to Musse as he announces his intentions angrily, "Give me some of that wine, you big ugly bastard!"

Musse, without skipping a beat, throws a jug of wine to his friend Lugg. Krom then takes two large chunks of deer meat, then tosses them to his pet tigers.

Krom calls out to his tigers as he tosses each one a chunk of meat. "Mean ass, here! Tooth, catch! That should hold you two over for a bit."

179

Now being the smart-ass that he is and apparently can't help himself, Musse jokes, "Those are very beautiful creatures, Krom. Which one do you bed first?"

Every Centaur lets out a loud laugh, except Musse, who remains stoic while continuing to eat. Krom, being caught off guard while drinking, has wine shoot out of his nose as he reacts to Musse's comments.

An unhappy Krom speaks as he is wiping the wine from his nose and chin, "Damn! You ass! Look what you made me do!"

Now everyone is laughing even harder than before and pointing at Krom's wine-covered face.

Now even Krom lets out a chuckle as he then threatens Musse, "Jest of me or my friends again and I shall have Mean One mount you in your sleep!"

Not missing a beat and in his usual stoic demeanor, Musse replies nonchalantly, "My bears would eat him before he mounts me!" Musse continues eating without a care in the world.

The Centaurs all laugh even harder now as some have wine shoot out from their noses; the others begin to fall onto the ground, laughing at them. It is quite the comic display of the twelve very massive and imposing warriors that even their leader Nor can't stop laughing. Sometime later, when all have calmed down, Nor looks to his friend Ivan.

A serious Nor asks, "Ivan, can you shoot that magnificent bow of yours as well as Lugg can his?"

Confidently, Ivan responds, "Yes, even better, but not on horse-back like Lugg can. He is truly a master horse archer!"

Lugg's facial expression changes from an angry glare to a pleas-ant smile after the compliment.

Nor nods in agreement. "Yes! Yes, he is that!" Nor smiles and nods to Lugg as Lugg then reciprocates the gesture back to his leader.

* * *

We now journey to the dark fortress of the warlock Grimmcock. We enter the fortress and make our way into Grimmcock's chambers where he is standing with an evil, concerned gaze upon his brow as he stares into his vision well. Grimmcock is joined by Brummel and Cetan; each takes their place beside their leader.

A concerned Brummel asks, "You look concerned, oh, great one. Did you see an unpleasant sight?"

Grimmcock responds, "My look is well warranted! This reunion we see here may be the beginning of the end for us. It does not look good at all!"

In a cocky and presuming fashion, Brummel speaks out, "With the armies and creatures we have at our disposal, we have nothing to fear, my lord!"

Grimmcock shouts, "At our disposal! You speak as if you are the warlock and leader! Remember your place Brummel and never forget who your lord is!"

Now embarrassed and appearing somewhat frightened, Brummel steps back bowing and then apologizes, "Forgive me, my lord! I meant to say your army and your creatures!"

Grimmcock lectures Brummel, "Yes! It will serve thy well never to forget this! Always remember, Brummel, I created you and I can destroy you!"

A very humble Brummel nods, then speaks in a very soft voice, "Yes Master! I meant no disrespect!"

Grimmcock orders Brummel, "Now go and prepare my army for battle and send a message to the Tartans to have them send troops here at once. We will need every man, creature, and warrior we can summon, I fear. Now go! Cetan, come here!"

A confident Cetan steps up to his master. "Yes, my lord!"

A somewhat shaken Grimmcock instructs his loyal servant, "Take your beasts and set your trap in the Forest of Shadows. Then when this is done, take your creatures and set an ambush in the river between the forest and my fortress. I will need you here when you are done. So make haste!"

With a grin and a bow, Cetan confirms his master's wishes, "Yes, my lord. I shall do as you desire. I shall return as soon as I have set the river ambush."

Now at the Centaur village, in Cantor's residence, we find Cantor in bed sleeping when he suddenly awakens in a cold sweat as he sits up in a panic. Cantor has a very worrisome look upon his thin, aged, scar-ridden, and ugly face. He grabs a cup and a jug, then pours what appears to be wine into his cup; he then chugs the liquid down in a rush, then bows his head in apparent despair.

* * *

As we return to the bear cave, we find the Centaur twelve preparing to depart their camp. Krom and Ivan appear to be talking.

In a sincere yet humorous tone, Krom asks, "So, my friend, are you ready to meet your fate?"

In a calm yet cocky tone, Ivan responds, "I am not concerned. I have no regrets and should I die, I die. But worry not my friend. I shall kill the one that kills you first."

The two let out a laugh and then smile at each other.

Listening in on the conversation is Magnus, who, in a commanding and confident voice states, "We shall not die today, my friends! We have been through too much and have come too far! Our destiny will not end at the hands of a piece of shit like Cantor!"

Standing next to Magnus, we hear a cold, angry response from Doom. In his deep and confident voice, we hear Doom speak, "I shall kill Cantor! Should Nor allow me, I shall behead that piece of shit!"

Now in a commanding voice, Nor instructs his friends, "Worry not, my friends! Once I know our families are safe, we will have our vengeance on that piece of shit! Just remember the plan and wait for my signals."

Doom, with a serious and fearsome look and in a threating manner, confirms Nor's orders, "Yes, wait for Nor's signals or you will answer to me!" Without concern and in a commanding manner, Doom turns and continues to prepare his horse for travel.

As a concerned gaze forms upon his brow, Krom leans over, then in a low voice, speaks to Moordock, "You know, other than Nor, Doom is the only man I would not want to fight!"

Smiling with an agreeable nod, Moordock responds, "Hell, remember when Doom was twelve? He beat the hell out of those three guards for insulting his mother!"

Just then, Magnus leans in and comments in a serious voice, "It's in his eyes. There is nothing there, except when he is angry, then it is pure evil!"

Sternly, the three all nod in agreement.

Now with serious look in his eyes, Moordock warns his friends, "You had better heed Nor's commands or Doom will surely have your ass under his boot or his boot in your ass!"

Magnus speaks up with a slight chuckle in his voice, "Just think. Nor used to protect Doom when we were young and stupid children. Remember Nor would kick the shit out of us when we would tease Doom about his speech problems."

Krom interjects his memory, "Hell yes, I remember! Ever since that last beating he gave us, Doom, Ox, and Musse have been like brothers to Nor!"

Just then, Lugg shout out, "Nor! Where do you want me and Ivan when we get there?"

Seriously, Nor looks to his fellow Centaurs; he then motions with his hand for them to join him. Nor bends to a knee as the rest of his men join him, kneeling down in a circle.

With confidence, Nor lays out his plan to enter the Centaur village. "Gather around, men. This is what we shall do when we enter our village and pay homage to that piece of shit sitting on my father's throne!"

With a stick and drawing into the dirt, Nor begins to draw the Centaur village and his designs for his plan to enter the Centaur village. Soon enough, the men begin to nod in agreement and approval; soon after, they begin to smile and even laugh as Nor continues to draw out his plan.

Several hours later, we find ourselves at the Centaur village where a platform has been built outside the main hall. Up on top the platform is Cantor's throne, where we find sitting in his lonely throne is an aged and somewhat sickly-looking Cantor. Cantor is not only aged and wrinkled but also straggly gray hair skirts his now narrow shoulders. Standing in a defensive stature behind their deteriorated king are Cantor's loyal guards. The Centaur villagers have been lined up on each side of the path leading to the king's platform. Out from a distance, two riders appear; as the pair draws near, it is plain to see that they are Cantor's men. The riders appear to be not only in a hurry but also excited and yet frightened. The two riders reach the platform where Cantor appears anxious about the news to which the riders are carrying. Both riders now stop just in front of the platform; one of the riders dismounts rapidly, then rushes up to kneel in front of Cantor. The rider bows to Cantor, then steps up and whispers into Cantor's ear. The rider bows again, then steps down and makes his way back to his horse and takes the horse's reins into his hand, then stands as if he is awaiting orders.

Now with a scared gaze upon his aged and withered brow, Cantor rises to his feet, then addresses his people, "Make ready, for the banished are approaching!"

Moments later, several figures appear in a distance from the edge of the path. As the figures grow closer and closer, it is apparent that the figures are all decked out in different types of armor, uniforms, and battle gear. The horses are magnificently adorned, some in sheets of armor, others in thick chain mail, and some decked out in brilliant-colored cloth. In a matter of seconds, the riders reach the edge of where the villagers are standing. It is clear that there are only ten riders in the group, and the riders have an awe-inspiring effect on the villagers as they pass by adorned in their impressive attire, mounted on their magnificent steeds, and brandishing some rather unique, yet very impressive weapons. One of the lead riders stands out in his darkened metal, some of it black and silver chain mail armor that make it appear as if it were made of pure evil and the downward pointing horns from the helmet make it even more sinister looking and fearsome. As the group reach Cantor's platform, Cantor stares the men down, then appears as if to be counting the riders now in front of him.

Confidently, Cantor leans forward, then addresses the riders, "So you have returned! It appears that you are two friends short of a dozen as it was when I banished you."

Calmly and confidently, Nor responds, "No, Cantor, you are wrong as usual. They are with us, just not in your presence." Nor then dismounts his noble steed to stand facing Cantor.

Now in an upset tone, Cantor shouts, "They must present themselves to me now!" Cantor appears to get angrier as he dwells on the situation.

In a sign of disrespect, Nor shrugs his shoulders and shakes his head in disgust of Cantor's behavior. This blighted disrespect cannot stand unpunished by Cantor, so Cantor attempts to stand in anger, but as Cantor attempts to stand, suddenly Nor nods his head as it is guarded by his impressive and beautifully designed Corinthian bronze helmet laden with a mohawk-like row of black nicely trimmed horse hair topping his magnificent helmet. Suddenly, two arrows strike Cantor's fur cape, pinning him to his throne, one arrow on each side of his shoulders, but only striking the fur, not Cantor himself. Quite a feat of archery and everyone can see this as all gasp in reaction and amazement. At first, Cantor appears shocked, then gets enraged as he attempts to raise his hand to remove the arrows pinning him. Nor shakes his head from left to right, and right on cue, two more arrows pierce the air, then strike Cantor's sleeves, one on the left arm and the other on the right arm, pinning Cantor to his throne and frightening him at the same time. Cantor looks to Nor in complete fear and shock.

In a commanding and fearsome tone, Nor addresses Cantor, "You shall not rise to me! You shall not command my people! You shall no longer sit upon my father's throne, you piece of shit!"

All the villagers, guards, soldiers, and Cantor look to Nor in amazement and some in glee.

Now in fear for his life and in a very frightened manner, Cantor speaks out, "What! What are these lies you speak of! You are my son, Nor! That is what that whore of a mother of yours told me!"

Angrily, Nor raises his voice, "Shut your mouth! You piece of shit! You are no father of mine! William is my father! William, son of Thor, is my father! Now I am here to reclaim what is rightfully mine! Now you shall tell me where my mother is, you ugly piece of shit! My mother shall confirm every word I have spoken here! Now, Cantor, where is my mother!"

Everyone looks on in shock and amazement as they begin to whisper among themselves.

A worried and uncertain Cantor speaks softly so as not to anger the very man he once called son, "Your mother is no longer with us."

Everyone lets out a sigh as some of Nor's men, even the nasty-looking, intimidating warriors, get a tear in their eye.

Now more determined and becoming even angrier, Nor asks, "Where the hell is my mother! I shall not ask thy again!"

A horrified Cantor leans back in his throne in a frightened manner. "Wait, wait, your mother is with Grimmcock, you fool. You shall not seek her, for whether you like it or not, I am king. I am your king and your father still. Like it or not!"

Suddenly, in a flash and in a rage, Doom dismounts his steed and, at the same time, removes his wicked-looking helmet, then storms over and stands to Nor's right. Doom and Nor are now joined by the giant in his white fur coat Musse to Nor's left, and it is a very impressive sight to see as these three behemoths stand in a formidable and aggressive stance in front of Cantor. Now aggressively, Doom steps up, then gives a frightening glare to Cantor.

"No, Cantor! Nor is not your son! Nor is the son of William! I, Father, am your son! You son of a bitch! You raped my mother and removed her tongue so she would not speak your name! Well, I will, I shall, and I do not fear you! I despise you! I shall kill you if my king, our true king, and my brother will allow me this vengeance!"

All, including Nor, look to Doom in shock and with a grief-stricken gaze upon their faces. Doom gives Nor a look as if to ask for approval. Nor is caught off guard by his friend's statement and is in a gasp as his eyes begin to fill with tears; he gives Doom an unfamiliar gaze of emotion. Doom, as usual, has his prototypical stoic gaze upon him. Nor, with tear-filled eyes, begins to nod slowly as he looks to Doom with a mournful gaze.

At first in a choked-up voice, then as it clears, Nor speaks to his beloved friend, "How can I…how can I refuse such a request from my dear brother! Doom, please kill that piece of shit! To battle!" Nor unsheathes his impressive sword and raises it into the air.

Now all those who were once-banished Centaurs dismount their steeds, then begin to charge Cantor's platform and start to battle those warriors, soldiers, and guards still loyal to Cantor. Cantor is aided by his guards as they remove the arrows from his sleeves and cape, then Cantor and several of his men make a dash for his residence, escaping the now-enraged Doom and Nor. As the battle begins, the families of the once banished that have been taken hostage are being held in a makeshift cell behind the main hall. Unaware of the presence of Ivan and Lugg, the guards that are assigned to detain the families of the once banished are caught off guard as arrows from Lugg's and Ivan's bows pierce the guards' bodies, killing all six of them in an impressive display of speed and accuracy. Lugg and Ivan then rush down to free the families. The families are directed into the nearby woods to seek freedom and shelter from the battle. Lugg and Ivan then proceed to join their friends in the ongoing battle. As Cantor rushes to escape, Doom has eliminated six of Cantor's guards in an extraordinary display of swordsmanship.

In a loud and confident voice, Doom shouts, "It is time to die, Father! Do not flee. Let us embrace this one last time!" Doom continues his determined march toward his father.

As the battle wages on, Doom makes his way to the two guards, protecting the doorway to Cantor's residence. Doom dispenses of the two guards in less time than it takes for him to kick Cantor's door open. Doom now stands in the doorway, blocking the exit. Cantor turns to see Doom, who is holding a giant bloodied ax and blood-stained massive sword in his huge rugged hands, ready to enact the long-awaited justice Doom has sought to exact upon his terrified father. Cantor, with his hands full of gold jewelry and other precious items, now trembles in fear for his life as he attempts to talk his way out of the reckoning Doom is prepared to administer upon him.

In a frightened exhibition, with tears in his eyes, Cantor pleads, "My son! I...I did not know she was with child! Please forgive me. I did not know you were mine!"

Now from behind Doom, arrive two of Cantor's guards. Cantor looks at the two and then orders his guards in a loud voice, "Kill him!"

Doom ducks, then spins around with his massive and sharp blades at the ready, whereby slicing the two guards in half, then in the same motion, Doom steps toward Cantor. Cantor steps back as he drops the precious items he was once holding.

Placing his hands in front of him, motioning Doom to stop, Cantor pleads, "I have no weapon! Would you kill your defenseless unarmed father? Where is the honor in that?"

With a slight smile and in a calm voice, Doom announces, "There is no honor in that. There is only your death, and that is what I wish for you, Father!" Now without hesitation and in a single swing, Doom cuts Cantor in half. Cantor's upper body falls to the ground in front of Doom's feet. Doom gazes down at the split body in front of him, then spits down on what was once his father. With a slight grin on his rugged mug, Doom casually turns, then exits the residence. Doom now rushes over to join the ongoing battle where he finds Nor has just killed two soldiers of Cantor's with a single swing of his magnificent sword. Doom advances in front of Nor, then nods as if to indicate he is pleased. Nor looks to his friend, then removes his helmet.

In a concerned manner, Nor asks, "Is it done?"

Removing his helmet, then taking a knee, Doom responds, "Yes. He has left this world forever."

All the remaining soldiers, villagers, and even the once banished notice Doom kneeling to Nor, so they all kneel in respect to Nor.

In a calm and grateful voice, Doom speaks to Nor, "Thank you, my friend, my brother, my king. I am forever in your debt and shall always be forever loyal!"

Now in a somewhat offended manner Nor speaks, "Rise, Rise!"

Doom rises to his feet with his head bowed to Nor.

In a sincere tone and manner, Nor addresses his dear friend, "I am your friend and brother first, your king second! You do not kneel to me, ever!" Nor then looks around and can see all have knelt to him. In a commanding voice, Nor commands, "Let it be known, from this day forth, the Centaur people will no longer take our children to the Forest of Shadows! Grimmcock is now our enemy, and we shall go to his evil fortress and put an end to this monster of a warlock and anyone or anything that stands in our way!"

The people all look to one another with smiles, then turn to Nor and let out a loud cheer and clap in approval of Nor's decision. Just then, an old lady approaches Nor with a smile on her old withered face, then hands him a wrapped leather pouch. The old lady then looks up to Nor and, in an scruffy voice, tells Nor, "My king, this was given to me by your mother. She asked me to give this to you once you returned. She loved you very much."

Nor smiles at the old lady, then leans down and gives the old lady a kiss on the cheek with a bit of a slight wink and then a smile. The old lady blushes as she steps back away from Nor.

Politely and gratefully, Nor speaks out, "Thank you, my lady. My mother chose her messenger well." Nor nods in appreciation and respect to the old lady. The old lady appears both smitten and embarrassed as she smiles at her new king.

The old lady blushes as she responds to Nor, "Thank you, my king!"

With a smile on his handsome mug, Nor looks down as he unravels the pouch. Nor removes a large gold ring from the pouch, then unravels what appears to be a short letter written on the leather package. Nor reads the message, then with a sad face, he places the magnificent ring on to his left-hand little finger. Then in a determined manner, Nor speaks out, "Men! Make ready! We shall depart in the morning to free my mother from that evil bastard Grimmcock. We shall show no mercy and give no quarter to any of our enemies! Is that understood!"

All his friends, soldiers, and villagers shout and cheer in approval.

CHAPTER 14

A GIFT OF LOVE AND TIME

IN THE CENTAUR village, we find Nor and his small but mighty army preparing to depart. Many of the men have joined Nor as they prepare their horses to ride as do some of the young men. It is very apparent that the mothers of the younger men do not wish their sons to join in the battle as they weep and plea with their sons not to go. As the mothers continue their weeping and pleading with their sons not to go, their actions do not fall on deaf ears or blind eyes. Nor looks the situation over and decides that he has enough men to accomplish the task ahead, so he makes an announcement.

In a loud and commanding voice, Nor shouts, "Men! Centaurs! This journey shall take many of our warriors from their families and loved ones. I shall ask some of you younger brave men to guard and protect our people here. This is a honor and a favor I shall not forget, so those warriors who have not seen at least twenty winters shall stay and protect our homes and, more importantly, our women and children. This sacrifice I ask of you shall not go unrewarded, and it shall never be forgotten by me, your king!"

The mothers all smile at Nor and mouth the words *thank you* as they all then bow to their king. The young men, though, seem a bit disappointed but show a brave face as they dismount their horses and unload what once was loaded upon their steeds for the journey and battle that was sure to come. Moments later, Nor begins to lead his mounted warriors through the Centaur village as the procession passes by the young children stand at attention as they place their wooden swords to their hearts in a sign of respect to their brave heroes and their brave handsome king. As Nor passes each of these children, he reciprocates the gesture with his sword to his chest, with a wink of the eye, and a slight smile. This kind gesture of Nor brings out the happiest of smiles from the children and the respect of all those who see the reaction.

Many days later, Nor's army finally reaches the edge of the Forest of Shadows. Nor's army has been riding hard, then as commanded by Nor, the army comes to a stop. Soon enough, two of Nor's scouts are spotted on top a hillside as the two riders appear to be riding without haste to contact their king. Moments later, Nor and his army are joined by the two scouts, both Lugg and a Centaur soldier, who ride up to Nor's position excitedly.

In a confident yet suspicious tone, Nor asks, "So, my friend, what news do you bear?"

In a stoic yet cocky manner, Lugg responds, "The Tartans are riding toward our position. They should arrive within the hour."

With a smile, Nor asks, "What are their numbers?"

In his typical stoic and cocky manner, Lugg replies, "Awe, only three hundred men or so, a good warm-up for the main battle to come."

With a slight chuckle, Nor smiles. "They only outnumber us nine to one then. They should have brought more men for this fight."

Nor then motions for his men to ride up and gather around, and they comply.

In his confident and commanding voice, Nor issues his orders, "Lugg! Ivan! Take the archers to the edge of the forest there and prepare to fire on my signal. Moordock! Take the rest of the men to the top of the hill behind us. Doom! Musse! Come with me, but first send those three bears of yours into the forest with the archers. Krom, you do the same with those two tigers of yours, then take your position upon the hill." Both Musse and Krom lead their furry large-toothed friends to the forest and position them in a secure area away from one another, then the two men take up their positions as instructed by Nor.

Sometime later, the Tartans make their presence known as they appear on top the hillside opposite that of the Centaur army. As the Tartan army begins to arrive, they spread out their cavalry in a line that covers the top and sides of the hilltop. The Tartan infantry then takes up positions behind the cavalry as do their archers. Just moments after their line forms, the Tartan king rides forward with two riders to confront Nor and his two men. The two kings are now in talking range as Nor then respectfully bows his head to the Tartan king, then looks to Tartan king with a cocky glare.

With a sharp tongue, Nor addresses the Tartan king, "I am honored to meet you, great Tartan king! Have you come to surrender your great army?"

The Tartans look to one another, then let out a laugh.

The Tartan king, in an insulted and cocky tone, retorts, "Surrender!"

Without hesitation and in a sarcastic manner, Nor speaks out, "I must apologize, great king! But I cannot accept your surrender right now as we do not have the provisions or, for that matter, the time to take you all prisoners!"

Now in a very angry mood and with an enraged voice, the Tartan king shouts, "What! What gall! You insult me with your insolence and lack of wisdom, boy! I will personally take your head and stick it on a pig pole, you swine!"

Again, without hesitation and with a smile on his handsome face, Nor responds, "Good! Then there will be no need for others to die today, just you. I accept your challenge to one-on-one battle."

The Tartan king suddenly has a change of tone in his mannerism and level of voice. "What! No! I shall not honor the likes of you with a one-on-one battle of combat!"

Now the two Tartans flanking their king appear surprised and embarrassed by their king's response and his demeanor to Nor's challenge.

The Tartan king arrogantly speaks out, "I am a king!"

In an immediate response, Nor speaks, "As am I! However, unlike you, I am not a coward! I accepted your challenge to cut off my head, yet you fear one-on-one battle with a man whom you believe you are better than?"

Now enraged and embarrassed, the Tartan king orders his general, "Eric! Kill him! Kill this insolent bastard!"

Embarrassed and disgusted, Eric addresses his king, "You do it! You told him you would take his head! Now you decline his challenge! You disgust me, you coward!" Eric nods to Nor, then turns his horse and rides back to join his men up on the hill. Now the Tartan guard to the Tartan king's left glares at his king in disgust, then shakes his head in disbelief, then he too nods to Nor and turns his horse and rides up to join the rest of the Tartan army.

Now with a smile and a very cocky tone, Nor address the Tartan king, "It appears that you are all alone. Will you yield your head with honor or must my men and I kill all your soldiers to take what is mine?"

Embarrassed and frightened, the Tartan king replies, "No! No, I shall not give you my head so easily!"

The Tartan king turns his horse, then rides up the hill to join his army. As the Tartan king makes his way halfway up the hill, he can see that Eric is leading the cavalry away from the rest of the Tartan army. The Tartan king reaches what is left of his army, then has them set up a square position around him to protect their cowardly king.

The Tartan king commands his remaining army, "Attack them! Kill them all! Charge! No mercy! No prisoners!"

The Tartan infantry charges downhill to engage the Centaurs as their king is centered in the middle of the Tartan army rather than leading his army; his men do not appear encouraged by this cowardly behavior. As the Tartans advance closer to Nor, Musse, and Doom, an array of arrows from within the forest strike the Tartans in force and with accuracy as many of the Tartan soldiers fall to their deaths and roll down the hill in front of the other Tartan soldiers. Many of the Tartan soldiers see the results of the arrow strikes, which strikes fear into them, resulting in a slower charge then initially anticipated by their king.

The Tartan king begins to holler at his men, "Charge, you cowards! Charge! Faster!"

The Tartan soldiers do not seem too eager to comply with their king's orders. With haste, the Centaur army rushes down the hillside and are now close enough to the Tartan army that the arrows have stopped flying. Almost instantly, the Centaur warriors and animals have rushed out of the forest to join in the attack. Nor, Doom, and Musse have engaged the Tartan infantry, and to the Tartan king's dismay, his men fall to the trio as if they were dead leaves falling from their branches in autumn during a windstorm. From on top of a nearby hilltop, Eric has his trumpeter blow his horn, which draws the attention of all. Eric waves his banner but with a white flag of truce upon his colors. The Tartan infantry soldiers who have engaged the Centaurs surrender their swords and spears to the Centaurs upon hearing the horn and seeing the banner fly. The Tartan king is all but unprotected and in a vulnerable position now. All but three of the Tartan infantry soldiers have surrendered, and they surround their king in a show of loyalty and courage, which impresses Nor. Nor, Doom, and Musse advance on the three guarding their king, then stop just out of reach of the Tartan spears the three possess.

In a show of respect and in a complimentary manner, Nor address the three, "You three have displayed courage, and I respect that, but do not be foolish with your lives. Put your weapons down. Don't force us to kill three brave men that could help serve a brave leader like Eric."

The three men look to one another, then to their king, who appears somewhat unsure of what to do. The three men place their weapons on to the ground, then kneel to Nor. With a smile on his handsome mug, Nor gazes at the Tartan king. The Tartan king bows his head in shame and in defeat to his younger foe.

Respectfully, Nor addresses the Tartan king, "I will accept your surrender, sword, and spare your life on two conditions. First, you denounce your throne, and second, you declare Eric king of all Tartans."

The Tartan king looks to Nor with a pathetic glare, then announces timidly, "I shall denounce my throne, but I cannot pass the crown to Eric. It is not the Tartan way."

In response to the Tartan king's comments, Nor commands confidently, "Lugg! Ride up to Eric's position and ask him if he would be kind enough to join us here, tell him I have a gift for him."

Lugg smiles, then nods his head as he then turns and jumps on his horse. Lugg then rushes over to Eric's position; once Lugg reaches Eric, he appears to tell Eric that which Nor has told him to say. Now Lugg, Eric, and his general guard all ride down the hill, then make their way over to Nor's position. The three all dismount once they reach Nor. Eric steps up to Nor, and in a show of respect, Eric kneels down in front of Nor.

Confidently, Eric addresses Nor, "King Nor! I am at service."

With a grin and a slight chuckle, Nor addresses Eric, "Rise, Eric. You do not need to kneel to me. I am not your king."

With a baffled look, Eric rises to his feet, then gazes at Nor. "I am somewhat confused. Did not our king surrender to you?"

With a slight chuckle, Nor replies, "Yes, your king has surrendered to me, but I did not accept his crown. I give it to you."

Confused and surprised, Eric speaks out, "I don't understand."

With a smile and in a confident manner, Nor addresses Eric, "It is simple, my friend. I give to you the gift of rule! Your behavior warrants it! The Tartans deserve a king that is brave, wise, considerate of the lives of his men, and, most of all, honorable! You, my friend, have those qualities!"

In a modest and humble reaction, Eric replies, "I am not worthy to be king, and besides, it is not our way." Eric begins shaking his head in disapproval and with humility.

Looking around to all the Tartans, Nor then speaks out, "Well, my friend, things change. That is how we grow. So tell me, Tartans, in your eyes, is Eric worthy of leading the Tartans as general and king?"

The Tartan soldiers and officers all begin to look to one another and begin to nod with slight smiles on their rugged faces. Suddenly, the Tartan soldiers begin to speak Eric's name and add the title of king in front of Eric's name.

The Tartan soldiers and officers begin to shout, "Eric! Eric! King Eric! King Eric! King Eric! King Eric!"

Eric humbly raises his hands into the air, and with that, he attempts to quiet his men where he then addresses his new friend, "King Nor, I shall accept this gift, but only in your absence. You should be the rightful king of the Tartans since you accepted the crown from our former king."

Now with a serious gaze and in a commanding voice, Nor addresses Eric, "I am king of the Centaurs. You are the king of the Tartans. I will not rule any others but the Centaurs. You have created a new friend and ally in the Centaurs. Unlike our forefathers, my friend, we shall work together to defend each other and help each other grow, yes!"

With a disbelieving grin on his face, Eric responds, "You truly are a fine example of a great king! I shall model my rule after yours, and if I may, King Nor, when you defeat Grimmcock and return, may I seek your advice and wisdom?"

With a slight chuckle, Nor responds, "Yes, my friend. I would be honored."

Proudly and confidently, Eric asks, "King Nor, we Tartans would be honored if you would allow us to join you on you crusade to defeat Grimmcock and his evil army."

In a concerned tone, Nor replies, "That would be a great honor for us. However, I would be more grateful if you and your brave men could guard this pass should Grimmcock send a force this way or may the gods allow us to fail in our quest. You and your men will be the only army left to stop him. So if you would be kind enough to guard this pass, I would be forever grateful."

Proudly and with a sincere smile, Eric replies, "We would be honored, King Nor! We would be honored, and we shall be here when you return victoriously!"

All the Tartans nod in agreement and with pride as they display their pleasure of the current events by cheering for their newfound alliance. They all cheer for King Nor.

The Tartans cheer, "King Nor! King Nor! King Nor!"

With the new alliance now established, Nor leads his men toward the road that leads to Grimmcock's fortress. Eric has his men establish a camp and they begin to set up fortification in preparation of defending the pass as agreed to with King Nor.

* * *

At the same time that Nor and Eric have created a new alliance, we find ourselves in Grumpa's village. The people of Grumpa's village appear to be preparing for a feast. There are several tables outside in rows with several different types of food and drink laid upon the tables. Walking around the tables adjusting the settings on the tables walks a beautiful auburn colored-haired woman with the most mesmerizing emerald green eyes and a body that would make any goddess jealous as she glides around in her almost-sheer white form-fitting gown. Following closely behind the auburn beauty are three younger stunningly beautiful ladies, and all have the same goddess figure as the lady they are following, just smaller versions. One of the beauties has long golden blond hair with sapphire blue eyes; the next beauty has long flowing thick light brown hair and the same sapphire blue eyes, and finally, behind her is the last beauty with long black shiny hair and the same sapphire blue eyes. All three of the young beauties are dressed in the same type of white form-fitting gowns as they are listening astutely to the lady they are following. It is apparent that the auburn beauty is a thirteen-year-older Ynew, and apparently she is being followed by her three stunningly beautiful sultry daughters as they prepare the tables.

In a very sweet and pleasant tone, Ynew announces, "My daughters, I have a surprise for you!"

All three of her daughters appear very pleased by this announcement as they stand with their eyes gleaming and smiles as they gaze at their beautiful mother.

The golden-haired daughter excitedly asks, "What is it, Mother?"

With a huge smile covering her beautiful face, Ynew responds happily, "Grumpa tells me that your father shall be returning soon and you will all finally get to meet him!"

All three daughters appear very excited and gleeful in their demeanor.

Excitedly, the brown-haired daughter speaks up, "Mother, is Father handsome?"

With a smile on her face, as she wraps her arms around her midriff, Ynew speaks, "Oh yes! He is so handsome and strong! He is wise beyond his years! He is the perfect man in every way!"

Now the black-haired daughter asks, "Is he smart, kind, and gentle?"

With a heavenly gaze and a smile, Ynew announces, "Oh yes, he is very gentle and very kind! He took my breath away the first time I set eyes upon him, and he never disappointed me. He must be smart. He chose me!" Ynew smiles and then begins to laugh.

Ynew's daughters join in as they all begin to laugh.

* * *

We now join Nor and his army entering the Forest of Shadows in a distance. Nor and his army draw nearer and nearer; as they cautiously approach the dark path, they can see a single figure standing, blocking the path. As Nor and his army draw closer to the figure, they can see the figure is decked out in some very malevolent-looking red and spiked silver armor. As Nor draws nearer to the figure, the figure places his large sword in front of him, then raises his head to give Nor an evil stare. The strange-looking man is wearing a very strange and sinister-looking helmet which covers his face, then the figure begins to speak. Nor raises his hand to indicate to his men to stop, and they comply with his command.

The figure asks in a very serious voice, "What are you doing in my forest?"

In a sarcastic tone, Nor responds, "Our most humble of apologies, sir! We did not know this was your forest!"

The figures gives Nor a snarl, then responds, "I do not accept your apology, Nor!"

With a slight grin and in a chuckling manner, Nor states, "So you know who I am and why I am here, yes?"

With an evil stare, Cetan speaks out, "Yes! My lord has ordered me to meet you here!"

In a pleased manner, Nor quips, "Your lord? You must be a servant to Grimmcock. So why are you here to meet me? Perhaps to escort me to Grimmcock's fortress so that I may put an end to his evil life?"

Now enraged and in an exacting voice, Cetan replies, "You have presumed correctly, Nor. I am, in fact, an officer of my Lord Grimmcock. Now you and your men must die!"

With a chuckle and a smile, Nor retorts, "So you challenge me to a duel, yet I do not know the name of the creature whose life I shall be taking?"

Now even more incensed, Cetan responds in a loud voice, "I am called Cetan! I am the master of all the creatures and beasts that all men fear! I am the most fearsome warrior to ever walk these lands! I am Cetan, and you are but a flea! I do not duel with fleas!"

Suddenly, Musse angrily shouts, "You insolent bastard! I shall cut your tongue from your ugly mouth!"

As Musse addresses Cetan, Doom has already dismounted his armored steed, fully armed. With his large battle ax in his right hand and his magnificent large sword in his left, Doom rushes toward Cetan.

In a rage and in a very violent manner, Doom shouts, "Bastard! You die now!"

In a calm yet commanding manner, Nor orders Doom, "Doom! Stop!"

As commanded, Doom stops, then crisscrosses his weapons in front of his chest. Cetan leans back, as if ready to fight.

Just then, Nor addresses Cetan in a firm tone, "I just spared your life! You may be the fiercest warrior to ever walk your lands, but this is Doom! He is the greatest warrior to have ever lived!"

With a startled look in his eyes, Cetan looks to Doom, then responds, "I know this name. Who are you to make such a claim?"

A serious Nor replies, "Doom claims nothing. I have proclaimed him this and with good cause! Can you defeat him and prove me wrong?"

Now swaying side to side and in a very angry manner, Cetan shouts to Nor, "No man is a greater warrior than Cetan!"

Laughing, Nor replies confidently and calmly, "I am. So are any one of my warriors!"

Cetan stops his swaying, then calmly answers back, "You are cunning, Nor! You tempt me to fight you with your insolence and sharp tongue. But on this day, it shall not be as you wish!" Cetan, now in a calm and self-confident manner, turns his head from left to right slowly. "You must first reach my master's fortress to battle me! For now, I shall leave you to my hairy and sharp-toothed beasts."

Cetan jumps like no man should be able to as he turns, then leaps out of sight into the forest. Now in the dark of the forest, many pairs of eyes are seen staring back at Nor and his men. They do not appear to be human eyes but rather some type of creature's eyes as they are shiny red in color. As many pairs of eyes surround the Centaurs, a growling sound can be heard coming from these creatures. As the creatures grow in numbers and draw ever closer, the growling becomes louder and louder.

In a curious but confident tone, Musse asks, "What the hell is that noise? What in hells name is that?"

Suddenly, with a loud command, Nor shouts, "To arms! To arms!" Nor and all his men draw their weapons in preparation for battle.

Just then, from out of the dark of the forest, a large figure jumps out onto the path in front of the Centaurs. This is a vicious-looking creature covered in thick hair, with huge sharp claws; its teeth are huge and sharp as it stared at Nor with its glaring red eyes and foam dripping from its mouth. This creature appeared to be a giant wolf standing on its hind legs and walking up right as if it were a man. Suddenly, the creature is joined by two more of its kind and just as large and fearsome as the first one.

Impressed and surprised, Nor nods his head in approval, "Impressive! They are magnificent creatures!"

Suddenly, many more of these creatures appear and now surround the entire Centaur army. Both Musse and Doom give a smile as they look around at these fascinating creatures which are called wolfaraptors.

Laughing now, Nor shouts out, "Well, don't just stand there gawking at them! Attack!"

Now the Centaurs charge at the creatures and the creatures reciprocate with loud roars and growls as they leap toward the Centaurs. A fierce battle ensues as blood flies and weapons are swung. Several of the Centaur soldiers are taken down from their mounts, and many more of the wolfaraptors are killed as the battle ensues and gets even bloodier. Musse's polar bears have joined in the battle as have Krom's tigers, and the wolfaraptors show no fear of even these massive animals who have charged in and engaged them in a gruesome exchange of claws and fangs. Nor wades through many of the wolfaraptors, as does Doom and Musse. The other Centaurs that were once banished fare well; however, many of the other Centaur soldiers do not. The wolfaraptors are not only powerful but also fast and agile as they leap from one position to the next. The polar bears are now red in color from all the blood being flung around and sprayed into the air.

Sadly, one of Krom's tigers is taken down by two of the wolfaraptors, and they manage to rip the tiger's throat, killing the fearsome tiger. Krom sees this and in a rage, stabs one of the wolfaraptors with his sword, then leaps on the back of the other attempting to strangle the beast with his bare hands. Nor sees this and in a flash with his mighty sword, chops the snout off the wolfaraptor, then in a spinning motion, Nor slices the wolfaraptor's throat with a swing of his sword, killing the wolfaraptor. Krom, now covered in blood, grabs at his now-fallen tiger, then hugs the dead tiger and weeps in the most heart-wrenching manner. This display of Krom incites his fellow warriors to battle even more fiercely as they kill even more of the gruesome beasts. With the losses they have suffered, the wolfaraptors suddenly disappear into the dark forest. Nor and his men surround the kneeling and weeping Krom as he continues to weep for his deceased friend. All the Centaurs bow their head in respect for the brave tiger and their friend Krom.

In a sincere and peaceful voice, Nor speaks out, "He fought bravely and died well my friend. He was as brave as his master. Come, we shall take him with us to Grumpa's village and give him a proper burial." Nor turns to his men, then gives his command, "Wrap their bodies in their blankets and place them on their horses. We shall burry and honor our fallen at Grumpa's village." As Nor has commanded, several of the men dismount and aid in the wrapping of the fallen Centaurs. Krom's other tiger lies next to its brother and is clearly saddened by the death of his brother. Krom hugs and comforts his sad tiger as they are all covered in blood. Musse kneels down next to his friend Krom, then speaks to Krom compassionately, "I shall place him on my horse, my friend."

Krom looks up to his giant friend, then speaks up, "I shall place him on mine, but thank you."

In a surprised manner, Ox tells Musse, "Musse, your bears are now red bears!"

In a frustrated manner, Musse responds to Ox, "They are covered in blood, you idiot!"

Angrily, Ox shouts to Musse, "What did you call me?"

In a display of dominance, an angry Nor orders, "Not now, you two! Not now!"

With a glare in his eyes, Ox tells Musse, "At Grumpa's village then!"

With a cocky smile, Musse retorts, "Yes! At Grumpa's it shall be then!"

Now that all the deceased have been placed on horseback, Nor reviews the situation, then gives his command.

In a commanding voice, Nor shouts, "We ride!" Nor then leads his men through the darkened forest.

* * *

Now back at Grimmcock's fortress, we find Grimmcock staring into his viewing well with a very angry look upon his concerned brow as he lifts he weathered and aged face.

As this day continues, at Grumpa's village, we can see young children running and playing. Suddenly, there are screams being heard from the children as they dash back to the center of the village. This prompts the adults to rush over to the children to inquire as to their screaming.

Taking charge is the elegant beauty Ynew. "What is it, children? What is happening?" The young beauty is dressed in a form-fitting plain body-hugging gown with her beautiful auburn hair flowing down to her ankles, revealing her mesmerizing emerald green eyes and luscious red lips.

In a panic and frightened voice, Ynew's blonde daughter replies, "Mother! There are three very large red creatures chasing us!"

Firmly, Ynew orders her daughters and the other children, "Quickly! All of you rush over and get Grumpa! Take your sisters and the others into our home and latch the door!" Her daughters and the other children comply as they rush toward Grumpa's residence. Ynew grabs a carving knife, then proceeds toward the path the children were playing near. Ynew is now joined by several other adults, as well as Grumpa. Grumpa has his staff in hand, ready to engage these creatures.

Grumpa suspiciously asks, "What is it, my daughter? The children said there were several large creatures trying to eat them."

Just then, the polar bears appear from the bend in the road. The villagers, including Ynew and Grumpa, appear to make ready for a fight. Just as Grumpa raises his staff, he notices several very large well-dressed warriors appear from behind the three massive bears. Grumpa then lowers his staff, then begins to laugh. Ynew and the other villager look at Grumpa as if he is crazy.

A confused Ynew asks, "Why do you laugh, Father? Who are they?"

Grumpa smiles at his beautiful daughter, then responds happily, "He has returned! It is Nor, my daughter!"

Ynew, in a very pleased voice, "My love has returned to me!"

203

Ynew becomes teary-eyed and a large smile overtakes her elegant beautiful face as she begins to walk toward her beloved to greet him. Just then, Grumpa places his staff in front of her, preventing her from advancing any farther.

Grumpa advises his daughter, "No, daughter! You must wait! The beasts will think you intend them harm. Let us wait for Nor to meet us here."

Ynew accepts the advice her wise old father has given her, and she stands with a happy smile as her eyes continue to fill with tears of joy. Just then, Musse commands his three blood-covered bears.

Musse shouts, "Teeth! Claw! Bear! Stop! Come! You are frightening our friends!" Musse then leads his bears away from Grumpa and the elegant beauty Ynew.

Nor now rides up to Grumpa and his beloved Ynew. Nor looks to Grumpa and then at his beloved Ynew; he then removes his shiny Corinthian helmet, then smiles.

Nor looks down at Grumpa, then happily announces, "It does my heart good to see that old face of yours once again old man!"

With Ynew standing next to Grumpa and gazing at her beloved with tears in her eyes and glowing smile, she is speechless and simply gazes at Nor.

With a sour scowl on his face, Grumpa speaks in a grumpy voice, "Old? This face is but 375 winters. It is middle-aged, not old!" He lets out a laugh, then happily says, "Welcome back, my brave young friend! It does these old eyes good to see you once again and alive!"

Now with a grin and gleaming eyes, Nor looks down at his beautiful beloved Ynew. With a calmness and in a steadfast manner, Nor dismounts his horse, then steps toward his Ynew. With his right hand and with the edges of his fingertips, Nor gently places them under Ynew's chin, raising her face up ever so slightly where he may gaze into her beautiful tear-filled and sparkling emerald eyes. In awe of her beauty, Nor leans back as he can't help but gaze in a mesmerized state at Ynew's beauty.

Calmly and passionately, Nor states, "You are so beautiful my love! I have missed you so!"

Ynew is motionless and can only manage a tear in her eye as she gazes at the man she is hopelessly in love with. Nor's men are all taken in by Ynew's beauty as they simply stare at her with mouths dropped and eyes popped open. Nor just continues to stare into Ynew's mesmerizing and gleaming eyes.

All but Musse are speechless as he looks to his fearless leader with a shake of his head. Musse can't help but speak up in his usual cocky tone, "Well, kiss her or I will!"

With this, Nor leans in and kisses his stunningly beautiful beloved with a kiss that every woman would die for. Ynew, now covered in chills, slowly raises her arms, then wraps them in a very passionate manner around Nor's massive neckline. The two embrace in a very long and romantic kiss. All the women that see this tear up as does a sensitive Ox. Ox wipes the tears from his eyes as he looks on with a slight grin. This does not go unnoticed by Musse.

In a demeaning voice, Musse tells Ox, "You weep like a woman, Ox!"

Ox becomes enraged. Ox immediately jumps off his horse onto Musse as they begin to fight. Some of the other warriors just laugh and shake their heads in disbelief while others throw their arms up in disgust. The villagers, as well as Ynew, are alarmed by the two massive warriors' confrontation.

Surprised by this fight, Ynew asks her beloved, "Will you not stop them?"

Unable to take his eyes away from Ynew, Nor calmly says, "No need my love."

In a confused manner, Ynew asks, "Will they not harm themselves?"

Still staring in awe at his beautiful Ynew, Nor simply replies in somewhat of a dazed state, "Every time. Worry not my love. Their wounds are never serious."

Just then, Ynew notices that there is a scratch on Nor's arm. Ynew then reacts with urgency. In a concerned manner Ynew speaks out, "Oh no! You are wounded my love!"

In a manly manner, Nor responds, "It is but a scratch, my love. It is nothing to be concerned over."

Suddenly, Ynew bends down, then rips the bottom of her gown, tearing a strip from her gown as Nor looks on in a surprised manner. Ynew then grabs Nor's massive arm, then pulls it toward her, she begins wrapping the wound with the cloth she has removed from her gown. In a surprised move, Nor attempts to pull away as if he disapproves of Ynew's actions. This does not sit well with Ynew, who gives Nor a stern gaze, then pulls his arm tighter and closer to her. Ynew finishes wrapping the wound, then gives Nor a scolding gaze.

In a very sultry manner, Ynew smiles at Nor, then asks, "There, that wasn't so bad now, was it?"

Unable to respond in any other fashion, Nor looks down at his beloved with a smile and a loving gaze. Grimm sees this and suddenly falls from his horse, as if wounded, as he grasps his leg in apparent pain. Grimm looks over to see if Ynew notices his actions, and she does.

All of a sudden, Grimm cries out, "My leg, my leg! There is so much pain! I fear I shall fade into the darkness if my wound is not tended to!"

A concerned Ynew looks to Grimm, then ask Nor, "He is injured seriously. Should you not help him?"

Shaking his head, Nor shouts at Grimm, "Grimm! Cease your behavior and get to your feet!"

In a quick and uninjured fashion, Grimm stands up, then dusts himself off as he grins and winks at Ynew.

A relieved Ynew, in a concerned tone, asks Grimm, "You are not injured?"

A sarcastic sad look on his face, Grimm states, "Only my heart!"

With a chuckle, Nor reprimands Grimm, "Okay, Grimm, you have met Ynew. Now you may leave us."

Pleadingly, Grimm gazes at Ynew. "You are much too beautiful for this man!" Grimm glances over to look at Nor, then gives Nor a subtle wink. "You most fortunate man you. If only I were king, she would be mine!"

Both Nor and Ynew give a chuckle, then stare back at each other with the most loving of gazes.

With a very suspicious grin, Ynew tells Nor, "Come my love. I have a surprise for you!"

Ynew grabs Nor's arm, then pulls him with her toward the center of the village. The two near Grumpa's home, then stop just a short distance away.

A smiling Ynew shouts, "Girls! Come out! It is safe now!"

Suddenly, there is a noise of the door being unlatched and then the door opens wide. Out from the doorway, Ynew's three daughters make their way out, then stand in a line in front of Ynew. The three young beauties stare at Nor with grins on their beautiful faces. Suddenly, in a curious and excited voice, Ynew's golden-haired daughter speak up, "Mother! Is this him?"

Surprised by this, Nor's grin turns into a slight frown, then he asks in a somewhat depressed voice, "Mother? You're a mother? Who is their father?"

With an astonished glare, Ynew slaps Nor's arm, then responds, "Yes, I am their mother and you, my love, are their father!"

Now with a very strained and bewildered look as he surveys his daughters, Nor speaks out, "These are my daughters? I am their faaaa…"

Suddenly and without any indication, Nor faints and falls backward on to the ground on his back, creating a puff of dust and a thud of a sound. Now with a grin and chuckle, Ynew looks down at her beloved, then at her daughters. In a soft voice, Ynew then announces to her daughters, "Girls, this is your father."

Ynew and her daughters let out a slight chuckle as the daughters cover their mouths to display a bit of respect, but unable to control their laughter, they laugh even louder and are very visible to Nor's men. Nor's men suddenly rush over to their fallen king as even Ox and Musse cease their fight and rush over to investigate the situation.

Doom now angrily looks to Ynew, then questions her, "What have you done to him?"

Still with a grin on her beautiful face and a chuckle in her voice, Ynew responds, "I simply told him that these three are his daughters!"

Shocked and surprised, Doom responds, "Wait! What? These three are Nor's daughters?"

Suddenly, Doom and all the other warriors burst out in laughter as they look down at their king.

In a humorous guise, Magnus speaks, "So the man who makes war like a god, who fights like a demon, is as wise as time is long, faints when he discovers he is the father of three beautiful daughters!"

All continue laughing as they all look down at the still-unconscious Nor. A concerned Olff looks around, then down to his king. Olff asks, "Well, are we just going to let him lie there, or are we going to lift him up?"

A fast-acting Doom looks to a woman holding a jug filled with liquid. In his rough voice, Doom orders the woman, "Here, give me that jug woman! Forgive me my king!" With a slight grin, Doom begins pouring the contents onto Nor's face.

Surprised by Doom's comments, Ynew asks, "Your king! Nor is your king?" Ynew looks at Doom as she questions him.

Distracted by Ynew, Doom continues pouring the contents on Nor, not realizing the liquid he is pouring is wine as he replies to Ynew in his rough voice, "Yes! Nor is king of the Centaurs and of all the northern tribes." Doom now looks down at Nor as the liquid continues to pour down on a now-awakened Nor. Doom stops pouring the wine, then apologizes to his king.

Apologetically, Doom speaks up, "Oops! I thought it was water!"

Everyone laughs, including Ynew and her daughters. Now sitting up, covered in wine, Nor wipes the wine from his face as he then looks up to Ynew.

A now-humbled Nor speaks out, "I have children! I have three beautiful daughters!" Nor now looks up at his men with a slight angry glare. "Don't just stand there, you big dumbasses! Help me to my feet so that I may meet my daughters!"

As ordered, Doom and Grimm aid their beloved king to his feet where he can now gaze upon his three beautiful daughters. Now on his feet, Nor looks at each of them with a proud gaze and a smile on his face. In a concerned manner, Ynew looks to her beloved, then questions him sweetly, "Are you yourself now, my love?"

With a huge grin upon his handsome face, Nor responds, "Yes, my love. I am myself now." In a proud manner, Nor asks, "So, my love, what are my daughters' names?"

In her typical sweet and confident voice, Ynew announces, "Well, my love, for now they are called the oldest, middle, and youngest daughters of Nor. I would not deprive you of your right to name your children."

In a very proud manner and with gratitude, Nor takes Ynew's hand, then kisses it as he gazes into her eyes. Nor smiles as he confidently makes an announcement, "Well, let it be known that from this day forth, first daughter of Nor, you shall be called Yelhsa! Second daughter of Nor, you shall be called Annaerb! Youngest daughter of Nor, you shall be called Ynaffit!" Nor steps back to take in the scene, and with a huge proud grin on his handsome face, he crosses his arms, then gazes at his beloved with the same proud mannerism.

The daughters of Nor are pleased with their names, as is Ynew; they all look to one another as they all smile and nod in agreement to Nor's decision.

With a proud and pleased smile upon her beautiful face, Ynew sweetly comments, "Your daughters are very pleased with their father's return and with the names you have bestowed upon them. You have done well this day, my love."

Proudly, Nor addresses his Ynew, "What beautiful young women you have given us my love!" Nor gazes upon his beautiful offspring.

With a proud grin, Ynew replies complimentarily, "Of course, they have their father's bloodline." She embraces Nor's giant bicep very affectionately and firmly.

Immediately, Nor responds in the same manner, "No, my love, they are beautiful and graceful, like their beautiful and perfect mother!" Nor bends down, then kisses his beloved on top the head.

From out of nowhere, Grimm interjects himself into the beautiful moment with his usual sexist bravado, "I definitely agree! Wow! What beauties we have here!" Grimm gazes at each of Nor's three beautiful daughters.

Grimm's comments change the moment as Nor becomes enraged as his face displays his every emotion of displeasure. Suddenly in a rage, Nor turns to his men in a manner to which they are unaccustomed, and Nor's face is as red as the wine they drink, but his eyes have changed as if every evil force was captured within his once-stunning blue eyes.

Angrily, Nor looks to all the men, then loudly hollers, "Should any man dishonor any of my daughters, I shall take his manhood with a dull knife, shove it down his mouth, then I will gut him like a pig! Understand?"

All look on in amazement and fear, especially Grimm, who is now shocked and visibly frightened by the looks of Nor, then in a frightened manner, Grimm reacts in a bit of a stutter, "My...my king, I was just agreeing with you!"

Just then, Ynew grabs her Nor and very sternly gives Nor a pull toward her with a lecturing look, combined with overtones of enough, but not a word is needed to make her point to her beloved. Nor's daughters are all taken aback by this action and display, a show of fear to their ruggedly handsome but enraged father. This behavior does not go unnoticed by Nor, so he tends to his emotions, then calms himself as he looks into his Ynew's calming eyes.

In a more composed manner now, Nor addresses his people, "You must all understand! I must now deal with all of you men in a manner to which I am not accustomed to. I now have three beautiful daughters, and I can only think of protecting them from men such as you. So you understand now. So stay away from my daughters!" Nor ends his words but not in the tone in which he began and with a look of discontent, followed by a scowling evil piercing eye, which everyone notices. All the men, except Grumpa and Doom, show fear in their manner and expressions.

In a calm voice, Grumpa speaks, "Having one beautiful daughter is hard enough on any man, but three beautiful daughters, surely that would be a test for any good man, especially a wise king."

Grumpa's words hit Nor like a ton of bricks, and Nor demonstrates the wisdom he has been given as he looks to Grumpa with a smile as he lets out a slight chuckle.

In a calmer voice, Nor speaks out, "Wise words from an even wiser man. Your words have hit their target, my wise old friend. I shall refrain from getting too angry in the future. Thank you."

Grumpa simply smiles as he gives Nor a simple nod. Everyone else gives a sigh of relief as Nor has his confident grin back on his handsome and rugged face once more.

Now in a sultry manner, Ynew glides her hand down Nor's massive arm. Nor gazes down at his beautiful Ynew as she gazes back up at him. Softly and seductively, Ynew asks, "Well, Your Highness? If I could have a moment of your time, there is something that I would like you to assist me with. You know something that I have not done since you were last here!" Ynew gives Nor a very seductive and sultry smile.

The realization of what Ynew is asking hits Nor like a heart attack, and he reacts accordingly as he lifts Ynew into the air with both hands to his eye level so that he may look directly into her mesmerizing beautiful eyes.

A very pleased and confident Nor speaks softly to his love, "I have dreamed of that for too long my love. Let us waste no more time." Nor then kisses his beloved passionately, which surprises his three daughters as they first appear shocked and displeased, but then this emotion soon turns into a pleased gaze and grins as Nor takes Ynew into his arms, carrying her away as the two engage in the most romantic of kisses. All watch on with approving smiles and nods. Nor's men simply smile, then let out an approving chuckle. Musse, without any warning, punches Ox, who then falls to the ground, holding his jaw. Musse laughs, then Ox rises up and charges Musse as they begin to fight and roll on the ground. The rest of the Centaurs just look on and laugh as the villagers look on in amazement. Moordock looks to Doom, then they both nod to each other.

In a compassionate yet commanding voice, Moordock speaks out, "Come, my friends, let us tend to our fallen."

All the Centaur warriors, with the exception of Musse and Ox, join Moordock and Doom as they make their way over where all the fallen lay. Krom takes his fallen tiger from on top of a horse, then lays him on the ground, covered in a blanket still. The others begin to dig graves for their fallen friends. After a while, as the graves are being dug up, Musse and Ox are still going at it. Now on their knees, exhausted from their skirmish, both Musse and Ox cease, then help each other up to their feet where they then walk over to join and help out their friends but are laughing at each other's wounds as they point to each other. Doom gives the two a firm look, which silences both Musse and Ox as they now become serious as they aid in the digging. Now that their fallen friends are buried, all the warriors bow their heads in respect.

In a sad and soft voice and with tears in his eyes, Krom speaks out, "Goodbye, my friend! You shall be missed!"

* * *

Sometime later, we find Ynew's home where Nor's three daughters appear to be awaiting the appearance of their father and mother. Moments later, the door of Ynew's home opens as both Nor and Ynew appear with smiles upon their faces. Apparently unaware of their surroundings, Nor lifts Ynew into their air, then gives her a very affectionate kiss, causing their daughters to giggle. The sound of their daughters catches both Nor and Ynew by surprise and causes them a bit of embarrassment, so Nor places his beauty back on to the ground where the two compose themselves, then react to their daughters. Nor then takes Ynew by the hand and walks with her, followed by their daughters to where they see Grumpa sitting at the feast area.

With a smile on his face and in a pleasant tone, Grumpa welcomes the young family. "Come, my large friend and my little beauties. Here, sit next to me so that we may speak of your travels and your many experiences."

In a pleased voice, Nor replies, "That, my old friend, would be an honor."

In a romantic move, Nor lifts Ynew up as if she were a dainty flower and places her on to the bench next to Grumpa. As Nor places Ynew down, their daughters look on and giggle. Nor, with a pleasant smile, sits down between Grumpa and his Ynew. As Nor sits down, they are joined by all the Centaur warriors who make themselves comfortable as they begin serving themselves both food and drink.

In a pleased yet curious tone, Grumpa questions Nor, "So, my large friend, tell me of your travels to the Greek lands, especially Sparta and Athens. I am very curious as to what you have experienced there."

In a very good mood, Nor replies, "The lands there are fruitful, the people are very honorable, and the warriors are fearsome. In Sparta, they are very well trained as they train to be warriors from the time they are seven winters of age, then continue until they are thirty. In Athens, they are more concerned of art and building amazing structures. Some so magnificent that one wonders how they can achieve such works."

Curiously, Grumpa speaks, "I have heard of this. It is said that in Athens they build their structures of white stone and decorate them in gold. Is this true?"

Nodding in agreement, Nor answers, "Yes, this is true. The people of Athens use a white stone called marble, and they sometimes use gold or polished bronze to decorate their structures and they are amazing works of art and the structures are quite the sight!"

As she gives Nor a curious and somewhat jealous gaze, Ynew asks, "What of their women? Are they beautiful and friendly?"

It is plain to see that Nor has become very uncomfortable and somewhat red-faced with Ynew's question as he begins to squirm ever so slightly in his seat. Nor takes a drink of wine, as if to buy himself some time, before responding as his beloved gives him a steady gaze with a slight scowl in her eyes.

Now in an unusual and shaky voice, Nor looks to Ynew with a nervous smile, then responds, "No! No! Not at all! They are manly looking and fat. Not friendly at all. None compare to your beauty, my love!"

As Nor speaks to Ynew in his nervous voice, his warriors and Grumpa all begin to grin as some chuckle in disbelief at what Nor has stated. Suddenly and in his usual troublemaking manner, a sarcastic and cocky Grimm declares, "That is not what you said when we all met up at the bear cave." Grimm smiles as he looks away from Nor, then takes a drink from his large cup.

All of a sudden, the Centaur men begin to laugh and chuckle; as Musse is taking a drink of his wine, he starts to laugh, then the wine squirts out of his nose, causing the rest of the Centaur warriors to laugh even harder. Now everyone begins to laugh even harder, all expect Ynew, who appears to become agitated by Grimm's comments. Ynew begins to stare at Nor with an even angrier glare. As this is happening, Nor gives Grimm a very angry scowl. Grimm refuses to look at his king and turns his head to avoid any eye contact, knowing that Nor was not pleased with his comments. Now becoming even more enraged, Ynew grabs Nor's ear, then turns his head so that he faces her as she questions him.

Unhappily, Ynew asks, "So, my love, father of my daughters and love of my life, what did you say of these women at the bear cave where I was not present?"

Nor, now facing his beloved with a reddened face and appearing very nervous, attempts to shake his head in disagreement, but Ynew's grasp on his ear will not allow him to move as she stares even angrier at her love.

All Nor can do is attempt a smile as he attempts to explain, "He jests, my love! Grimm is always joking and causing unnecessary trouble!" Nor shifts his eyes back at Grimm's position as he attempts an angry scowl toward Grimm, who still refuses to look at Nor. Ynew pulls at Nor's ear, forcing him to reset his eyes back on her. In a nervous voice, Nor attempts to calm his beloved, "None of the women I encountered have even a grain of your beauty, my love. None compare to your stunning beauty or amazing body, my beloved, the love of my life! You are all that I live for, my love!"

With a scowl on her beautiful face and staring into Nor's nervous eyes, Ynew asks in a very serious tone, "Did you bed any of these women?"

Now even more anxious and uncertain, Nor responds the only way he can, "No! Of course not! I...I...I would never! You are the only love for me, my love, my beauty, my life!"

All but Nor and Ynew begin to chuckle as they can see Nor is in trouble and that Ynew has complete control over this massive man and fearless king. As this transpires, Grimm being Grimm can't help but interject his thoughts. A cocky and sarcastic Grimm fake coughs as he woefully attempts to cover his mouth. "Bullshit! Bullshit! Lie! Lie!"

This does not go unnoticed by Ynew, who becomes even more enraged as she releases Nor's ear, then slaps Nor in the back of the head, causing Nor's head to snap forward a bit. All are surprised at her action, then once over their astonishment, they all begin to laugh—all but a very angry Ynew. Nor is very embarrassed, and it is very prevalent to all. Unsure of how to react, Nor simply looks down at his food with a shameful, dumbfounded gaze upon his disheartened ruggedly handsome face. The beautiful Ynew then places her hands on Nor's face, turning his handsome mug to her as she then gives Nor a very seductive but firm gaze.

In a very sultry but firm voice, Ynew tells Nor, "From this time on, you will not look to any other women but me! Is that understood, King Nor of the Centaurs, father of my daughters, love of my life, and man whom I have worried about and never strayed from since we first met?"

It is very obvious to all that Nor is very embarrassed and feeling guilty as he gazes at his beloved starstruck eyes.

In a soft and guilty tone, Nor replies, "You and only you, my beloved beauty! You and only you, love of my life!"

With this, Ynew pulls Nor toward her, and she leans in and kisses her man with the most sensual kiss, which astonishes everyone, including Nor. Then with a smile, Ynew releases Nor's face, as she stares directly into his now-vulnerable blue eyes.

In a somewhat cocky yet consoling tone, Ynew states, "That should take care of it then, yes?"

Now taken in by her forgiveness and love, Nor is unable to resist. Nor stares into Ynew's mesmerizing sparkling emerald green eyes in very heartfelt manner as he forms a grin upon his handsome face and nods in agreement.

In the same manner as before, Ynew tells her love, "Fine. I am the only woman you will ever need or for that matter, desire!" Then confidently, Ynew smiles as she turns to look at her daughters who are in awe of her performance and control of their father. The Centaur warriors look on in amazement as to how this tiny beauty just dominated their fearless leader and wise king. They all show a newfound respect for Ynew as they all, in unison, bow their heads in total and complete respect of this beautiful and powerful tiny lady who has displayed an immense amount of courage and control, not to mention with such elite candor.

With a slight chuckle and a grin on his old withered face, Grumpa tells Nor, "She will make a great and wise queen, Nor, son of William. Oh, and she shall bear you more children and sons to retain your throne."

With a dazed grin, Nor nods in agreement, then speaks out, "Yes, yes she will." Suddenly, Nor realizes what Grumpa said, then reacts in a surprised manner. "She will?"

Grumpa just smiles and nods to indicate yes as he continues to drink from his mug.

As they all continue to eat and drink, Olff speaks up in a serious and eager tone, "My king, when do we depart for Grimmcock's fortress to put an end to this evil warlock?"

Suddenly, everyone stops what they were doing as they now all look to Nor. Nor grins, then responds to his friend.

In a calm and commanding manner, Nor responds, "Soon, my friend, soon. For now, we shall feast and enjoy the pleasure of our hosts and friends. Besides, I would like to take some time to come to know my beautiful daughters and once again, place a satisfying smile upon my future bride's beautiful face." Nor again gazes at his beautiful and elegant Ynew with a stupid, loving smile.

With this being said, all are taken by surprise as most begin to smile and nod; a curious gaze overtakes Ynew. Ynew looks to Nor in a suspicious manner, and in cunning fashion with a guarded tone, Ynew asks, "Future bride? Why would I marry you, Nor, king of the Centaurs?"

With her words, Ynew has put everyone in a frozen state, and no one dare move as they are all aghast at her reaction, all but Nor who smiles at his strong-willed and beautiful Ynew.

In a calm and loving tone, Nor speaks clearly and plainly to his love, "You will marry me because you are the woman I love! You are the mother of my children! Because I have loved you ever since the day I laid my eyes upon you! Because only a woman with your beauty, grace, elegance, and courage that you would slap a king upside his head, then you should at least do him the honor of marrying him after causing such pain and embarrassment! A woman such as this should at least marry this king she has struck and become his queen, as only this lady could ever be just that, my queen, my love, my wife, and mother of all my children!"

Now all the men grin and chuckle as the women all giggle, covering their mouths, as do Nor's daughters. Ynew sees this and becomes even more emboldened and more determined to make Nor plead just a bit more.

Proudly and stubbornly, Ynew raises her head just a bit, then in a determined tone, she states, "If you wish me to marry you, Nor, king of the Centaurs, you must ask me properly!"

Now Grumpa, drinking his wine, has some of the wine shoot out from his nose as he is caught off guard by his daughter's demands of this king. The Centaur warriors, who are clearly smitten with and respect Ynew, have made it clear that they are very pleased with Ynew's actions and proud yet demanding response as they all nod and smile in approval.

Now in a show of disbelief, Nor questions, "You would have me kneel to you in front of all these people, my daughters, and my warriors?"

Without hesitation and in a very confident manner, Ynew replies, "Yes! Yes, I would! Now bend a knee to me, King Nor, and ask me properly!"

All the Centaur warriors begin to shout, "On your knee, beg her! On your knee, beg her! On your knee, beg her!" They all laugh as Nor gives them a huge smile and shakes his head in disbelief, but as instructed by his beloved, Nor then takes to one knee in front of Ynew, causing his men to clap and nod in approval. Everyone is pleased as they smile, laugh, and clap in approval of Nor's act of loyalty and capitulation to his beloved's demands.

Now staring into Ynew's mesmerizing eyes sincerely and romantically, Nor asks, "My love, my life, my everything! I cannot live another day without you. You are the only reason for my existence! You are the only woman I have ever loved and desired. My love, will you do this humble man, this lonesome warrior, this unworthy king the honor of becoming my wife, my queen, and my companion for the rest of life?"

As Ynew gazes hopelessly into Nor's beaming blue eyes, Ynew smiles ever so slightly, then in a soft and sultry manner, she responds, "I have always loved thee. Yes, my love. I will marry you!"

Nor rises up as he takes Ynew into his arms and lifts his beloved into the air, then kisses her with a long loving embrace; this prompts everyone to cheer and clap for the future bride and groom. Unexpectedly, this show of affection and love causes both Musse and Ox to tear up, then cry openly.

Weeping in a choked-up manner, Ox announces, "That was beautiful!"

Nodding in agreement, Musse also weeping and choked up, comments, "Yes, yes, it was!"

The two giants lean toward each other as they place their foreheads against each other, then they both begin to pat each other on the shoulder. A disgusted Dread looks on as he shakes his head and grins at the two giants showing their sensitive side once again. Suddenly, Nor makes an announcement.

In a loud and proud voice, Nor shouts, "Rejoice everyone! For on the morrow, we shall have us a grand wedding!" With a huge grin on his face, Nor then looks to his beautiful Ynew, then announces, "Then I shall have the most beautiful of brides and then the most beautiful wife and queen!"

Everyone cheers as they raise their cups and mugs to drink in celebration of the announcement.

Happily, Moordock shouts, "This is a very good day! We shall have a very worthy and beautiful queen once again!"

This prompts Grumpa to speak, "Yes! Ynew shall truly be a great queen, a loving mother, and a perfect wife!" A tear can be seen forming in his eye.

Now hollering happily, Magnus stands, "Tonight! Tonight we shall drink in honor of our king and future queen!"

All the men shout and cheer as they all raise their drinks into the air.

Much later that evening, we find all the Centaur warriors and Grumpa sitting around a large table as they all appear very drunk as they continue drinking wine and ale from very large bowls, cups, pitchers, and mugs, basically anything that can hold liquid, they use to drink from.

A very drunk Nor shouts out, "Grimm! You shit! You must pay for your remarks today! You caused your king to be struck and something else happen too." Nor appears slightly confused as he can't remember what else he was going to say.

Visibly drunk but in a brave and loud manner, Grimm asks, "What would you have me do? Just say it and I shall obey my king, my friend!"

Shouting out and very drunk, Musse suggests, "You should have him kiss Ox!"

All laugh but Dread and Ox.

With a bewildered gaze, a very drunk Ox asks, "How is that a punishment?"

All the others laugh as wine shoots out of Musse's nose, which causes him to make a sour face.

Nor attempts to stand but is unable so he shouts from where he is seated. "No! He might like that! I have seen him kiss worse!"

Not hesitating and in an aggressive manner, Dread grabs Ox's face, then kisses Ox, and just as sudden, he releases Ox, then wipes his own mouth and lets out a shout.

Loudly, Dread shouts, "There! I kissed the ugly big bastard! What else would you have your most loyal servant do to satisfy his king's wishes?"

Ox looks around surprised, but not sure what just happened as he appears confused by Dread's actions.

Now drunken Magnus adds in his two cents, "You should have him kiss Musse's ugly bears!"

Taking offense to Magnus's comment, Musse appears to have had his feelings hurt as he states sadly, "My bears are not ugly!"

In an exerted effort, finally making it to his feet, swaying back and forth, Nor then commands, "Nope, for getting your king!" He now pauses to burp and lets out a very loud and long burp. "In trouble with our future queen and my future wife!" He sees a boy walking carrying a jug. "You, Grimm, shall drink without stopping all the contents from that jug that that boy is carrying!"

Doom is the nearest to the boy, so Doom grabs the jug from the boy, scaring the boy half to death and causing the boy to jump back. Doom gives the boy a half-cocked drunken smile, then nods to the boy. Doom then throws the jug to Grimm as Doom shouts out to Grimm.

In a drunken shout, Doom calls out to Grimm, "Here! Drink!"

With both hands, Grimm manages to catch the jug, then confidently speaks out, "I shall drink this to honor my king, for I have caused my king to be struck in the head by a very beautiful woman! Our! Our! A soon to be queen! So I say to you, my king, my friend, you are a lucky bastard! Ynew is too beautiful for even you! So I accept my punishment! To Nor and Ynew! May they live forever and love each other till then!"

Grimm stagers as he raises the jug to his lips. Now Nor raises his mug as he sways back and forth with his right-hand fist to his chest as he addresses Grimm in a complimentary manner, "You honor your king! Now quit stalling and drink, you shit!"

Holding the jug up to his face, Grimm can barely stand but announces, "To my king! To my friend! To Nor! My deepest apologies!" Grimm begins to chug from the jug.

All the men begin to chant, "Chug! Chug! Chug!" With the jug tilted up, the contents seemingly all gone, Grimm removes the jug from his mouth. Grimm makes a sour face, then shakes his head rapidly.

In a half voice, Grimm asks Grumpa, "What the hell was that? That shit is good, but it burns my mouth, my throat, and my gut!

A laughing Grumpa replies, "It should! I make it to use as torch fuel! It is good though!"

A swaying Nor asks, "What is it made from?"

A swaying and smiling Grumpa responds, "It is made of a mixture I call burning water. I make it myself with grains, potatoes, and other things. It is good for wounds, starting fires, but I like to drink it. But sadly, I am the only one who enjoys it."

Not wanting to miss out, Musse grabs a jug from another boy who is walking by carrying a jug of burning water. Musse begins drinking the contents.

Removing the jug from his mouth to burp, Musse then speaks up, "This is good! To Nor! My friend! My brother in arms! My kiiii!" Just then, Musse passes out face-first onto the table but manages to place the jug onto the table where it sits safely from harm.

A laughing and very drunk Grimm addresses Nor, "You are a lucky man, my friiii!" Grimm passes out, but he falls face-first onto the ground.

A very drunk Nor looks around confused and a bit angered, it appears from Grimm's comments but doesn't remember who he was speaking to. "What did he call me? A what?" Scratching his head and looking confused, Nor looks around to see who was talking to him. "I'll kick his ass!"

Now a drunken Moordock speaks out, "He called you a friii."

Angrily, Nor states, "How dare he call me that! What is a friii?"

Shaking his head and raising his shoulders to indicate he doesn't know, a drunken Moordock states, "I don't know. Maybe it's a new word he learned."

A very drunk Nor responds, "Oh. It's a good thing he left! I would have had to have kicked his ass again!" In a fit, Nor grabs the jug sitting on the table, he begins to chug from it then hands the jug to Moordock. "He did not finish the jug! The bastard! Here, Moordock! Have some of this. It is good!"

Moordock drinks from the jug, then smiles at Nor. "This good! It warms the butt and burns the goat. No, I mean it burns the gut and warns the goat. No, I meant it burns the throat and warms the gut!" Now appearing confused, he looks to Nor and asks, "Right?"

A very drunken Grumpa hands Nor a large bowl. "Here, Nor, have some of this. It has a berry taste to it."

With a drunken smile, Nor takes the bowl. "I don't mind if I do." Tilting the bowl to his mouth, Nor begins to chug from the container, then with a burp and a smile, Nor comments, "This is good!" With a silly grin on his face, Nor passes out face-first into the bowl of berry-flavored burning water. Soon enough, bubbles begin to form from Nor's nose. Grumpa, in an irritated manner, pulls the bowl from under Nor's face, causing Nor's face to hit the table.

An angered Grumpa scolds a passed-out Nor. "How dare you! Don't waste this fine drink on your nose!" Grumpa then pulls Nor's head up, then speaks to him, "You will make a great queen. Ynew is a good mother and will make you a great king and wife, my son. I meant wife and a good king. No, I meant a great mother and a good king. No!" Grumpa then appears to ponder his words, then speaks again, "I meant a great queen and an excellent wife! Yes! That is what I meant! Yes!"

With his face facing Grumpa, Nor speaks out in his sleep, "I love you, Ynew! You're my wife."

Grumpa retorts for Ynew, "She loves you too." Grumpa smiles, then drops Nor's face back onto the table. Grumpa drinks the rest of the burning water, then comments as all the Centaurs are now passed out, "One should never waste good drink!" Grumpa then looks around and realizes he is the only conscious one left. "They are great warriors but terrible drinkers!" Grumpa now stands up, then turns and walks away from the table, not watching where he is going; he runs into a tall pole where a torch is mounted and burning on top of it. Grumpa falls to the ground, then makes his way back to his feet. He then addresses the pole, "Forgive me, madam. I did not see you standing there." Grumpa nods, then walks off toward his home.

CHAPTER 15

A TRUE GIFT FROM THE GODS

THE NEXT DAY, we find Nor dressed in his Spartan uniform, shiny and polished with his crimson red Spartan cape covering his massive back. Standing to Nor's left is Doom dressed in his shiny black-and-silver armor; the two are standing facing Grumpa. Behind Nor and Doom, we find all the villagers and Nor's men. It is very apparent that Nor's men are very hungover as they stand with bloodshot eyes all dressed and cleaned from the previous night.

Suffering from the hair of the dog, Nor leans over and whispers to Doom, "My head feels as if twenty horses have stomped on it!"

Feeling the same way, Doom speaks up, "We need more drink, that will surely rid us of this horrible feeling!"

With a smile and chuckle, it is clear that Grumpa is not suffering from any hangover, so he comments, "I have much more of that burning water in my storage room."

Suddenly, flutes begin to play, which prompts all to stand to attention as everyone then looks back in the direction of a decorated tent opposite of Nor's position. From out of the decorated tent appear Nor's three beautiful daughters; they are all dressed in elegant long light blue-colored gowns which are practically painted on the girls, revealing their hourglass figures as their long beautiful hair flows freely behind them. The three are all carrying a bouquet of flowers as they line up to march down the flower-laden path ahead of them, leading to their handsome and massive father's position.

Leading the three is the beautiful Yelhsa, followed by the radiant Annaerb, and then the stunning Ynaffit. The three beauties make their way toward their father who appears very proud as he stares at his three little beauties. Nor notices the looks his men are giving his beautiful daughters, then an angry glare overcomes his smile as he gives his men an angry glare. The men notice their king is displeased with their gawking of Nor's daughters, so they instantly all remove their eyes from Nor's stunning daughters, then focus them back on their king. In subtle manner, Nor gives his men a nod of approval, then a slight smile. Now from the decorated tent appears Nana; she is dressed in a simple white gown as she appears to hold the tent open for Ynew, who appears shortly after Nana.

Ynew is a true vison of beauty as she makes her way out of the tent. Ynew is dressed in a very form-fitting off-white gown with two very long slits down the dress, which are revealing her perfectly shaped legs as her long beautiful auburn hair flows freely down past her ankles as it sways ever so slightly in the breeze. Ynew's body is enhanced by this gown, and everyone can't help but drop their jaws as she and Nana make their way down the flowered path toward Nor. Unable to restrain his feelings, Nor stands with his eyes tightly affixed to his love with his jaw dropped open as drool drips down his lip. Doom is just as taken but manages to nudge Nor.

In a very complimentary manner, Doom speaks out, "You, my friend, are a very lucky man!"

Not missing a beat, Nor responds very proudly, "Yes, I am! She is breathtaking! She is a true gift from the gods!"

Ynew draws ever closer and closer to Nor; she can't help but notice the expression on Nor's face, and she begins to smile with a slight giggle. She then gazes at Nor and wipes at her mouth, indicating to Nor to wipe the drool from his mouth. Unable to respond due to the lock Nor has on his beloved beauty with his piercing eyes, Nor simply stands staring at the love of his life as even more drool drips from his mouth, causing Ynew to giggle even more. Ynew and

Nana finally reach Nor. Nana nods to Nor as he reciprocates the nod, then takes Ynew's left hand in his right hand. Ynew, with a chuckle and a beautiful smile, takes her right hand and wipes the drool from Nor's mouth, then simply smiles as she gazes lovingly into his blue eyes. Grumpa takes a long piece of cloth, a string of the same length, a thin chain of the same length, and a strand of Ynew's auburn hair. Grumpa then begins to twist the four together, and once he is satisfied with the binding, Grumpa then pulls the couple's hands into to his, then he wraps the strands around the couple's touching wrists.

In a solemn voice, Grumpa asks, "My daughter, is this the man you choose to wed and become his wife for life?"

With a gazing smile as she stares into Nor's eyes, Ynew replies, "Yes, Father. This is he. This is my love until the end of time."

In a more pleased tone, Grumpa asks again, "My daughter, will you love this man till your last day? Will you please this man with your mind, body, and heart? Will you care for this man, and will you give your life to him?"

As she gazes with a smile and in a very confident manner, with the sweetest voice, Ynew responds, "Yes, Father, I shall do this all and more till my last day!"

Grumpa then turns to Nor and asks, "King Nor, is this the woman you have chosen to wed and love for the rest of your life?"

As he gazes down at his Ynew with a silly grin, Nor replies, "Yes, this is she. My Ynew is the only woman I choose to wed, whom I give my life to until the end of time."

In a more assertive voice and manner, Grumpa asks, "King Nor, will you give your life for this woman? Will you protect her from harm? Will you give her your mind, body, and heart? Will you care for my daughter with your last breath, and would you die for her?"

Without hesitation, Nor responds, "Yes, I shall do all this and more, whatever my love desires of me, until the end of time!"

A very pleased Grumpa smiles, then announces, "Then as your father, I do hereby bind the two of you in marriage and for the rest of your lives! May you bear many children and live long, loving, and happy lives. Now you must kiss to complete this marriage."

Immediately, Nor lifts Ynew up, then wraps his massive arms around her tiny waist and gazes into her mesmerizing eyes as he kisses Ynew passionately and romantically. Ynew then wraps her arms around Nor's massive neck and reciprocates the kiss.

A very pleased and excited Grumpa shouts out, "I hereby proclaim you husband and wife! Now let us drink and feast!"

Everyone cheers and claps as Nor and Ynew continue their long, tender, and passionate embrace and kiss.

Tenderly and lovingly, Nor gazes into his wife's stunning eyes, then speaks, "You have made me a very happy man, my love!"

Out of nowhere, Grumpa takes Nor by the arm, then speaks to Ynew, "My daughter, I need to speak to your husband for a bit. It will only take a short time, I assure you. Come, Nor, let us talk as father and son for a moment."

Ynew gives an uncertain smile as the two men walk away from her and toward Grumpa's house. As Grumpa pulls at Nor, Nor looks back with a sad face at Ynew but continues to walk with Grumpa. Ynew makes her way over to the large wedding table and takes her place at the table near her three daughters and Nana. Now inside Grumpa's home, Grumpa pulls out two mugs, then pours some burning water into the containers. Suspiciously, Nor sits down where he is joined by Grumpa at a table.

Curiously, Nor asks, "So tell me, Grumpa, what is it that you wish to speak to me about?"

Grumpa smiles, then gets very serious, "You must never repeat what I am going to tell you. Do you agree as a man and as king?"

With a curious look, Nor asks, "Not even to Ynew?"

Grumpa then gives Nor a very serious gaze. "No! Ynew must never know of what I am going to tell you. No one and I mean no one but you, Nana, and I shall ever know this!"

Surprised, Nor responds, "Okay then, yes, I agree."

Being very serious, Grumpa begins to speak, "Ynew is my blood daughter! Nana gave birth to her one hundred twenty-six winters ago. You know wizards are not supposed to have children, but I am exceptional, as you know! Now Ynew never really knew how old she was and we never told her. We would just change the subject, and we never allowed anyone to stay with us for too long. Worry not, Nor, for when you bedded my daughter some thirteen winters ago, you made her become somewhat mortal. You see, because when she gave you her heart, it changed her in some ways. Ynew started to age as other humans do, so her ageing started the day you took her into that cave. Unfortunately for Nana and me, Ynew will live a human life span, and one day, we will lose her. This is why you must give us many grandchildren. Ynew will live on in them and so on, yes!"

In a very sorrowful mode now, Nor tells Grumpa, "Had I known this, I would not have bedded her!"

Grumpa laughs, then speaks out, "As if you had a chance to deny my daughter's beauty! I ask you, Nor, would you rather our Ynew never know what true love was? Would you deny my daughter the existence to have children? Would you deny her a life filled with the love of children or the man she has always loved? This chance meeting was never an option for either of you. You two were destined for each other. Why do you not think I did not stop you two from entering that cave? I could have you know!" Grumpa gives Nor a cocky and confident grin.

Surprised by this, Nor replies, "I don't understand, Grumpa. Why did you allow me to bed Ynew?"

Laughing at first, then Grumpa responds, "I didn't allow you to bed her! Ynew did. She chose you, not me! And may I say, my son, Ynew chose wisely, very wisely. Just look at your daughters. They are perfect, as shall your sons and other daughters be. They shall all be."

Now taken aback, Nor asks, "Did she use magic on me? Did she make me fall in love with her?"

Grumpa laughs out again. "No! No, Nor! Ynew is no sorceress, at least not now anyway. Besides, she is not that kind of female. Let's face it. You fell in love with my beautiful daughter the second you laid eyes upon her! Did you not? Besides, no one has that strong of magic anyway, not even me! Let's face it, Nor, Ynew did not need magic to take your heart. She stole it and still has it now, and it appears she shall keep it forever."

With a chuckle and a smile, Nor responds, "Yes, this is true. My Ynew owns my heart and my life forever!"

Seriously, Grumpa leans in, then tells Nor, "You must know this, Nor! Now that you have wed my Ynew, should you ever stray and bed another, Ynew shall turn her true age before your very eyes and die of a broken heart! This is the trade-off she has made without even knowing it. This is all due because she chose to wed a human! So you must never stray again, or I shall be forced to kill you, yes?"

Appearing angered, Nor responds, "That will never happen! I am so in love with my Ynew. It breaks my heart just to be away from her for a short time. Even now seems like an eternity!"

Relieved and in a cocky tone, Grumpa comments, "Good, I would hate to have to kill the father of my grandchildren!"

Surprisingly, Nor asks, "Are you disappointed that Ynew chose me rather than a wizard or a warlock?"

In a pleased tone, Grumpa replies, "This is what Ynew wanted, and we are happy for her. Surely we will be saddened upon the time that death does seek her! But remember, her life goes on in her children, so please have many!" He laughs out loudly, then pats Nor on the shoulder. "Ynew chose wisely, my son. You are everything we ever hoped she would find and fall in love with. You are a good man, Nor, king of the Centaurs! We know you shall never disappoint us or our daughter!"

Gratefully, Nor nods, then asks in a curious manner, "Will Ynew or my children have magical powers?"

Confidently, Grumpa speaks up, "No! Well, I don't think so. Perhaps! I guess only time will tell! I am not sure! This should be a thing to watch for. Interesting? Why did I not ever ponder this before? Hmm! I guess we'll both have to find out in time. If they do, then I shall teach them how to harness their powers. Yes. I shall help them harness their powers should they possess any." Grumpa smiles at Nor.

Now taken by surprise by Grumpa's words, Nor gives Grumpa a scowl and a shake of the head, as if to indicate he is not pleased by Grumpa's response.

In a concerned voice, Nor tells Grumpa, "Well, I guess we'll just have to wait and see. Be assured, ole wise one, I shall never speak of this conversation to anyone, not even Ynew. This, of course, will be hard to do. You do realize this? Ynew has a way about her of getting me to tell her exactly what she wants to know. Those eyes of hers just make me melt to her will. It shall be a test, that is without a doubt, but I shall prevail. I hope!" Nor smiles at a Grumpa, who gives Nor a concerned glare. "Shall we join the others now?" Nor stands up, then reaches his hand out to aid Grumpa up.

Grumpa now rises to his feet as he is aided by Nor, then he advises Nor, "I knew this, you know. I just wanted to see your face when I told you. It is a father's right, you know!" The two laugh as Nor nods his head in agreement. They exit the home, then make their way to the celebration.

Moments later, Nor and Grumpa join the celebration as Nor walks up from behind Ynew; he places his large hands around his beautiful elegant wife's tiny waist, then places his lips on her neck, just brushing his lips ever so slightly upon her neck. Ynew closes her eyes, then leans her head in the opposite direction as she enjoys the affection her husband has demonstrated, and she has no power to stop this as she is helpless to his gentle kiss and display of affection.

In a soft and warm voice, Nor asks, "Is my beautiful bride enjoying her celebration?"

With her eyes still closed, Ynew answers in a soft sultry voice, "I am now that my husband is with me and so close with his touch."

In a surprised move, Ox stands up and addresses his new queen, "My queen, of all the women I have bed, I would gladly trade them all for a bride as beautiful as you, my lady!" Ox then nods to his queen.

Unsure of how to respond to this, Ynew being the class act that she is, simply smiles, then thanks Ox. "Thank you, Ox! That was such a kind thing to say!"

As usual, Dread can't help but interject his opinion in his usual sarcastic manner, "All what women? You have only had but only one!"

Then a very drunk Musse intercedes his thoughts in a cocky tone, "Yes! And she was as ugly as you are, Ox!" Musse then bursts out laughing as do many of the others.

Calmly, Ox retorts, "You should not speak of your mother in such a horrible manner!"

Now just about everyone bursts out in laughter as wine shoots out of Musse's nose. Musse wipes the wine from his face, then stands up angrily. A very upset Musse shouts at Ox, "What! I! I shall! Ahhhh!" Musse attempts to charge at Ox.

In a split second, Doom reaches out his arm, stopping Musse in his tracks, then advises Musse and Ox, "No! You two will not fight today! Not on this day, not on Nor's wedding day. No one fights today! Is that understood?" Doom gives his typical scowl to every one of the Centaurs. Each look to Doom, then nod in agreement as they fear Doom's wrath and fighting skills.

A very upset Musse speaks out, "But, Doom, he called my mother ugly!"

A calm and stoic Doom speaks, "No, he did not. He said he bed your mother."

Now in a bewildered manner, Musse responds, "Oh yeah!"

A disgusted Doom rolls his eyes and shakes his head in disbelief as everyone else grins or chuckles.

In a soft and curious voice, Ynew asks Nor, "Is Doom a great warrior?"

Calmly and proudly, Nor answers "Yes! Perhaps the greatest I have ever seen."

Now curiously, Ynew asks, "Is he better than you?"

With a slight chuckle, Nor responds, "We shall never know, for I would never raise a hand to him. He is my brother, my right hand."

Curious, Ynew asks Nor, "Who is his father?"

With a stoic look on his face, Nor answers, "He is the bastard son of Cantor. We speak of this not, for it angers and saddens him at the same time."

Apologetically, Ynew whispers to Nor, "I am sorry, my love. I did not know this."

Ynew then leans over and whispers in Grumpa's ear. Just as this is happening, Nana questions Doom inquisitively, "So, Doom, do you have a special lady waiting for you somewhere?"

Proudly and excitedly, Doom responds in a very un-Doom-like manner, "Yes! My little Angel awaits me with my sons back at her father's home."

Suspicious, Grumpa speaks out, "Nor! Doom! Come with me to my lodge and assist me to carry some more burning water."

Now in a sly manner, Ynew leans over and whispers to Nana, "Doom is Cantor's bastard son."

Nana is overcome by a flabbergasted gaze as it takes over her wrinkled old sweet face.

Moments later, now in Grumpa's lodge stand Nor, Doom, and Grumpa. In a friendly gesture, Grumpa takes a jug from his shelf and three cups; he then places the cups on the table near the three. Grumpa begins pouring burning water into the three cups, then suggests, "Nor! Doom! Here, let us drink alone for a bit. Here, sit."

All three of the men sit around the table, then begin to consume the liquid from within the cups.

Grumpa clears his throat, then asks, "So, Doom, I understand that you are the bastard son of Cantor. Is this true?"

Nonchalantly, Doom responds, "Yes, sadly this is true, but thanks to Nor, I was allowed to end his pathetic life."

It is apparent that Grumpa is very taken by Doom's armor as he continues to inspect the malevolent work of art and its fine craftsmanship. Grumpa suddenly touches the armor, then asks, "The armor you wear, the craftsmanship has a familiar look to it. May I ask where did you obtain this magnificent dark armor?"

In his usual stoic manner, Doom replies, "It was a gift."

Grumpa suspiciously asks, "From whom, may I ask?"

Again, in his usual stoic manner, Doom responds, "I received it from a master blacksmith called the Alchemist. Why do you ask?"

Doom appears to be getting somewhat agitated by Grumpa's questions, so in a friendly yet commanding manner, Nor places his hand on Doom's shoulder, then gives Doom a nod.

Calmly, Nor speaks to Doom, "My friend, I believe Grumpa is trying to tell you something. Am I correct in this assumption, Grumpa?"

Both Nor and Doom look now to Grumpa with curious faces.

With a slight smile and in a calm voice, Grumpa speaks up, "Yes, my son. You are correct." Now with a more serious look than before, Grumpa looks directly at Doom, then announces, "The Alchemist is my brother! That is why I asked about the armor you wear, Doom. The craftsmanship looked very familiar to me. So correct me if I am wrong, but Holga is your mother then, yes?"

In his usual stoic manner and tone, Doom replies, "Yes."

In a melancholic fashion, Grumpa places his hand upon Doom's shoulder, then announces in a very apologetic voice, "I am sorry, my friend! Your mother died last winter!"

Doom sits motionless and without expression as a single tear manages to roll down his rugged hard face. Nor places his hand on Doom's other shoulder and respectfully bows his head to Doom.

Now showing some emotion, Doom asks in a very disheartened manner, "How? How did my mother die?"

In a very dejected tone, Grumpa replies, "She fell and struck her head. By the time we found her, there was nothing we could do, so we did what we could and gave her a proper burial out near the woods and marked her grave with carved stone. Perhaps later I can show you where she rests."

Compassionately, Nor gives his friend a very sad look as tears form in Nor's eyes.

With a gloomy gaze upon his hardened face, Doom speaks out in very sad voice, "I thank you, Grumpa. Thank you for tending to my mother." Even with his attempts to mask his sorrow, Doom's face is now like an open book as tears begin to roll down his hardened face.

Seeing his best friend's face filled with tears, Nor places his tear-filled face onto Doom's shoulder as he pats Doom on the back in a display of affection and respect. Doom bows his head as he attempts to weather his sorrow.

In an effort to change to mournful mood, Grumpa attempts a smile as he asks, "Tell me, Doom, when you were a guest at my brother's, did you meet a young lady with the blackest of hair living with them?"

Doom raises his head with a bit of a strange look on his hard face, and in a less sullen voice, he responds, "Yes, his daughter Angel!"

With a smile and a upbeat persona, Grumpa asks, "She is blind, tiny, long black hair, and mesmerizingly beautiful?"

With a silly smile upon his rough face, Doom replies, "Yes!"

In a pleasant tone, Grumpa announces, "I have great news for you then! She is your half sister. She, too, is Cantor's bastard daughter! Is that not great news?"

A very emotional Doom begins to weep as he places his head down to his knees, weeping openly; all Doom could manage to speak are the words, "No! No! No! It cannot be true! No! No!"

In a surprised fashion, Nor leans back and asks, "What is it, my brother? Why is this not pleasant news? Please tell me why you weep so. Please tell me. What is wrong?"

Weeping in the most pathetic of fashions, Doom responds, "I have dishonored my sister!" Doom continues weeping in the most mournful of manners.

Bewildered as he shrugs his shoulders looking to Nor, Grumpa asks, "I don't understand. I thought this would be welcome news." Grumpa suddenly becomes overcome with remorse and guilt.

With a look of confusion and in the same manner, Nor asks, "What do you mean? How? How did you dishonor you sister?"

A very dejected and sorrowful Doom replies as he continues to weep, "My Angel! She is my sister! My Angel has given me two sons and was with child when I departed to kill Cantor!" Doom continues to weep as he places his head down and shakes his head side to hide in disbelief and disgrace.

With a dejected gaze of disappointment, Grumpa exclaims, "I did not know this! I am so very sorry, Doom."

In the most pitiful manner, Doom speaks out, "I cannot live with this shame! I can never return to my beloved Angel! My sons! What have I done?"

With eyes filled with tears, Nor asks Grumpa, "This will not do, no. This cannot remain. Is there something you can do?"

In a confused emotional state, Grumpa shakes his head as if to indicate no, then he replies, "I, I don't know. What would you have me do, Nor? I cannot lie to him now. I cannot take it back or undo their meeting."

Angrily, Nor shouts, "Do something! Anything! Use your damn magic or something!"

In a weakened and melancholic manner, Doom rises to his feet, then looks to Nor. "My king, I must ask for your pardon and leave of my services! I will be of no good service to you in the battles to come! Please forgive me, my brother."

In a surprised and shocked manner, Nor responds, "My brother! I cannot do this thing you ask of me! To go to battle without you by my side! I would have you hack off my right arm from my body rather than go to battle without you! I cannot do this, my brother! I need you by my side now more than ever before! Please, brother! Do not ask this of me please!"

In a much-destressed manner and a show of respect and affection, Doom places his weeping face upon Nor's chest and continues to weep uncontrollably.

Barely understandable, Doom mutters, "My heart is heavy as shall my sword be my brother."

Desperately, Nor looks to Grumpa and ask in the most pathetic manner, "Please! There must be something you can do for him please."

Looking more confident and upbeat, Grumpa responds, "Perhaps there is something we can do! I shall need time to prepare, and I will need to draw on Nana's and Ynew's healing powers. You must understand, Nor, this will weaken Ynew!"

Concerned, Nor asks, "Will it harm her?"

In a very confident yet sly manner, Grumpa states, "No! She will only be tired for several days." Now Grumpa places his hand on Doom's shoulder as he looks down at Doom with a serious gaze. "Doom! Nor will need you in this upcoming battle! You must defeat Cetan! For only a king or a wizard can kill a warlock! It is not possible for us to succeed as even Nor cannot battle a warlock and a supreme warrior such as Cetan at the same time!"

Now in a more commanding manner, Nor asks, "Grumpa, how much time do you need?"

Grumpa replies with a grin, "A night or two."

Concerned, Nor responds, "That will not please her!"

Just then, Ynew barges into the domicile with a wide-open door behind her.

Firmly, Ynew tells her father, "Father! You have had my husband to yourself long enough!" Suddenly, Ynew realizes that there is more going on than she originally expected. Now in a more concerned and sensitive manner, Ynew asks, "What is the matter? What is going on here?"

In a rushed commanding manner, Nor steps up to his beautiful bride, and placing his massive hands around her tiny waist, Nor then begins to whisper in her ear.

Ynew's expression begins to change as Nor whispers to her. Ynew blurts out, "Oh! No! No!"

Ynew's face becomes filled with a mournful expression of both sadness and concern. Ynew then touches Nor's cheek with the back of her hand, then being Ynew, she sidesteps her husband and tells her father, "I shall help you, Father! Together we shall make this right as once before!" Now in the most sincere and desperate of manners, a tear-filled-eyed Ynew kneels down in front of a very depressed and mournful Doom. Placing both hands on Doom's pitiful yet hardened face, raising his to face hers, Ynew gazes into Doom's eyes with the most woeful gaze, then speaks in the saddest voice, "My husband needs you Doom! I would gladly trade one night of pleasure with my beloved for many, many more! But this will not be if you are not by his side! Doom, I need you to bring him back to me! Please!"

Ynew begins weeping even more as she attempts to restrain her tears and her emotions. "Doom, your heart knows what true love is! Would you take this from me? Would you take this from Nor? Would you take this from your Angel? You did not know who she was! This is what Cantor would want of you, to break you and he shall win! Do not give him his victory! Your heart is pure and I can see this! I can see this in you as I saw it in Angel! She deserves to be happy and be with the one she loves as do you, yes? Please! I implore you Doom! I beg you! Please let us help you! Please! I cannot live without my beloved and neither can Angel!"

Now in a more calm and consolable manner, Doom responds with a still-mournful face, "I cannot refuse you, for you have my Angel's way about you. I shall do as you ask, my queen."

Ynew, in a sign of complete and unmitigated affection and gratitude, hugs Doom, then speaks in the most humble of manners, "Thank you! Thank you, thank you Doom!" In the most graceful of displays, Ynew holds Doom's face with both her tiny gentle hands, then kisses Doom on his forehead, causing a now-embarrassed Doom to blush ever so slightly.

Pleasantly, Doom tells his queen, "Thank you, my queen. Thank you for the courage and resolve you have given me."

A now very pleased and smiling Nor and Grumpa both nod in satisfaction and approval.

A very happy and emotional Ynew gazes into Doom's eyes, then tells the big brute, "No! No Doom, thank you! Thank you for giving us all a future and the chance for the love we all so desire and require!"

In a commanding manner and with a stern gaze, Nor speaks up, "What has happened here must never leave this room, and we should never speak of this to anyone!"

All look to Nor and nod in agreement.

Back outside, around the feasting area, we find Nor's three beautiful daughters talking and giggling as Nor's men are all eating, talking, laughing, and drinking as are the villagers.

A curious Krom speaks out, "Where are our king and queen?"

A wisecracking Grimm interjects his opinion in his usual joking manner, "I don't know, but if Ynew were my bride, I know where I would be!" Grimm laughs out.

Responding laughingly, Krom comments, "Yes, I as well!"

Several others laugh with Grimm, but his comments do not sit well with some of the others.

Not pleased with the words he has heard spoken by his friends, Olff scolds them, "Ynew is your queen and our friend's wife! Do not disrespect her!"

In a jesting manner, Krom speaks up, "We are just jesting, Olff!"

A serious Magnus then speaks up, "Then you should stop! Ynew is our queen, wife of our king and friend. You insult his honor with such thoughts and words! Do it again and I shall have your asses at the end of my boot!"

An offended Krom interjects his thoughts out loud, "Who do you think you are? Doom?"

Now a angered Moordock intercedes, "He is Nor's friend as am I! Now shut your mouths and speak of our queen like that never again! Heed my warning, for if Doom hears you say these things of our queen, he will do much worse than just warn you!"

Magnus speaks up, "Doom would do much worse and with no warning, much worse!"

All the men nod in agreement.

Apologetically, Krom states, "We shall jest of this never again. You are right my friends."

Happily, Musse speaks out, "Come my friends! Grumpa has finally brought out our king and queen, and they have more firewater!"

All of Nor's men walk over to meet Nor, Ynew, and Grumpa to help with the firewater they are carrying. The men take possession of the jugs the three are carrying, then take them back to the feast and rejoin the festivities. All seem to be enjoying themselves as they continue to eat, drink, talk, and laugh.

A drunk Musse approaches Nor and asks, "My king, where is our friend Doom? I should like to drink with his ugly bald head once again."

A smiling Nor responds, "Doom is meditating and will not be disturbed by anyone. Let all know that no one is to disturb Doom!"

Musse nods in acceptance, then turns and walks away, drinking from a jug he has been holding on to for some time now, and he is visibly drunk.

The next morning, we find many of the men passed out on the ground, tables, benches, chairs, on each other, and two more on top of two horses. Nor and Ynew make their way around the sleeping men, cautious not to awaken them. The couple finally makes their way to Grumpa's domicile where they enter quietly. Now inside, Nor closes the door behind them. Sitting around the table is Doom, Nana, and Grumpa as they appear to be consoling Doom. Nor and Ynew take a seat next to Doom and between Nana.

An impatient Nor asks, "So will we be proceeding soon?"

In her sweet and calm voice, Ynew responds, "Yes, my husband. We shall get started in a moment. There are a few more preparations to make, but they will not take too long, oh great king. Be patient, my love." Ynew gives Nor a very seductive smile as she runs her delicate fingers down Nor's rugged yet handsome cheek.

Blushing with a goofy smile, Nor responds, "Yes, my beautiful queen, as you command."

Grumpily, Grumpa speaks up, "Enough of that nonsense!" Grumpa shakes his head in disgust and disapproval.

In a show of displeasure with Grumpa's reaction, Nana speaks out in an angrily, "Enough of that, you old fool! Perhaps you could learn from Nor how to treat your beautiful wife!"

Grumpa chuckles, then looks around sarcastically and announces, "If I had such a beautiful wife, perhaps I would treat her in such a manner, but all I have is you, you old witch!"

Without hesitation, Nana reaches over and smacks Grumpa on the back of the head, causing Grumpa to jolt forward.

Caught off guard, Nor, Ynew, and Doom let out a chuckle as they cover their mouths, attempting to guard their responses.

Without hesitation, Nana replies, "Perhaps that tap on the back of your head has resolved the problem you have with your eyes!" Nana gives Grumpa a stare of discontentment.

In response, Grumpa places his left hand on the back of his head as he turns to Nana with a snarl on his old weathered face and in a cocky tone replies, "Do not disrupt my concentration, old woman!"

With a squint of her eyes, Nana tells her husband, "You were not concentrating on your task. You were trying to remember what you were doing, old fool!"

Insulted and angry, Grumpa stands up, then speaks out, "What! What are you talking about, old woman? I was calculating the formula for the size of Doom. He is rather large you know and this is science, not a guessing game, you old witch!"

Nor, Ynew, and Doom all attempt in vain to restrain from showing their emotions but are unsuccessful as they all laugh out and lower their heads to hide their reaction. Both Grumpa and Nana give each other a smile as Grumpa turns, then approaches his mixing table. The table has many powders, jars, bowls, roots, plants, dried-up insects, mushrooms, and many other strange items upon it. Grumpa now stands in front of his table and begins mixing items together as he adds different items into the bowl he is utilizing.

In a sly motion, Grumpa turns his head, then asks cockily, "Nor, did you sleep well?" Grumpa then chuckles as his shoulders tremble as he laughs quietly.

This angers Nana as she stands up and walks over to Grumpa, smacking Grumpa on the head once again with her hand. This causes Grumpa to lurch forward once again and let out a grunt.

Instantly, Grumpa turns to Nana and asks angrily, "What did you do that for this time, you old witch?"

With a glare in her old eyes and an angry stare, Nana replies, "You know why, you old goat! Now stop teasing Nor! Make haste and help that poor boy now! Or would you like another adjustment on the back of that old feeble head of yours again?"

With a slight growl in his voice and a snarl upon his old weathered face, Grumpa turns and continues working on the mixture for Doom. Grumpa is heard in a low mumble, "Bossy old witch!"

With a glare in her eyes and in an angry tone Nana asks, "What was that? What did you call me, you old goat?"

Nor, Ynew, and Doom bow their heads down, attempting once again to hide their laughter.

Now in an unsure yet almost frightened tone, Grumpa replies, "I said, I said, yes, my love."

Now confidently and harshly, Nana grabs Grumpa's ear with her fingers, then asks, "What was that, old man? What did you say?"

Grumpa acts as if the grab is painful as he comments, "Ouch! Ouch! Ouch! Let go of my ear you old witch! I need that to hear with. You know my other ear does not hear well!"

In a scolding manner, Nana demands, "Apologize and I shall release you so that you may hear every word I shall be calling you!"

Apologetically, Grumpa speaks out, "I am sorry! I am sorry that you're a mean old witch!"

Nana begins to twist Grumpa's ear, causing Grumpa to shout out loudly, Grumpa tells Nana, "Okay, okay, okay! I am sorry, my beautiful witch of a wife!"

This prompts Nana to release Grumpa's ear and then she gives Grumpa a smile and a kiss on his cheek, then Nana replies, "There, I accept your apology because you called me beautiful."

With a chuckle, Nor address Ynew, "I now see where you get your persuasive forehand from my love!"

Ynew gives Nor a smile, then lays her delicate head on his massive arm in a show of affection.

Standing next to Grumpa, Nana asks, "Well? Are you ready to proceed old man?"

Grumpa nods his head to indicate yes. Nana then walks over to Doom.

Nana bends down and looks Doom in the eyes, then asks, "Doom, come sit over here in that chair there. Daughter, come join us."

Ynew stands up, then walks over to the chair where Doom is now seated and where he has Nana standing next to him on his left side. Ynew then stands to Doom's right side. Nana places her hand on Doom's head, then pushes his head down as Doom complies with Nana's action. Grumpa then takes his staff crystal ball and rubs some of the mixture he has concocted over the top of the crystal, then places the staff back next to him. Grumpa then adds some of his firewater to the concoction and begins to mix it.

An impatient Nana asks, "Well! Are you ready yet?"

Agitated, Grumpa replies, "Hush old woman!" Can't you see that I am working here, woman? This is complicated and not for amateurs like you, old woman, so hush!" Grumpa mouths Nana's words as he shakes his head in a motion, as if to duplicate Nana's head motion.

This does not sit well with Nana, so she replies angrily, "What did you say to me, old man? Are you having trouble holding your big head steady? How would you like me to come over there and hold your skinny feeble neck to stop your big head from moving about so?"

In a futile effort, Nor and Ynew begin to giggle as they cover their mouths, attempting to cover their response from the old couple yet again.

In a low but cocky tone, Grumpa speaks up, "You would like that, wouldn't you? So you could break it!"

In a snarky tone, Nana replies with smug grin, "It would not take much to break that skinny neck of yours!

Grumpa turns his head, then replies as if shocked by Nana's words, "So! You would like to break my neck! Would you not?"

In a disgusted manner, Nana instructs Grumpa, "Shut that old mouth of yours, you old fool, before I smack that white head of yours once again."

Nor and Ynew continue to chuckle as they cover their mouths.

Now a confident Grumpa speaks up, "Daughter, take Doom's hand into yours and woman, you do the same with his other hand. Now begin the silent chant of Neba as you pass your thoughts to Doom."

Now Grumpa turns with the mixture in his hand as well as his staff; he then approaches Doom.

Confidently, Grumpa looks at Nana, then states, "There! It is ready! No thanks to you, you old witch! Now make yourself useful for once and give this to Doom so that he may drink all the contents."

Nana takes the bowl from Grumpa and lifts Doom's head as she places the bowl to Doom's lips. Doom proceeded to drink the concoction as all watch him with optimistic faces, all but Grumpa.

Sincerely, Grumpa ask Doom, "Doom, close your eyes and focus on your Angel. Now I want you to think of your favorite vision of Angel. Think of her at her most beautiful moment in your life, yes! Let me know when you see her and have the image frozen in your head."

In deep concentration, Doom announces to Grumpa, "I have her in my mind. She is so beautiful and frail I can—ouch!"

All of a sudden, Grumpa smacks Doom in the head with the round crystal part of his staff. This causes Doom to drop the bowl, which is nearly empty. Doom grabs the top of his head and slightly rubs it as Nor and Ynew burst out with a short laugh, then slightly chuckle and grin.

A now very unhappy Doom asks, "Why did you strike me with your staff?"

Apologetically, Grumpa speaks to Doom, "I apologize Doom. My staff slipped out of my old, weak, and feeble hand. So you were telling us about this beautiful woman of yours. You say her name is Angel, yes?"

Proudly and happily, Doom raves, "Yes! Her name is Angel! She is so beautiful! She has the most beautiful long black shiny hair, lips that would pale the rose, and she is so kind and sweet. Unfortunately, however, my beautiful Angel is blind." Doom sits with the goofiest of smiles on his rugged mug.

A now-serious Grumpa interjects, "That is good, Doom! She sounds wonderful! You can tell us more later, but for now, I need you to remove your shirt so Ynew may heal that wound in your chest!"

With a bewildered look on his face, Doom responds, "The wound is on my head, not my chest." As he looks at Grumpa, Doom rubs his head with his hands. In her usual sweet and persuasive voice, Ynew advises, "Trust me Doom. Just remove your shirt and relax."

Doom removes his shirt and sits as Ynew places her hands upon his heart and his head with her eyes closed; she makes Doom tremble for short time, then removes her hands. As she steps back, she appears a little woozy, so without hesitation, Nor takes Ynew into his arms to prevent her from falling.

Concerned Nor asks, "Are you okay my love?"

Ynew gathers herself, then responds in her calm and sweet voice, "Yes, my love." Ynew then touches Doom upon his shoulder, then instructs him, "You will need to rest now Doom."

Doom nods his tired head as he yawns.

In a commanding tone, Nor tells Doom, "You heard your queen. Rest now my brother! For we depart for Grimmcock's fortress in the morn. Come let us allow Doom to get some rest while we speak outside."

An agreeable Grumpa nods his head, then states, "Yes, of course. He will need to sleep for a while to regain his strength."

All but Doom exit the dwelling. Now outside the residence and walking down the path, a curious Nor looks to his bride suspiciously. In an inquisitive tone, Nor asks, "What just happen in there?"

Nonchalantly, Grumpa replies, "Did you not see me strike Doom upon his head with my staff crystal?"

Inquisitively, Nor asks, "Yes, of course, but why did you strike him?"

In a cocky yet humorous tone, Grumpa replies, "Well, how else would you replace a one memory with another? I had to knock out the bad one to replace it with a better one! Then Ynew mended his broken heart and healed his head. Simple!"

Somewhat bewildered, Nor asks, "But you said Ynew would be tired and weak! She appears to be neither."

A smiling and chuckling Grumpa answers, "It was you that needed the rest! For it was your strength and love for your friend that made it possible for us to succeed!"

Now somewhat agitated by this, Nor speaks out, "Why did you just not tell me the truth?"

A upset Nor stops with Ynew on his arm as they await a response from Grumpa.

Seriously, Grumpa smiles, then replies, "Because you would not resist my daughter unless you feared it may bring her harm, and Ynew would not risk your friend's state of mind for fear of losing you! Simple."

With a smirk and a shrug of his shoulders, Grumpa steps up to Ynew, then kisses her on the forehead; he then turns and walks off hand and hand with a smiling Nana in the direction of the storage cave. The old couple turns and smiles simultaneously at the newlyweds, then both Nana and Grumpa announce, "We shall keep your daughters busy so you may have your wedding night now!" The old couple let out a giggle as they walk away toward the cave.

A smiling and yet baffled Ynew speaks in her soft voice, "You know, he never ceases to amaze me with his wisdom and way!"

With a gleam in his eye and a smile on his face, Nor tells his beloved, "He is right! I could not resist you, not now, not ever!"

Ynew turns and gives Nor a very sultry gaze and smile, then replies, "And I you! Now husband, my parents will keep our daughters busy, so perhaps you can do the same to me."

Now a huge grin forms on Nor's face as if the tide washed over the beach. Nor eagerly, with both arms, takes his beauty into his arms, then announces excitedly, "Well, how can I refuse such an elegant beauty's request? I must do as my wife demands, and I shall with pleasure!" Nor turns, then takes Ynew in the direction of her home.

The next morning, out in the open, we find all of Nor's warriors preparing their mounts for travel. The warriors are loading supplies, food, drink, and weapons on their horses as they appear in very good spirits.

At this time, Nor and Ynew, are lying in bed in Ynew's bedroom. The newlyweds are apparently naked, lying in a warm embrace as they are gazing into each other's eyes with loving smiles.

A grinning Nor tells his love, "Upon my return, we will need to make preparations to move to the Centaur village. Do think our daughters will be pleased with this move?"

A confident Ynew responds, "They will do as their father tells them to. How long should I tell them their father shall be gone?"

Nor answers, "We shall return upon the rising of the third new moon. The fortress is not much farther from here, but I am sure Grimmcock will have several surprises in store for us and they will surely delay our movement."

A now pouting Ynew speaks softly, "They will feel like three long winters to me my love!"

A consoling Nor kisses his love upon her forehead, then tells her, "One must never weep before a battle my love."

An excited and very naked Ynew jumps out of bed, then tells Nor, "I almost forgot!" Ynew bends over and opens up a case lying on the floor, then removes a wrapped-up bundle and stands and turns toward Nor. Ynew steps up, then in the most sultry manner, kneels down in front of a now-seated Nor. Ynew hands the bundle to Nor with a very gleeful smile covering her beautiful face. "Here, my love. I want you to wear this under your clothing. Your daughters and I made this, and it shall help protect you."

With a huge smile upon his face, Nor reaches over and grabs a package which he hands to Ynew. "Here, my love. This is for you. I want you to wear this upon my return."

An impatient Ynew unwraps the package, then stands up and holds a very elegant and beautiful gown up in front of her still-naked perfect body, and in a very grateful and pleased manner, she tells Nor, "Oh my! This is the most beautiful gown I have ever seen!" Suddenly, Ynew realizes that she will be without her beloved for some time, then becomes saddened. "But I shall miss you, and that is such a long time!"

Standing up with a piercing gaze in his eyes, Nor speaks softly to his Ynew, "I shall miss thy more than you will ever know my love! I shall miss those beautiful eyes, those pouting lips, your perfect body, and those amazing perfect plump breasts, but most of all, I shall miss your soft beautiful calming voice."

Without hesitation and in the most seductive manner, Ynew tells her husband, "Then you shall have them all once more before you depart so that you would miss them even more and hasten your return back to them!" Ynew then drops the gown and wraps her arms around Nor's massive neck, then in the same motion, she places her beautiful plush lips onto Nor's and gives him a very passionate kiss. Ynew then releases Nor, then pushes Nor onto the bed, then sits on top his naked body, taking his hands, then placing them onto her perfect breasts as she tells him, "They shall eagerly await your return as shall the rest of me!"

Nor just gazes up at his beautiful wife with a very pleased smile.

Sometime later, we find Nor followed by Ynew exiting the dwelling. The couple make their way over to the other warriors as they continue to load their horses in preparation for the upcoming battles. Nor and Ynew are soon joined by their three beautiful daughters.

Moments later, we find Grumpa leading his saddled horse with Nana at his side toward Nor and his families position.

Both concerned and curious, a radiant Ynew asks, "Father! Why do you have Dark Star saddled?"

With a gaze of bewilderment and in sarcastic tone, Grumpa replies, "Because he is easier to ride with the saddle on!" Grumpa then gives Ynew a smile and a nod.

A more serious and levelheaded Nana comments, "Your father shall accompany Nor to make sure our daughter's husband returns in the same manner in which he departs her. Besides, my daughter, they will need your father once they get to the fortress gates."

In a show of respect, Nor nods to Grumpa, then humbly states, "We are honored to have you join us Grumpa!" Nor then places his right fist to his chest and bows to Grumpa.

Being Grumpa and as cocky and as proud as a rooster, he tells Nor, "Of course you are! I am not just a great wizard. I am also a supreme grand warrior you know!"

A not-so-happy and scolding Nana interjects, "Sure you were two hundred years ago! Just stick to your magic, old man!"

A now insulted Grumpa fires back, "Silence old woman! I have not lost a step in over two hundred years! I am still a force to reckoned with you know!"

Now a concerned and fearful Ynew interrupts, "Father! You will always be a great warrior, but for now and for me, please just use your magic. Please!"

A now humbled Grumpa says, "Fine! I will only use my staff!" Grumpa gives Nana then Ynew a nod. "Will that make you happy, ladies?"

Both Ynew and Nana nod in agreement with large grins on their faces.

In a grateful tone, Ynew tells her father, "Thank you Father!"

Grumpa gives Ynew a grin and wink of the eye, then turns to Nana with a grumpy gaze. "Come here old woman! Give me a kiss so I can ride with these young warriors and show them how to make war!"

Nana walks up to Grumpa, then gives him an affectionate kiss and a warm hug.

Grumpa leans in and whispers into Nana's ear, "I sent for them."

Nana smiles and nods, then mouths the words, "Thank you."

Grumpa gives her a smile, then a slight wink of the eye.

Nana speaks out to Grumpa, "Take caution and make haste my lover! We shall expect your safe return upon the third new moon!" She then blows Grumpa a kiss which he pretends to catch, then acts as if he places it in his pouch for later, then gives Nana a wink of the eye.

Grumpa mounts his horse, then looks down at Nor and in his usual cocky tone, says, "Let get this party started!"

A proud Nor calls his daughters, "Come to me my daughters!" All three of Nor's daughters come and hug him as he reciprocates the affection they give him. Nor kisses each one on the forehead, then addresses them, "Fret not my beautiful daughters, for we shall return soon!"

All three of Nor's daughters' eyes are filled with tears and lips pouting as they slightly quiver with tears rolling down their beautiful young faces.

Suddenly, Nor's eldest daughter Yelhsa, turns to Ynew, then asks, "Mother! Did you tell Father the good news?"

Now all three of Nor's daughters look to their mother.

A slightly embarrassed and blushing Ynew gazes at Nor.

Now curious, Nor asks, "What news do have my love?"

With a pleasant smile and rubbing her belly, Ynew tells her husband, "I am with child! It is your son!"

A proud and excited Nor steps up to his Ynew and gives her a gentle hug and an affectionate kiss, then asks her, "A son! You would not tell me this before I departed? Why?"

A concerned Ynew, in her soft and apologetic voice, replies, "I did not want to burden you with more worry! I had hoped you would realize this upon your return."

In a proud and calm tone, Nor tells his love, "Noting from your beautiful lips could ever burden to me my love, nothing!" Nor smiles, then steps back and turns as he mounts his horse with a huge smile on his face.

A now very impatient Grumpa grumpily tells Nor, "Tell her you love her, then let us ride! I am not getting any younger you know!"

A laughing then a serious Nor gazes at his love, then tells her, "I do love you so my lady, my queen, my wife, my love! We shall return soon! Daughters, take care of your mother and Nana! I love you all so very much!" Nor turns to his men, then to Grumpa. "We ride!"

Nor then leads his men away in a cloud of dust as the army rides off.

CHAPTER 16

A COSTLY RECKONING

NOR AND HIS army reach the river near Grimmcock's darkened fortress. Nor raises his hand up into the air, indicating to his men to halt their progress. Nor sits upon is noble steed as he gazes upon the river and the banks on each side. With Grumpa at his side, Nor looks to Grumpa with a smirk on his rugged face. Grumpa smiles back at Nor, then gives Nor a nod of approval.

Confidently and eagerly, Nor draws his large sword from its sheath, then shouts, "Evil awaits us in the river men! There are creatures in these waters men! To arms! Let us send these creatures to the netherworld where they belong! Are we ready for some fun?"

Nor's men all eagerly shout and cheer as they draw then raise their weapons into the air as they make ready for their charge into battle against these malevolent-looking creatures.

In a confident and eager manner, Nor announces, "Kill them all! No mercy! Charge!" With an eager Grumpa at his side, Nor charges into the wide river.

The Centaur army follows their fearless leader into the river. As the army rushes into the river, the water begins to fly into the air from the horses' hooves reaching for the river bottom; this charge prompts the creatures to make themselves visible. Suddenly and without warning, two of these large creatures jump out of the water in front of Nor. These creatures are massive with large sharp teeth and claws; they are an evil-looking dark green color with large whitish-colored horns protruding from each side of their heads, and they are clearly reptilian in nature as they swim like that of crocodiles with large red eyes. Without hesitation, Nor swings his large sword, beheading both creatures with one swing. A disappointed and upset Grumpa gives Nor an angry glare, as if he was disappointed that Nor killed both creatures, thereby not allowing Grumpa the pleasure of the kill. With a smile on his face, Nor gives Grumpa a confident gaze which suddenly turns into a look of surprise as a giant creature rises out of the water right next to Grumpa. Realizing Nor's reaction, Grumpa swings his staff blindly to his side, striking the creature and causing the massive creature to explode into thousands of pieces. This strike causes blood, guts, bone, skin, and other body parts to fly all over the river and upon the Centaur warriors.

As Musse and his three bears are crossing the river, one of the large creatures lurches out in front of him, so with a smile on his face, Musse swings his giant sharp halberd, decapitating the creature. Musse lets out a laugh, but then three more creatures appear one in front of him, then one to each side. Musse chops the creature in front of him in half, but before he can unleash his giant blade on the other two, he sees that Claw has taken the creature to his left out of action, and Bear has the one on the right by its neck and is shredding it with his claws.

As the battle ensues, Olff's horse is grabbed by the neck by one of the creatures. This angers Olff, who responds rapidly.

Angrily, Olff shouts at the creature, "You ugly bastard!" Then he strikes the creature across the face, causing the creature to release Olff's horse, then on the back swing, Olff decapitates the creature then makes his horse trample the dead creature as he attempts to continue to cross the river.

As Nor is cutting down several more of these creatures with Grumpa at his side, they reach the shore both drenched in the blood of the creatures they have eliminated.

Excitedly, Grumpa shouts out, "Watch out for their tails. They have some kind of armor spikes on the ends of them! Nor, these are Cetan's evil creatures!"

With a smile, Nor nods to Grumpa, then as Nor looks back, he sees that some of the Centaur soldiers are not faring well in the water, so he commands them, "Hurry! Force them to fight on land!" Just then, Doom joins Nor and Grumpa but only to get covered in blood from the creature Nor has just beheaded as the creatures' blood sprays all over Doom. Doom looks down at his armor and sees that is covered in dark blood from the creature, which prompts Doom to give Nor a very dissatisfied glare.

With a grin on his blood-covered face, Nor chuckles, then tells Doom, "Better it's their blood than yours!"

In his usual stoic manner and tone, Doom responds, "It stinks!"

A more serious Nor tells Doom, "Duck!"

Doom does as Nor instructs, then with his magnificent large sword, Nor swings it just over Doom's head, killing a creature that jumped up to engage Doom. The swing from Nor's blade causes even more blood to spew all over Doom's magnificent armor and this is very displeasing to Doom based on the expression he has displayed to Nor, once again Nor responds to Doom's gaze.

With a grin on his face, Nor tells Doom, "Like I said, better theirs than yours!"

In a very happy voice and laughing, Grumpa shouts gleefully, "This is fun!" In a dominant manner, Grumpa strikes two more creatures, obliterating them with his magical staff.

Dread has made his way close to the group on land, then laughs as he hears Grumpa shout in glee, "He's a madman!"

In a commanding manner, Nor hollers, "Ivan! Lugg! Take to the bank and use your bows on these creatures! They just keep coming and coming!"

As Nor commands, Lugg and Ivan take to the riverbank and utilize their bows to eliminate the creatures. The creatures arise from the water as if they themselves were created by the river as a seemingly endless flow of creatures continue to emerge from the river.

Now we see that most of the men have made it out of the river and are now fighting on land. All but two Centaur soldiers have made it to land and as the two attempt to rejoin the rest of the army, they are taken down and ripped apart by four of the creatures. This angers Nor, who charges back into the river to kill the creatures. In a rage, Nor strikes down seven more creatures, but more continue to replace those that he has struck down. Now Doom and Musse charge in to aid their king and they begin to cut down many more, but they realize the creatures are too many. Grumpa, now realizing the situation is dire, begins to chant with his staff raised, he appears to make the river change direction around Nor, Doom, and Musse as they all look on in amazement! Seeing their chance, Nor commands his men, "Back! Back to the riverbank!"

Now Nor, Doom, and Musse make their way back to land, rejoining his men.

Just then, Ox is heard shouting, "Musse, behind you! Duck!" A creature leaps into the air behind Musse, but as Musse ducks, Ox hurls his sword at the creature, killing it as the giant sword slices through the creature's body as if it were made of melted butter. Musse turns to Ox with a smile, then gives the giant Ox a nod. Ox reciprocates the nod and smile.

Pointing to the river, Nor shouts, "Look! They are retreating down the river! Come on men, let us regain our breath then we shall pursue them!"

Now deep inside Grimmcock's fortress, we find the door to Grimmcock's viewing room open. Inside, we find three figures standing around the viewing well. Looking into his viewing well, we find Grimmcock where he is flanked by Cetan and Brummel. Grimmcock does not appear pleased by the current events. Grimmcock stands back, then orders his acolytes, "Cetan! Brummel! Fill the tunnels with our men and creatures! Do not fail me again!"

Back outside Grimmcock's fortress, we can see Nor and his army approaching from the road near the river. As Nor's army moves ever forward, the lake next to Grimmcock's fortress now comes into sight. In the woods surrounding the lake, we can see many of the beasts called Wolfaraptors trolling the lake's edges while many of the creatures called Demasaurs are lurking and swimming in the lake. Nor and his army draw even closer to the lake well armed and prepared for battle. Now in a position, Nor feels that the area can be easily defended, so he orders his men to halt by simply raising his hand into the air. Nor then points to the lake and forest.

Looking to Doom, then Grumpa, Nor speaks, "Do you see them there? They are waiting for us. We shall prepare for attacks from all sides here. It is a good position with clear sight all around, and now we have clear sight of the fortress gates."

Confidently, Doom states, "We will be ready!"

Inquisitively, Grumpa asks, "Will we set up camp before we assault the gates?"

With a nod and a smile, Nor replies, "Yes. We will appear ill prepared as to entice them to attack us first. This will work to our advantage."

All nod in agreement with Nor's strategy.

Doom orders the men, "Men, set up camp in a circular manner so we may have sight all around us. No one sleeps! No one!"

Now Nor commands, "I want a large fire so that Grimmcock can see that we are here and that we are coming for him!"

Grumpa adds, "Yes, he shall see that his old friend is back and we have some unfinished business to attend to. He wanted a rematch, so I shall give him one."

In a bit of a humorous tone, Dread points out that the gates of the fortress are opening. "Look there! It appears you are about to get your wish!"

All the Centaurs look to the fortress gates as they open up, some with concerned gazes, others with smiles.

Now at the fortress gates, we see an army of cavalry charge out led by Brummel. The cavalry is some three hundred strong, whereby outnumbering the Centaurs by some ten to one. The army of Brummel's appear to be very confident and in good spirits as they cheer and shout at the Centaurs.

As the cavalry of Brummel makes its presences known, Nor and his army do not react as Brummel had anticipated.

Calmly, Nor instructs his men, "Men, show them no care. Do not react to their display or presence."

Nor's army continues making camp, feeding and watering their horses, building the fire, sitting as they eat and drink, completely ignoring Brummel's army. This lack of concern appears to be getting under Brummel's skin as he appears to get angrier and angrier.

On his armored mount, Brummel commands his army, "Stay here! I shall return shortly!"

Brummel turns and rides back to the gates where we find a very unhappy and concerned Grimmcock. Brummel rides up to Grimmcock apologetically.

A very displeased Grimmcock asks Brummel, "What is it? Why have you not attacked and destroyed them?"

In a very confounded tone, Brummel responds, "My lord, we rode out to meet them and they just sat there! They do not appear concerned, and I fear it may be a trap! So I held the charge until we could form a strategy!"

Frustrated and in a loud voice, Grimmcock commands, "We must not allow them any rest! We must deplete their numbers! Now go and crush them!"

Brummel nods then turns his horse back in the direction of his cavalry, then charges off to rejoin his men. Now back at the front of his cavalry, Brummel raises his hand as he looks side to side to see that his front line had formed up; he lowers his hand.

In a loud voice, Brummel commands his men, "First line, charge!"

As Brummel's first line of men charge toward the Centaurs, he sits back to determine the outcome before committing more of his men.

Meanwhile, Nor and his men continue to ignore Brummel's cavalry as they continue to eat and drink around the now-large fire they have built.

Looking up, a cocky Dread announces, "Nor, they are coming."

With a smile and in a very nonchalant manner, Nor commands, "Lugg. Ivan. Take your archers and drop them with your arrows while we prepare for the main course."

As Nor commands, both Lugg and Ivan rise up, then motion for their archers to join them. Now Lugg, Ivan, and ten more Centaur archers make their way between the charging mounted riders and Nor position. Nor's archers form a line, then load their bows and take aim at the charging cavalry.

With Lugg and Ivan at the center of the line, in a cocky tone, Lugg challenges his friend, "I bet you your jug of firewater that I take down more than you!"

Full of bravado and very cocky, Ivan laughs, then states, "Your loss, my gain!

Lugg shouts, "Release hell!"

Just then, the Centaur arrows fly, and like falcons attacking their prey, each arrow finds its mark, killing their target, then within a blink of an eye, another group of arrows strike their target. In less than twenty seconds, the entire first line of charging cavalry is demolished and lying on the ground dead as their horses turn and run off back into the fortress. As the now-unmounted horses make their way past Brummel, he again raises his hand into the air.

A now-angry Brummel shouts, "Second wave, attack their archers!" Brummel then lowers his arm, prompting the second cavalry charge to commence.

Now charging toward the Centaur archers, the cavalry fall as fast as drops of rain onto the ground. Within seconds, the second wave is destroyed just like the first.

Brummel sees his second wave destroyed just like the first, so in a very angry manner, he raises both arms into the air.

Shouting, Brummel commands, "Everyone, attack now!" Brummel throws down both his arms angrily.

Now what remains of Brummel's cavalry charges the Centaur position.

Calmly, Lugg turns to Nor, then advises, "Nor, we are running low on arrows, and they are sending the rest."

Disgusted, Nor rises to his feet, then announces, "Everyone, draw your weapons. Form our line, then disperse of these fleas so that we may finish our food and drink. Archers, down your bows and draw your swords. No need to waste any more of your arrows!"

The Centaurs form their line to engage the charging cavalry, and it is a magnificent sight with Nor in the center with Doom at his right and Musse to his left; they appear fearsome and mighty. With Krom's tiger at his left and with Musse's three bears to his left, this is truly a fearsome sight to see and a terrifying one for their enemies. As many of Brummel's men charge the Centaurs, they are knocked off their horses in a brutal and bloody manner as the Centaurs leap in toward the horsemen, killing them in hordes. To most, this is a gruesome and violent battle, but as the Centaurs begin to dominate their enemy, the Centaurs appear to be enjoying themselves as they wade through their enemies, as if they were mindless scarecrows mounted on horseback. The brutal battle is over almost as soon as it started as the Centaurs, now drenched in blood and entrails, look to one another with smiles and nods of approval. The victorious Centaurs raise their weapons in victory but do not shout; they just simply look to one another with gazes of approval and relief.

A very disgruntled and embarrassed Brummel rides back to the fortress where he finds an angry Grimmcock and a disapproving Cetan. Brummel dismounts his horse, then steps up to his lord. Brummel bows to Grimmcock, then apologizes as only Brummel would.

In a solemn tone, Brummel addresses Grimmcock, "They are good, very good!" Now Brummel looks up to the men on the top of the ramparts of the fortress, then shouts to them, "Close the gates now!"

With gaze of disapproval, Cetan gives Brummel a snarl and a shake of his disapproving head.

Cetan then speaks up, "Yes, they were for you, but tomorrow they will all die at the hands of my creatures and beasts."

A very unhappy Grimmcock interrupts, "Set your guards and have them keep a cautious and sharp eye."

With a disgusted glare, Cetan looks at Brummel, then again shakes his head in disappointment and speaks up, "Yes, my lord." Now shouting at the men on the walls, Cetan commands, "Triple the guard! No one sleeps tonight!" As a captain of the guard walks by, Cetan hollers to him, "You there! Take three men with you and guard the path outside the gate, and if they move anywhere, you had best warn our men immediately or my creatures shall feast upon your body as you watch!"

The Captain of the guard nods in a frightful manner; he then steps back and makes his way toward the gate.

Early the next morning, we find the Centaur camp bustling with activity. The Centaurs appear to be preparing for the upcoming battle as they sharpen their weapons, gather arrows, get dressed, exercise, and pack their belongings. Nor, with Grumpa, Doom, Moordock, and Musse walking with him, all kneel down as Nor signals for his men to join him he calls out, "Men! Gather around and form a circle around this area." Now with his dagger, Nor begins to draw shapes and figures into the ground before him as his men gather in a closed circle around his position.

Later, in Grimmcock's viewing chambers, we find a stressed-out Grimmcock talking with Brummel as Brummel, with a stick, is poking a hood-covered woman donned in a bloody dress as the woman moans in pain; she is chained to the ceiling in the chamber, unable to escape the torment that Brummel is causing her. Suddenly, the door bursts open as Cetan rushes in panting and excited, Cetan speaks up, "My lord! The Centaurs appear to be on the move!"

Grimmcock turns in a worrisome manner as he then addresses his acolytes, "Brummel, stop poking that bitch and make ready! Get over here. Cetan, execute the plan as we had discussed." Cetan rushes out of the chamber as Brummel stands next to Grimmcock, appearing to listen to Grimmcock's orders.

Back at the Centaurs' location, we find the Centaurs spreading out the large fire they have kept going. Now from the direction where the river joins the lake, we see a very pleased Grumpa approaching the group with a very self-gratifying smile upon his old mug. Dread notice the old man's smiling face, then calls out to Nor.

In a humorous tone, Dread tells Nor, "Looks like Grumpa is very happy with himself!"

Turning to see Grumpa approaching, Nor grins then asks, "So tell me Grumpa, are you pleased with the effect?"

In a glorious and laughing manner, Grumpa speaks out, "Those creatures will be of no use for at least two days!" Grumpa then points to the lake. Grumpa begins to laugh almost uncontrollably as this has an infectious reaction on those Centaurs watching; they can't help but join Grumpa in his infectious laughter as the see the effects of Grumpa's actions.

As they glance toward the lake, they can see the giant green Demasaurs attempt to walk, stumble, crawl, and pass out as they attempt to make their way out of the waters of the lake. It is a hilarious sight for the Centaurs to see and a welcome sight at that.

With a huge grin on his face, Nor speaks up, "This is good, Grumpa. Fewer enemies to face! That was a good use of your burning water though I think our men will not be happy knowing you used so much of it to get those creatures drunk!"

Grumpa smiles and nods, then replies, "We have plenty more for the victory afterward!"

As Ivan, Lugg, and several other Centaur archers gather the arrows from the bodies they penetrated, Ivan accidentally kicks off one of the helmets once covering the face of one of the fallen. Surprised by the disfigured and hideous face uncovered, Ivan steps back, then comments, "What the hell is this? Look at these ugly bastards. They must all be sick or something!"

As Musse is helping gather arrows, he also knocks off the helmet of one of the fallen, then comments after viewing the disfigured face, "Damn! They are all as ugly as Ox!" Musse lets out a chuckle as he looks to Ox with a smirk.

Ox turns to Musse with a smile, then knocks off the helmet of another fallen warrior of Brummel's, then comments after glancing down at the dead body, "Look! This one looks like your mother and he is ugly!" Ox lets out a laugh.

Hearing these comments by his own men, Nor becomes aggravated, then scolds his men, "Enough! They died bravely! Do not dishonor them!"

Now in a less happy tone, Grumpa advises, "They were once your brethren! Some were Centaur children and others were Tartan children. Then Grimmcock changed them into these monstrous creatures you see before you!"

Now out of respect and shame, the Centaur men all bow their heads in honor of these fallen warriors and former brethren.

In a determined voice, Nor commands, "Come! Let us put an end to this evil bastard and all his sheep once and for all! Smoke the fires!"

With this command, several warriors lay heavy green foliage on top the now-spread-out burning fires, and just as the green vegetation catches on fire, the men pour water on top the fires. These two actions cause heavy smoke to form, shielding the Centaurs' movements from Grimmcock's armies' vision. Now with a heavy smoke covering their movements, the Centaurs go into action and begin moving into position as some disappear into the surrounding vegetation as others begin to mount their horses and prepare for their advance.

Now that his men are in position and ready, Nor commands, "Ivan! Lugg! Take them out!"

Immediately after Nor shouts, both Lug and Ivan fire their arrows through the thick smoke and fly toward the fortress. The arrows strike their targets, killing one guard after the other in just seconds; the guards once guarding the ramparts and gate are now no more and none are left to call out for help.

Now with all the guards fallen, Nor commands, "To the gates men!"

With the command given, the Centaur army advances toward the gates, reaching them in just seconds. Now at the front of the gates, Grumpa raises his staff, then begins chanting very quietly as he rises his head and closes his eyes. Moments later, the ground begins to shake and the gates begin to open. With the gates now open, Nor and his men charge in and eliminate what few warriors were remaining guarding the fortress entrance. Now that the entrance of the fortress is secure, Nor takes action in protecting their rear and flanks.

In his usual commanding presence, Nor orders, "Moordock! Grimm! Take some men and close the gates so we are not attacked from behind. Lugg! Krom! Watch our left flank. Ivan! Olff! Watch our right flank! The rest of you, focus on that tunnel. From the position that the Centaurs are in, they can see the large tunnel leading toward the main fortress and there appears to be some activity within in the darkness of the tunnel. With the gates closed and secured, Moordock and Grimm rejoin Nor. Nor and Grumpa appear to be speaking as they look toward the darkened tunnel.

In a bold move, Nor asks, "Grumpa, how much of that burning water do you have in that barrel there?"

Reacting rather suspiciously, Grumpa replies, "That barrel is full, enough for all of us for the next three days, but this is not the time for drink or do you have something else in mind?"

With a confident gaze upon his ruggedly handsome face, Nor instructs, "Ox, grab that barrel of burning water from Grumpa's horse and bring it here."

As commanded, Ox fetches the barrel and brings it to Nor.

Innocently, Ox asks, "Where do you want me to put it?"

Nor commands, "Place it there in front of the tunnel."

Again, as commanded, Ox places the barrel in front of the tunnel then turns to Nor. Again in his naive manner, Ox asks, "Is this where you want it?"

With a smile and in a calm voice, Nor instructs Ox, "Yes. Now join the others."

In a surprise move, Nor takes possession of Doom's battle ax, then strikes the burning water barrel and kicks it, forcing it to roll into the tunnel. All look at Nor in shock, dismay, disappointment, and even some with clear heartbreak.

Shouting, Grumpa asks, "Why did you do that? That is a waste of good drink!"

With a smile on his face, Nor turns, then grabs a burning torch next to them and without looking, Nor tosses the burning torch into the tunnel causing the burning water to catch fire, then an explosion is seen within the tunnel. Suddenly, figures can be seen in the tunnel on fire and in a panic.

Nor draws his mighty sword, then commands, "Make ready men, all hell is about to break loose!"

The Centaurs all draw their weapons and just then, several Demasaurs, Wolfaraptors, and soldiers of Grimmcock come rushing out on fire. The Centaurs chop them down as soon as they are within range; it is a massacre and a bloodbath as the Centaurs battle without a loss.

Now with a curious smile on his face, Grumpa comments, "That was a great idea, Nor!"

With a curious grin, Nor responds, "I am pleased that you approve, Grumpa!"

Not very pleased and in a very saddened tone, Musse speaks out, "What a waste of good drink!"

With a chuckle and a smile, Nor shrugs his shoulders, then Grumpa nudges Musse with an elbow.

With a smile and in a happy tone, Grumpa tells Musse, "I have three more barrels on that horse!"

This news brings smiles back to all that hear Grumpa speak of the additional burning water he has brought.

A very excited Musse hollers, "I love you, old man!"

Suddenly and without notice, a very enthusiastic Musse picks up Grumpa and practically crushes the old man with his giant arms and Herculean strength. Grump does not appear pleased at all by the actions of Musse.

A very angry Grumpa scolds Musse, "Put me down, you clumsy fool! Put me down!"

Musse places Grumpa back on to the ground, then happily proclaims, "You sneaky old wizard! I love you old man!"

A very grumpy Grumpa attempts to straighten out his cloak, then scolds and threatens Musse, "Do that again and I shall turn you into an ugly toad!" Grumpa continues grumpily to adjust his cloak as he glares at Musse, who is unfazed by Grumpa's displeasing stare.

A cautious Nor analyzes the situation as he looks around, then commands, "Follow me and bring those torches."

A protective Doom, with sword and ax in his hands, rushes ahead of Nor as he grabs one of the soldiers carrying a torch, then instructs him, "You light, I'll fight!" Doom then looks back to Nor.

"It may be a trap, so he and I will lead the way!" Doom turns, then proceeds with the soldier deeper into the tunnel.

As the Centaurs reach deeper and deeper into the tunnel, they see many dead burnt bodies of men, demasaurs, and wolfaraptors lying on the floor as they make their way past these fallen hideous creatures and men. Now through the main tunnel, the Centaurs enter a large room made of stone with several more tunnels connecting to the room leading in different directions. Suddenly, from out of each tunnel, the Centaurs are attacked by even more soldiers, Demasaurs, and Wolfaraptors. One of Musse's bears is attacked from behind by two Wolfaraptors but are knocked away by one of the other bears and the two Wolfaraptors are brutally mauled and killed by Krom's tiger and the third of Musse's bears. The battle is fearsome and bloody, but the Centaurs are victorious, but at a cost; they have lost three more soldiers. The floor of the room is laden with blood, dead bodies, and hacked-off body parts. Standing and observing the aftermath, Olff stands over several dead bodies, and he himself is bleeding. This does not go unnoticed by Nor.

Concerned, Nor asks, "Olff, is that a bad wound or just a scratch?"

Olff looks at his leg and reacts, "I did not know I was injured. It is a clean cut."

Being the natural leader he is, Nor issues his orders, "Olff, stay here and tend to that wound. Krom, stay here and aid Olff, guard this room and make sure no one or thing enters and lives. You five, stay here with Krom and help him guard this room. We will have to split up to search each tunnel for Grimmcock and my mother."

Interjecting, Grumpa advises, "My brother the Alchemist had been here before and he stated that three of these tunnels join near Grimmcock's chambers. Some, if not all, of these tunnels have secret passageways so beware of traps and ambushes."

Lugg asks sarcastically, "Did he happen to mention which ones?"

A smiling Grumpa replies, "Nope! He did not."

Now as he surveys the tunnels, Nor commands his men, "It does not matter. We will have to clear each tunnel. We must eliminate every creature, soldier, acolyte, and Grimmcock himself to rid us of this cursed tradition we have had to endure for all this time, but no more. We shall separate into seven groups." In a commanding tone, Nor begins to point to each tunnel as he gives his instructions, "This is tunnel one, this is two, three, four, five, six, and seven. Doom, you are with me in tunnel four. Grumpa and Moordock, take tunnel five. Lugg and Magnus, take tunnel three. Musse with your bears and you two, take tunnel two. Dread and you two will take tunnel six. Grimm and you two will take tunnel seven, and Ox with Ivan, take tunnel one. Now once you have cleared your tunnel, come back here and wait. Whoever reaches Grimmcock's chambers, wait there for me and call out the tunnel number so I may rush over to aid you. Do not engage Grimmcock or Brummel unless you are attacked. Understand!"

All of Nor's men nod in agreement to Nor's command.

Grumpa interjects, "Remember men, only a wizard or king can kill a warlock like Grimmcock and Brummel, so don't be foolish with your lives! Call out for aid. There is no shame in this. Trust me, you don't want to engage them without me or Nor to kill them."

Agreeing, Nor speaks out, "I agree and watch for traps. Now let us rid ourselves of this scourge once and for all."

Confidently Nor turns to enter tunnel four, but Doom grabs a torch in his left hand and holds his battle ax in his right as he jumps ahead of Nor.

Doom looks back at Nor, then announces, "I shall go first, just in case we walk into a trap." Doom gives Nor a smile and a wink of his eye.

Nor gives Doom a shake of the head with a grin, then motions for Doom to proceed and Doom does exactly that.

Now deep inside the tunnel where Ox is leading the way, he sees a sign in a language he does not recognize, then as he points, he asks Ivan "What is that?"

Nodding with a smirk on his face, Ivan explains, "My friend, it appears that we have come to the entrance of Grimmcock's chambers."

Just then, Ivan is knocked hard into the stone wall on the opposite side of the large room and knocked out. Cetan now appears from within a secret passageway; he then stands directly in front of Ox with an evil grin on his deformed ugly mug. Cetan looks Ox up and down as he nods his head in approval.

Not lacking in arrogance and confidence, Cetan comments, "You are a big one!" Cetan laughs. "Ha, ha, ha, ha! I shall enjoy chopping you down into tiny pieces."

A very angry Ox, "I shall have your head for killing my friend, you ugly bastard!"

Ox and Cetan charge each other and engage in an extremely fierce battle. The two exchange blow after blow, but neither is wounded; however, Ox is clearly tired, then in a swinging and turning motion, Cetan bends down, chopping off Ox's right leg, causing Ox to fall to the ground. Lying next to Ox is his now-detached leg, Ox attempts to reattach the leg but to no avail as he looks up to Cetan with a courageous smile, then speaks to Cetan bravely, "Finish it, you ugly bastard!"

A smiling Cetan retorts, "In pieces, big man, small pieces!"

As Cetan steps up and raises his sword, he is charged and knocked against the wall by a very determined Grimm. Grimm can see his friends lying on the ground as Ox lies on the floor bleeding profusely from his leg wound.

A very emotional Grimm shouts, "You ugly fucking bastard!"

An enraged Grimm charges Cetan, but Cetan blocks Grimm's blade with his as the two engage in a fierce and intense battle. Cetan, in a very fanciful move, spins, then knocks Grimm to the ground. Just then, two more Centaur soldiers charge in at Cetan but have no chance against the skilled and ruthless warrior. In an impressive maneuver, Cetan beheads the two with one swing of his sword as he leaps into the air over the two, then lands on his feet at the same time the two heads meet the ground.

Now back on his feet, a courageous Grimm shouts, "Come here, you ugly bastard!"

A smiling Cetan turns to face Grimm, then proclaims, "Now you die!"

Again, Cetan and Grimm engage in a fierce battle but unable to sustain the movement and speed of Cetan. Grimm is badly wounded and knocked to the ground. Lying on the ground facing Cetan, a spiteful Grimm grins then proclaims, "Eat shit!" then spits at Cetan.

Cetan advances toward a tired and wounded Grimm lying on the floor. Suddenly, Cetan is cut off by a now-awakened and fresh Ivan. Ivan stands between Grimm and Cetan with his sword at the ready as he stares at Cetan. No words are exchanged, only swords and the two send sparks flying as their swords collide in numerous strikes. Suddenly, Ivan is knocked to the ground from a blow to the stomach from Cetan. An injured Ivan, now on his knees, looks up to Cetan with a scorn gaze.

In a bitter tone, Ivan shouts, "Come on, you ugly shit! Finish it!"

Now from the opposite side of the room, a barely standing Grimm hollers, "Over here, you ugly bastard! Come to Grimm so I may take your ugly soul!" Grimm is barely able to stand much less raise his sword to fight Cetan, but he is all heart and willing to do whatever it takes to save his dear friend.

Cetan lurches over, then strikes Grimm across the head with the back of his mighty axe, whereby knocking Grimm to the floor unconscious. Ivan, now back on his feet with his sword raised in front of him is clearly exhausted and can barely defend himself when Cetan strikes Ivan's sword with his, causing Ivan to fall to the ground. Cetan, now standing above Ivan ready to strike the final blow, is suddenly knocked to the ground by the giant Musse.

Musse shouts, "No! No! No!"

Musse's two soldiers enter the area and see Musse looking down at a seriously injured Ox. Musse becomes teary-eyed as he looks down at his good friend. Now seeing this, Cetan rises to his feet then laughs. With an evil grin, Cetan speaks out, "I shall cut him into small pieces as I shall do the same with you!"

Screaming, Musse directs his attention back to Cetan. "Damn you!"

With his anger at a new level, Musse charges in at Cetan. The two battle fiercely and for some time as the two appear evenly matched, but suddenly, Musse is struck on the shoulder, causing him to fall back onto the ground next to Ox. Musse appears winded;

however, Cetan appears fresh as he is now charged by the two soldiers who accompanied Musse. Cetan sees the two preparing their charge, so Cetan crouches down, then leaps into the air, doing a flip over the two brave Centaur soldiers; as he does his flip over the two, he uses his blades to decapitate the two brave men, killing them instantly. Suddenly, Cetan appears concerned as he steps back to reevaluate the situation as he appears to notice a figure appear from one of the tunnels. Cetan crouches down with his weapons at the ready.

Now lying next to Ox, Musses comments to his wounded friend in a sarcastic manner, "I should have brought my bears, but I left them in the other cave to guard our backs! Shit!"

A struggling Ox smiles in a pitiful manner at Musse, then states, "I shall miss you my friend." Ox then lays his giant head on Musse's shoulder.

A teary-eyed and very distraught Musse begins to weep as he grabs his giant friend Ox and attempts to put his leg back on Ox's body. Just then, Doom enters the area with his weapons in hand; as he surveys the situation, he can see his friends strewn all around him. Cetan makes his way in front of the door leading to Grimmcock's chambers, then makes his stance.

In his stoic mannerism, Doom looks to Cetan, then speaks, "You!"

Just then, Nor enters the area and can see the havoc Cetan has created. This of course angers Nor, who now appears both angry and saddened as a tear fills his eye; he then commands his friend.

Both raging and emotional Nor shouts out, "Doom! Kill that ugly son of a bitch now!"

A cocky yet weary Cetan addresses Doom, "You shall join your friends soon."

This does not sit well with Doom as he turns to Cetan very determined and with confidence. Doom speaks out, "Time to die, ugly one."

Suddenly, Cetan lurches toward Doom but is unable to slow down or make stop a charging determined Doom. Doom spins and turns as his blades flail through the air and strike Cetan, separating his right arm and left leg from his body. Cetan falls to the ground.

Clearly Cetan is grimacing from pain as he addresses Doom, "What kind of magic is this? Cetan cannot be defeated!"

Angrily, Doom shouts, "I need no magic to defeat the likes of you!"

Cetan now rises on his one leg to battle Doom, but as soon as he is upright, Doom slashes down with sword and ax, striking Cetan on both shoulders, cutting his body into pieces. Cetan lets out a painful scream, then in one motion, Doom spins and with his mighty ax, he decapitates Cetan. Cetan's head and body fall to the ground, spewing blood all around. Doom leans down, then picks up Cetan's head and in a surprising act, bitterly, Cetan speaks his last words, "We shall meet again!"

Holding Cetan's head away from him, Doom responds, "Good, then I shall enjoy killing you once again!" Doom then tosses the now-lifeless head into one of the dark tunnels.

Just then, we can hear a weeping and mournful Musse cry out in the most pitiful manner. "No! No! You stay with me!"

A badly wounded Ox looks at Musse with a slight smile as a tear runs down his massive cheek.

An openly crying and very emotional Musse tells Ox, "Just hang on! We'll take you to Grumpa! He can fix this! He can heal you! Please Ox, don't leave me! Please! I beg you!" Musse frantically attempts in vain to restore the hacked-off leg back on Ox, but his efforts are futile as Ox looks one last time at his old friend with his eyes filled with tears.

In an almost lifeless tone, Ox whispers, "I shall see you in the next life, my friend." Just then, Ox's head drops onto Musse's lap as Ox dies and breathes his last breath onto Musse's lap.

Musse lets out a horrible scream as he holds his friend's lifeless body as if it were his own child in his arms. Musse is inconsolable as he weeps in the most pathetic and mournful manner. Musse's cries bring all to tears as they all clearly loved the big man lying on Musse's lap. A tear-filled Nor steps up to Musse, then raises Musse's head up as he then tells a mournful Musse what should be done.

In a compassionate and sorrowful tone, Nor commands his men, "Musse, we shall all miss our Ox. You must take him to the gate and await my arrival. Grimm! Ivan! Take our wounded to the gate and tend to your wounds."

As commanded, Nor's men comply with his orders. A mournful Musse lifts the lifeless body of Ox, then exits the area along with Ivan and Grimm. Nor and Doom stand alone at the door leading to Grimmcock's chambers; the large and thick door is the only thing standing between them and their hated enemy.

Inquisitively, Nor asks Doom, "Can that magnificent ax of yours cut through that door?"

Doom simply smiles, then nods in a positive manner as he then begins to chop his way through the door.

In one of the other tunnels, we find Lugg and Magnus searching till they reach the end of the tunnel, then as the two look to each other with a smirk, they turn back to join their friends.

Now in another tunnel, we find Dread and two Centaur soldiers who have stumbled upon an empty barracks and the end of their assigned tunnel. With this empty end, the men turn back to join the rest of their friends.

In a separate tunnel, we find Grumpa and Moordock who have entered what appears to be a prison and torture chamber. Grumpa and Moordock rush to release the prisoners. Moordock almost vomits from the sight of excrement, vomit, blood, and entrails lying about on the floor. It is a terrible sight and a horrible place to be in, much less live in. The foul looks on Grumpa and Moordock's faces reveal their displeasure in being in there.

A disgusted Grumpa orders, "All those able to walk, help those that are unable to walk and get out of this wretched place. Then meet us at the gate. Make haste!" As Grumpa looks around, he comments, "I do not see Nor's mother!"

A disgusted Moordock gazes at Grumpa, then states, "Let us join the others. Perhaps Nor has found her!"

We now join Olff, Krom, the five Centaur soldiers, Krom's tiger, and, surprisingly, Musse's three bears, which appear to be covered in blood. All are engaged in a fierce battle with Wolfaraptors, Demasaurs, and Grimmcock's soldiers. The battle is finally over, and the Centaurs are victorious but a very expensive cost as Olff and three other Centaur soldiers lay dead upon the bodies of creatures and soldiers they have killed. A teary-eyed Krom lifts and moves his friend to a clear spot, then places Olff's lifeless body down where he removes his cape and covers Olff's face and body. A weeping Krom kneels down over his friend as he is joined by his tiger, the remaining two Centaur soldiers, and amazingly, Musse's three bears.

A somber Krom, bids farewell to his fallen friend, "I am sorry my friend! I am so very sorry! I could not aid you in your time of need!"

Just then, Lugg and Magnus arrive from out of a tunnel. Then Dread and his two Centaur soldiers appear as does Grumpa and Moordock, along with all the once-held prisoners that were saved by Grumpa and Moordock.

A very sad Moordock asks, "Is that Olff?"

With tears in his eyes, a mournful Krom replies, "Yes! He died saving my life!"

As a good commander would respond, Moordock speaks to Krom, "You would have done the same for him Krom. Come now! We must find Nor so we can finish Grimmcock, find Nor's mother, and leave this evil place."

Krom looks up to Moordock, then informs him, "Nor and Doom returned, then entered tunnel two and I have not seen or heard from them since."

Without hesitation, Grumpa speaks up, "Then all who can fight, come with me and we shall all go into tunnel two. Come, Moordock! Lugg! Magnus! The rest of you, head toward the campsite and we shall join you as soon as we are able. Now go!" Grumpa turns, then proceeds into and down tunnel two, followed by Moordock, Lugg, and Magnus.

Back at the door of Grimmcock's chambers, we find Doom has broken down the massive and thick door leading into Grimmcock's chambers. Now with a clear view of the inside of the chambers, we can see a frightened Grimmcock sitting on a chair with Brummel at his side, standing with a knife at the throat of a beaten, battered, and still-beautiful Einirt.

In a calm yet frightened voice, Grimmcock speaks to Nor, "So, Nor, you have come for my head, haven't you?"

Nor steps into the chamber, then responds to Grimmcock, "Finally, we meet Grimmcock! This ugly bastard must be Brummel."

With an unsure gaze, Grimmcock stares at Nor, "You are very observant Nor. Do you recognize the woman to which Brummel is holding and prepared to kill?"

With tears in her eyes, a weeping Einirt shouts to Nor, "Kill them my son! I'm already dead! Avenge me and your father whom I go to be with!"

With tear-filled eyes, an angry Nor shouts, "Release her! Now!"

Unsure of how to respond, Grimmcock asks, "Should I release her? Do I have your word that you will allow me to leave and live?"

A quick-to-respond Brummel asks, "You! Just you live! What of me?"

Suddenly and without provocation, Brummel slices Einirt's throat, then grabs a thick well ornate and malevolent-looking book from the table near Grimmcock. Brummel cowardly pushes Einirt's dead body toward Nor, then rushes to the open window where he then stands and looks back at the group. A shaken and weeping yet angry Nor grabs his mother's body, preventing her from falling to the ground. Nor holds his mother close to him as he weeps gazing into his mother's now-closed eyes. A startled Grimmcock turns to Brummel. Hollering in fear and in anger, Grimmcock looks to Brummel, "No! No! You fool! What have you done! You have killed us both!"

A rage-filled Doom rushes toward Grimmcock. Grimmcock does not appear frightened of Doom as he stands with a hand up and open.

Without fear and looking at Doom, Grimmcock shouts, "Fool! Only Nor can kill me and he is still outnumbered!" Doom appears frozen in his tracks by some sort of magic spell Grimmcock has just hit him with. Suddenly, Grumpa appears from nowhere.

A cocky and angered Grumpa flashes his hand at Doom, freeing Doom from the spell of Grimmcock's, then immediately addresses his former friend and now enemy, "Nor is alone no more, my old friend!"

Grumpa now turns his attention to Grimmcock as he points his crystal ball and staff at Grimmcock. Some kind of magic has emerged from the crystal of the staff, which causes Grimmcock to fly into the wall behind him. Grimmcock is knocked out temporarily. Nor lifts, then places his mother into Doom's arms and with a nod of Nor's head, Doom immediately takes Einirt's body out of the chamber. Nor draws his sword from its sheath, then rushes toward Grimmcock and without hesitation, Nor pierces Grimmcock's heart with his magnificent sword. This kills Grimmcock instantly, which causes Grimmcock's body to all but disintegrate; all but bones and his cloak remain. Nor then turns his attention to Brummel who now looks to Nor in fear as Brummel then turns and jumps out of the window. Nor rushes over to locate Brummel, but there is not sign of Brummel as he has disappeared into the darkness of the evil forest which surrounds this evil fortress. Nor turns to Grumpa, then addresses the situation in a calmer voice, "This is not over. I shall find that creature and finish him once and for all. For now, let us tend to our fallen and make our way back to those which we love. He will die at my hand! This I swear!"

Now back at the Centaur camp, we find all that is left of the Centaur army. There are many wrapped-up bodies lying on the ground and many saddened faces looking down at them. Nor is kneeling down at what must be his mother's body wrapped in a blanket.

A slightly weeping and teary-eyed Nor speaks to his mother, "You are with my father now. May you both be as happy as me and my Ynew! I wish you could have met her and my daughters. I shall miss you Mother! I wish I could have met my father. I only wish I could be the man and king you once were Father! May the gods grant thee peace and the love you once held for each other be restored in the next life and every life thereafter. Farewell Mother. I love thee!" Weeping softly, Nor looks down and wipes the tears from his ruggedly handsome face. Nor stands, then turns and addresses his men.

In a compassionate and exhausted voice, Nor commands, "Let us take our fallen back to the Centaur village and give them a proper burial, but first we shall make our way to Grumpa's village for a well-deserved rest. Grumpa, can you keep their bodies from decay and smell?"

A humble Grumpa responds with a nod, then proceeds to cast a spell upon the fallen bodies to preserve them for the long trip ahead of them.

Many days later, we find the Centaur army entering Grumpa's village. Sitting around a festive table laden with food and drink, we find Ynew dressed in the beautiful form-fitting Grecian gown which Nor presented to her before he departed. Ynew is a vision of pure beauty as she has her long auburn hair flowing freely with her three daughters seated next to her with Nana sitting across the table from the four. They appear to be talking when suddenly, Nana notices the army entering the village. Suddenly, Grumpa breaks away from the group where he rushes over to meet Nana and Ynew. Once Grumpa reaches Nana, he dismounts his horse, then hugs his wife where he also begins to speak to her and now standing near Ynew. The news is very apparent as the once gleeful faces of both Nana and Ynew have now turned to a look of sadness. Now the rest of the army reaches the area where Ynew is standing, awaiting her beloved. Nor dismounts his horse, he then steps up to Ynew then takes and lifts her into his arms, giving her hug and a long-awaited kiss.

An excited and emotional Ynew tells Nor, "I have missed you so much my love! I am so sorry to hear of your mother my love! I am so sorry!" Tears are now flowing from Ynew's beautiful eyes and down her beautiful face.

A solemn Nor responds, "I wish you could have met her!"

Without hesitation, Ynew replies "Your mother is with her true love once again as am I!"

With a slight smile, Nor speaks out, "This is true my love."

Just then, Nor's three daughters join him and Ynew in a well-deserved and long-awaited family hug. Just then, Doom approaches the group.

Ynew looks to her husband, then to Doom as she states with a smile, "We have a surprise that will please you and Doom." Ynew then whispers into Nor's ear. This brings a huge smile to Nor's ruggedly handsome face.

In his usual stoic manner and tone, Doom announces, "Surprise! I have had enough damn surprises to last me a life time as of late."

Just then, Nana and Grumpa approach Doom from the direction Doom is now facing and in Grumpa's possession, he is holding a newborn baby. Suddenly, the baby begins to cry, so Grumpa hands the crying infant to Doom.

Grumpa calmly tells Doom, "Here Doom, hold this for me until his mother arrives."

Caught off guard, Doom takes the crying baby from Grumpa with a confused gaze. Doom looks at Grumpa as Grumpa simply stands there looking at Doom with a silly grin upon his old weathered face. Now from behind Doom arrive his two sons, leading their beautiful blind mother toward Doom. With a dumfounded gaze upon his hard and rugged face, Doom asks, "Grumpa, did you say to hold this crying baby until his mother arrives?" Doom does not appear very comfortable holding the infant. Those around him including Nor, all smile as some giggle at Doom as he appears somewhat nervous now. Nor just can't resist but make a comment.

In a sarcastic tone, Nor comments, "All be damn Doom. That child looks just like you. Bald head, grumpy frown, and he even has your eyes!"

Doom, with his standard stoic gaze, looks at Nor, then snarls as he comments, "That's not funny!"

Just then, the beautiful Angel, dressed to kill in a form-fitting white long leg slit, with cleavage-showing V-neck gown, addresses Doom, "Is that how you hold your son, my love?"

A shocked and happily surprised Doom turns abruptly with a goofy smile on his hardened face. Doom suddenly begins to rush over to greet his Angel. Immediately rushing over to Angel, Ynew grabs the baby from Doom as Doom relinquishes the hold on the infant to allow Ynew to take the child. Doom with free hands, places his giant paws around his Angel's tiny waist, he lifts her into the air where he pulls her into him and kisses her in the most romantic of manners. Angel simply complies and retorts Doom's affection and actions. A very excited Doom then inquires of his Angel, "My Angel! My sons! How did you get here and how did you know where I was?"

A very happy but calm Angel replies, "Grumpa sent for us when you departed for that evil place."

Doom gazes over to Grumpa, then nods, "Thank you Grumpa! Thank you from the bottom of my heart! This is a great surprise!"

Grumpa nods as all the others just smile.

Just then, Nor looks to Grumpa, "That was a very nice surprise, old man! A very nice surprise indeed! Thank you, Father!"

A smiling and cocky Grumpa nods as he comments, "A king called me father! Imagine that!"

A smiling Ynew, now surrounded by her loving daughters, asks Nor, "So, my love, when do we depart for our new home?"

A very content and smiling Nor replies, "In time my love. For now, we celebrate and get a well-deserved rest." In a not so subtle manner, Nor gives Ynew a very seductive gaze as his daughters look on with grins that soon turn to giggles.

Ynew grins at her man, then states, "By the way my king, that young man over there in the black shirt wishes to court your eldest daughter, Yelhsa."

Both Nor and Doom hear these words and are not too pleased as the smiles that once lit their faces have now turned bitter and sour. Both Nor and Doom proceed toward the young once-smiling young man who suddenly stands, then turns and begins to run toward the forest. Both Nor and Doom began to pick up the pace as they pursue the young man. As this pursuit takes place, a shadow appears from behind a large tree. From deep in the forest and lurking around, appearing to be spying on the group, is the ugly and evil-looking Brummel, who does not appear to be in good spirits.

PRONUNCIATION OF NAMES

Annaerb—Anna-erb
Yelhsa—Ela-sa
Ynaffit—In-a-fit
Ynew—E-new

CPSIA information can be obtained
at www.ICGtesting.com
Printed in the USA
BVHW031038230821
615023BV00001B/4

9 781662 435638